Johnny left soon afterward and wandered along the street toward the building on the northern outskirts of the town where Pecos Kane ran a gambling house and hotel. Johnny ignored the hotel half and lolled against the door as he sized up the interior of the gambling hall, and instantly became the center of well-disguised interest. While he paused inside the threshold a lean, tall man arose from a chair against the wall and sauntered carelessly out of sight through a narrow doorway leading to a passage in the rear. Kit Thorpe was not a man to loaf on his job when a two-gun stranger entered the place, especially when the stranger appeared to be looking for someone. Otherwise there was no change in the room, the bartender polishing his glasses without pause, the card players silently intent on their games and the man at the deserted roulette table who held a cloth against the ornate spinning wheel kept on polishing it. They seemed to draw reassurance from Thorpe's disappearance.

Clarence E. Mulford books from
Tom Doherty Associates

Clarence E. Mulford

THE BAR-20 THREE

FORGE ®

A TOM DOHERTY ASSOCIATES BOOK
NEW YORK

This is a work of fiction. All the characters and events portrayed in this book are either products of the author's imagination or are used fictitiously.

THE BAR-20 THREE

A Forge Book
Published by Tom Doherty Associates, Inc.
175 Fifth Avenue
New York, NY 10010

www.tor-forge.com

Forge® is a registered trademark of Tom Doherty Associates, Inc.

ISBN-13: 978-0-7653-5940-7
ISBN-10: 0-7653-5940-5

First Tor Edition: April 1998
Second Tor Edition: November 2007

Printed in the United States of America

0 9 8 7 6 5 4 3 2 1

CONTENTS

CHAPTER I

"Put a 'T' in It"

IDAHO NORTON, laughing heartily, backed out of the barroom of Quayle's hotel and trod firmly on the foot of Ward Corwin, sheriff of the county, who was about to pass the door. Idaho wheeled, a casual apology trembling on his lips, to hear a biting, sarcastic flow of words, full of profanity, and out of all proportion to the careless injury. The sheriff's coppery face was a deeper color than usual and bore an expression not pleasant to see. The puncher stepped back a pace, alert, lithe, balanced, the apology forgotten, and gazed insolently into the peace officer's wrathful eyes.

"—an' why don't you look where yo're steppin'? Don't you know how to act when you come to town?" snarled the sheriff, finishing his remarks.

Idaho looked him over coolly. "I know how to act in any company, even yourn. Just now I ain't actin'—I'm waitin'."

The sheriff's eyes glinted. "I got a good mind—"

"You ain't got nothin' of th' sort," cut in the puncher, contemptuously. "You ain't got nothin' good, except, mebby, yore reg'lar plea of self-defense. I'm sayin' out loud that *that* ain't no good, here an' now; an' I'm waitin' to take it away from you an' use it myself. You been trustin' too cussed much to that nickel badge."

Bill Trask, deputy, who had a reputation not to be overlooked, now took a hand from the rear, eager to add to his list of victims from any of that outfit. The puncher was between him and the sheriff, and hardly could watch them both. Trask gently shook his belt and said three unprintable words which usually started a fight, and then glared over his shoulder at a sudden interruption, tense and angry.

"Shut up, you!" said the voice, and he saw a two-gun stranger slouching away from the hotel wall. The deputy took him in with one quick glance and then his eyes returned to those of the stranger and rested there while a slick prickling sensation ran up his spine. He had looked into many angry eyes, and in many kinds of circumstances, but never before had his back given him a warning quite so plainly. He grew restless and wanted to look away, but dared not; and while he hung in the balance of hesitation the stranger spoke again. "Two to one ain't fair, 'specially with the lone man in middle; but I'll make th' odds even, for I'm honin' to claim self-defense, myself. It's right popular. I saw it all—an' I'm sayin' you are three chumps to get all het up over a little thing like that. Mebby his toes *are* tender—but what of it? He ain't no baby, leastawise he don't look like one. An' I'm tellin' you, an' yore badge-totin' friend, that *I* know how to act, too." A twinkle came into the hard, blue eyes. "But what's th' use of actin' like four strange dogs?"

Somewhere in the little crowd a man laughed, others joined in and pushed between the belligerents; and in a minute the peace officers had turned the corner, Idaho was slowly walking toward the two-gun stranger and the crowd was going about its business.

"Have a drink?" asked the puncher, grinning as he pushed back his hat.

"Didn't I just say that I knowed how to act?" chuckled the stranger, turning on his heel and following his companion through the door. "You musta met them two before."

"Too cussed often. What'll you have? Make mine a cigar, too, Ed. No more liquor for me today—Corwin don't forget."

The bartender closed the box and slid it onto the back-bar again. "No, he don't," he said. "An' Trask is worse," he added, looking significantly at the stranger, whose cigar was now going to his satisfaction and who was smilingly regarding Idaho, and who seemed to be pleased by the frank return scrutiny.

"You ain't a stranger here no longer," said Idaho, blowing out a cloud of smoke. "You got two good enemies, an' a one-hoss friend. Stayin' long?"

"About half an hour. I got a little bunch of cows on th' drive west of here, an' they ought to be at Twitchell an' Carpenter's corrals about now. Havin' rid in to fix up bed an' board for my little outfit, I'm now on my way to finish deliverin' th' herd. See you later if yo're in town tonight."

"I don't aim to go back to th' ranch till tomorrow," replied Idaho, and he hesitated. "I'm sorry you horned in on that ruckus—there's mebby trouble bloomin' out of that for you. Don't you get careless till yo're a day's ride away from this town. Here, before you go, meet Ed Doane. He's one of th' few white men in this runt of a town."

The bartender shook hands across the bar. "Pleased to meet up with you, Mr.— Mr—?"

"Nelson," prompted the stranger. "How do you do, Mr. Doane?"

"Half an' half," answered the dispenser of liquids, and then waved a large hand at the smiling youth. "Shake han's with Idaho Norton, who was never closer to Idaho than Parsons Corners, thirty miles northwest of here. Idaho's a good boy, but shore impulsive. He's spent most of his life practicin' th' draw, et cetery; an' most of his money has went for ca'tridges. Some folks say it ain't been wasted. Will you gents smoke a cigar with me?"

After a little more careless conversation Johnny nodded his adieus, mounted and rode south. Not long thereafter he came within sight of the Question-Mark, Twitchell and Carpenter's local ranch.

Its valley sloped eastward, following the stream winding down its middle between tall cottonwoods, and the horizon was limited by the tops of the flanking hills, which dipped and climbed and zigzagged into the gray of the east, where great sand hills reared their glistening tops and the hopeful little creek sank out of sight into the dried, salty bed of a one-time lake. Near the trail were two buildings, a small stockaded corral and a wire-fenced pasture of twenty acres; and the Question-Mark brand, known wherever cattlemen congregated, even beyond the Canadian line, had been splashed with red paint on the wall of the larger building. The glaring, silent interrogation-mark challenged every passing eye and had started many curious, grim, and cynical trains of thought in the minds of tired and thirsty wayfarers along the trail. To the north of the twenty-acre pasture a herd of SV cattle grazed, spread out widely, too tired, too content with their feeding to need much attention.

Johnny saw the great, red question-mark and instantly drew rein, staring at it. "Why?" he muttered, and then grew silent for a moment. Shaking his head savagely he urged the horse on again, and again glanced at the crimson interrogation. "Damn you!" he growled. "There ain't no man livin' can answer."

He passed the herd at a distance and rode up to the larger building, where a figure suddenly appeared in the doorway, looked out from under a shielding hand, and quickly stepped forward to meet him.

"Hello, Nelson!" came the cheery greeting.

"Hello, Ridley!" replied Johnny. "Glad to see you again. Thought I'd bring 'em down to you, an' save you goin' up th' trail after 'em. Why don't you paint out that glarin' question-mark on th' side of th' house?"

Ridley slapped his hands together and let out a roar of laughter. "Has it got you, too?" he demanded in unfeigned delight.

"Not as much as it would before I got married," replied Johnny. "I'm beginnin' to see a reason for livin'."

"Good!" exclaimed Ridley. "If I ever meet yore wife I'll tell her somethin' that'll make her dreams sweet." The expression of his face changed swiftly. "Do you know—" he considered, and changed the form of his words. "You'd be surprised if you knew th' number of people hit by that painted question-mark. I've had 'em ride in here an' start all kinds of conversations with me; th' gospel sharps are th' worst. One man blew his brains out in Quayle's hotel because of what that sign started workin' in his mind. Go look at it: it's full of bullet holes!"

"I don't have to," replied Johnny, and quickly answered his companion's unspoken challenge. "An' I can sleep under it, an' smile, cuss you!" He glanced at the distant cattle. "Have you looked 'em over?"

Ridley nodded. "They're in good shape. Ready to count 'em now?"

"Be glad to, an' get 'em off my han's."

"Bring 'em up in front of th' pasture, an' I'll wait for you there," said Ridley.

Johnny wheeled and then checked his horse. "What kind of fellers are Corwin an' Trask?" he asked.

Ridley looked up at him, a curious expression on his face. "Why?"

"Oh, nothin'; I was just wonderin'."

"As long as you ain't aimin' to stop around these parts for long, th' less you know about 'em th' better. I'll be waitin' at th' pasture."

Johnny rode off and started the herd again, and when it stopped it was compacted into a long V, with the point facing the pasture gate, and it poured its units from this point in a steady stream between the two horsemen at the open gate, who faced each other across the hurrying procession and built up another herd on the other side, one which spread out and grazed without restraint, unless it be that of a wire fence. And with the shrinking of the first and the expanding of the second the SV ownership changed into that of the Question-Mark.

The shrewd, keen-eyed buyer for Twitchell and Carpenter looked up as the gate closed after the last steer and smiled across the gap at the SV foreman as he announced his count.

Johnny nodded. "My figgers, to a T," he said. "That 2-Star steer don't belong to us. Joined up with us somewhere along th' trail. You know 'em?"

"Belongs to Dawson, up on th' north fork of th' Bear. I'll drop him a check in a couple of days. This feller musta wandered some to get in with yourn. Well, yourn is a good bunch of four-year-olds. You'll have to wait till I get to town, for I ain't got a blank check left, an' I shore ain't got no one thousand one hundred and forty-three dollars layin' around down here. Want cash or a check?"

"If I took a check I'd have to send somebody up to Sherman with it," replied Johnny. "I might take it at that, if I was goin' right back. Better make it cash, Ridley."

Ridley grinned. "I've swept up this part of th' country purty good."

Johnny shook his head. "I'm lookin' for weaners—an' not in this part of th' country. I'll see you in town."

"Before supper," said Ridley. "You puttin' up at Quayle's?"

"You called it," answered Johnny, wheeling. He rode off, picked up his small outfit and led the way to Mesquite, where he hoped to spend but one night. The little SV group cantered over the thin trail in the wake of their bobbing chuck wagon, several miles ahead of them, and reached the town well ahead of it, much to the cook's vexation. As they neared Quayle's hotel Johnny pulled up.

"This is our stable," he said. "Go easy, boys. We leave at daylight. See you at supper."

They answered him laughingly and swept on to Kane's place, which they seemed to sense, each for his favorite drink and game.

The afternoon shadows were long when Ridley, just from the bank, left his rangy bay in front of the hotel and entered the office, nodding to several men he knew. He went on through and stopped at the bar.

"Howd'y, Ed," he grunted. "That SV foreman around? Nelson's his name."

Ed Doane mopped up the bar mechanically and bobbed his head toward the door. "Here he comes now. Make a deal?"

Ridley nodded as he turned. "Hello, Nelson! Read this over. If it's all right, sign it, an' we'll let Ed disfigure it as a witness. I allus like a witness."

Johnny signed it with the pen the bartender provided and then the bartender labored with it and blew on it to dry the ink.

"Disfigure it, hey?" chuckled Ed, pointing to his signature, which was beautifully written but very much overdone. "That bill of sale's worth somethin' now."

Johnny admired it frankly and openly. "I allus did like shadin', an' them flourishes are plumb fetchin'. Me, now; I write like a cow."

"I'm worse," admitted Ridley, chuckling and giving Johnny a roll of bills. "Count 'em, Nelson. Folks usually turn my writin' upside down for th' first try. Speakin' of witnesses, there's another little thing I like. I allus seal documents, Ed. Take 'em out of that bottle you hide under th' bar. Three of 'em. Somehow, Ed, I allus like to see you stoop like that. Well, Nelson; does it count up right? Then, business bein' over, here's to th' end of th' drought."

It went the rounds, Ed accumulating three cigars as his favorite beverage, and as the glasses clicked down on the bar Ridley felt for the makings. "Sorry th' bank's closed, Nelson. It might be safer there over night."

"Mebby—but it's safe enough, anyhow," smiled Johnny, shrugging his shoulders. "Anyhow th' bank wouldn't be open early enough in th' mornin' for us. Which reminds me that I better go out an' look around. My four-man outfit's got to leave at daylight."

"I'll go with you as far as th' street," said Ridley. As they neared the door Johnny hung back to let his companion pass through first and as he did so he heard a soft call from the bartender, and half turned.

"Come here a minute," said Doane, leaning over the bar. "It ain't none of my business, Nelson, but I'm sayin' *I* wouldn't go into Kane's with th' wad of money you got on you; an' if I did I shore wouldn't show it nor get in no game. You don't have to remember that I said anythin' about this."

"I never gamble with money that don't belong to me," replied Johnny, "nor not even while I've got it on me; an' already I've forgot you said anythin'. That place must be a sort of 'sink of iniquity,' as that sanctified parson called Abilene."

"Huh!" grunted Doane. "You can put a 'T' in that 'sink,' an' there's only one place where a 'T' will fit. Th' money would be enough, but in yore case there's more. Idaho said it."

"He's only a kid," deprecated Johnny.

" 'Out of th' mouths of babes—' " replied Doane. "I'm tellin' you—that's all."

Ridley stuck his head in at the door. "So-long, fellers," he said.

"Hey, Ridley!" called the bartender hurriedly. "Would you go into Kane's if you had Nelson's roll on you?"

"Not knowin' what I might do under th' infloonce of likker, I can't say," answered Ridley; "but if I did I wouldn't drink in there. So-long, an' I mean it, this time," and he did.

Johnny left soon afterward and wandered along the street toward the building on the northern outskirts of the town where Pecos Kane ran a gambling-house and hotel. Johnny ignored the hotel half and lolled against the door as he sized up the interior of the gambling-hall, and instantly became the center of well-disguised interest. While he paused inside the threshold a lean, tall man arose from a chair against the wall and sauntered carelessly out of sight through a narrow doorway leading to a passage in the rear. Kit Thorpe was not a man to loaf on his job when a two-gun stranger entered the place, especially when the stranger appeared to be looking for someone. Otherwise there was no change in the room, the bartender polishing his glasses without pause, the card players silently intent on their games and the man at the deserted roulette table who held a cloth against the ornate spinning wheel kept on polishing it. They seemed to draw reassurance from Thorpe's disappearance.

One slow look was enough to satisfy Johnny's curiosity. The room was about sixty feet long by half as wide and on his left-hand side lay the bar, built solidly from the floor by close-fitting planks running vertically, which appeared to be of hardwood and quite thick, and the top was of the same material. Several sand-box cuspidors lay before it. The backbar was a shelf backed by a narrow mirror running well past the middle half, and no higher than necessary to give the bartender a view of the room when he turned around, which he did but seldom. Round card-tables, heavy and crude, were scattered about the room and a row of chairs ran the full length along the other side wall. Several loungers sat at the tables, one of them an eastern tough, judging from his clothes, his peaked cap pulled well down over his eyes. At the farther end was a solid partition painted like a checkerboard and the few black squares which cunningly hid several peepholes were not to be singled out by casual observation. Those who knew said that they were closed on their inner side by black steel plates which hung on oiled pivots and were locked shut by a pin. At a table in front of the checkerboard were four men, one flung forward on it, his head resting on his crossed arms; another had slumped down on the edge of his chair, his chin on his chest, while the other two carried on a grunted, pessimistic conversation across their empty glasses.

Johnny's face flickered with a faint smile and he walked toward them, nodding carelessly at the man behind the bar.

Arch Wiggins looked up, a sickly grin on his flushed face. "Hullo," he grunted, foolishly.

"Not havin' nothin' else to do I reckoned I'd look you up," said Johnny. "Fed yet?"

Arch shrugged his shoulders and Sam Gardner sighed expressively, and then prodded the slumped individual into a semblance of intelligence and erectness. This done he kicked the shins of the prostrate cook until that unfortunate raised an owlish, agonized, and protesting countenance to stare at his foreman.

"Nelson wants to know if yo're hungry," prompted Sam, grinning.

"Take it—away!" mumbled the indignant cook. "I *won't* eat! Who's goin' to make me?" he demanded with a show of pugnacity. "I won't!"

Joe Reilly, painfully erect in his chair, blinked and focussed his eyes on the speaker. "Then don't!" he said. "Shut yore face—others kin eat!" He turned his whole body, stiff as a ramrod, and looked at each of the others in turn. "Don't pay no 'tention to him. I kin—eat th'—damned harness," he asserted, thereby proving that his stomach preserved family traditions.

Johnny laughed at them. "Yo're a hell of an outfit," he said without conviction. "What do you say about goin' up to th' hotel an' gettin' somethin' to eat? It's past grubtime, but let's see if they'll have th' nerve to try to tell us to get out. Broke?" he inquired, and as they silently arose to their feet, which seemed to take a great deal of concentration, he chuckled. Then his face hardened. "Where's yore guns?" he demanded.

Arch waved elaborately at the disinterested bartender. "That gent loaned us ten apiece on 'em," he said. " 'Bli-gin' feller. Thank you, friend."

"Yo're a'right," said the cook, nodding at the dispenser of fluids.

"An' yo're a fine, locoed bunch, partin' with yore guns in a strange town," snapped Johnny. "You head for th' hotel *pronto*! G'wan!"

The cook turned and waved a hand at the solemn bartender. "Goo'-bye!" he called. "I *won't* eat! Goo'-bye."

Seeing them started in the right direction, Johnny went in and up to the bar. "Them infants don't need guns," he asserted, digging into a pocket, "but as long as they ain't shot themselves, yet, I'm takin' a chance. How much?"

The bartender, typical of his kind, looked wise when it was not necessary, finished polishing the glass in his hand and then slowly faced his inquisitor, bored and aloof. He had the condescending air of one who held himself to be mentally and physically superior to any man in town, and his air of preoccupation was so heavy that it was ludicrous. "Ten apiece," he answered nonchalantly, as behove the referee of drunken disputes, the adviser of sodden men, the student of humanity's dregs, whose philosophy of life was rotten to the core because it was based purely on the vicious and the weak, and whose knowledge, adjudged abysmal and cyclopedic by an admiring riffraff of stupefied mentality, was as shallow, warped, and perverted as the human derelicts upon which his observations were based. As Johnny's hand came up with the roll of bills the man of liquor kept his face passive by an act of will, but there crept into the ratlike eyes a strange gleam, which swiftly faded. "Put it 'way," he said heartily, a jovial, free-handed good fellow on the instant. "We got it back, an' more. It was worth th' money to have these where they wouldn't be too handy. We allus stake a good loser—it's th' policy of th' house. Take these instead of th' stake." He slid the heavy weapons across the bar. "What'll you have?"

"Same as you," replied Johnny, and he slowly put the cigar into a pocket. "Purty quiet in here," he observed, laying two twenty-dollar bills on the bar.

"Yeah," said the bartender, pushing the money back again; "but it's a cheerful ol' beehive at night. Better put that in yore pocket an' drop in after dark, when things are movin'. I know a blonde that'll tickle you 'most to death. Come in an' meet her."

"Tell you what," said Johnny, grinning to conceal his feelings. "You keep them bills. If I keep 'em I'll have to let them fools have their guns back for nothin'. I'm aimin' to take ten apiece out of their pay. If you don't want it, give it to th' blonde, with Mr. Nelson's compliments. It won't be so hard for me to get acquainted with her, then."

The bartender chuckled and put the bills in the drawer. "Yo're no child, I'm admittin'. Reckon you been usin' yore head quite some since you was weaned."

One of the card players at the nearest table said something to his two companions and one of them leaned back, stretched and arose. "I'm tired. Get somebody to take my place."

The sagacious observer of the roll of bills started to object to the game being broken up, glanced at Johnny and smiled. "All right; mebby this gent will sit in an' kill a little time. How 'bout it, stranger?"

Johnny smiled at him. "My four-man outfit ain't leavin' me no time to kill," he answered. "I got to trail along behind 'em an' pick up th' strays."

The gambler grinned sympathetically. "Turn 'em loose tonight. What's th' use of herdin' with yearlin's, anyhow? If you get tired of their company an' feel like tryin' yore luck, come in an' join us."

"If I find that I got any heavy time on my han's I'll spend a couple of hours with you," replied Johnny. As he turned toward the door he glanced at the bartender. "Don't forget th' name when you give her th' forty," he laughed.

The bartender chuckled. "I got th' best mem'ry of any man in this section. See you later, mebby."

Johnny nodded and departed, his hands full of guns, and as he vanished through the front door Kit Thorpe reappeared from behind the partition, grinned cynically at the bartender and received a wise, very wise look in return.

Reaching the hotel Johnny entered it by the nearest door, that of the barroom, walked swiftly through with the redeemed guns dangling from his swinging hands and without pausing in his stride, flung a brief remark over his shoulder to the man behind the bar, who was the only person, besides himself, in the room: "You was shore right. It should ought to have a 'T' in it," and passed through the other door, across the office and into the dining-room, where his four men were having an argument with a sullen waiter and a wrathy cook.

Ed Doane straightened up, his ears preserving the words, his eyes retaining the picture of an angry, hurrying two-gun man from whose hands swung four more guns. He cogitated, and then the possible significance of the numerous weapons sprang into his mind. Ed did not go around the bar. He vaulted it and leaped to the door, out of which he hopefully gazed at the tranquil place of business of Pecos Kane. Slowly the look of hope faded and he returned to his place behind the bar, scratching his frowsy head in frank energy, his imagination busy with many things.

CHAPTER II

Well-Known Strangers

THE DESERT and a paling eastern sky. The penetrating cold of the dark hours was soon to die and give place to a punishing heat well above the hundred mark. Spectral agaves, flinging their tent-shaped crowns heavenward, seemed to spring bodily from the radiating circlet of spiny swords at their bases, their slender stems still lost in the weakening darkness. Pale spots near the ground showed where flower-massed yuccas thrust up, lance-like, from their slender, prickly leaves. Giant cacti, ghostly, bulky, indistinct, grotesque in their erect, parallel columns, reached upward to a height seven times that of a tall man. They are the only growing things unmoved by winds. The sage, lost in the ground-hugging darkness, formed a dark carpet, mottled by lighter patches of sand. There were quick rustlings over the earth as swift lizards scurried hither and yon and a faint whirring told of some "side-winder" vibrating its rattles in emphatic warning against some encroachment. Tragedies were occurring in the sage, and the sudden squeak of a desert rat was its swan song.

In the east a silvery glow trembled above the horizon

and to the magic of its touch silhouettes sprang suddenly from vague, blurred masses. The agave, known to most as the century plant, showed the delicate slenderness of its arrowy stem and marked its conical head with feathery detail. The flower-covered spikes of the Spanish bayonets became studies in ivory, with the black shadows on their thorny spikes deep as charcoal. The giant cacti, boldly thrown against the silver curtain, sprang from their joining bases like huge, thick telegraph poles of ebony, their thorns not yet clearly revealed. The squat sage, now resolved into tufted masses, might have been the purplish leaden hollows of a great sea. The swift rustlings became swift movements and the "side-winder" uncoiled his graceful length to round a nearby sage bush. The quaking of a small lump of sand grew violent and a long, round snoot pushed up inquiringly, the cold, beady eyes peering forth as the veined lids parted, and a Gila monster sluggishly emerged, eager for the promised warmth. To the northeast a rugged spur of mountains flashed suddenly white along its saw-toothed edge, where persistent snows crowned each thrusting peak. A moment more, and dazzling heliographic signals flashed from the snowy caps, the first of all earthly things to catch the rays of the rising sun, as yet below the far horizon. On all sides as far as the eye could pierce through the morning twilight not a leaf stirred, not a stem moved, but everywhere was rigidity, unreal, uncanny, even terrifying to an imaginative mind. But wait! Was there movement in the fogging dark of the north? Rhythmic, swaying movement, rising and falling, vague and mystical? And the ghostly silence of this griddle-void was broken by strange, alien sounds, magnified by contrast with the terror-inspiring silence. A soft creaking, as of gently protesting saddle leather, interspersed with the frequent and not unmusical tinkle of metal, sounded timidly, almost hesitatingly out of the dark along the ground.

Silver turned into pink, pink into gold, and gold into crimson in almost a breath, and long crimson ribbons became lavender high in the upper air, surely too beautiful to be a portent of evil and death. Yet the desert hush

tightened, constricted, tensed as if waiting in rigid sus-
pense for a lethal stroke. Almost without further warning
a flaming, molten arc pushed up over the far horizon
and grew with amazing bulk and swiftness, dispelling
the chill of the night, destroying the beauty of the silhouettes, revealing the purple sage as a mangy, leaden cover-
let, riddled and thin, squatting tightly against the tawny
sand, across which had sprung with instant speed long,
vague shadows from the base of every object which
raised above the plain. The still air shuddered into a
slow dance, waving and quivering, faster and faster like
some mad dance of death, the rising heat waves distort-
ing with their evil magic giant cacti until their fluted,
thorny columns weaved like strange, slowly undulating
snakes standing erect on curving tails. And in the distance but a few leagues off blazed the white mockery of
the crystal snow, serene and secure on its lofty heights,
a taunt far-flung to madden the heat-crazed brain of
some swollen, clawing thing in distorted human form
slowly dying on the baking sands.

The movement was there, for the sudden flare of light
magically whisked it out of the void like a rabbit out of a
conjurer's hat. Two men, browned, leather-skinned,
erect, silent, and every line of them bespeaking reliance
with a certainty not to be denied, were slowly riding
southward. Their horses, typical of their cow-herding
type, were loaded down with large canteens, and suggested itinerant water peddlers. Two gallons each they
held, and there were four to the horse. One could imagine these men counted on taking daily baths—but they
were only double-riveting a security against the hell-fires
of thirst, which each of them had known intimately and
too well. The first rider, as erect in his saddle as if he had
just swung into it, had a face scored with a sorrow which
only an iron will held back; his squinting eyes were cold
and hard, and his hair, where it showed beneath the
soiled, gray sombrero, was a sandy color, all of what was
left of the flaming crimson of its youth. He rode doggedly
without a glance to right or left, silent, sullen, inscrutable.
When the glorious happiness of a man's life has gone out

there is but little left, often even to a man of strength. Behind him rode his companion, five paces to the rear and exactly in his trail, but his wandering glances flashed far afield, searching, appraising, never still. Younger in years than his friend, and so very much younger in spirit, there was an air of nonchalant recklessness about him, occasionally swiftly mellowed by pity as his eyes rested on the man ahead. Now, glancing at the sun-cowed east, his desert cunning prompted him and he pushed forward, silently took the lead and rode to a thicket of mesquite, whose sensitive leaves, hung on delicate stems, gave the most cooling shade of any desert plant. Dismounting, he picketed his horse and then added a side-line hobble as double security against being left on foot on the scorching sands. Not satisfied with that, he unfastened the three full canteens, swiftly examined them for leaks and placed them under the bush. Six gallons of water, but if need should arise he would fight to the death for it. Out of the corner of his eye he watched his companion, who mechanically was doing the same thing. Red Connors yawned, drank sparingly and then, hesitating, grinned foolishly and fastened one end of his lariat to his wrist.

"That dessicated hunk of meanness don't leave this hombre afoot, not nohow," said Red, looking at his friend; but Hopalong only stared into the bush and made no reply.

Nothing abashed at his companion's silence, Red stretched out at full length under the scant shade, his Colt at his hand in case some Gila monster should be curious as to what flavor these men would reveal to an inquisitive bite. Red's ideas of Gilas were romantic and had no scientific warrant whatever. And it was possible that a "side-winder" might blunder his way.

"It's better than a lava desert, anyhow," he remarked as he settled down, having in mind the softness of the loose sand. "One whole day of hell-to-leather fryin', an' one more shiverin' night, an' this stretch of misery will be behind, but it shore saves a lot of ridin', it does. I'll bet I'm honin' for a swim in th' Rio Placer—an' I ain't carin' how much mud there is, neither. Ah, th' devil," he growled in great disgust, slowly arising. "I done forgot to sprinkle them cayuses' insides. One apiece, they get, which is only insultin' 'em."

Hopalong tried to smile, arose and filled his hat, which his thirsty horse frantically emptied. When the canteen was also empty he went back to the sandy couch, to lay awake in the scorching heat, fighting back memories which tortured him near to madness, his mental torments making him apathetic to physical ones. And so dragged the weary, trying day until the cooling night let them go on again.

Three days later they rode into Gunsight, made careless inquiries and soon thereafter drew rein before the open door of the SV, unconscious of the excited conjectures rioting in the curious town.

Margaret Nelson went to the door, her brother trying to push past her, and looked wonderingly up at the two smiling strangers.

Red bowed and removed his hat with a flourish. "Mrs. Johnny?" he asked, and at the nodded assent smiled broadly. "My name's Red Connors, an' my friend is Hopalong Cassidy. He is th' very best friend yore fool husband ever had. We came down to make Johnny's life miserable for a little while, an' to give you a hand with his trainin', if you need it."

Margaret's breath came with a rush and she held out both hands with impulsive friendliness. "Oh!" she cried. "Come in. You must be tired and hungry—let Charley turn your horses into the corral."

Charley wriggled past the barrier and jumped for Hopalong, his shrill whoop of delighted welcome bringing a smile to the stern face of the mounted man. A swoop of the rider's arm, a writhing twist of the boy's body, coming a little too late to avoid the grip of that iron hand, and Charley shot up and landed in front of the pommel, where he exchanged grins at close range with his captor.

"I knowed you first look," asserted the boy as the grip was released. "My, but I've heard a lot about you! Yo're goin' to stay here, ain't you? I know where there's some black bear, up on th' hills—want to go huntin' with me?"

Hopalong's tense, wistful look broke into a smile, the first sincere, honest smile his face had known for a month. Gulping, he nodded, and turned to face his friend's wife. "Looks like I'm adopted," he said. "If you don't mind, Mrs. Johnny, Charley an' me will take care of th' cayuses while Red helps you fix up th' table." He reached out, grasped the bridle of Red's horse as its rider dismounted, and rode to the corral, Charley's excited chatter bringing an anxious smile to his sister, but a heart-felt, prayerful smile to Red Connors. He had great hopes.

Red paused just inside the door. "Mrs. Johnny," he said quietly, quickly, "I got to talk fast before Hoppy comes back. He lost his wife an' boy a month ago—fever—in four days. He's all broke up. Went loco a little, an' even came near shootin' me because I wouldn't let him go off by hisself. I've had one gosh-awful time with him, but finally managed to get him headed this way by talkin' about Johnny a-plenty. That got him, for th' kid allus was a sort of son to him. I'm figgerin' he'll be a lot better off down here on this south range for awhile. Even crossin' that blasted desert seemed to help—he loosened up his talk considerable since then. An' from th' way he grabbed that kid, I'm sayin' I'm right. Where is Johnny?"

"Oh!" Margaret's breathed exclamation did not need the sudden moisture in her eyes to interpret it, and in that instant Red Connors became her firm, unswerving friend. "We'll do our best—and I think he should stay here, always. And Johnny will be delighted to have him with us, and you, too—Red."

"Here he comes," warned her companion. "Where is Johnny? When will he get here?"

"Why, he took a herd down to Mesquite," she replied, smiling at Hopalong, who limped slowly into the room with Charley slung under his arm like a sack of flour. "He should be back any day now. And won't he be wild with delight when he finds you two boys here! You have no idea how he talks about you, even in his sleep—oh, if I were inclined to jealousy you might not be so welcome!"

"Ma'am," grinned Red, tickled as a boy with a new gun, "you don't never want to go an' get jealous of a couple of old horned toads like us—well, like Hoppy, anyhow. We'll sort of ride herd on him, too, every time he goes to town. Talk about revenge! Oh, you wait! So he went off an' left you all alone? Didn't he write about some trouble that was loose down here?"

"It was—but it's cleaned up. He didn't leave me in any danger—every man down here is our friend," Margaret replied, quick to sense the carefully hidden thought which had prompted his words, and to defend her husband.

"Well, two more won't hurt, nohow," grunted Red. "You say he ought to get here any day?"

"I'm spending more time at the south windows every day," she smiled. "I don't know what will happen to the housework if it lasts much longer!"

"South windows?" queried Hopalong, standing Charley on his head before letting loose of him. "Th' trail is west, ain't it?" he demanded, which caused Red to chuckle inwardly at how his friend was becoming observant again.

"The idea!" retorted Margaret. "Do you think my boy will care anything about any trail that leads roundabout? He'll leave the trail at the Triangle and come straight for this house! What are hills and brush and a miserable little creek to *him*, when he's coming home? I thought you knew my boy."

"We did, an' we do," laughed Red. "I'm bettin' yore way—I hope he's got a good horse—it'll be a dead one if it ain't."

"He's saving Pepper for the homestretch—if you know what *that* means!"

"Hey, Red," said Charley, slyly. "Yore gun works, don't it?"

"Shore thing. Why?"

"Well, mine don't," sighed the boy. "Wonder if yourn is too heavy, an' strong, for a boy like me to shoot? *Bet* it ain't."

Margaret's low reproof was lost in Red's burst of laughter, and again a smile crept to Hopalong's face, a smile full of heartache. This eager boy made his memories painfully alive.

"You an' me an' Hoppy will shore go out an' see,"

promised Red. "Mrs. Johnny will trust you with us, I bet. Hello! Here's somebody comin'," he announced, looking out of the door.

"That's my dad!" cried Charley, bolting from the house so as to be the first one to give his father the good news.

Arnold rode up laughing, dismounted and entered the house with an agility rare to him. And he was vastly relieved. "Well! Well! Well!" he shouted, shaking hands like a pump handle. "I saw you ride over the hill an' got here as fast as Lazy would bring me. Red an' Hopalong! Our household gods with us in the flesh! And that scalawag off seeing the sights of strange towns when his old friends come to visit him. I'm glad to see you boys! The place is yours. Red and Hopalong! I'm not a drinkin' man, but there are times when—follow me while Peggy gets supper!"

"Can I go with you, Dad?" demanded Charley.

"You help Peggy set the table."

"Huh! *I* don't care! Me an' Hoppy an' Red are goin' after bear, an' I'm goin' to use Red's gun."

"Seems to me, Charley," reproved Arnold, "that you are pretty familiar, for a boy; and especially on such short acquaintance. You might begin practicing the use of the word 'Mister.' "

"Or say 'Uncle Red' and 'Uncle Hopalong,' " suggested Margaret.

" 'Red' is my name, an' I'm shore 'Red' to him," defended that person.

"Which goes for me," spoke up his companion. "I'm Hopalong, or Hoppy to anybody in this family—though 'Uncle' suits me fine."

"Then we'll have a fair exchange," retorted Margaret, smiling. "The family circle calls me 'Margaret' or 'Peggy.' "

"If you want to rile her, call her Maggie," said Charley. "She goes right on th' prod!"

"I'm plumb peaceful," laughed Red, turning to follow his host. "You help Mrs.—Margaret, an' when I come back you an' me'll figger on goin' after bear as soon as we can."

CHAPTER III

A Question of Identity

JOHNNY SAUNTERED into Quayle's barroom and leaned against the bar, talking to Ed Doane. An hour or two before he had finished his dinner, warned his outfit again about the early start on the morrow, advanced them some money, and watched them leave the hotel for one more look at the town, and now he was killing time.

"What do you think about Kane's?" asked Ed carelessly, and then looked up as a customer entered. When the man went out he repeated the question.

Johnny cogitated and shrugged his shoulders. "Same as you. Reg'lar cow-town gamblin'-hall, with th' same fixin's, wimmin', crooked games, an' wise bums hangin' 'round. Am I right?"

A group entered, and when they had been served they went into the hotel office, the bartender's eyes on them as long as they were in sight. He turned and frowned. "Purty near. You left a couple of things out. I'm not sayin' what they are, but I *am* sayin' this: Don't you ever pull no gun in there if you should have any trouble. Wait till you get yore man outside. Funny thing about that—sort of a spell, I reckon—but no stranger ever got a gun out an' workin' in Kane's place. They died too quick, or was put out of workin' order."

Johnny raised his eyebrows: "Mebby no good man ever tried to get one out, an' workin'."

"You lose," retorted Ed emphatically. "Some of 'em was shore to be good. It's a cold deck—with a sharp-shooter. There I go again!" he snorted. "I'm certainly shootin' off my mouth today. I must be loco!"

"Then don't let that worry you. I ain't shootin' mine off," Johnny reassured him. "I'm tryin' to figger—"

A voice from the street interrupted him. "Hey, stranger! Yore outfit's in trouble down in Red Frank's!"

Johnny swung from the bar. "Where's *his* place?" he asked.

"One street back," nodded the bartender, indicating the rear of the room. "Turn to yore right—third door. It's a dive—look sharp!"

Johnny grunted and turned to obey the call. Walking out of the door, he went to the corner, turned it, and soon turned the second corner. As he rounded it he saw stars, reached for his guns by instinct, and dropped senseless. Two shadowy figures pounced upon him, rolled him over, and deftly searched him.

Back in the hotel Idaho stuck his head into the bar-room. "Seen Nelson?" he asked.

"Just went to Red Frank's this minute—his gang's in trouble there!" quickly replied Ed.

"I'll go 'round an' be handy, anyhow," said Idaho, loos-ening his gun as he went through the door. Rounding the first corner, he saw a figure flit into the darkness across the street and disappear, and as he turned the second corner he tripped and fell over a prostrate man. One glance and his match went out. Jumping around the cor-ner, he saw a second man run across an open space between two clumps of brush, and his quick hand chopped down, a finger of flame spitting into the night. A curse of pain answered it and he leaped forward, hot and vengeful; but his search was in vain, and he soon gave it up and hastened back to his prostrate friend, whom he found sitting up against the wall with an open jackknife in his hand.

"What happened?" demanded Idaho, stopping and bending down. "Where'd he get you?"

"Somethin' fell on my head—an' my guns are gone," mumbled Johnny. "I—bet I've been robbed!" His slow, fumbling search revealed the bitter truth, and he grunted. "Clean! Clean!"

"I shoved a hunk of lead under th' skin of somebody runnin'—heard him yelp," Idaho said. "Lost him in th' dark. Here, grab holt of me. I'll take you to my room in th' hotel. Able to toddle?"

"Able to kill th' skunk with my bare han's," growled the unfortunate, staggering to his feet. "I'm goin' to Kane's!" he asserted, and Idaho's arguments were exhausted before he was able to have his own way.

"You come along with me—I want to look at yore head. An', besides, you ought to have a gun before you go huntin'. Come on. We'll go in through th' kitchen— that's th' nearest way. It's empty now, but th' door's never locked."

"You gimme a gun, an' I'll know where to go!" blazed Johnny, trembling with weakness. "I showed my roll in there, like a fool. Eleven hundred—hell of a foreman *I* am!"

"You can't just walk into a place an' start shootin'!" retorted Idaho, angrily. "*Will* you listen to sense? Come on, now. After you get sensible you can do what you want, an' I'll go along an' help you do it. That's fair, ain't it? How do you know that feller belongs to Kane's crowd? May be a Greaser, an' a mile away by now. Come on—be sensible!"

"Th' SV can't afford to lose that money—oh, well," sighed Johnny, "yo're right. Go ahead. I'll wash off th' blood, anyhow. I must be a holy show."

They got to Idaho's room without arousing any unusual interest and Idaho examined the throbbing bump with clumsy fingers, receiving frank statements for his awkwardness.

"Shucks," he grinned, straightening up. "It's as big as

an egg, but besides th' skin bein' broke an' a lot of blood, there ain't nothin' th' matter. I'll wash it off—an' if you keep yore hat on, nobody'll know it. I reckon that hat just about saved that thick skull of yourn."

"What did you see when you found me?" asked Johnny when his friend had finished the job.

Idaho told him and added: "Hoped I could tell him by th' yelp, but I can't, unless, mebby, I go around an' make everybody in this part of th' country yelp for me. But I don't reckon that's hardly reasonable."

"Yo're right," grinned Johnny. "Well," he said, after a moment's thought, "I don't go back home without eleven hundred dollars, U.S., an' my guns; but I got to send th' boys back. They can't help me none, bein' known as my friends. Besides, we're all broke, an' they're needed on th' ranch. If I *knowed* that Kane had a hand in this, I'd cussed soon get that money back!"

"Yo're shore plumb set on that Kane idear."

"I showed that wad of bills in just two places: Ed's bar, an' Kane's joint."

"Ed's bar is out of it if nobody else was in there at th' time."

"Only Ridley, Ed, an' myself."

"Somebody could 'a' looked in th' window," suggested Idaho.

"Nobody did, because I was lookin' around."

"If you go in Kane's an' make a gunplay, you'll never know how it happened or who done it; an' if you go in, without a gunplay, an' let 'em know what you think, some Greaser'll hide a knife in you. Then you'll never get it back."

"Just th' same, that's th' place to start from," persisted Johnny doggedly. "An' from th' inside, too."

Idaho frowned. "That may be so, but startin' it from there means to end it there an' then. You can't buck Kane in his own place. It's been tried more'n once. I ain't shore you can buck him in this town, or part of th' country. Bigger people than you are suspected of payin' him money to let 'em alone. You'd be surprised if I named names. Look here: I better speak a little piece about this part of th' country. This county is unorganized an' ain't got no courts, nor nothin' else except a peace officer which we calls sheriff. It's big, but it ain't got many votes, an' what it has is one-third Greaser. Most Greasers don't amount to much in a stand-up fight, but their votes count. They are all for Kane. We've only had one election for sheriff, an' although Corwin is purty well known, he won easy. Kane did it, an' when anybody says 'Corwin,' they might as well say 'Kane.' He is boss of this section. His gamblin'-joint is his headquarters, an' it's guarded forty ways from th' jack. His gang is made up of all kinds, from th' near decent down to th' night killer. When Kane wants a man killed, that man don't live long. Corwin takes his orders before an' after a play like this one. Yo're expected to report it to him. Comin' down to cases, th' pack has got to be fed, an' they have got to make a killin' once in a while. Even if Kane ain't in on it direct, he'll get most of that money across his bar or tables. To wind up a long speech, you better go home with yore men, for that ain't enough money to get killed over."

"Mebby not if it was mine!" snapped Johnny. "An' I ain't shore about that, neither. An' there's more'n money in this, an' more than th' way I was handled. Somebody in this wart of a town has got Johnny Nelson's two guns—an' nobody steals *them* an' keeps 'em! I got friends, lots of 'em, in Montanny, that would lend me th' money quick; but there ain't nobody can give me them six-guns but th' thief that's got 'em. I'm rooted—solid."

"All right," said Idaho. "Yo're talkin' foolish, but cussed if I don't like to hear it. So me an' you are goin' to hog-tie that gang. If I get Corwin in th' ruckus, I'll be satisfied."

"Yo're th' one that's talkin' foolish," retorted Johnny, fighting back his grin. "An I'm cussed if *I* don't like to hear it. But there's this correction: Me an' you ain't goin' to bulldog that gang at all. *I* am. Yo're goin' to sprawl on yore saddle an' light out for wherever you belong, an' stay there. Yo're a marked man an' wouldn't last th' swish of a longhorn's tail. Yore brand is registered—they got you in their brand books; but they ain't got mine. I'm not wearin' no brand. I ain't even ear-notched, 'though I musta been a 'sleeper' when I let 'em put this walnut on my head. I'm a plain, ornery maverick. Think I'm comin' out in th' open? I don't want no brass band playin' when I go to war. I'm a Injun."

"Yo're a little striped animal in this town—one of them kind that's onpleasant up-wind from a feller," snorted Idaho. "How can you play Injun when they know yo're hangin' 'round here lookin' for yore money? Answer me that, maverick!"

"I'm comin' to that. Can you get me an old hat? One that's plumb wore out?"

"Reckon so," grunted Idaho, in surprise. "Th' clerk might be able to dig one up."

"No, not th' clerk; but Ed Doane," corrected Johnny. "Now you think hard before you answer this one: Could you see my face plain when you found me? Could *they* have seen it plain enough to be shore it was me?"

Idaho stared at him and a cheerful expression drifted across his face. "I'm gettin' th' drift of this Injun business," he muttered. "Mebby—mebby—cuss it, it *will* work! I couldn't see nothin' but a bump on th' ground along that wall till I lit a match. I'll get you a hat an' I'll plant it, too."

Johnny nodded. "Plant anythin' else you want that don't look like anythin' I own. Be shore that hat ain't like mine."

Idaho raised his hand as a sudden tramping sounded on the stairs. "That yore outfit?" he asked as a loud, querulous voice was heard.

Johnny went to the door and called, whereupon Arch waved his companions toward their quarters and answered the summons, following his foreman into the room. Johnny was about to close the door when Idaho arose and pushed past him.

"We been talkin' too loud," whispered the departing puncher. "You never can tell. I'm goin' out to sit on th' top step where there's more air," and he went on again, the door closing after him.

Johnny turned and smiled at Arch's expression. "You

boys leave at daylight on th' jump. I got to stay here. You can say I'm waitin' for th' chance to pick up some money—buyin' a herd of yearlin's cheap, or anythin' you can think of. Anythin' that'll stick. You'll have plenty of time to smooth it out before you get back home. I want you boys to scratch up every cent you've got an' turn it over to me. Any left of that I gave you after supper?"

"Shore—quite some," grinned Arch. "We had better luck, down th' street. You must be aimin' to get a-plenty yearlin's, with that roll you got. What are *we* goin' to do, busted?"

"I want a couple of Colts, too," continued Johnny. "You won't need any money. Th' waggin is well stocked—an' when you get back you can draw on Arnold."

"We was goin' to stop at Highbank for a good time," protested Arch.

"Have it in yore old man's hotel an' owe it to him," suggested Johnny.

"Have a good time in my old man's place!" exclaimed Arch. "Oh, *hell*!" He burst out laughing. "That'll tickle th' boys, *that* will!" The puncher looked searchingly at his foreman. "Hey, what's all th' trouble?"

Johnny thought it would be wiser to post his companion and crisply told what had happened.

Arch cleared his throat, hitched up his belt, and looked foolish but determined. "It's been comin' rapid, but I got it all. Yo're talkin' to th' wrong man. You want to fix up that story for th' ranch with some soft-belly that's ridin' that way. Better send a letter. We're all stayin' here. *Fine* bunch of—"

"You can help me more by goin' back like nothin's happened," interrupted Johnny. "Th' ranch won't be worryin' me then, an' if you stayed here it might give th' game away. Besides, one man can live longer on th' money we got than four can, only have a quarter of th' chance to drink too much, an' only talk a fourth as much. That's th' natural play, an' everythin' has *got* to be natural."

"That's th' worst of havin' a smooth face," grumbled

Arch, ruefully rubbing his chin. "If I only had whiskers, I could shave 'em off an' be a total stranger; but I don't reckon I could grow a good enough bunch to get back here in time."

Johnny laughed, his heart warming to the puncher. "Take *you* a year or two; an' there's more'n whiskers needed to hide from a *good* man. There's little motions, gait, voice—oh, lots of things. You can help me more if you go north. See Dave Green, tell him on th' quiet, an' ask him to send me down a couple hundred dollars. He can buy a check from th' Doc, payable to George Norton. There's a bank in this town. He's to send it to George Norton, general delivery."

"Dave will spread it far an' wide," objected Arch. "He tells all he knows."

"If he did," smiled Johnny, "it shore would be an eddication for th' man that heard it. He talks a lot—an' says nothin'. If he told all he knew, hell would 'a' popped long ago on them ranges. I'm only wishin' he could get a job in Kane's!"

"Gosh!" exclaimed Arch. "Mebby he can. He's a bang-up bartender."

Johnny shook his head and laughed.

"Well, I reckon you know best," said Arch. "If you say so, we'll go home—but it hurts bad as a toothache. An' as long as we're goin', we can start tonight—this minute."

"You'll start at daylight, like honest folks," chuckled Johnny. "Think I want Kane to sit down an' figger why a lazy outfit got ambitious all at once? An' th' two boys that lend me their guns want to be ridin' close to th' waggin, on its left side, until they get out of town. I don't want anybody noticin' they ain't got their guns. Mebby their coats'll hide 'em, anyhow. But before you do anythin' else, get me a copy of that weekly newspaper downstairs. There's some layin' around th' office. Shore you got it all?"

Arch nodded, and his foreman opened the door. Idaho glanced around and then went down the stairs and through the office, stopping at the bar, where he held a low-voiced conversation with the man behind it. Ed looked a little surprised at the unusual request, but Idaho's earnestness and anxiety told him enough and he asked no questions. A few minutes later, after Idaho had disappeared into the kitchen, Ed told the clerk to watch the bar, and went up to his room, and dropped several articles out of the window before he left it again.

When Idaho had finished scouting and planting the sombrero, a broken spur, and a piece torn from a red kerchief, he went into the barroom and grinned at his friend Nelson, who leaned carelessly back against the wall; and then his eyes opened wide as he saw the size of the roll of bills from which Johnny was peeling the outer layer. For two hours they sat and played California Jack in plain sight of the street as though nothing unusual had occurred, Johnny's sombrero pushed back on his head, the walnut handle of one of his guns in plain sight, his boots not only guiltless of spurs, but showing that they never had borne them, and his faded, soiled, blue neckerchief was as it had been all day. His mood was cheerful and his laughter rang out from time to time as his friend's witticisms gave excuse. To test his roll, he pulled it out again under his friend's eyes and thumbed off a bill, changed his mind, rolled it back again, and carelessly shoved the handful into his pocket.

Idaho leaned forward. "Who th' devil did *you* slug?" he softly asked.

"Tell you later—deal 'em up," grunted Johnny, a sigh of satisfaction slipping from him. It had been one of Tex Ewalt's maxims never to be broke, even if carefully trimmed newspapers had to serve as padding, and in this instance, at least, Johnny believed his old friend to be right. The world finds bluff very useful, and opulence seldom receives a cold shoulder.

At daylight three horsemen and a wagon went slowly up the little street, two men sticking close to each other and the vehicle, and soon became lost to sight. Two or three nighthawks paused and watched the outfit, and one of them went swiftly into Kane's side door. Idaho drew back from the corner of the hotel where he had been watching, nodded wisely to himself, and went into the stable to look after his horse.

The little outfit of the SV stopped when a dozen miles had been put behind and prepared and ate a hurried breakfast. As he gulped the last swallow of coffee, Arch arose and went to his horse.

"Thirty miles a day with a waggin takes too long," he said. "One of you boys ride in th' waggin an' gimme a lead hoss. Nelson's a good man, an' it's our job to help him all we can. I can do it that way between sleeps, if I can keep my eyes open to th' end of it. By gettin' a fresh cayuse from my old man at Highbank, I'll set a record for these parts."

Gardner nodded. "Take my cayuse, Arch. I'm crucifyin' myself on th' cross of friendship. Cook, give him some grub."

Ten minutes later Arch left them in a cloud of dust, glad to get away from the wagon and keen to make a ride that would go down in local history.

After breakfast Johnny sauntered into the barroom, nodded carelessly to the few men there, and seated himself in his favorite chair.

"Thought mebby you might be among th' dear departed this mornin'," remarked Ed carelessly. "Heard a shot soon after you left last night, but they're so common 'round here that I didn't get none excited. Have any trouble in Red Frank's?"

"You better pinch yoreself," retorted Johnny. "You saw me an' Idaho settin' right in this room, playin' cards long after that shot. I was upstairs when I heard it. Didn't go to Red Frank's. Changed my mind when I got around at th' side of th' hotel, an' went through th' kitchen, upstairs lookin' for Idaho. What business I got playin' nurse to four growed-up men? A lot they'd thank me for cuttin' in on their play."

"Did they have any trouble?"

"No; they wasn't in Red Frank's at all—anyhow, that's what they said. Somebody playin' a joke, or seein' things, I reckon. Seen Idaho this mornin'?"

"No, I ain't," answered Ed sleepily. "Reckon he's still

abed. Say, was that yore outfit under my winder before dawn? I come cussed near shootin' th' loud-mouthed fool that couldn't talk without shoutin'."

Johnny laughed. "I reckon it was. They was sore about havin' to go home. Know of any good yearlin's I can buy cheap?"

Ed yawned, rubbed his eyes, and slowly shook his head. "Too close to Ridley. Folks down here mostly let 'em grow up an' sell 'em to him. Prices would be too high, anyhow, I reckon. Better hunt for 'em nearer home."

"That's what I been doin'," growled Johnny. "Well, mebby yo're right about local prices an' conditions; but I'm goin' to poke around an' ask questions, anyhow. To tell you th' truth, a town looks good to me for a change, 'though I'm admittin' this ain't much of a town, at that. Sorta dead—nothin' happens, at all."

"That's th' fault of th' visitor, then," retorted Ed, another yawn nearly disrupting his face. "Ho-hum! Some day I'm goin' out an' find me a cave, crawl in it, close it up behind me, an' sleep for a whole week. An' from th' looks of you, it wouldn't do you no harm to do th' same thing." He nodded heavily to the other customers as they went out.

"I'll have plenty of time for sleep when I get home," grinned Johnny. "I got to get some easy money out of this town before I think of sleepin'. Kane's don't get lively till dark, does it?"

Ed snorted. "Was you sayin' easy money?" he demanded with heavy sarcasm.

"I was."

"Oh, well; if you must I reckon you must," grunted the bartender, shrugging his shoulders.

"A new man, playin' careful, allus wins in a place like Kane's, if he's got a wad of money as big as mine," chuckled Johnny, voicing another maxim of his friend Tex, and patting the bulging roll in his pocket.

Ed looked at the pocket, and frowned. "Huh! Lord help that wad!" he mourned.

"It's got all th' help it needs," countered Johnny. "I'm

its guardian. I might change it for bigger bills, for it's purty prominent now. However, that can wait till it grows some more." He burst out laughing. "Big as it is, there's room for more."

"Better keep some real little ones on th' outside," suggested Ed wisely. "You show it too cussed much."

"Do you know there's allus a right an' a wrong way of doin' everythin'?" asked his companion. "A man that's got a lot of money will play safe an' stick a few little ones on th' outside; but a man that's got only little bills will try to get a big one for th' cover. One is tryin' to hide his money; th' other to run a bluff. Wise gamblers know that. I got little bills on th' outside of mine. You watch 'em welcome me."

Despite his boasts, he did not spend much time in Kane's, but slept late and hung around the hotel for a day or two, and then, one morning, he got a nibble on his bait. He was loafing on the hotel steps when he caught sight of the sheriff coming up the street. Corwin had been out of town and had returned only the night before. Seeing the lone man on the steps, the peace officer lengthened his rolling stride and headed straight for the hotel, his eyes fixed on the hat, guns, kerchief, and boots.

"Mornin'," he said, nodding and stopping.

"Mornin'," replied Johnny cheerily. "Bright an' cool, but a little mite too windy for this hour of th' day," he observed, watching a vicious little whirlwind of dust racing up the middle of the street. It suddenly swerved in its course, struck the sheriff, and broke, covering them with bits of paper and hurling dust and sand in their faces and mouths. Other furious little gusts sent the light debris of the street high in the air to be tossed about wildly before settling back to earth again.

"Yo're shore shoutin'," growled Corwin, spitting violently and rubbing his lips. "Don't like th' looks of it. Ain't got no love for a sand storm." He let his blinking eyes rest for a moment on his companion's boots, noted an entire absence of any signs of spur straps, glanced at the guns and at the opulent bump in one of the trouser pockets, noted the blue neckerchief, and gazed into the light blue eyes, which were twinkling at his expression of disgust. "Damn th' sand," he grunted, spitting again. "How do you like this town of ourn, outside of th' dust, now that you've seen more of it?"

Johnny smiled broadly. "Leavin' out a few things besides th' dust—such as bein' too quiet, dead, an' lackin' 'most everythin' a town should have—I'd say it is a purty fair town for its kind. But, bad as it is, it ain't near as bad as that bed I've been sleepin' in. It reminds me of some of th' country I've rid over. It's full of mesas, ridges, canyons, an' valleys, an' all of 'em run th' wrong way. Cuss such a bed. I gave it up after awhile, th' first night, an' played Idaho cards till I was so sleepy I could 'a' slept on a cactus. After that, though, it ain't been so bad. It's all in gettin' used to it, I reckon."

The sheriff laughed politely. "Well, I reckon there ain't no bed like a feller's own. Speakin' of th' town bein' dead, that is yore fault; you shouldn't stay so close to th' hotel. Wander around a little an' you'll find it plumb lively. There's Red Frank's an' Kane's—they are high-strung enough for 'most anybody." The momentary gleam in his eyes was not lost on his companion.

"Red Frank's," cogitated Johnny. Then he laughed. "I come near goin' in there, at that. Anyhow, I shore started."

"Why didn't you go on?" inquired the sheriff, speaking as if from polite, idle curiosity. "You might 'a' seen some excitement in there."

"Somebody tried to play a joke on me," grinned Johnny, "but I fooled 'em. My boys are shore growed up."

"How'd yore boys make out?"

"They said they wasn't in there at all. Reckon somebody got excited or drunk if they wasn't tryin' to make a fool out of me. But, come to think of it, I *did* hear a shot."

"They're not as rare as they're goin' to be," growled the sheriff. "But it's hard to stop th' shootin'. Takes time."

Johnny nodded. "Reckon so. You got a bad crowd of Greasers here, too, which makes it harder—though they're generally strong on knifeplay. Mexicans, monte, an' mescal are a bad combination."

"Better tell yore boys to look sharp in Red Frank's. It's a bad place, 'specially if a man's got likker in him. An' they'll steal him blind."

"Don't have to tell 'em, for I sent 'em home," replied Johnny, and then he grinned. "An' there ain't no man livin' can rob 'em, neither, for I wouldn't let 'em draw any of their pay. Bein' broke, they didn't kick up as much of a fuss as they might have. I know how to handle my outfit. Say!" he exclaimed. "Yo're th' very man I been lookin' for, an' I didn't know it till just this minute. Do you know where I can pick up a herd of a couple or three hundred yearlin's at a fair figger?"

Corwin shook his head. "You might get a few here an' there, but they ain't worth botherin' about. Anyhow, prices are too high. Better look around on yore way back, up on some of them God-forsaken ranges north of here. But how'll you handle a herd with yore outfit gone?"

His companion grinned and winked knowingly. "I'll handle it by buyin' subject to delivery. Let somebody else have th' fun of drivin' a lot of crazy-headed yearlin's all that distance. Growed-up steers are bad enough, an' I've had all I want of them for awhile. Well," he chuckled, "not havin' no yearlin's to buy, I reckon I've got time to wander around nights. Six months in a ranchhouse is shore confinin'. I need a change. What do you say to a little drink?"

Corwin wiped more sand from his lips. "It's a little early in th' day for me, but I'm with you. This blasted wind looks like it's gettin' worse," he growled, scowling as he glanced about.

"It's only addin' to th' liveliness of yore little town," chuckled Johnny, leading the way.

"We ain't had a sand storm in three years," boasted the sheriff, hard on his companion's heels. "I see you know th' way," he commented.

Johnny set down his empty glass and brought up the roll of bills, peeled the outer from its companions, and tossed it on the bar. "You got to take somethin' with us, Ed," he reproved.

Ed shrugged his shoulders, slid the change across the counter, and became thoughtfully busy with the arrangement of the various articles on the backbar.

Corwin treated, talked a few moments, and then departed, his busy brain asking many questions and becoming steadily more puzzled.

Ed mopped the bar without knowing he was doing it, and looked at his new friend. "Where'd you pick *that* up?" he asked.

"Meanin'?" queried Johnny, glancing at the windows, where sand was beating at the glass and pushing in through every crack in the woodwork.

"Corwin."

"Oh, he rambled up an' got talkin'. Reckon I'll go out, sand or no sand, an' see if I can get track of any yearlin's, just to prove that you don't know anythin' about th' cow business."

"Nobody but a fool would go out into that unless they shore had to," retorted Ed. "It's goin' to get worse, shore as shootin'. I know 'em. Lord help anybody that has to go very far through it!"

Johnny opened the door, stuck his head out and ducked back in again. Tying his neckerchief over his mouth and nose, he went to the rear door, closed his eyes, and plunged out into the storm, heading for the stable to look to the comfort of his horse. Pepper rubbed her nozzle against him, accepted the sugar with dignity, and followed his every move with her great, black eyes. He hung a sack over the window and, finding nails on a shelf, secured it against the assaults of the wind.

"There, Pepper Girl—reckon you'll be right snug; but don't you go an' butt it out to see what's goin' on outside. I'm glad this ain't no common shed. Four walls are a heap better than three today."

"That you, Nelson?" came a voice from the door. Idaho slid in, closed the door behind him with a bang, and dropped his gun into the holster. "This is shore a reg'lar storm; an' that's shore a reg'lar hoss!" he exclaimed, spitting and blowing. He stepped toward the object of his admiration.

"Look out!" warned Johnny. "She's likely to brain a stranger. Trained her that way. She'll mebby kill anybody that comes in here; but not hardly while I'm around, I reckon. Teeth an' hoofs—she's a bad one if she don't know you. That's why I try to get her a stable of her own. What was you doin' with th' six-gun?"

"Keepin' th' sand out of it," lied Idaho. "Thiefproof, huh?" he chuckled. "I'm sayin' it's a good thing. Ever been tried?"

"Twice," answered Johnny. "She killed th' first one." He lowered his voice. "I'm figgerin' Corwin knows about that little fracas of th' other night. Did you tell anybody?"

"Not a word. What about yore outfit?"

"Tight as fresh-water clams, an', besides, they didn't have no chance to. They even left without their breakfast. But I'm dead shore he knows. How did he find it out?"

"Looks like you might be right, after all," admitted Idaho. "I kept a lookout that mornin', like I told you, an' th' news of yore outfit leavin' was shore carried, which means that somebody in Kane's gang was plumb interested. How much do you think Corwin knows about it?"

"Don't know; but not as much now as he did before he saw me this mornin'," answered Johnny. "When he sized me up, his eyes gave him away—just a little flash. But now he may be wonderin' who th' devil it was that got clubbed that night. An' he showed more signs when he saw my money. Say: How much does Ed know?"

"Not a thing," answered Idaho. "He's one of my best friends, an' none of my best friends ask me questions when I tell 'em not to. An' now I'm glad I told him not to, because, of course, you don't know anythin' about him. No, sir," he emphatically declared; "anythin' that Corwin knows come from th' other side. What you goin' to do?"

"I don't know," admitted Johnny. "I got to wrastle that out; but I *do* know that I ain't goin' out of th' hotel today. It looks like Californy Jack for us till this blows over. Yore cayuse fixed all right?"

"Shore; good as I can. Come on, if yo're ready."

"Hadn't you better carry yore gun in yore hand, so th' sand won't get in it?" asked Johnny gravely.

Idaho looked at him and laughed. "Come on—I'm startin'," he said, and he dashed out of the building, Johnny close at his heels.

CHAPTER IV

A Journey Continued

POUNDING INTO Highbank from the south, Arch turned the two fagged-out horses into his father's little corral, roped the better of the two he found there, saddled it, and rode around to the front of the hotel, where he called loudly.

Pete Wiggins went to the door and scowled at his son. "What you doin' with that hoss?" he demanded in no friendly tone.

"Breakin' records," impudently answered his young hopeful. "Left Big Creek, north of Mesquite, at six-twenty this mornin', an' I'm due in Gunsight before dark. Left you two cayuses for this one—but don't ride 'em too hard. So-long!" and he was off in a cloud of dust.

Pete Wiggins stepped forward galvanically and called, shaking his fist. "Come back here! Don't you kill *that* hoss!"

His beloved son's reply was anything but filial, but as long as his wrathful father did not hear it, perhaps it may better be left out of the record.

The shadows were long when Arch drew up in front of the "Palace" in Gunsight, and dismounted almost in the door. He looked at his watch and proudly shouted the miles and the time of the ride before looking to see who was there to hear it. As he raised his head and saw Dave Green, Arnold, and two strangers staring at him, he called himself a fool, walked stiffly to a chair, and lowered himself gently into it.

"That's shore some ridin'," remarked Dave, surprised. "What's wrong? What's th' reason for killin' cayuses?"

"Wanted to paste somethin' up for others to shoot at," grinned Arch, making the best of the situation.

"How'd you come to leave ahead of Nelson?" demanded Arnold, his easy-going boss. "Where is he? An' where's th' rest of th' boys?" The SV owner was fast falling into the vernacular, which made him fit better into the country.

"Oh, he's tryin' to make a fortune buyin' up a herd of fine yearlin's," answered the record-maker with confident assurance. "It ain't nothin' to him that th' owner don't want to sell 'em. I near busted laughin' at 'em wranglin'. They was near fightin' when I left. You should 'a' heard 'em! Anybody'd think that man didn't own his own cattle. But I'm bettin' on Nelson, just th' same, for when I left they had got to wranglin' about th' price, an' that's allus a hopeful sign. He shore will tire that man out. I used a lead hoss as far as Highbank, changin' frequent', an' got a fresh off th' old man. Nelson told us all to go home, where we're needed—but he'll be surprised when he knows how quick *I* got there. Sam an' th' others are with th' waggin, comin' slower."

"I should hope so!" snorted Arnold. "An' you ain't home yet. What's th' real reason for all this speed, an' for headin' here instead of goin' to th' ranch? A man that's born truthful makes a poor liar; but I'll say this for you, Arch—with a little practice you'll be near as good as Dave, here. Come on; tell it!"

Arch looked wonderingly at his employer, grinned at Dave, and then considered the two strangers. "I've done told it already," he affirmed, stiffly.

"Shake hands with Red Connors an' Hopalong Cassidy," said Arnold. "You've heard of them, haven't you?"

"Holy cats! I *have*!" exclaimed Arch, gripping the

hands of the two in turn. "I certainly have. Have you two ever been in Mesquite?" he demanded, eagerly. "Good! Now, wait a minute; I want to think," and he went into silent consultation with himself.

"Mebby he's aimin' to improve on me," said Dave. "Judgin' from th' studyin', I figger he's trying to bust in yore class, Arnold."

Arch grinned from one to the other. "Seein' as how we're all friends of Nelson, an' his wife ought to be kept calm, I reckon I ought to spit it out straight. Here, you listen," and he told the truth as fully and completely as he knew it.

Arnold shook his head at the end of the recital. The loss of the herd money was a hard blow, but he was too much of a man to make it his chief concern. "Arch," he said slowly, "yo're so fond of breakin' records that yo're goin' to sleep in town, get another horse at daylight, an' break yore own record gettin' back to Mesquite. Tell that son-in-law of mine to come home right away, before Peggy is left a widow. It's no fault of his that he lost it— it's to his credit, goin' to the aid of his men. I wouldn't 'a' had it to lose if it wasn't for what he's done for th' SV. He earned it for me; an' if he's lost it, all right."

"Most generally th' East sends us purty poor specimens," observed Dave. "Once in awhile we get a thoroughbred. Gunsight's proud of th' one it got."

"Arnold," said Arch eagerly, "I'll get to Mesquite tomorrow if it's moved to th' other side of hell!"

Hopalong took the cigar from his mouth. "Wait a minute," he said. He slowly knocked the ashes from it and looked around. "While I'm appreciatin' what you just said, Arnold, I don't agree with it." He thought for a moment and then continued. "You don't know that son-in-law of yourn like I do. Somebody knocked him on th' head, stole his money an' his guns. Don't forget th' guns. Bein' an easterner, that mebby don't mean anythin' to you; but bein' an old Bar-20 man, it means a heap to me. He won't leave till he's squared up, all around. I *know* it. Seein' how it is, we got to accept it; an' figger out some way to make his wife take it easy, an' not do no worryin'.

Here!" he exclaimed, leaning forward. "Arnold, you sit down an' write him a letter. Write it now. Tell him to stay down there until he gets a good herd of yearlin's. Then Arch has got to start back in th' mornin' an' join th' wag-gin, an' come home like he ought to. He stays here tonight, an' nobody has seen him, at all."

"An' Dave don't need to bother with any check," said Red. "Hoppy an' me has plenty of money. We'll start for Mesquite at daylight, Arch, here, ridin' with us till we meet th' waggin. Of course, Hoppy don't mean that yo're really goin' to write a letter, Arnold," he explained.

"That's just what I *do* mean," said Hopalong. "He's goin' to write th' letter, but he ain't goin' to send it. He'll give it to Arch, an' then it can be torn up. What's th' use of lyin' when it's so easy to tell th' truth? 'Though I'm ad-mittin' I wasn't thinkin' of that so much as I was that a man can allus tell th' truth better'n he can lie. When he tells about th' letter, he's goin' to be talkin' about a real letter, what won't get to changin' around in a day or two, or when he gets rattled. Mrs. Johnny is mebby goin' to ask a lot of questions."

"I'll give odds that she does," chuckled Dave, looking under the backbar. "Here's pen an' ink," he said, push-ing the articles across the counter. "There's paper an' envelopes around here some—here it is. Go ahead, now: 'Dear Johnny: I take my—' "

"Shut up!" barked Arnold, glaring at him. "I guess I know how to write a letter! Besides, I don't take my pen in hand. It's your pen, you grinnin' chump! As long as we're ridin' on th' tail of Truth, let's stick to it, all th' way. Shut up, now, an' gimme a chance!" He glared around at the grinning faces, jabbed the pen in the ink, and went to work. When he had finished, he read it aloud, and handed it to Arch, who tore it up and threw the pieces on the floor.

Hopalong reached down, picked up the pieces, and gravely, silently put them on the bar. Dave raked them into his hand, dropped them into a tin dish, and put a match to them. Arnold looked around the little group and snorted.

"Huh! You an' Dave musta gone to th' same school!"

Dave nodded. "We have, I reckon. Experience is a good school, too."

"Th' lessons stick," said Hopalong, looking at Dave with a new interest.

Arch chuckled. "Cuss it! I'll shore hate to stop at that waggin. I'm sayin' Mesquite is goin' to be terrible upset some day soon. Why *ain't* I got whiskers? I'd like to see his face when he sets eyes on you fellers. Bet he'll jump up an' down an' yell!"

"Mebby," said Hopalong, "for if there's any yellin', he'll shore have to start it. He sent you fellers away because you was known to be friends of his, didn't he?"

Dave slapped the bar and laughed outright. "If I wasn't so fat, I'd go with you! I'm beginnin' to see why he thought so much of you fellers. Here—it's time for a drink."

"What are we goin' to tell Margaret?" asked Arnold. "She may get suspicious if you leave so suddenly."

"You just keep repeatin' that letter to yoreself," laughed Red, "an' leave th' rest to better liars. Yo're as bad a liar as Arch, here. Me an' Hoppy may 'a' been born truthful, but we was plumb spoiled in our bringin' up. Reckon we better be leavin' now. Arch, where'll we meet you about two hours after daylight tomorrow?"

Arch groaned. "Shucks! About daylight it'll take Fanning that long to get me out of bed—oh, well," he sighed, resignedly. "I'll be at th' ford, waitin' for you to come along. Come easy, in case I'm asleep."

"South of here, on this trail?" asked Red. "Thought so. All right. So-long," and he followed his slightly limping friend out to the horses.

Dave hurried to the door. "Hey!" he shouted. "Hadn't I better send him that check, anyhow? He may need it before you get there."

A roar of laughter from behind answered him, and he wheeled to face Arch. "When does th' mail leave?" asked the puncher.

"Day after tomorrow," answered Dave, and swung around as a voice from the street rubbed it in.

"You musta played hookey from that school, Dave," jeered Arnold.

"He's fat clean to th' bald spot," shouted Arch. "Come on in, Dave. We ain't got time to hold back for no mail to get there first." He stuck his head out of the window. "So-long, fellers! See you at th' ford."

Dave watched the three until they were well along the trail and then he turned slowly. "I never did really doubt th' stories Nelson told about that old outfit, but if I had any doubts I ain't got them no more. Did you see th' looks in their eyes when you was tellin' about Nelson?"

"I did!" snapped Arch. "Why in hell ain't I got whiskers?"

Reaching the SV, Arnold and his companions put up the horses and walked slowly toward the house, seeing a flurry of white through the kitchen door.

"Think it'll reach him in time?" asked Red, waiting outside the door for Arnold to enter first.

"Ought to. Slim said he would mail it at Highbank as soon as he got there," answered Arnold.

"I shore hope so," said Red. "I'd hate to have that ride for nothin'—an' it would just be our luck to pass him somewhere on th' way, an' get there after he left."

"He'd likely foller th' reg'lar trail up, anyhow," said Hopalong. "It ain't likely we'll miss him."

Margaret put down the dish and looked at them accusingly. "What are you boys talking about?" she demanded.

"Only wonderin' if yore father's letter will get to Johnny in time to catch him before he leaves," said Hopalong. "Dave says it will as long as that Slim feller is takin' it to Highbank with him. Slim live down there?" he asked his host.

"No; goin' down for th' Double X, I suppose," replied Arnold. "Supper ready, Peggy?"

"Not until I learn more about this," retorted Margaret, determinedly. "What letter are you talking about?"

"Oh, I told Johnny to look around and see if he could pick up a good herd of yearlings cheap," answered her father, going into the next room.

Margaret compressed her lips, but said nothing about it, whereupon Red silently swore a stronger oath of allegiance. "The table is waiting for you. I've had to keep the supper warm," she said.

Red nodded understandingly. "Men-folks are shore a trial an' tribulation," he said, passing through the door.

"Hadn't ought to take him very long, I suppose?" queried Arnold, passing the meat one way and the potatoes the other.

Red laughed. "You don't know him very well, yet," he replied. "Give him a chance to dicker over a herd an' he's happy for a week or more. He shore does like to dicker."

"I never saw anything in his nature which would indicate anything like that," said Margaret, tartly. "He always has impressed me with being quite direct. Perhaps I did not understand you correctly?"

"Peggy! Peggy!" reproved her father. "It means bread and butter for us."

"I can eat my bread without butter," she retorted. "As a matter of fact I've seen very little butter out in this country."

Red screwed his face up a little and wriggled his foot. "I don't reckon you've ever seen him buyin' a herd, ma'am?"

"You are quite right, Mr. Connors. I never have."

Red did not take the trouble to inform her that *he* never had seen her husband buy a herd. "I reckon it's his love for gamblin'," he said, carelessly, and instantly regretted it.

"Gambling?" snapped Margaret, her eyes sparking. "Did you say gambling?"

Hopalong flashed one eloquent look at his friend, whose hair now was not the only red thing about him, and removed the last of the peel from the potato. "Red is referrin', I reckon, to th' love of gamblin' that was born in yore husband, Margaret. It allus has been one of his, an' our, fears that it would get th' best of him. But," he said, proudly and firmly, "it never did. Johnny is gettin' past th' age, now, when a deck of cards acts strong on him. An' it's all due to Red. He used to whale him good every time he caught th' Kid playin'."

Red's sanctimonious expression made Hopalong itch to smear the hot potato over it, and the heel of his boot on Red's shin put a look of sorrow on that person's face which was not in the least simulated.

"We all had a hand in that, Margaret," generously remarked the man with the shuddering shin. "Tex Ewalt watched him closest. But, as I was sayin', out at th' corral, I don't believe he's got men enough to handle no herd of yearlin's. Them youngsters are plumb skittish, an' hard to keep on th' trail. Me an' Hoppy are aimin' to go down an' help him—an' see him all th' sooner, to tell you th' truth."

"That will please him," smiled Margaret. She looked at her father, whose appetite seemed to be ravenous, judging by the attention he was giving to the meal. "What did you write, Dad?"

Arnold washed down a refractory mouthful of potato, which suffered from insufficient salivation, and looked up. He repeated the letter carelessly and reached for another swallow of coffee, silently thanking Hopalong for insisting that the letter actually be written.

The meal over, they sat and chatted until after dark, Margaret doing up a bundle of things which she thought her husband might need. When morning came she had breakfast on the table at daylight for her departing friends, and she also had a fat letter for her husband, which she entrusted to Red, the sterling molder of her husband's manly character.

When they had ridden well beyond sight of the house Hopalong thoughtfully dropped the bundle to the ground, turned in the saddle and looked with scorn at his friend. "You shore are a hard-boiled jackass! For two bits I'd 'a' choked you last night. How'd you like to have somebody shoot off his mouth to yore wife about your gamblin'?"

"I've reformed, an' she knows it!"

"Yes, you've reformed! You've reformed a lot, you have!"

"You ain't got no business pickin' on th' man that taught th' Kid most all he knows about poker!" tartly retorted Red.

"Cussed little you ever taught him," rejoined Hopalong. "It was me an' Tex that eddicated his brain, an' fingers. He only used you to practice on."

And so they rode, both secretly pleased by this auspicious beginning of a new day, for the day that started without a squabble usually ended wrong, somehow. Picking up Arch, who yawningly met them at the ford, they pushed southward at a hard pace, relying on the relay which their guide promised to get at Highbank. Reaching this town Arch led them to his father's little corral, and exulted over the four fresh horses which he found there. Saddles were changed with celerity and they rolled on southward again.

Peter Wiggins in the hotel office held the jack of hearts over the ten of the same suit and cocked an ear to listen. Slowly making the play he drew another card from the deck in his hand, and listened again. Reluctant to bestir himself, but a little suspicious, he debated the matter while he played several cards mechanically. Then he arose and walked through the building, emerging from the kitchen door. Three swiftly moving riders, his son in the middle, were taking the long, gentle slope just south of town. Pete's laziness disappeared and he made good time to the corral. One look was enough and he shook a vengeful fist at his heir and pride.

"Twice!" he roared, kicking an inoffensive tomato can over the corral wall. "Twice! Mebby you'll try it again! All right; *I'm* willin'. I never heard of anybody around here thraskin' a twenty-three-year-old son, but as long as yo're bustin' records an' makin' th' Wigginses famous, I ought to do *my* share. Yo're bustin' ridin' records—I'm aimin' to bust th' hidin' records, if you don't smash th' sprintin' records, you grinnin' monkey!"

Pete went into the hotel, soon returning with the cards and a box; and for the rest of the morning played solitaire with the steadily rising sun beating on his back, and swarms of flies exploring his perspiring person.

The three riders were going on, hour after hour, their speed entirely controlled by what they knew of horse-flesh, and when they espied the wagon Arch suggested another change of mounts, which was instantly over-ruled by Hopalong.

"Some of them Mesquite hombres will be rememberin' them cayuses," he said. "We're doin' good enough as we are."

When they reached the wagon and drew rein to breathe their mounts, Joe Reilly grinned a welcome. "Thought you was goin' to Gunsight!" he jeered.

Arch laughed triumphantly. "I've done been there, but got afraid you fellers might get lost. Meet Hopalong Cassidy an' Red Connors, friends of th' foreman."

"Why'n hell didn't you bring my hoss with you, you lo-coed cow?" blazed Sam Gardner from the wagon seat. "You never got to Gunsight. You musta hit a cushion an' bounced back."

"Forgot all about yore piebald," retorted Arch. "But if you must have a cayuse you can ask my old man for one when you get to Highbank. I'd do it for you, only me an' him ain't on th' best of terms right now." He turned to his two new friends. "All you got to do now is foller th' wagon tracks to town."

"So-long," said the two, and whirled away.

They spent the night not many miles north of Big Creek and were riding again at dawn. As they drew nearer to their objective the frisking wind sent clouds of dust whirling around them to their discomfort.

"That must be th' town," grunted Red through his ker-chief as his eyes, squinting between nearly closed lids, caught sight of Mesquite through a momentary opening in the dust-filled air to the southeast.

"Hope so," growled his companion. "Cussed glad of it. This is goin' to be a whizzer. Look at th' tops of them sand hills yonder—streamin' into th' air like smoke from a roarin' prairie fire. Here's where we separate. I'm takin' to th' first shack I find. Don't forget our names, an' that we're strangers, for awhile, anyhow."

Red nodded. "Bill Long an' Red Thompson," he muttered as they parted.

Not long thereafter Hopalong dismounted in the rear of Kane's and put his horse in the nearer of the two stables, doing what he could for the animal's comfort, and then stepped to the door. He paused, glanced back at the "P.W." brand on the horse and smiled. "Red's is a Horseshoe cayuse. That's what I call luck!" and plunged into the sand blasts. Bumping into the wall of Kane's big building he followed it, turned the corner, and groped his way through the front door.

At the sudden gust the bartender looked around and growled. "Close that door! *Pronto!*"

The newcomer slammed it shut and leaned against the wall, rubbing at his eyelids and face, and shed sand at every movement.

The bartender slid a glass of water across the bar. "Here, wash it out. You'll only make 'em worse, rubbin'," he said as the other began rubbing his lips and spitting energetically.

Bill Long obeyed, nodded his thanks and glanced furtively at the door, and became less alert. "Much obliged. I didn't get all there was flyin', but I got a-plenty."

The dispenser of drinks smiled. "Lucky gettin' in out of it when you did."

"Yes," replied Bill, nervously. "Yes; plumb lucky. This will raise th' devil with th' scenery."

"Won't be a trail left," suggested the bartender, watching closely.

Bill glanced up quickly, sighed with satisfaction and then glanced hurriedly around the room. "Whose place is this?" he whispered out of the corner of his mouth.

"Pecos Kane's," grunted the bartender, greatly pleased about something. His pleasure was increased by the quick look of relief which flashed across the other's face, and he chuckled. "Yo're all right in here."

"Yes," said Bill, and motioned toward a bottle. Gulping the drink he paid for it and then leaned over the counter.

"Say, friend," he whispered anxiously, "if anybody comes around askin' for Bill Long, you ain't seen him, savvy?"

"Never even heard of th' gent," smiled the other. "Here's where you should ought to lose yo're name," he suggested.

Bill winked at him and slouched away to become mixed up in the crowd. The checkerboard rear wall obtruded itself upon his vision and he went back and found a seat not far from it and from Kit Thorpe, bodyguard of the invisible proprietor, who sat against the door leading through the partition. Thorpe coldly acknowledged the stranger's nod and continued to keep keen watch over the crowd and the distant front door.

The day was very dull, the sun's rays baffled by the swirling sand, and the hanging kerosene lamps were lit, and as an occasional thundering gust struck the building and created air disturbances inside of it the lamps moved slightly to and fro and added a little more soot to the coating on their chimneys. Bill's natural glance at the unusual design of the rear wall caught something not usual about it and caused an unusual activity to arise in his mind. He knew that his eyes were sore and inflamed, but that did not entirely account for the persistent illusion which they saw when his roving glance, occasionally returning to the wall, swept quickly over it. There were several places where the black was a little blacker, and these spots moved on their edges, contracting and lengthening as the lamps swung gently. Pulling the brim of his hat over his eyes, he faced away from the wall and closed his burning eyelids, but his racing thoughts were keen to solve any riddle which would help to pass the monotonous time. Another veiled glance as he shifted to a more comfortable position gave him the explanation he sought. Those few black squares had been cut out, and the moving strips of black which had puzzled him were the shadows of the edges, moving across a black board which, set back from the thickness of the partition, closed them.

"Peekholes," he thought, and then wondered anew.

Why the lower row, then, so low that a man would have to kneel to look through the openings? "Peekholes," persisted hide-bound Experience, grabbing at the obvious. "Perhaps," doubted Suspicion; "but then, why that lower row?" Suddenly his gunman's mind exulted. "Peekholes above, an' loopholes below." A good gunman would not try to look through such small openings, nearly closed by the barrel of a rifle. But why a rifle, for a *good* gunman? "He'd need all of a hole to look through, an' a *good* gunman likes a hip shot. That's it: Eyes to th' upper, six-gun at th' lower, for a range too short to allow a miss."

He stirred, blinked at the gambling crowd and closed his eyes again. The sudden, gusty opening of the front door sent jets of soot spouting from the lamp chimneys and bits of rubbish skittering across the floor; and it also sent his hand to a gun-butt. He grunted as Red Thompson entered, folded his arms anew and dozed again, as a cynical smile flickered to Thorpe's face and quickly died. Bill shifted slightly. "Any place as careful in thinkin' out things as *this* place is will stand a lot of lookin' over," he thought. "Th' Lord help anybody that pulls a gun in this room. An' I'll bet a man like Kane has got more'n loopholes. I'm shore goin' to like his place."

Kit Thorpe had not missed the stranger's alert interest and motion at the opening of the door, but for awhile he did not move. Finally, however, he yawned, stretched, moved restlessly on his chair and then noisily arose and disappeared behind the partition, closing the checkered door after him. It was not his intention to sit so close to anyone who gave signs which indicated that he might be engaged in a shooting match at any moment. It would be better to keep watch from the side, well out of the line of fire.

Bill Long did not make the mistake of looking at the holes again, but dozed fitfully, starting at each gust which was strong enough to suggest the opening of the door. "I got to find th' way, an' that's all there is to it," he muttered. "How am I goin' to be welcome around here?"

CHAPTER V

What the Storm Hid

THE SQUEAKING of the door wakened Johnny and his gun swung toward the sound as a familiar face emerged from the dusk of the hall and smiled a little.

"Reckon it ain't no shootin' matter," said the sheriff, slowly entering. He walked over to a chair and sat down. "Just a little call in th' line of duty," he explained.

"Sorry there wasn't a bell hangin' on th' door, or a club, or somethin'," replied Johnny ironically. "Then you could 'a' waited till I asked you to come in."

"That wouldn't 'a' been in th' line of duty," chuckled Corwin, his eyes darting from one piece of wearing apparel to another. "I'm lookin' around for th' fellers that robbed th' bank last night. Yore clothes don't hardly look dusty enough, though. Where was you last night, up to about one o'clock?"

"Down in th' barroom, playin' cards. Why?"

"That's what Ed says, too. That accounts for you durin' an' after th' robbery. I've got to look around, anyhow, for them coyotes."

"You'd show more sense if you was lookin' around for hoss tracks instead of wastin' time in here," retorted

Johnny, keeping his head turned so the peace officer could not see what was left of the bump.

"There ain't none," growled Corwin, arising. "She's still blowin' sand a-plenty—a couple of shacks are buried to their chimneys. I'm tellin' you this is th' worst sand storm that ever hit this town, but it looks like it's easin' up now. There won't be a trail left, an' th' scenery has shifted enough by this time to look like some place else. Idaho turn in when you did?"

"He did. Here he is now," replied Johnny, for the first time really conscious of the sand blasts which rasped against the windows.

Idaho peered around the door, nodded at Corwin and looked curious, and suspicious. "If I ain't wanted, throw me out," he said, holding up his trousers with one hand, the other held behind his back. "Hearin' voices, I thought mebby somebody was openin' a private flask an', bein' thirsty, I come over to help. My throat is shore dusty. An' would you listen to that wind? It shore rocked this old hotel last night. Th' floor of my room is near ankle deep in places."

"Th' bank was robbed last night," blurted Corwin, watching keenly from under his hat brim. "Whoever done it is still in town, unless he was a damned fool!"

Idaho grunted his surprise. "That so? Gee, they shore couldn't 'a' picked a better time," he declared. "Gosh, there's sand in my hair, even!"

Johnny rubbed his scalp, looked mildly surprised and slammed his sombrero on his head. "It ain't polite," he grinned, "but I got enough of it now." He sat up, crossed his legs under the sand-covered blankets and faced his visitors. "Tell us about it, Sheriff," he suggested.

"Wait till I get a belt," said Idaho, backing out of the door. When he returned he carried the rest of his clothes and started getting into them as the sheriff began his recital.

"John Reddy, th' bank watchman, says he was a little careless last night, which nobody can hardly blame him for. He sat in his chair agin' the rear wall, th' whole place under his eyes, an' listened to th' storm. To kill time he got to makin' bets with hisself about how soon th' second crack in th' floor would be covered over, an' then th' third, an' so on. 'Long about a little after twelve he says he hears a moan at th' back door. He pulls his gun an' listens close, down at th' crack just above th' sand drift. Then he hears it again, an' a scratchin' an clawin'. There's only one thing he's thinkin' about then—how he'd feel if he was th' poor devil out there, lost an' near dead. I allus said a watchman should ought to have no feelin's, an' a cussed strong imagination. John ain't fillin' th' bill either way. He cleared away th' drift on his side of th' door an' opens it—an' beyond rememberin' somethin' sandy jumpin' for him, that's all he knows till he come to later on an' found hisself tied up, with a welt on th' head that felt big as a doorknob."

If the sheriff expected to detect any interchange of glances between his auditors at his reference to the watchman's bump on the head he was disappointed. Johnny was looking at him with a frank interest seconded by that of Idaho, and neither did anything else during the short pause.

"John got his senses back enough to know what had happened, an' one glance around told him that he was right," continued Corwin. "Finally he managed to get his legs loose enough to hobble, an' he butted out into th' flyin' sand with his eyes shut an' his nose buried agin' his shoulder so he could breathe; an' somehow he managed to hit a buildin' in his blind driftin'. It was McNeil's, an' by throwin' his weight agin' th' door an' buttin' it with his shoulders an' elbows, he woke up Sam, who let him in, untied his arms an' th' rest of him, fixed him up as well as he could in a hurry an' then left him there. Sam got Pete Jennings, next door, sent Pete an' a scattergun to watch over what was left in th' bank, an' then started out to find me. He had to give it up till it got light, so he waited in th' bank with Pete. Th' bank fellers are there now, checkin' up. Th' big, burglar-proof safe was blowed open neat as a whistle—but they plumb ruined th' little one. They overlooked the biggest of all, down in th' cellar. Well," he sighed, arising, "I got to go on with my callin'—an' it's one fine day to be wanderin' all over town."

"If I was sheriff I wouldn't have to do much wanderin'," said Idaho. "But, anyhow, it can't last," he grinned.

Johnny nodded endorsement. "Th' harder, th' shorter. It's gettin' less all th' time," he said, pivoting and sitting on the edge of the bed. "But, just th' same," he yawned, stretching ecstatically, "I'm shore-e-e—g-l-a-d *I* can stay indoors till she peters out. Yo're plumb right, Corwin; them fellers never left town last night. An' if I was you I'd be cussed suspicious of anybody that seemed anxious to leave any time today."

"They never did leave town last night," said Idaho, a strange glint showing in his eyes.

"An' nobody can leave today, neither," said Corwin. "If they try it they will be stopped," he added, pointedly. "I've got a deputy coverin' every way out, sand or no sand. So-long," and he tramped down the bare stairs, grumbling at every step.

Johnny removed his hat to put on his shirt, and then replaced it. "You speakin' about sand in yore hair gave me what I needed," he grinned.

"That's why I said it," laughed his companion. "I saw that yore neck was stiff an' felt sorry for you. Now what th' devil do you think about that bank?"

"Kane," grunted Johnny, pouring sand from a boot.

"That name musta been cut on th' butt of th' gun that hit you," chuckled Idaho. "It's been drove in solid. Get a rustle on; I'm hungry, an' my teeth are full of sand. I'm anxious to hear what Ed knows."

An unpleasant and gritty breakfast out of the way, they went in to visit with the bartender and to while away a few hours at California Jack.

"Hello," grunted Ed. "Sheriff come pokin' his face in *yore* room?" he asked.

"He did," answered Johnny; "an' he'll never know how close he came to pokin' it into hell."

"My boot just missed him," regretted Ed. "He sung out right prompt when he felt th' wind of it. Damned four-flush."

"I'm among friends an' sympathizers," chuckled Idaho. "He says as how he's goin' wanderin' around in th' sand blasts doin' his duty. Duty nothin'! I'm bettin' he's settin' in Kane's, right now, takin' it easy."

"Then he can't get much closer to 'em," snorted Ed. "He can near touch th' men that did it." He paused as Johnny laughed in Idaho's face and, shrugging his shoulders, turned and rearranged the glasses on the backbar: "All right; laugh and be damned!" he snorted; "but would you look at that shelf an' them glasses? Cuss any country that moves around like that. I bet I got some of them Dry Arroyo sand hills in them glasses!"

"There was plenty in th' hash this mornin'," said Idaho; "but it didn't taste like that Dry Arroyo sand. It wasn't salty enough. Gimme a taste of that."

"Just because you'll make a han'some corpse ain't no reason why you should be in any hurry," retorted Ed. "Here!" he snorted, tossing a pack of cards on the bar. "Go over an' begin th' wranglin' agin—'though th' Lord knows I ain't got nothin' agin' Nelson." He glanced out of the window. "Purty near blowed out. It'll be ca'm in another half-hour; an' then you get to blazes out of here, an' stay out till dark!"

"I wish I had yore happy disposition," said Idaho. "I'd shore blow my brains out."

"There wouldn't be anythin' to clean up, anyhow!" retorted Ed. "Lord help us, here comes Silent Lewis!"

"Hello, fellers!" cried the newcomer. "Gee but it's been some storm. Sand's all over everythin'. Hear about th' bank robbery?"

"Bank robbery?" queried Ed, innocently. "What bank robbery? Sand bank?" he asked, sarcastically.

"Sand bank! Sand bank nothin'!" blurted Silent. "Ain't you heard it yet? Why, I live ten miles out of town, an' I know all about it."

"I believe every word you say," said Ed. "Tell us about it."

"Gee, where have you-all been?" demanded Silent. "Why, John Reddy, settin' on his chair, watchin' th' safe, hears a moanin', so he opened th' door—"

"Of th' safe?" asked Idaho, curiously.

"No, no; of th' bank. Th' bank door, th' rear one. He hears a moan—"

"Which moan; first, or second?" queried Ed, anxiously.

"Th' first—th' second didn't come till—hey, I thought you didn't hear about it?" he accused.

"I didn't; but you mentions two moans, separate an' distinct," defended Ed.

"You shore did," said Idaho, firmly.

Johnny nodded emphatically. "Yessir; you shore did. Two moans, one at each end."

"But I didn't get to th' second moan at all!"

"Now, what's th' use of tellin' us that?" flared the bartender. "Don't you think we got ears?"

"If you can't tell it right, shut up," said Idaho.

"I can tell it right if you'll shut up!" retorted Silent. "As I said, he hears a moan, so he leaves th' safe an' goes to th' door. Then he hears a second moan, scratchin', an'—"

"Hey!" growled Ed indignantly. "What you talkin' about? Who in hell ever heard of a second moan scratchin'—"

"It was th' first that scratched," corrected Idaho. "He said it plain. You must be listenin' with yore feet."

"If you'd gimme a chance to tell it—" began Silent, bridling.

"Never mind my hearin' you," snapped Ed at Idaho. "I know what I heard. An' lemme tell you, Silent, you can't cram nothin' like that down my throat. Before you go any further, just explain to me how a moan can scratch! I'm allus willin' to learn, but I want things explained careful an' full."

"He ain't quick-witted, like you an' me," said Johnny. "We understand how a scratch moans, but he's too dumb. Go on an' tell th' ignoramus."

"If yo're so cussed quick-witted, will you please tell me what'n blazes you are talkin' about?" demanded Silent, truculently. "What do you mean by a scratch moans?"

"That's what I want to know," growled Idaho. "You

can't scratch moans. Cuss it, reckon I ought to know, for I've tried to do it, more'n once, too."

"Yo're dumber than Nelson," jeered Ed. "It's all plain to me."

"What is?" snapped Idaho.

"Moanin' scratches, that's what!"

"Of a safe?" asked Johnny. "Then why didn't you say so? How'd *I* know that you meant that. Go on, Silent."

"You was at th' second moan," prompted Ed.

"He scratched that," said Idaho. "He got as far as leavin' th' safe, 'though what he was doin' in there with it, I'd like to know. Reddy let you in?"

"Look here, Idaho," scowled Silent. "I wasn't in there at all. You'll get me inter trouble, sayin' things like that. I was ten miles away when it happened."

"Then why didn't you say so, at th' beginnin'?" asked Ed.

"Ah!" triumphantly exclaimed Johnny. "Then you tell us how you could hear th' scratchin' an' moanin'; tell us that!"

"That's all right, Nelson," said Idaho, soothingly. "He can hear more things when he's ten miles away than any man you ever knowed. Go ahead, Silent."

"You go to hell!" roared Silent, glaring. "You think yo're smart, don't you, *all* of you? I was goin' to tell you about th' robbery, but now you can cussed well find it out for yoreselves! An' don't let me hear about any of you sayin' I was in that bank last night, neither! Damned fools!" and he stamped out, slamming the door behind him. "Blow an' be damned!" he growled at the storm. "I'd ruther eat sand than waste time with them ijuts. 'Scratch moans!' Scratch *hell!*"

Silent's departure left a more cheerful atmosphere in the barroom. The three men he had forsaken were grinning at each other, the petty annoyances of the storm forgotten, and the next hour passed quickly. At its expiration the wind had died down and the storm-bound town was free again. Ed finished cleaning the bar and the glassware about the time that his two friends had swept the last of the sand into the street and cleared away a drift which blocked the rear door. They were taking a congratulatory drink when Ridley, coming to town for the mail himself because he would not ask any of his men to face the discomforts of that ride, stamped in, and his face was like a thunder cloud.

"Gimme a drink!" he demanded, and when he had had it he swung around and glared at Idaho. "Lukins have any money in that bank? Yes? You better be off to let him know about it. Hell of a note: Thirty thousand stole! An' Jud Hill holdin' a gun on *me* when I rode into town, askin' fool questions! An' let me tell you some-thin'—judgin' from th' tools they forgot to take with 'em, it wasn't no amatachures that did that job. Diamond drills an' cow-country crooks don't know each other. An' that Jud Hill, a-stoppin' *me*!"

"Mebby he won't let you leave town," suggested Idaho. "Corwin's given orders like that."

Ridley crashed his fist on the bar, and then to better express his feelings he leaned over and stuck out his jaw. "Y-a-a-s? Then I'm invitin' you-all to Hill's funeral, an' Corwin's, too, if he cuts in! *Thirty thousand*! Great land of cows!"

"Corwin's out now, huntin' for 'em," said Ed.

"Is he?" sneered Ridley. "Then he wants to find 'em! Th' firm of Twitchell an' Carpenter owns near half of that bank—every dollar th' Question-Mark has was in it. There's a change comin' to this part of th' country!" and he stamped out, mounted his horse and whirled down the trail. When he reached the sentry he rode so close to him that their legs rubbed and Hill's horse began to give ground.

"Do I go on?" snapped Ridley.

Jud Hill nodded pleasantly. "Shore. Seein' as how you come in this mornin' I reckon you do."

Ridley urged his horse forward without replying, reached the ranchhouse, wrote a letter which was a masterpiece of its kind and gave it to one of his men to post in Larkinville, twenty miles to the south. That done, all he could do was impatiently await the reply.

After Ridley had left, Johnny went out to look after

Pepper, found her all right, cleaned the sand out of the feed box and then went down to look at the bank. Four men with rifles were posted around it and waved him away. He could see several other men busy in the building, but beyond that there was nothing to claim his attention. Joining the small crowd of idlers across the street he listened to their conjectures, which were entirely vague and colorless, and then wandered back to look for Idaho in Quayle's. His friend was not to be seen and after exchanging a few words with the jovial proprietor he went in to talk with the bartender.

"No wind now, but my throat's dry. Gimme a drink, half water," and holding it untasted for the moment he jerked his head backward in the direction of the bank. "Nothin' to see, except some fellers inside lookin' for 'most anythin', an' four men with Winchesters on th' outside."

While he was speaking a man had entered and seated himself in the rear of the room. Johnny glanced carelessly at him, and the glass cracked sharply in his convulsive grip, the liquor squirting through his fingers and gathering a deeper color as it passed. A thin trickle of blood ran down his hand and wrist.

Ed had started at the sound and his head was bent forward, his unbelieving eyes staring at the dripping hand.

Johnny opened it slowly, shook the fragments from it and let it fall to his side, mechanically shaking off blood and liquor. "Cuss it, Ed," he gently reproved, looking calmly into the bartender's questioning face, "you should ought to pick out th' bad ones an' throw 'em away—yes, an' bust 'em first."

Ed picked up the bottom of the glass and critically examined it, noting a discolored strip along one of the sharp edges, where dirt had accumulated from numberless washings. The largest fragment showed the greasy line to the rounded brim. "I usually do," he growled. "Thought I had this one, too. Musta got back somehow. Hurt bad?"

"Nothin' fatal, I reckon," answered Johnny, drawing the injured member up his trousers leg. "But I'm sayin' you owe me another drink; an' leave th' water out, this time. Water in whisky never does bring good luck, nohow."

Ed smiled, pushing out bottle and glass. "We might say *that* one was on th' house—all that didn't get on you." He instinctively reached for and used the bar cloth as he looked over at the stranger. "I can promise you one that ain't cracked," he smiled.

"I'll take mine straight," said Bill Long. "I don't want no more hard luck."

"Wonder where Idaho is?" asked Johnny. "Well, if he comes in, tell him I'm exercisin' my cayuse. Reckon I'll go down an' chin with Ridley this afternoon. Th' south trail is less sandy than th' north one."

"An' give Corwin a chance to say things about you?" asked Ed, significantly. "He'll be lookin' for a peg to hang things on."

"Then mebby he won't never look for any more."

"That may be true; but what's th' use?"

"Reckon yo're right," reluctantly admitted Johnny. "Guess I'll go up to Kane's an' see what's happenin'. If Idaho comes in, or any more of my numerous friends," he grinned, "send 'em up there if they're askin' for me. I'll mebby be glad to see 'em," and he sauntered out.

Ed smiled pleasantly at the other customer. "Bad thing, a glass breakin' like that," he remarked.

Bill Long looked at him without interest. "Serves him right," he grunted, "for holdin' it so tight. Nobody was aimin' to take it away from him, was they?"

Johnny entered Kane's too busy thinking to give much notice to the room and the suppressed excitement occasioned by the robbery, and sat down at a table. As he leaned back in the chair he caught sight of a red-headed puncher talking to one of Kane's card-sharps and he got another shock. "Holy maverick!" he muttered, and looked carelessly around to see if any more of his Montana friends had dropped into town. Then he smiled as the card-sharp looking up, beckoned to him. As he passed down the room he noticed the quiet easterner hunched up in a corner, his cap well down over his eyes, and Johnny wondered if the man ever wore it any other way. He was out of place in his cow-town surroundings—perhaps that was why he had not been seen outside of Kane's building. Ridley's remark about the tools came to him and he hesitated, considered, and then went on again. He had no reason to do Corwin's work for him. Dropping into a vacant chair at the gambler's table he grunted the customary greeting.

"Howdy," replied the card-sharp, nodding pleasantly. "No use bein' lonesome. Meet Red Thompson," he said, waving.

"Glad to meet you," said Johnny, truthfully, but hiding as well as he could the pleasure it gave him. "I once knowed a Thompson—short, fat feller. Worked up on a mountain range in Colorado. Know him?"

Red shook his head. "Th' world's full of Thompsons," he explained. "You punchin'?"

"Got a job on th' SV, couple of days' ride north of here. Just come down with a little beef herd for Twitchell an' Carpenter. Ain't seen no good bunch of yearlin's that can be got cheap, have you?"

Red shook his head: "No, I ain't."

The gambler laughed and poked a lean thumb at the SV puncher. "Modest feller, *he* is," he said. "He's foreman, up there."

Red's mild interest grew a little. "That so? I passed yore ranch comin' down. Need another man?"

The SV foreman shook his head. "I could do with one less. Them bank fellers picked a good time for it, didn't they?"

"They shore did," agreed the gambler. "Couldn't 'a' picked a better. Kane loses a lot by that, I reckon. Well, what do you gents say to a little game? Small enough not to cause no calamities; large enough to be interestin'? Nothin' else to do that I can see."

Red nodded and, the limit soon agreed upon, the game began. As the second hand was being dealt Bill Long wandered in, talked for a few moments with the bartender and then went over to a chair. Tipping it back against the wall he pulled down his hat brim, let his chin sink on his chest and prepared to enjoy a nap. Naturally a man wishing to doze would choose the darkest corner, and if he was not successful who could tell that the narrow slit between his lids let his keen eyes watch everything worth seeing? His attention was centered mostly on the tenderfoot stranger with the low-pulled cap and the cutout squares in the great checkerboard partition at the rear of the room.

The poker game was largely a skirmish, a preliminary feeling out for a game which was among the strong probabilities of the future. Johnny and the gambler were about even with each other at the breaking up of the play, but Red Thompson had lost four really worth-while jack pots to the pleasant SV foreman. As they roughly pushed back their chairs Bill Long stirred, opened his eyes, blinked around, frowned slightly at being disturbed and settled back again. "Red couldn't 'a' got that money to him in no better way," he thought, contentedly.

The three players separated, Johnny going to the hotel, Red seeking a chair by the wall, and the gambler loafing at the bar.

"An' how'd you find 'em?" softly asked the wise bartender. "Goin' after that foreman's roll?"

The gambler grunted and shifted his weight to the other leg. "Thompson ain't very much; but I dunno about th' other feller. Sometimes I think one thing; sometimes, another. Either he's cussed innocent, or too slick for me to figger. Reckon mebby Fisher ought to go agin' him, an' find out, for shore."

"How'd you make out, last night, with Long?"

"There's a man th' boss ought to grab," replied the gambler. "He didn't win much from me—but it's his first, an' last, chance with me. I don't play him no more. I'd like to see him an' Fisher go at it, with no limit. Fisher would have th' best of it on th' money end, havin' th' house behind him in case he had to weather a run of hard luck; but mebby he'd need it."

As the gambler walked away the easterner arose, slouched to the bar and held a short whispered conversation with the man behind it.

The bartender frowned. "You can't get away before night. Sandy Woods will take care of you before mornin', I reckon. Go upstairs an' quit fussin'. Yo're safe as hell!"

The bartender's prophecy came true after dark, when Sandy Woods and the anxious stranger quietly left town together; but the stranger had good reason to be anxious, for at dawn he was careless for a moment and found himself looking into his escort's gun. He had more courage than good sense and refused to be robbed, and he died for it. Sandy dragged the body into a clump of bushes away from the trail and then rode on to kill the necessary time, leading the other's horse. He was five thousand dollars richer, and had proved wrong the old adage about honor among thieves.

CHAPTER VI

The Writing on the Wall

WHEN THE senior member of the firm of Twitchell and Carpenter read Ridley's letter things began to happen. It was the last straw, for besides being half-owners in the bank the firm had for several years been annoyed by depredations committed by Mesquite citizens on its herds. The depredations had ceased upon payment of "campaign funds" to the Mesquite political ring, but the blackmail levy had galled the senior member, who was not as prone as Carpenter was to buy peace. Orders flew from the firm's office and the little printing-plant at Sandy Bend broke all its hazy precedents, with the result that a hard-riding courier, relaying twice, carried the work of the job-print toward Mesquite. Reaching Ridley's domain he turned the package over to the local superintendent, who joyously mounted and carried it to town.

Tim Quayle welcomed his old friend, listened intently to what Ridley had to say and handed over an assortment of tacks and nails, and a chipped hammer. " 'Tis time, Tom," he said, simply.

Ridley went out and selected a spot on the hotel wall,

and the sound of the hammer and the sight of his unusual occupation caused a small crowd of curious idlers
to gather around him. When the poster was unrolled
there were sibilant whispers, soft curses, frank prophe-
cies, and some commendations, which were entirely a
matter of the personal viewpoint. Half an hour later, the
last poster placed, Ridley took a short cut, entered the
hotel through the kitchen and went into the barroom.
What he had published for the enlightenment, edifica-
tion, or disapprobation of his fellow-citizens was pointed
and business-like, and read as follows:

$2,500.00 REWARD!
For Information Leading to the Capture
and Conviction of the Men Who Robbed
the Mesquite Bank.
STRICTLY CONFIDENTIAL
TWITCHELL & CARPENTER
Sandy Bend   TOM RIDLEY, Local Supt.

Quayle turned and smiled at the T & C man. "Ye've
slapped their faces, Tom. Mind yore eye!"

"They've prodded th' old mosshead once too often,"
growled Ridley, looking around at Johnny, Idaho, and
the others. "I reckon this stops th' blackmail to th' gang.
When I wrote my letter I expected somethin' would
happen, an' th' letter I got in return near curled my hair.
Twitchell's fightin' mad."

"Th' reward's too big," criticized Idaho.

"I'm fearin' it ain't big enough," said Ed Doane, shaking his head.

Ridley laughed contentedly. "It's more than enough.
There's men in this town, an' that gang, who would
knife anybody for half of that. When they can get twenty-
five hundred by simply openin' their mouths, without
bein' known, they'll do it. Loyalty is fine to listen about,
but there's few men in th' gang we're after that have any
twenty-five hundred dollars' worth. This is th' beginnin'
of th' end. Mark my words."

"A lot depends on how many were in on it," suggested Johnny, "an' how many of th' others know about it."

"He's throwin' money away," doggedly persisted Idaho. "A thousand would buy any of 'em, that an' secrecy."

"He ain't throwin' it away," retorted Ridley, "considerin' his letter. He's after results, amazin' results, an' he shore knows how to get 'em. It'll be sort of more pleasant if th' gang is sold out. He figgers a reward like that will save time an' be self-actin', for my orders are to stay in th' ranchhouse an' wait. That's what I'm goin' to do, too; an' I'll be settin' there with all guns loaded. No tellin' what'll happen now an', not bein' able to say how soon it will happen, I'm leavin' you boys. So-long."

He walked out to his horse and mounted. As he settled into the saddle there was a flat report, his hat flew from his head and he toppled from the horse, dead before he struck the ground.

Quayle swiftly reached over the desk and took a Winchester from its pegs, Irish tears in his eyes; and waited hopefully, Irish rage in his heart, watching the dirty windows and the open door. "It's to a finish, byes," he grated in a brogue thickened by his emotions, the veins of his forehead and neck swelling into serpentine ridges. "They read th' writin' on th' wall, an' they read ut plain. D'ye mind what some of thim divils would be after doin' for all that money? They'd cut their own mither's throat—an' Kane knows ut! An' I'm thinkin' they'll be careful now—Kane has served his notice."

The idlers in the street stood as if frozen, gaping, not one of them daring to approach the body, nor even to stop the horse as it kicked up its heels and trotted down the street. Ed Doane was the third man through the door and he brought in the dead man's hat as Johnny and Idaho placed the warm body on the floor of the office. They hardly had stepped back when hurried footsteps neared the door and the sheriff, with two of his deputies, entered the office, paused instinctively at sight of the rifle in Quayle's hands, and then slowly, carefully bent over to examine the body. The sheriff reached forth a hand to turn it over, but stopped instantly and froze in his stooped position, his arm outstretched.

"Kape ut off him!" roared Quayle, his eyes blazing. "What more d'ye want to see?"

"From behind?" asked Corwin, slowly straightening up, but his eyes fixed on the proprietor.

"An' where'd ye be thinkin' 'twas from?" snarled Quayle, the veins standing out anew. "No dirty pup of that pack would dare try ut from th' front, an' ye know ut! An' need ye look twice to see where th' slug av a buffalo-gun came out? Don't touch him, anny av ye! Kape yore paws off Tom Ridley! An' *I'm* buryin' him, mesilf."

"But, as sheriff—" began Corwin.

"Aye, *but*!" snapped Quayle. "We'll be after callin' things be their right names. Ye are no sheriff. Ye was choosed by th' majority av votes cast by th' citizens av an unorganized county, like byes choose a captain av their gangs. There's no laws to back ye up, an' ye took no oath. As long as th' majority will it, yore th' keeper av th' peace—an' no longer. Sheriff?" he sneered. "An' 'tis a fine sheriff ye'll be makin', runnin' in circles like a locoed cow since th' robbery, questionin' every innocent man in town, an' hopin' 'twould blow over, an' die a natural death. But it's got th' breath av life in it now! What do ye think old Twitchell will be sayin' to *this*?" he thundered, his rigid arm pointing to the body on the floor. "Clear out, th' pack av ye! Ye've seen all ye need to!"

Corwin glanced at the body again, from it around the ring of set and angry faces, shrugged his shoulders and motioned to his deputies to leave. "We'll hold th' inquest here," he said, turning away.

"Ye'll hold no inquest!" roared Quayle. "Show me yore coroner! Inquest, is ut? I've held yore inquest already. There's plenty av us here an' we say, so help us God, Tom Ridley was murdered, an' by persons unknown. There's yer inquest, an' yer findin's. What do ye say, byes?" he demanded. A low growl replied to him and he sneered again. "There! There's your inquest! As long as yer playin' sheriff, go out an' do yer duty; but look out ye don't put yer han's on a friend! Clear out, an' run yer bluff!"

Corwin's eyes glinted as he looked at the fearless speaker, but with Idaho straining at a moral leash, Johnny's intent eagerness and the sight of the rifle in the proprietor's hands, he let discretion mold his course and slouched out to the street, where another quiet crowd opened silently to let him through.

Johnny passed close to Idaho. "Go to your ranch for a few days, or they'll couple you to me!" he whispered.

Bill Long, feeding his borrowed Highbank horse in the northernmost of the two stables at the rear of Kane's, heard the jarring crash of a heavy rifle so loud and near that he dropped instantly to hands and knees and crawled to a crack in the south wall. As he peered out he got a good, clear view of a pock-marked Mexican with a crescent-shaped scar over one eye and who, Sharp's in hand, wriggled out of the north window of the adjoining stable, dropped sprawling within five feet of the watcher's eyes, scrambled to his feet and fled close along the rear of Bill's stable. The watcher sprang erect, sped silently back to his horse and stirred the grain in the feed box with one hand, while the other rested on a six-gun in case the Mexican should be of an inquisitive and belligerent frame of mind. His view of the street had been shut off by the corner of the southern stable and he had not seen the result of the shot. Wishing to show no undue curiosity he did not go down the street, but returned to the gambling-hall. He had not been seated more than a few minutes when one of Kane's retainers ran in from the street with the news of Ridley's death. There was a flurry of excitement, which quickly died down, but under the rippling surface Bill sensed the deeper, more powerful currents.

"This man Kane, whoever an' wherever he is," he thought, "has shore trained this bunch of scourin's. I'm gettin' plumb curious for a look at him. Huh!" he muttered, as the window-wriggling, pock-marked Mexican emerged from behind the partition, bent swiftly over Kit Thorpe and betook his tense and nervous self to the roulette table. "I've got yore ugly face carved deep in my mem'ry, you Greaser snake!" he growled under his breath. "If it wasn't for loosin' bigger game I'd turn you over to Ridley's friends before night. You can wait."

Not long after the appearance of the Mexican, the sheriff came in by the front door, pushed through the crowd near the bar and walked swiftly toward the rear of the room. Speaking shortly to Kit Thorpe in a low voice he passed through the door of the checkerboard partition.

"I'm learnin'," muttered Bill. "I don't know who Kane is, but I'm dead shore I know *where* he is. An' I'm gettin' a better line on this killin'. I'll shore have to get a look behind that door, somehow."

Suddenly the doorkeeper arose and stuck his head around behind the partition and then, straightening up, closed the door, went up to the bar, spoke to several men there and led them to the rear. Opening the door again he let them through and resumed his vigil; and none of them reappeared before Bill went into the north building to eat his supper.

CHAPTER VII

The Third Man

KANE'S GAMBLING-HALL was in full blast, reeking with the composite odor of liquor, kerosene lamps, rank tobacco, and human bodies, the tables well-filled, the faro and roulette layouts crowded by eager devotees. The tenseness of the afternoon was forgotten and curses and laughter arose in all parts of the big room. The two-man Mexican orchestra strumming its guitars and the extra bartenders were earning their pay. Punchers, gamblers, storekeepers, two traveling men, a squad of cavalrymen on leave from the nearest post, Mexicans, and bums of several races made up the noisy crowd as Johnny Nelson pushed into the room and nodded to the head bartender.

"Well, well," smiled the busy barman without stopping his work. "Here's our SV foreman, out at night. Thought mebby you'd heard of some yearlin's an' hit th' trail after 'em."

"I don't reckon there was ever a yearlin' in this section," grinned Johnny.

"That so? There's several down at th' other end of th' bar," chuckled the man of liquor. "That blonde you left th' forty dollars for has shore been strainin' her eyes lookin' for you. Says she knows she's goin' to like you. Go back an' soothe her. Gin is her favorite."

"I ain't lookin' for her yet," replied Johnny. "That's somethin' you never want to do. It's th' wrong system. Don't pay no attention to 'em if you want 'em to pay attention to you. Let her wait a little longer. Where's that Thompson feller? I like th' way he plays draw, seein' as how I won some of his money. Seen him tonight?"

"Shore; he's around somewhere. Saw him a little while ago."

Johnny noticed a quiet, interested crowd in a far corner and joined it, working through until he saw two men playing poker in the middle. One was Bill Long and the other was Kane's best card-sharp, Mr. Fisher, and they were playing so intently as to be nearly oblivious of the crowd. On the other side of the ring, sitting on a table, was Red Thompson, his mouth partly open and his eyes riveted on the game.

The play was getting stiff and Fisher's eyes had a look in them that Johnny did not like. The gambler reached for the cards and began shuffling them with a speed and dexterity which bespoke weary hours of earnest practice. As he pushed them out for the cut his opponent leaned back, relaxed and smiled pleasantly.

"I allus like to play th' other fellow's game," Bill observed. "If he plays fast *I* like to play fast; if he plays 'em close, *I* like to play 'em close; if he plays reckless, *I* like to play reckless; if he plays 'em with flourishes, *I* like to play 'em with flourishes. I'm not what you might call original. I'm a imitator." He slowly reached out his hand, held it poised over the deck, changed his mind and withdrew it. "Reckon I'll not cut this time. They're good as they are. I like yore dealin'.'"

Fisher yanked the deck to him and dealt swiftly. "I'm not very bright," he remarked as he glanced at his hand, "so I'm gropin' about yore meanin'. Or didn't it have none?"

"Nothin', only to show that I'm so polite I allus let th' other feller set th' pace," smiled Bill. "As he plays, I play."

He picked up the cards, squared them into exact alignment and slid them from the table and close against his vest, where a deft touch spread them for a quick glance at the pips. "They look good; but, I wonder?" he muttered. "Reckon that's best, after all. Gimme two cards when you get time."

Fisher gave him two and took the same number.

"I find I'm gettin' tired," growled Bill, "an' it shore is hot an' stiflin' in here. As it stands I'm a little ahead—not more'n fifty dollars. That bein' so, I quit after this hand and two more. There ain't much action, anyhow."

"If yo're lookin' for action mebby you feel like takin' off th' hobbles," suggested Fisher, carelessly.

"Hobbles, saddles an' anythin' else you can think of," nodded Bill. "Do we start now?"

Fisher nodded, saw the modest bet and doubled it.

Bill tossed his four queens and the ace of hearts face down in the discard and smiled. "Didn't get what I was lookin' for," he grinned into the set face across from him. "Got to have 'em before I can play 'em."

Fisher hid his surprise and carelessly tossed his four kings and the six of diamonds, also face down, into the discard, fumbled the deck as he went to pass it over and spilled it on top of the cards on the table. Cursing at his clumsiness, he scrambled the cards together and pushed them toward his opponent. "My fingers must be gettin' all thumbs," he growled as he raked in the money. What had happened? Had he bungled the deal, or wasn't four queens big enough for the talkative fool across from him?

Bill smilingly agreed. "They do get that way at times," he remarked, shuffling with a swift flourish which made Johnny hide a smile. He pushed the pack out, Fisher cut it, and the flying cards dropped swiftly into two neat piles almost flush on their edges, which seemed to merit a murmur of appreciation from the crowd. Johnny shifted his weight to the other leg and prepared to enjoy the game.

Fisher glanced at his hand and became instant prey to a turmoil of thoughts. Four queens, with an eight of clubs! He looked across at the calm, reflective dealer who was rubbing the disgraceful stubble on his chin while he drew two cards partly from his hand and considered them seriously. He seemed to be perplexed.

"I been playin' this game for more years than I feel like tellin'," Bill grumbled, whimsically; "but I ain't never been able really to decide one little thing." Becoming conscious that he might be delaying the game he looked up suddenly. "Have patience, friend. *Oh,* then it's all right! You ain't discarded yet," he finished cheerfully. Throwing away the two cards he waited.

"Gimme one," grunted Fisher, discarding, "an' I'm sayin' fifty dollars," he continued, shoving the money out without glancing at the card on the table. "How many you takin'?" he asked.

"Two," answered Bill, looking at him keenly. He glanced down at the single back showing on the table before him and grinned. "Th' other's under it," he explained needlessly. "Well, I'm still an imitator," he chuckled. "Here's yore fifty, and fifty more. I'm sorry I ain't playin' in my own town, so I could borrow when it all gets up."

Whatever Fisher's thoughts were he hid them well, and he was not to be the first one to weaken and look at the draw. He had a reputation to maintain, and he saw the raise and returned it. Bill pushed out a hundred dollars and Fisher came back, but his tenseness was growing.

Bill considered, looked down at his unknown draw, shook his head and picked up one card. "I'm feelin' the strain," he growled, seeing the raise and repeating it. He glanced up at the crowd, which had grown considerably, and smiled grimly.

Fisher evened up and raised again, watching his worried opponent, who scowled, sucked his lips, shook his head and then, with swift decision, picked up the other card. "I can't afford to quit now," he muttered. "Here goes for another boost!"

His opponent having wilted first and saved the gambler's face, Fisher picked up his own draw and when he saw it he stiffened, his thoughts racing again. It was no coincidence, he decided. In all of his experience he had known but two men who could do that, and here was a third! But still there was a hope that there was no third, that it was a coincidence. And there was quite a sum of money on the table. The doubt must be removed and the truth known, and another fifty, sent after its brothers was not too big a price to pay for such knowledge. He pushed the money out onto the table. "I calls," he grunted.

Bill dropped his little block of cards and spread them with a sweep of one hand, while the other was ready to make the baffling draw which had made him famous in other parts of the country. Fisher glanced at the four kings and nodded, all doubts laid to rest—the third man sat across from him.

He slowly pushed back as the crowd, not knowing just what to expect, scattered. "I'm tired. Shall we call it off for tonight?" he asked.

Without relaxing Bill nodded. "Suits me. I'm tired, too; an' near suffocated. See you tomorrow?"

Fisher grunted something as he arose and, turning abruptly, pushed through the thinning crowd to get a bracer at the bar, while the winner slowly hauled in the money. Gulping down the fiery liquor the gambler wheeled to go into the dark and deserted dining-room where he could sit in quiet and go over the problem again, and looked up to see the other gambler in his way.

"What did you find out?" asked the other in a low voice.

"I found th' devil has come up out of hell!" growled Fisher. "Come along an' I'll tell you about it. He's th' third man! Old Parson Davies was th' first, but he's dead; Tex Ewalt was th' second, an' I ain't seen him in years—cuss it! I wondered why this man's play seemed familiar! He's got some of Tex's tricks of handlin' th' cards."

"Shore he ain't Tex?"

"As shore as I am that you ain't," retorted Fisher; "but I'm willin' to bet he knows Tex. Come on—let's get out of this hullabaloo. He's got a nerve, pickin' *my* cards, an' dealin' 'em alternate off th' top an' bottom, with *me* watchin' him!"

"We got to figger how to get it back," thoughtfully muttered the other, following closely. "Everythin's goin' wrong. They went after Nelson an' got somebody else; they stirred up th' T & C by robbin' th' bank, an' then had to go an' make it worse by gettin' Ridley! I'm admittin' I'm walkin' soft, an' ready to jump th' country right quick."

Fisher sank into a chair in the dining-room. "An' if Long hangs around here much longer Kane'll ditch me like a wore-out boot. A couple more losses like to-night an' he'll plumb forget my winnin's for th' past two years. An' me gettin' all cocked to strike him for a bigger percentage!"

Out in the reeking gambling-hall Bill put his empty glass on the bar and slid a gold piece at the smiling head man behind the counter. "Spend th' change on th' ladies in th' corner," he said. "It allus gives me luck; an' I had such luck tonight that I ain't aimin' to take no chances losin' it. Reckon I'll horn in on th' faro layout," and he did, where he managed to lose a part of his poker winnings before he turned in for the night.

Up late the next morning he hastened into the dining-room to beat the closing of the doors and saw the head bartender eating a lonely breakfast. The dispenser of liquors beckoned and pushed back a chair at his table.

Bill accepted the invitation and gave his order. "Well," he remarked, "yo're lookin' purty bright this mornin'."

"I'm gettin' so I don't need much sleep, I reckon," replied the bartender. "Did yore folks use a poker deck to cut yore teeth on?"

Bill laughed heartily. "My luck turned, an' Fisher happened to be th' one that got in th' way."

"He says you play a lot like a feller he used to know."

"That so? Who was he?"

"Tex Ewalt."

"Well, I ought to, for me an' Tex played a lot together, some years back. Wonder what ever happened to Tex? He ain't been down this way lately, has he?"

"No. I never saw him. Fisher knew him. He says Tex was th' greatest poker player that ever lived."

"I reckon he's right," replied Bill. "I'm plumb grateful to Tex. It ain't his fault that I don't play a better game. But I got an idea playin' like his has got to be born in a man." He ate silently for a moment. "Now that I'm spotted I reckon my poker playin' is over in here. Oh, well, I ain't complainin'. I can eat an' sleep here, an' find enough around town to keep me goin' for a little while, anyhow. Then I'll drift."

"Unless, mebby, you play for th' house," suggested the bartender. "What kind of a game does that SV foreman play?"

"I never like to size a man up till I play with him," answered Bill. "I was sort of savin' him for myself, for he's got a fat roll. Now I reckon I'll have to let somebody else do th' brandin'." He sighed and went on with his breakfast.

"Get him into a little game an' see how good he is," suggested the other, arising. "Goin' to leave you now." He turned away and then stopped suddenly, facing around again. "Huh! I near forgot. Th' boss wants to see you."

"Who? Kane? What about?"

"He'll tell you that, I reckon."

"All right. Tell him I'm in here."

The other grinned. "I said th' *boss* wants to see *you*."

"Shore; I heard you."

"People he wants to see go to him."

"Oh, all right; why didn't you say so first off? Where is he?"

"Thorpe will show you th' way. Whatever th' boss says, don't you go on th' prod. If yore feelin's get hurt, don't relieve 'em till you get out of his sight."

"I've played poker too long to act sudden," grinned Bill, easily.

His breakfast over, he sauntered into the gambling-room and stopped in front of Kit Thorpe, whose welcoming grin was quite a change from his attitude of the day before. "I've been told Kane wants to see me. Here I am."

Thorpe opened the door, followed his companion through it and paused to close and bolt it, after which he kept close to the other's heels and gave terse, grunted directions. "Straight ahead—to th' left—to th' right—straight ahead. Don't make no false moves after you open that door. Go ahead—push it open."

Bill obeyed and found himself in an oblong room which ran up to the opaque glass of a skylight fifteen feet above the floor, and five feet below the second skylight on the roof, in both of which the small panes were set in heavy metal bars. The room was cool and well ventilated. Before him, seated at the far side of a flat-topped, walnut desk of ancient vintage sat a tall, lean, white-haired man of indeterminate age, who leaned slightly forward and whose hands were not in sight.

"Sit down," said Kane, in a voice of singular sweetness and penetrating timbre. For several minutes he looked at his visitor as a buyer might look at a horse, silent, thoughtful, his deeply-lined face devoid of any change in its austere expression.

"Why did you come here?" he suddenly snapped.

"To get out of th' storm," answered Bill.

"Why else?"

Bill looked around, up at the graven Thorpe and back again at his inquisitor, and shrugged his shoulders. "Mebby you can tell me," he answered before he remembered to be less independent.

"I think I can. Anyone who plays poker as well as you do has a very good reason for visiting strange towns. What is your name?"

"Bill Long."

"I know that. I asked, what *is* your name?"

Bill looked around again and then sat up stiffly. "That ain't interestin' us."

"Where are you from?"

Bill shrugged his shoulders and remained silent.

"You are not very talkative today. How did you get that Highbank horse?"

Bill acted a little surprised and anxious. "I—I don't know," he answered foolishly.

"Very well. When you make up your mind to answer my questions I have a proposition to offer you which you may find to be mutually advantageous. In the meanwhile, do not play poker in this house. That's all."

Thorpe coughed and opened the door, and swiftly placed a hand on the shoulder of the visitor. "Time to go," he said.

Bill hesitated and then slowly turned and led the way, saying nothing until he was back in the gambling-hall and Thorpe again kept his faithful vigil over the checkered door.

"Cuss it," snorted Bill, remembering that in the part he was playing he had determined to be loquacious. "If I told him all he wanted to know I'd be puttin' a rope around my neck an' givin' him th' loose end! So he's got a proposition to make, has he? Th' devil with him an' his propositions. I don't have to play poker in his place— there's plenty of it bein' played outside this buildin', I reckon. For two-bits I'd 'a' busted his neck then an' there!"

"You'd 'a' been spattered all over th' room if you'd made a play," replied Thorpe, a little contempt in his voice for such boasting words from a man who had acted far from them when in the presence of Kane. He had this stranger's measure. "An' you mind what he said about playin' in here, or I'll make you climb up th' wall, you'll be that eager to get out. You think over what he said, an' drift along. I'm busy."

Bill, his frown hiding inner smiles, slowly turned and walked defiantly away, his swagger increasing with the distance covered; and when he reached the street he was exhaling dignity, and chuckled with satisfaction— he had seen behind the partition and met Kane. He passed the bank, once more normal, except for the armed guards, and bumped into Fisher, who frowned at him and kept on going.

"Hey!" called Bill. "I want to ask you somethin'."

Fisher stopped and turned. "Well?" he growled, truculently.

Bill went up close to him. "Just saw Kane. He says he has got somethin' to offer me. What is it?"

"My job, I reckon!" snapped the gambler.

"Yore job?" exclaimed his companion. "I don't want yore job. If I'd 'a' knowed that was it I'd 'a' told him so, flat. I'm playin' for myself. An' say: He orders me not to play no more poker in his place. Wouldn't that gall you?"

"Then I wouldn't do it," said the gambler, taking his arm. "Come in an' have a drink. What else did he say?"

Bill told him and wound up with a curse. "An' that Thorpe said he'd make me climb up th' wall! Wonder who he thinks he is—Bill Hickok?"

Fisher laughed. "Oh, he don't mean nothin'. He's a lookin'-glass. When Kane laughs, *he* laughs; when Kane has a sore toe, *he's* plumb crippled. But, just th' same I'm tellin' you Thorpe's a bad man with a gun. Don't rile him too much. Say, was you ever paired up with Ewalt?"

Bill put down his glass with deliberate slowness. "Look here!" he growled. "I'm plumb tired of answerin' personal questions. Not meanin' to hurt yore feelin's none, I'm sayin' it's my own cussed business what my name is, where I come from, who my aunt was, an' how old I was when I was born. I never saw such an' old-woman's town!"

Fisher laughed and slapped his shoulder. "Keep all four feet on th' ground, Long; but it *is* funny, now ain't it?"

Bill grinned sheepishly. "Mebby—but for a little while I couldn't see it that way. Have one with me, after which I'm goin' up an' skin that SV man before you can get a crack at him. He's fair lopsided with money. If I can't play poker in Kane's, I shore can send a lot of folks to his place with nothin' left but their pants an' socks!"

"Don't overdo it," warned Fisher. "Come on—I'm headin' back an' I'll leave you at Quayle's."

"How'd you ever come to let that yearlin'-mad foreman keep away from yore game?" asked Bill as they started up the street. "Strikes me you shore overlooked somethin'."

"Does look like it, from a distance," admitted Fisher, grinning. "Reckon we was goin' too easy with him; but we didn't know you was goin' to turn up an' horn in. We never like to stampede a good prospect by bein' hasty. We felt him out a little an' I was figgerin' on amusin' him right soon. There's somethin' cussed odd about him. We're all guessin', an' guessin' different."

"Yes?" inquired Bill carelessly. "I didn't notice nothin' odd about him. He acts a little too shore of hisself, which is how I like 'em. You ain't got a chance to get him now, for I'm goin' to set on his fool head an' burn a nice, big BL on his flank. So any little thing that you know shore will come in handy. I'd do th' same for you. I'm through spoilin' yore game in Kane's, an' I didn't take yore job. What's so odd about him?"

Fisher glanced at his companion and shook his head. "It ain't nothin' about cards. He figgered in a mistake that was made, an' don't know how lucky he was. Th' boss don't often slip up—an' there's a white man an' some Greasers in this town that are cussed lucky too. They blundered, but they got what they went after. An' nobody's heard a word about th' gent that was *un*lucky, which makes me suspicious. I got a headache tryin' to figger it." He shook his head again and then exclaimed in sudden anger: "An' I've quit tryin'! Kane was all set to throw me into th' discard as soon as you come along. He can think what he wants to, for all I care. But let me tell you this: If you win a big roll in this town, an' th' one you got now is plenty big enough, be careful how you wander around after dark. I reckon I owe you that much, anyhow."

Bill stopped in front of the hotel. "I don't know what yo're talkin' about, but that don't make no difference. Th' last part was plain. Come in an' have somethin'."

Fisher looked at him and smiled. "Friend, I'd just as soon be seen goin' in there *now* as I would be seen rustlin' a herd; an' it might even be worse for me. Let it go till you come up to our place. *Adios.*"

CHAPTER VIII

Notes Compared

ENTERING THE barroom of the hotel Bill bought a cigar, talked aimlessly for a few minutes with Ed Doane and then wandered into the office, where Johnny was seated in a chair tipped back against the wall and talking to the proprietor. Bill nodded, took a seat and let himself into the conversation by easy stages, until Quayle was talking to him as much as he was to Johnny, and the burden of his words was Ridley's death.

Bill spat in disgust. "*That* ain't th' way to get a man!" he exclaimed. "Looks like some Greaser had a grudge agin' him—somebody he's mebby fired off his payroll, or suspected of cattle-liftin'."

"You're a stranger here," replied the proprietor. "I can tell ut aisy."

"I am, an' glad of it," replied Bill, smiling; "but I'm learnin' th' ways of yore town rapid. I already know Fisher's poker game, Thorpe's nature, an' Pecos Kane's looks an' disposition. I cleaned Fisher at poker, Thorpe has threatened to make me climb up a wall, an' Kane told me, cold an' personal, to quit playin' poker in his place. I also learned that a white man an' some Greasers

made a big mistake, but got what they went after; that
Fisher figgers different from Kane an' th' others; an' that
Kane won't slip up th' next time, after dark, 'specially if
he don't use th' same fellers. All that I heard; but what it's
about I don't know, or care."

Johnny was laughing at the humor of the newcomer,
and waved from Bill to Quayle. "Tim, this is Bill Long, that
we heard about, for I saw him clean out Fisher. Long, this
is Quayle, an' my name's Nelson. Cuss it man! *I*'d say you
was gettin' acquainted fast. What was that you was sayin'
about th' white man an' th' Greasers, an' some mistake? It
was sort of riled up."

"It *is* riled up," chuckled Bill, crossing his legs. "I gave
it out just like I got it. As I says to Fisher last night, I'm a
imitator. Any news about th' robbery?"

Quayle snorted. "Fine chance! An' d'ye think they'd
be after tellin' on thimselves? That's th' only way for any
news to be heard."

"I may be a stranger," replied Bill; "but I'm no stranger
to human nature, which is about th' same in one place
as it is in another. If that reward don't pan out some
news, then I'm loco."

Quayle listened to a call from the kitchen. "It's th' only
chance, then," he flung over his shoulder as he left
them. "It's that damned Mick. I'll be back soon."

Johnny, with a glance at the barroom door, leaned
slightly forward and whispered one word, his eyes moist:
"*Hoppy!*"

Bill Long squirmed and grinned. "*You flat-headed
sage-hen!*" he breathed. "*I want to see you in secret.*"

Johnny nodded. "I reckon th' reward might start somethin' out in th' open, but I wouldn't want to be th' man that
tried for it." His voice dropped to a whisper. "*We'll take a
ride this afternoon from Kane's, plain an' open.*" In his
natural voice he continued. "But, Twitchell an' Carpenter
are shore powerful. An' they've got th' men an' th' money."

"Do you reckon anybody had a personal grudge?"
asked Bill. "*I'll fix it.*"

"I'm near as much a stranger here as you are," answered Johnny, "though I sold Ridley some cattle. I met

him before, on th' range around Gunsight. Nice feller, he was. *What time?*"

"He musta been a good man, to work for th' T & C," replied Bill. "*After dinner.*"

"He was."

"Oh, well; it ain't *my* funeral. Feel like a little game?"

"I used to think I could play poker," chuckled Johnny; "but I woke up last night. Seein' as how I still got them yearlin's to buy, I don't feel like playin'."

Quayle's voice boomed out suddenly from the kitchen. "If yer fingers was feet ye'd be as good! *Hould* it, now—if ut slips this time I'll be after bustin' yer head. I've showed ye a dozen times how to put it back, an' still ye yell fer me. *There,* now—*hould* it! Hand me th' wire— annybody'd think—blast th' blasted man that made ut! Some Dootchman, I'll wager."

"Shure an' we ought to get a new wan—it's warped crooked, an' cracked—"

"We should, should we?" roared the proprietor. "An' who are 'we'? Only tin years old, an' it's a new wan we'd be gettin', is ut? What we ought to be gettin' is a new cook, an' wan that's *not* cracked. Now, th' nixt time ye poke ut, poke gintly—ye ain't makin' post holes with that poker. An' *now* look at me—" A door slammed and a washbasin sounded like tin.

Ed Doane's laugh sounded from the barroom and he appeared in the doorway, where he grinned. "I hear it frequent, but it's allus funny. Sometimes they near come to blows."

"Stove?" queried Bill.

"Shore—th' grate's buckled out of shape, an' it's a lit-tle short. Murphy gets mad at th' fire an' prods it good— an' then th' show starts all over again. It's funnier than th' devil when th' old man gets a blister from it, for he talks so that nobody but Murphy can understand one word in ten. Easy! Here he comes."

"Buy a new wan, is ut?" muttered the proprietor, his red face bearing a diagonal streak of soot. "Shure—for him to spile, like he spiled this wan. Ah, byes, I'm tellin' ye th' hotel business ain't what it used to be."

"Yore face looks funny," said Ed.

Quayle turned on him. "Oh, it does, does ut? Well, if my face don't suit ye—now would ye look at that?" he demanded as he caught sight of his reflection in the dingy mirror over the desk. "But it ain't so bad, at that; th' black's above th' red!"

"Hey, Tim!" came from the kitchen. "Thought ye said ye fixed ut? Ut's down agin!"

"I—I—I!" sputtered Quayle wildly. He spread the soot over his face with a despairing sweep of his sleeve, leaped into the air and started on a lumbering run for the kitchen. "You—I—*damn* it!" he yelled, and the kitchen resounded to his bellowing demands for the cook.

Ed Doane wiped his eyes, looked around—and shouted, his out-thrust hand pointing to a window, where a red face peered into the room.

"Shure," said the cook, apologetically, "he's the divvil himself. If I stay here wan more day me name ain't Murphy. Will wan av yez, that ain't go no interest in th' dommed stove, tell that Mick to buy a new grate? An' would ye listen to him *now*?"

When he was able to Bill arose. "Well, I reckon I'll go up an' look in at Kane's. If I run this way, don't stop me."

Sauntering up the street he came to the south side of the gambling-hall and went along it, and when a certain number of paces beyond the fifth high window, the sill of which was above his head, he stumbled and fell. Swearing under his breath he picked up a Colt which had slipped from its holster and, arising to hands and knees, looked around and then stood up. He could see under the entire building except at the point where he had fallen, and there he saw that under Kane's private room the walls went down into the earth. When he reached the stables he entered the one which sheltered his horse, closed the door behind him and made a hasty examination of the building, but found nothing which made him suspect a secret exit. He came to the opinion that the boards went down to the earth below Kane's quarters for the purpose of not allowing anyone to crawl under his rooms. In a few minutes he led his horse outside, mounted and rode around to the front of the gambling-hall, where he dismounted and went in for a drink, scowling slightly at the vigilant and militant Mr. Thorpe, who returned the look with interest.

"Got a cayuse?" he asked the bartender.

The other shook his head. "No, why?"

"Thought mebby you'd like to ride along with me. That one of mine will be better for a little exercise. What's east of here?"

"Sand hills, dried lakes, an' th' desert."

"Then I'll go west," grinned Bill. "But mebby it's th' same?"

"It ain't bad over that way; but why don't you ride south? There's real good country down in them valleys."

"Ain't that where th' T & C is?"

The bartender nodded.

"West is good enough for me. Better get a cayuse an' come along."

"Can't do it, an' I ain't set a saddle in two years. I'd be a cripple if I stuck to you. Why don't you hunt up that Nelson feller? He ain't got nothin' to do."

"Just left him. Don't reckon he'd care to go. Huh!" he muttered, looking at the clock. "I reckon I'll eat first, an' ride after."

Shortly after dinner Johnny strolled in and nodded to the bartender, who immediately called to Bill Long.

"Here's Nelson now; mebby he'll go with you," he said.

"Go where?" asked Johnny, pausing.

"Ridin'."

"What for?"

"Exercise. He wants to take th' devilishness out of his horse. You got one, too, ain't you?"

"Shore have," answered Johnny. "An' she's gettin' mean, too. It ain't a bad idea. Where are you goin', Long?"

"Anywhere, everywhere, or nowhere," answered Bill carelessly. "I'm aiming to ride him to a frazzle, an' I got to cut down his feed more."

"All right, if you says so," agreed Johnny, joining the group.

Red Thompson rode up to the door and came in. "Hey, anybody that's goin' down th' trail wants to ride easy. That T & C gang are so suspicious that they're insultin'. Got four men ridin' along their wire, with rifles across their pommels. Looks like they was goin' on th' prod."

Thorpe silently withdrew, to reappear in a few minutes and resume his watch.

Bill arose and nodded to Johnny as he went out. "Ready, Nelson?" he asked.

In a few minutes they met in front of the gambling-hall, and the SV foreman's black caused admiring and covetous looks to show on the faces of the idle group.

"Foller th' trail leadin' to Lukins' ranch, over west," suggested Fisher. "It's better than cross-country. You'll strike it half a mile above."

Long nodded and led the way, both animals prancing and bucking mildly to work off some of their accumulated energy. Reaching the cross trail they swung along it at a distance-eating lope.

"Tell me about everythin'," suggested Johnny. "How'd you come to ride south?"

"Kid," said Hopalong, "you got th' best cayuse ever raised in Montanny. That Englishman was shore right: it pays to cross 'em with thoroughbreds." Moodily silent for a moment, he slowly continued. "Kid, I've lost Mary, an' William, Junior. Fever took 'em in four days, an' never even touched *me*! I'm all alone. Either you move up north, or I stay with you till I die. An' if I do that I'll miss Red an' th' others like th' devil. I'm goin' to have a good look at that Bar-H, that you chased them thieves off of. Montanny is too far north, an' I'm feelin' th' winters too hard. An' it's gettin' settled too fast, an' bein' ploughed up more every year. But all of this can wait: what's goin' on down here that I don't know?"

Johnny told him and when he had finished and listened to what his friend knew they spent the rest of the time discussing the situation from every angle and arranged a few simple signals, resurrected from the past, to serve in the press of any sudden need. They met two punchers riding in from Lukins' ranch, exchanged nods and then turned south into the cattle trail, crossed a crescent arroyo and turned again, when below the town, under the suspicious eyes of a Question-Mark sentry hidden in a thicket. Following the main trail north they entered the town and parted at Quayle's.

The evening passed uneventfully in Kane's and when the group began to break up Bill Long went up to his room. Gradually man after man deserted the gambling-hall, until only Johnny and the head bartender were left, and after half an hour's dragging conversation the dispenser of liquids yawned and nodded decisively.

"Nelson, I'm goin' to lock up after you. See you tomorrow."

"Most sensible words said tonight," replied Johnny, and he stepped out, the door closing behind him. The lights went out, one by one, with a tardiness due to their height from the floor, and he stood quietly for a moment, scrutinizing the sky and enjoying the refreshing coolness. Moving out into the middle of the street he sauntered toward the dark hotel, every sense alert as a previous experience came back to him. Suddenly a barely audible sound, like the cracking of a toe joint, caused him to leap aside. An indistinct figure plunged past him, so close that he felt the wind of it. His gun roared while he was in the air and when he alighted he was crouched, facing the rear, where another figure blundered into the second shot and dropped. Swiftly padding feet came nearer and he slipped further to the side, letting the sound pass without hindrance. Moving softly forward he turned and crept along the wall of a building, smiling grimly at the low Spanish curses behind him on the street. Again the kitchen door served him well and the deeper blackness of the interior silently engulfed him.

Up at Kane's, Red Thompson, who was awake and waiting until the building should be wrapped in sleep, heard the shots and crept to the window. He could see nothing, but he heard whispers and heavy, slow and shuffling steps, which drew steadily nearer. The Mexican tongue was no puzzle to Red, whose years largely had been spent in a country where it was constantly used and his fears, instantly aroused, were soon followed by a savage grin.

"That Nelson, he is a devil," floated up to him, the words a low growl.

"Again he got away. I will not face the Big Boss. It is the second failure, and with Anton dead, an' Juan's arm broken, I shall leave this town. Put him here, at the door. May God forgive his sins! *Adios!*"

"Wait, Sanchez!" called a companion. "We will all go, even Juan, for he'd better ride than remain. There will be trouble."

"What's all th' hellabaloo?" came Thorpe's truculent voice in English from the corner of the building, where he stood, clad only in boots and underwear, a six-shooter in his upraised hand. At the sudden soft scurrying of feet he started forward, and then checked himself.

"If them Greasers bungled it *this* time, may th' Lord help 'em. They'll shore get a-plenty. I wouldn't be—" he stopped and stared at the door, and then moved closer to it. "By God, they *got* him!" he whispered, and bent down, his hand passing over the indistinct figure. "Huh! I take it all back," he muttered in disgust. "That's a Greaser, by feel an' smell. They made more of a mess of it this time than they did before. Well, you ain't no fit ornament for th' front door. Might as well move you myself," and, grumbling, he grabbed hold of the collar and dragged the unresisting bulk around to the rear, where he carelessly dropped it and went back into the building. Soon two Mexicans, rubbing sleepy eyes, emerged with shovel and spade, that the dawn should find nothing more than a carefully hidden grave.

Red waited a little longer and then, knowing better than to go on his feet along the old floor of the hall, inched slowly over it on his stomach, careful to let each board take his weight gradually. Reaching the second door on his left he slowly pushed it open, chuckling with pride at his friend's forethought in oiling the one squeaking hinge. Closing it gently he scratched on the floor twice and then went on again toward the answering scratch. An hour passed in the softest of whispering and when he at last entered his own room again and carefully stood up, the darkness hid a rare smile on his tanned and leathery face, which an exultant thought had lighted.

"Th' Old Days: They're comin' back again!" he gloated. "Me, an' Hoppy, an' the Kid! Glory be!" and the smile persisted until he awakened at dawn, when it moved from the wrinkled face to the secrecy of his heart.

CHAPTER IX

Ways of Serving Notice

If Sandy Bend had been seized with a local spasm when the senior member of the T & C had learned of the robbery of the Mesquite bank, it now was having a very creditable fit. The little printing-shop was the scene of bustling activities and soon a small bundle of handbills was on its way to the office of the cattle king. McCullough, drive-boss *par excellence* and one of the surviving frontiersmen who not only had made history in several localities, but had helped to wear the ruts in the old Santa Fe Trail until the creeping roadbed of the railroad had put the trail with other interesting relics of the past, was rudely torn from his seven-up game with his cronies by one of the several couriers who lathered horses at the snapping behest of the senior partner. He hastened to the office, rumbled across the outer room and pushed open the door of the holy of holies without even the semblance of a knock. He was blunt, direct, and no respecter of persons.

"Hello, Charley!" he grunted. "What's loose now?"

"Hell's loose!" snapped Twitchell. "Ridley's been murdered by one of Kane's gang. Shot in th' back—head near blowed off. There's only four men up there now, an' they may be dead by this time. Take as many men as you need an' go up there—we just bought a herd of SV cows, if there's any left. But I want th' man that killed Ridley. That's first. I want th' man who robbed th' bank— that's second. An' I want Pecos Kane—that's first, second, an' third. Damn it! I growed up with Tom Ridley!"

"I'll take twenty men an' bring you th' whole gang—but some of 'em will shore spoil before we can get 'em here, this kind of weather. Do I burn that end of th' town?"

"You'll burn nothin'," retorted Twitchell. "You'll not risk a man until you have to. You'll stay on th' ranch an' watch th' cattle. I've lost one good man now, an' I'm spendin' money before I risk losin' any more. There's a bundle of handbills. When they've been digested by that bunch of assassins you can sit in th' bunkhouse an' have yore game delivered to you, all tied up, an' tagged."

"Orders is orders," growled McCullough; "but some are damned fool orders. If you want somebody to set on th' front porch an' whittle, why'n hell are you cuttin' *me* out of th' herd for th' job?"

"I'm cuttin' you out because I want my best man out there!" retorted the senior member heatedly. "You may find it lively settin', an' have to do yore whittlin' with rifles an' six-guns. Look out that somebody don't whittle you at eight hundred while yo're settin' on th' front porch! You talk like you think yo're goin' to a prayer meetin'!"

"I'm hopin' they come that close," said McCullough, picking up the package of bills. "So Tom's gone, huh? Charley, there ain't many of us left no more. Remember how you an' Ridley an' me used to go off trappin' them winters, hundreds of miles into th' mountains, with only what we could easy carry on our backs? That was livin'."

"You get out of here, you old fraud!" roared Twitchell. "Ain't I got enough to bother me now? Take care of yore-self, Mac; an' my way's worth tryin', an' tryin' good. If it don't work, then we'll have to try yore way."

"All right; I'll give it a fair ride, Charley; but it will be time wasted," replied the trail-boss. "In that case I'm takin' a dozen men. We relay at th' Squaw Creek corrals, an' again at Sweetwater Bottoms. Send a wagon after us—you'll know what we'll need. You send a new boss to th' Sweetwater, for I'm pickin' up Waffles. He's one of th' best men you got, an' he's been picketed at that two-bits station long enough."

"Good luck, Mac. Take who you want. Yo're th' boss. Any play you make will be backed to th' limit by th' T & C."

When McCullough got outside he found a crowd of men which the hard-riding couriers had sent in from all parts of the town. They shouted questions and got terse answers as he picked his dozen, the twelve best out of a crowd of good men, all known to him in person and by deeds. The lucky dozen smiled exultantly at the scowling unfortunates and dashed up the street in a bunch after their grizzled pacemaker. One of the last, glancing behind him, saw a stern-faced, sorrowful man in a black store suit standing in the office door looking wistfully after them; and the rider, gifted with understanding, raised his hand to his hat brim and faced around.

"Th' old man's sorry he's boss," he confided to his nearest companion.

"An' there's plenty up in Mesquite that will be th' same," came the reply.

Despite his years McCullough held his lead without crowding from the rear, for he was of the hard-riding breed and toughened to the work. When the first relay was obtained at Squaw Creek that evening there were several who felt the strain more than the leader. A hasty supper and they were gone again, pounding into the gathering dusk of the northwest. All night they rode along a fair trail, strung out behind a man who kept to it with uncanny certainty. Dawn found them changing mounts in Sweetwater Bottoms, but without the snap displayed at the Squaw. Waffles, one-time foreman of the O-Bar-O, needed all his habitual repression to keep from favoring them with a war dance when he heard his luck. Impatiently waiting for the surprised but enthusiastic cook to prepare their breakfasts, they made short work of the meal when it appeared and rolled on again, silent, grim, heavy-lidded, but cheerful. They gladly would do more than that for McCullough, Twitchell—and Tom Ridley. The second evening found them riding up to the buildings of the Question-Mark, guns across their pommels, and they were thankfully received.

Mesquite awakened the next morning to a surprise, for handbills were scattered on its few streets and had been pushed under doors, one of them under the front door of Kane's gambling-hall. When Johnny came down to breakfast the proprietor handed him the sheet, pointing to its flaming headline.

"Read that, me bye!" cried Quayle.

Johnny obeyed:

$2,500.00 REWARD!

For Information Leading to the Capture and
Conviction of the Murder of Tom Ridley
STRICTLY CONFIDENTIAL
TWITCHELL & CARPENTER, Sandy Bend
JOHN McCULLOUGH, Gen'l. Supt., Mesquite

He thoughtlessly shoved it into his pocket and shrugged his shoulders. "That man Twitchell thinks a lot of his money," he said. "But, if it's his way, it's his way. I'm glad to say it ain't mine."

Quayle looked at him from under heavy brows and smiled faintly. "Mac's here, hisself," he said. "They've raised th' ante, an' if I was as young as you I'd have a try at th' game. An', me bye, it isn't only th' money; 'tis a duty, an' a pleasure. Go in an' eat, now, before that wild Mick av a cook scalps ye."

Hoofbeats pounded up the street from the south and a Mexican galloped past toward Kane's, followed on foot by several idlers.

"There ye go!" savagely growled the proprietor; "an' I hope ye saw a-plenty, ye Greaser dog!"

After a hurried breakfast Johnny went up to Kane's and found an air of tension and suspicion. Men were going in and out of the door through the partition and the half-friendly smiles which he had received the night before were everywhere missing. Feeling the chill of his reception did not blunt his powers of observation, for he saw that both Red Thompson and Bill Long, being unaccredited strangers, drew an occasional suspicious glance. The former was seated in a chair at the lower end of the bar, his back to the wall and only a step from the dining-room door. Bill Long was leaning against the upper end of the counter, where it turned at right angles to meet the wall behind it. At Bill's back and only two steps away was the front door. His chin was in his hand and his elbow rested on the bar, where he appeared to be moodily studying the floor behind the counter, but in reality his keen, narrowed eyes were watching Thorpe and the loopholes in the checkerboard. From his position he caught the light on them at just the right angle to see the backing plates. He let Johnny go past him without more than a casual glance and nod.

Thorpe moved forward, cleaving a straight path through the restless crowd and stopped in front of the newcomer. "Nelson," he said, tartly; "th' boss wants to see you, *pronto!*" As he spoke he let his swinging hand rest against the butt of his gun.

Johnny took plenty of time for his answer, his mind working at top speed. If Kane had caused inquiries to be made around Gunsight concerning him he knew that the report hardly would please any man who was against law and order; and he knew that Kane had had plenty of time to make the inquiries. The thinly veiled hostility and suspicions on the faces around him settled that question in his mind. He slouched sidewise until he had Thorpe in a better position between him and the partition.

"You shore made a mistake," he drawled. "Th' boss never even heard of me."

"I said *pronto!*" snapped Thorpe.

"Well, as long as yo're so pressin'," came the slow, acquiescent reply, "you can *go to hell!*"

Thorpe's gun got halfway out, and stopped as a heavy Colt jabbed into his stomach with a force which knocked the breath out of him and doubled him up. Johnny's other gun, deftly balanced between his palm and the thumb on its hammer, freezing the expressions as it had found them on the faces of the crowd. "Stick up yore han's! All of you! You, in the chair!" he roared. "Stick 'em up!" and Red lost no time in making up for his delinquency. Bill Long, being out of the angry man's sight, raised his only halfway.

"I was welcome enough last night," snapped Johnny; "but somethin's wrong today. If Kane wants to see me, he can send somebody that can talk without insultin' me. An' as for this sick cow, I'm warnin' him fair that I shoot at th' first move, *his* move or anybody *else's*. Stand up, *you*!" he shouted; "an' foller me outside. Keep close, an' plumb in front of me. I'll turn you loose when I get to cover. *Come on!*"

As he backed toward the door, Thorpe following, Bill Long, seeing that Johnny was master of the situation, got his hands all the way up, but the motion was observed and Johnny's gun left Thorpe long enough to swing aside and cover the tardy one. "You keep 'em there!" he gritted. "You can rest 'em later!" and he cautiously backed against the door, moved along it the few inches necessary to gain the opening, and felt his way to the street. "Don't you gamble, Thorpe!" he warned. "Stick closer!"

Being furthest from the front door and soonest out of Johnny's sight, Red Thompson let his hands fall to his hips and cautiously peered over the top of the bar, ready to cover the crowd until Bill Long could drop his upraised hands.

Bill was unfortunate, since he would have to be the last man to assume a more natural position; but he was growing tired and suddenly flung himself sidewise beyond the door opening. As he left the bar there came a heavy report from the street and the bullet, striking the edge of the counter where he had stood, glanced upward and entered the ceiling, a generous cloud of dust moving slowly downward.

"He's a mad dog," muttered Bill, shrinking against the wall. "An' he can shoot like hell! I reckon he's itchin' to get me on sight, *now*. Somebody look out an' see where he is. But what'n blazes is it all about, anyhow?"

The chief bartender's head reappeared farther down the counter. "You fool!" he yelled. "Why didn't you let me know what you was goin' to do? Don't you never think of nobody but yourself? That parted my hair!"

Fisher swore disgustedly. "Look out, yourself, Long, if yo're curious! But why didn't you get him?" he demanded. "You was behind him!"

"I wasn't neither behind him; I was on th' side!" retorted Bill. "He was watchin' me out of th' corner of his eye, like th' damned rattler he is! I could see it plain, I tell you!"

"You can see lots of things when yo're scared stiff, can't you?" sneered a voice in the crowd.

"I wasn't scared," defended Bill. "But I wasn't takin' no chances for th' glory of it. He never done nothin' to me, an' I ain't on Kane's payroll—yet."

"An' you ain't goin' to be, I reckon," laughed another.

Fisher's face proclaimed that he had solved whatever problem there might be in Bill's lack of action. "Ain't had a chance to get it from him yet, huh?" he asked. Sneering, he gave a warning as he turned away. "An' don't you try for it, neither. If he won't come back here no more, I can get him playin' somewhere else."

Red arose fully and stretched, hearing a slight grating noise at a loophole in the partition behind him, where the slide dropped into place. "I'm dry; bone dry," he announced. "I never was so dry before. All in favor of a drink, step up. I'm payin' for *this* round."

All were in favor of it, and the bartender moved slowly behind the counter toward the front door, his head bent over far to the right. "Don't see him; but we better wait till Thorpe comes back. Great guns! Did you *see* it!" he marveled.

"I can see it better now than I could then," said Red, leaning against the bar. "Come on, boys; he's done gone. This means you, too, Long; 'though I ain't sayin' you hardly earned it. If he saw you before he backed up, I says he's got eyes in his ears. Why, cuss it, he was lookin' plumb at *me* all th' time. You got too hefty an imagination, Long."

Out in the street Johnny, backing swiftly from the building, saw Bill Long's sudden leap and fired, for moral effect, at the place vacated. Yanking his captive's gun from its holster, he was about to toss it aside when his fingers gripped the telltale butt and a colder look gleamed in his eyes. Slipping his right-hand gun into its holster he gripped the captured weapon affectionately, and then hazarded a quick glance around him. Someone was riding rapidly down the trail from the north, and a second sidewise glance told him that it was Idaho.

"Faster, you!" he growled to the doorkeeper. "Keep a-comin'—keep a-comin'. One false move an' Kane'll need another sentry. You may be able to make Bill Long climb up a wall, but I ain't in his class."

Idaho, who was riding in to appease his burning curiosity, felt its flames lick instantly higher as he saw his friend back swiftly from Kane's front door, with Thorpe apparently hooked on the sight of the six-gun. Drawing rein instantly in his astonishment, he at once loosened them and whirled into the scanty and scrawny vegetation on the far side of the trail. Going at a dead run he sent the wiry little pony over piles of cans, around cacti and other larger obstructions until he reached the rear of Red Frank's, facing on the next street. Here he pulled up and drew the Winchester from its scabbard, feeling that Johnny was capable of taking care of Kane's if not interfered with from behind.

Johnny, reaching the rear of the building which he had sought the night before, leaped back and to one side as he came to the end of the wall, glanced along the rear end and then curtly ordered Thorpe back to his friends.

"There'll be more to this," snarled Thorpe, white from anger, his face working. His courage was not of the fineness necessary to let him yield to the mad impulse which surged over him and urged him to throw himself, hands, feet, and teeth, in a blind and hopeless attack upon the certain death which balanced itself in the gun in Johnny's hand. His blazing eyes fixed full on his enemy's, he let discretion be his tutor and slowly, grudgingly stepped back, his dragging feet moving only inches at each shuffle, while their owner, poised and tense and ready to take advantage of any slip on Johnny's part, backed toward the sandy street and the scene of his discomfiture. At last reaching the front of the building he paused, stood slowly erect and then wheeled about and strode toward Kane's. At the door he glanced once more at his waiting adversary and then plunged into the room, striding straight for the partition door without a single sidewise glance.

Idaho's voice broke the spell. "I thought he was goin' to risk it," he muttered, a deep sigh of relief following the words. "He was near loco, but he just about had enough sense left to save his worthless life. You would 'a' blowed him apart at that distance."

"I'd 'a' smashed his pointed jaw!" growled Johnny. "I ain't shootin' nobody that don't reach for a gun. An' if I'd had any sense I'd 'a' chucked th' guns to you an' let him have his beatin'. Next time, I will. Fine sort of a dog he is, tellin' me what I'm goin' to do, an' when I'm goin' to do it!"

"Wait till payday, when I'll have more money," chuckled Idaho. "I can easy get three to two around here. He's th' champeen rough-an'-tumble fighter for near a hundred miles, but I'm sayin' any man with th' everlastin' nerve to pull Kit Thorpe out from his own kennel an' pack ain't got sense enough to know when he's licked. An' that bein' so, I'm bettin' on yore condition to win. He's gettin' fat an' shortwinded from doin' nothin'. Besides, I'm one of them fools that allus bets on a friend." He laughed as certain memories passed before him. "I've done had a treat—come on, an' let me treat you. How many was in there when you pulled him out? An' why didn't th' partition work like it allus did before?"

"Because th' man that worked it was out in front," answered Johnny. "Things went too fast for anybody else to get behind it." A sudden grin slipped to his face. "Hey, I got one of my pet guns back! He was wearin' it. I knowed it as soon as my fingers closed around th' butt, for I shaped it to fit my hand several years ago. Did you see th' handbills? Twitchell's put up another reward, this one for Ridley; an' McCullough is down on th' Question-Mark. Things ought to step fast, now."

CHAPTER X

Twice in the Same Place

THORPE REAPPEARED through the partition door armed anew with the mate to the gun he had lost, too enraged to notice that it was better suited to a left than to a right hand. An ordinary man hardly would have noticed it, but a gunman of his years and experience should have sensed the ill-fitting grip at once. He glared over the room, suspiciously eager to catch some unfortunate indulging in a grin, for he had been so shamed and humiliated that it was almost necessary to his future safety that he redeem himself and put his shattered reputation back on its pedestal of fear. There were no grins, for however much any of his acquaintances might have enjoyed his discomfiture they had no lessened respect for his ability with either six-guns or fists; and there was a restlessness in the crowd, for no man knew what was coming.

Fisher conveyed the collective opinion and broke the tension. "*Any* man would 'a' been fooled," he said to the head bartender, but loud enough for all to hear it. His voice indicated vexation at the success of so shabby a trick. "When he answered Thorpe I shore thought he was goin' prompt an' peaceful—why, he even *started*! Nobody reckoned he was aimin' to make a gunplay. How could they? An' I'm sayin' that it's cussed lucky for him that *Thorpe* didn't!"

"Anybody can be fooled th' *first* time," replied the man of liquor. He looked over at the partition door and nodded. "Come over an' have a drink, Thorpe, an' forget it. I got money that says there ain't no man alive can beat you on th' draw. He tricked you, actin' that way."

"He's th' first man on earth ever shoved a gun into me like that," growled Thorpe, slowly moving forward. "An' he's th' last! Seein' as there's some here that mebby ain't shore about it, I'll show 'em that I was tricked!" He stopped in front of Bill Long and regarded that surprised individual with a look as malevolent as it was sincere. "Any squaw dog can tote *two* guns," he said, his still raging anger putting a keener edge to the words. "When he does he tells everybody that he's shore bad. If he ain't, that's *his* fault. I tote one—an' yo're not goin' to swagger around these parts with any more than I got. Which one are you goin' to throw away?"

Bill blinked at him with owlish stupidity. "What you say?" he asked, as though doubting the reliability of his ears.

"Oh," sneered Thorpe, his rage climbing anew; "you didn't hear me th' first time, huh? Well, you want to be listenin' *this* time! I asked, which gun are you goin' to throw away, you card-skinnin' four-flush?"

"Why," faltered Bill, doing his very best to play the part he had chosen. "I—I dunno—I ain't goin' to—to throw any of 'em away. What you mean?"

"Throw one away!" snapped Thorpe, his animal cunning telling him that the obeyance of the order might possibly be accepted by the crowd as grounds for justification, if any should be needed.

Bill changed subtly as he reflected that the crowd had excused Thorpe's humiliation because he had been tricked, and determined that no such excuse should be used again. He looked the enraged man in the eyes and a contemptuous smile crept around his thin lips.

"Thorpe," he drawled, "if yo're lookin' for props to hold up yore reputation, you got th' wrong timber. Better look for a sick cow, or—"

The crowd gasped as it realized that its friend's fingers were again relaxing from the butt of his half-drawn gun and that three pounds of steel, concentrated on the small circumference of the barrel of a six-gun, had been jabbed into the pit of his stomach with such speed that they had not seen it, and with such force that the victim of the blow was sick, racked with pain and scarcely able to stand, momentarily paralyzed by the second assault on the abused stomach, which caved, quivered, and retched from the impact. Again he had failed, this time after cold, calm warning; again the astonished crowd froze in ridiculous postures, with ludicrous expressions graven on their faces, their automatic arms leaping sky-ward as they gaped stupidly, unbelievingly at the second gun. Before they could collect their numbed senses the master of the situation had backed swiftly against the wall near the front door, thereby blasting the budding hopes of the bartender, whose wits and power of move-ment, returning at equal pace, were well ahead of those of his friends. It also saved the man of liquor from being dropped behind his own bar by the gun of the alert Mr. Thompson, who felt relieved when the crisis had passed without calling forth any effort on his part which would couple him with the capable Mr. Long.

"Climb that wall!" said Bill Long, his voice vibrating with the sudden outpouring of accumulated repression. "I'm lookin' for a chance to kill you, so I ain't askin' you to throw away no gun. This is between you an' me—anybody takin' cards will drop cold. You got it comin', an' comin' fair. Climb that wall!"

Thorpe, gasping and agonized, fought off the sickness which had held him rigid and stared open-eyed, open-mouthed at glinting ferocity in the narrowed eyes of the two-gun man.

"Climb that wall!" came the order, this time almost a whisper, but sharp and cutting as the edge of a knife, and there was a certainty in the voice and eyes which was not to be disregarded. Thorpe straightened up a little, turned slowly and slowly made his way through the opening crowd to the wall, and leaned against it. He had no thought of using the gun at his hip, no idea of resistance, for the spirit of the bully within him had been utterly crushed. He was a broken man, groping for bearings in the fog of the shifting readjustments going on in his soul.

"*Climb!*" said Bill Long's voice like the cracking of a bull-whacker's whip, and Thorpe mechanically obeyed, his finger-nails and boot toes scarping over the smooth boards in senseless effort. He had not yet had time to realize what he had lost, to feel the worthlessness which would be his to the end of his days.

The two-gun man nodded. "I told you boys I was a imitator," he said, smiling; "an' I am. I imitated him in his play to kill me. I imitated that SV foreman, an' now I'm imitatin' Thorpe again. It's his own idea, climbin' walls."

Fisher, watching the still-climbing Thorpe, was using his nimble wits for a way out of a situation which easily might turn into anything, from a joke to a sudden shambles. He now had no doubts about the real quality of Bill Long, and he secretly congratulated himself that he had not yielded to certain temptations he had felt. Besides, his arms were growing heavy and numb. There came to his mind the further thought that this two-gun, card-playing wizard would be a very good partner for a tour of the country, a tour which should be lucrative and safe enough to satisfy anyone.

"Huh," he laughed. "We're imitatin', too; only we're imitatin' ourselves, an' we're gettin' tired of holdin' 'em up. I'm sayin', fair an' square, that I ain't aimin' to draw no cards in any game that is two-handed. I reckon th' rest of th' boys feel th' same as I do. How 'bout it, boys?"

Affirmation came slowly or explosively, according to the individual natures, and the two-gun man was confident enough in his ability to judge character to accept the words. He slowly dropped his guns back in the holsters and smiled broadly. Even the lower class of men is

capable of feeling a real liking, when it is based on auda-
cious courage, for anyone who deserves it; and he knew
that the now shifting crowd had been caught in the momentum of such a feeling. There was also another con-
sideration to which more than one man present gave
grave heed: They scarcely had quit marveling at the wiz-
ardy of one two-gun man when the second had appeared and made them marvel anew.

"All right, boys," he said. "Thorpe, you can quit climbin',
seein' that you ain't gettin' nowhere. Come over here an'
gimme that gun. I'm still imitatin'. This ain't been no lucky
day for you, an' just to show you that you can make it on-
luckier," he said as he took the Colt, "I'm goin' to impress
somethin' on yore mind." He threw the barrel up and
carelessly emptied the weapon into the checkerboard
partition with a rapidity which left nothing to be desired.
The distance was nearly sixty feet. "Reckon you can cover
'em all with th' palm of one hand," he remarked as he
shifted the empty gun to his left hand, where he thought it
would fit better. He looked at it and turned it over. Three
small dots, driven into the side of the frame, made him re-
press a smile. His own guns had two, while Red Thompson's lone Colt had four. He opened the flange and
shoved the gun down behind the backstrap of his trousers,
where a left-handed man often finds it convenient to
carry a weapon, since the butt points that way. Letting his
coat fall back into place he walked slowly to the door and
out onto the street, the conversation in the room buzzing
high after he left.

He next appeared in Quayle's, where he grinned at
Idaho, Quayle, Johnny, and Ed Doane.

"I just made Thorpe climb th' wall," he said. "He
looked like a pinned toad. Do you ever like to split up a
pair of aces, Nelson?"

Johnny considered a moment and then slowly shook
his head.

"Neither do I," replied the newcomer. His left hand
went slowly around under his coat and brought out the
captured Colt. "An' I ain't goin' to begin doin' it now.
Here," and he handed the weapon to Johnny.

Johnny took it mechanically and then quickly turned it over and glanced at the frame. Weighing it judicially he looked up. "Th' feel an' balance of this Colt just suits me," he said. "Want to sell it?"

"I don't hardly own it enough to *sell* it," answered Bill; "but I reckon I can give it away, seein' that Thorpe set th' fashion. I'm warnin' you that he *might* want it back. But you should 'a' seen him a-climbin' that wall!" and he burst into laughter.

"I'll gamble," grinned Johnny. "I'll get you a new one for it."

"No, you won't," replied Bill, still laughing. "I got more'n th' value of a wore-out six-gun watchin' yore show up there. Besides, if it was better'n mine I would 'a' kept it myself. I ain't expectin' you'll be there, tonight," he finished.

"Suits me right here," replied Johnny. "Much obliged for th' gun." He looked at Idaho and grinned. "I aim to clean out this sage-hen at Californy Jack, tonight."

"Which same you might do," admitted Idaho, slowly looking at the Colt in his friend's hand; "for you shore are a fool for luck."

CHAPTER XI

A Job Well Done

PECOS KANE looked up at the sound of shooting and signaled for the doorkeeper. Getting no response he pulled another cord and waited impatiently for the man who answered it.

"What was that shooting, and who did it?" demanded the boss. He cut the wordy recital short. "Tell Bill Trask to assume Thorpe's duties and send Thorpe to me."

Thorpe soon appeared, slowly closed the door behind him and faced the boss, who studied him for a silent interval, the object of the keen scrutiny squirming at the close of it.

"You are no longer suited for my doortender," said Kane's hard voice. "Report to the dining-room, or kitchen, or leave the hotel entirely. But first find Corwin and send him to me. That is all."

Thorpe gulped and shuffled out and in a few minutes the sheriff appeared.

"Sit down, Corwin," said Kane, pleasantly. "Trask has Thorpe's job now. Wait a moment until I think something out," and he sat back in his chair, his eyes closing. In a few moments he opened them and leaned forward.

"I have come to a decision regarding some strangers in this town. I have reason to believe that Long and Thompson know each other a great deal better than they pretend. I want to know more about Nelson, so you will send a good man up to his country to get me a report on him. Do it as soon as you leave me, and tell him to waste no time. That clear?"

Corwin nodded.

"Very well," continued the boss. "I want you to arrest both Long and Thompson before tomorrow, and throw them into jail. Since Long's exhibition today it will be well to go about it in a manner calculated to avoid bloodshed. There is no use of throwing men away by sending them against such gunplay. You are to arrest them without a shot being fired on *either* side. It is only a matter of figuring it out, and I will give you this much to start on: Whatever suspicions may have been aroused in their minds about their welcome here not being cordial must be removed. Because of that there should be no ill-advised speed in carrying out the arrests. They could be shot down from behind, but I want them alive; and it suits my purpose better if they are taken right here in this building. They are worth money, and a great deal more than money to me, to you, and to all of us. Twitchell and Carpenter are very powerful and they must be placated if it can be done in such a way as not to jeopardize us. I think it may be done in a way which will strengthen us. You follow me closely?"

The sheriff nodded again.

"All right," said Kane. "Now then, tell me where each of the three men, Nelson, Long, and Thompson, were on the occasions of the robbery of the bank and the death of Ridley. Think carefully."

Corwin gazed at the floor thoughtfully. "When th' bank was robbed Nelson was playin' cards with Idaho Norton in Quayle's saloon. Quayle an' Doane were in there with 'em. Long an' Thompson were here, upstairs, asleep."

"Very good, so far," commented Kane; "go on."

"When Ridley was shot Nelson was with Idaho Norton in Quayle's hotel, for both of them rustled into th' street an' carried him indoors. Thompson was in th' front room, here, an' Long come in soon after the shot was fired."

"Excellent. Which way did he come?"

"Through th' front door."

"Before that?" demanded the boss impatiently.

"I don't know."

"Why don't you?" blazed Kane. "Have I got to do *all* th' thinking for this crowd of dumbheads?"

"Why, why should I know?" Corwin asked in surprise.

"If you don't know the answer to your own question it is only wasting my time to tell it to you. Now, listen: You are to send four men in to me—but not Mexicans, for the testimony of Mexicans in this country is not taken any too seriously by juries. The four are not all to come the same way nor at the same time. The dumbheads I have around me necessitate that each be instructed separate and apart from the others, else they wouldn't know, or keep separate their own part. Is this plain?"

"Yes," answered the arm of the law.

"Very well. Now you will go out and arrange to arrest and jail those two men. And after you have arranged it you will *do* it. Not a shot is to be fired. When they are in jail report to me. That is all."

Corwin departed and did not scratch his head until the door closed after him, and then he showed great signs of perplexity. As he went up the next corridor he caught sight of a friend leaning against the back of the partition, and just beyond was Bill Trask at his new post. He beckoned to them both.

"Sandy, you are to report to th' boss, right away," ordered the sheriff. "He wants four white men, an' yo're near white. Trask, send in three more white men, one at a time, after Woods comes out. An' let me impress *this* on yore mind: It is strict orders that you ain't to fire a shot tonight, when somethin' happens that's goin' to happen; you, nor nobody else. Got that good?"

"What do you mean?" asked the sentry, grinning.

"Good God!" snorted the sheriff. "Do I have to do *all* th' thinkin' for this crowd of dumbheads?"

"Yo're a parrot," retorted Trask. "I know that by heart.

You *don't* have to. You don't even do yore *own*. You may go!"

Corwin grunted and joined the crowd in the big room and when Bill Long wandered in and settled down to watch a game the sheriff in due time found a seat at his side. His conversation was natural, not too steady and not too friendly and neither did he tarry too long, for when he thought that he had remained long enough he wandered up to the bar, joked with the chief dispenser, and mixed with the crowd. After a while he went out and strolled over to the jail, where a dozen men were waiting for him. His lecture to them was painfully simple, in the simplest words of his simple vocabulary, and when he at last returned to the gambling-hall he was certain that his pupils were letter-perfect.

Meanwhile Kane had been busy and when the first of the four appeared the clear-thinking boss drove straight to his point. He looked intently at the caller and asked: "Where were you on the night of the storm, at the time the bank was robbed?"

"Upstairs playin' cards with Harry."

"Do you know where Long and Thompson were at that time?"

"Shore; they was upstairs."

"I am going to surprise you," said Kane, smiling, and he did, for he told his listener where he had been on that night, what he had seen, and what he had found in the morning in front of the door of Bill Long's room. He did it so well that the listener began to believe that it was so, and said as much.

"That's just what you must believe," exclaimed Kane. "Go over it again and again. Picture it, with natural details, over and over again. Live every minute, every step of it. If you forget anything about it come to me and I'll refresh your memory. I'll do so anyway, when the time comes. You may go."

The second and third man came, learned their lessons and departed. The fourth, a grade higher in intelligence, was given a more difficult task and before he was dismissed Kane went to a safe, took out a bundle of large bills and handed two of them to his visitor, who nodded, pocketed them, and departed. He was to plant them, find them again and return them so that the latter part of the operation would be clear in his memory.

Supper was over and the big room crowded. Jokes and laughter sounded over the quiet curses of the losers. Bill Long, straddling a chair, with his arms crossed on its back, watched a game and exchanged banter with the players during the deals. Red Thompson, playing in another game not far away, was winning slowly but consistently. Somebody started a night-herding song and others joined in, making the ceiling ring. Busy bartenders were endeavoring to supply the demand. The song roared through the first verse and the second, and in the middle of the following chorus, at the first word of the second line there was a sudden, concerted movement, and chaos reigned.

Unexpectedly attacked by half a dozen men each Bill and Red fought valiantly but vainly. In Bill's group two men had been told off to go for his guns, one to each weapon, and they had dived head-first at the signal. Red's single gun had been obtained in the same way. Stamping feet, curses, grunts, groans, the soft sound of fist on flesh, the scraping of squirming masses of men going this way and that, the heavy breathing, and other sounds of conflict filled the dusty, smoky air. Chairs crashed, tables toppled and were wrecked by the surging groups and then, suddenly, the turmoil ceased and the two bound, battered, and exhausted men swayed dizzily in the hands of their captors, their chests rising and falling convulsively beneath their ragged shirts as they gulped the foul air.

Two men rocked on the floor, slobbering over cracked shins, another lay face down across the wreck of a chair, his gory face torn from mouth to cheekbone; another held a limp and dangling arm, cursing with monotonous regularity; a fifth, blood pouring from his torn scalp and blinding him, groped aimlessly around the room.

Corwin glanced around, shook his head and looked at his two prisoners in frank admiration. "You fellers shore can lick hell out of th' man that invented fightin'!"

Bill Long glared at him. "I didn't see—you—nowhere

near!" he panted. "Turn us—loose—an' we'll clean—out th' place. We was—two-thirds—licked before we—knew it was comin'."

"Don't waste yore—breath on th'—damned bastard," snarled Red. "There's a few I'm aimin' to—kill when I—get th' chance!"

"What's th' meanin' of—this surprise party?" asked Bill Long.

"It means that you an' Thompson are under arrest for robbin' th' bank; an' you for th' murder of Ridley," answered the peace officer, frowning at the ripple of laughter which arose. A pock-marked Mexican, whose forehead bore a crescent-shaped scar, seemed to be unduly hilarious and vastly relieved about something.

Thorpe came swiftly across the room toward Bill Long, snarled a curse, and struck with vicious energy at the bruised face. Bill rolled his head and the blow missed. Before the assailant could recover his balance and strike again a brawny, red-haired giant, whose one good eye glared over a battered nose, lunged swiftly forward and knocked Thorpe backward over a smashed chair and overturned table. The prostrate man groped and half arose, to look dazedly into the giant's gun and hear the holder of it give angry warning.

"Any more of that an' I'll blow you apart!" roared the giant. "An' that goes for any other skunk in th' room. Bear-baitin' is barred." He looked at Corwin. "You've got 'em—now get 'em out of here an' into jail, before I has to kill somebody!"

Corwin called to his men and with the prisoners in the middle the little procession started for the old adobe jail on the next street, the pleased sheriff bringing up the rear, his Colt swinging in his hand. When the prisoners had been locked up behind its thick walls he sighed with relief, posted two guards, front and rear, and went back to report to Kane that a good job had been well done.

The boss nodded and bestowed one of his rare compliments. "That was well handled, Sheriff," he said. "I am sorry your work is not yet finished. A zealous peace officer like you should be proud enough of such a capture as to be anxious to inform those most interested. Also," he smiled, "you naturally would be anxious to put in a claim for the reward. Therefore you should go right down to McCullough and lay the entire matter before him, as I shall now instruct you," and the instructions were as brief as thoroughness would allow. "Is that clear?" asked the boss at the end of the lesson.

"It ain't only clear," enthused Corwin; "but it's gilt-edged; I'm on my way, now!"

"Report to me before morning," said Kane.

Hurrying from the room and the building the sheriff saddled his horse and rode briskly down the trail. Not far from town he began to whistle and he kept it up purposely as a notification of peaceful and honorable intentions, until the sharp challenge of a hidden sentry checked both it and his horse.

"Sheriff Corwin," he answered. "What you holdin' *me* up for?"

A man stepped out of the cover at the edge of the trail. "Got a match?" he pleasantly asked, the rifle hanging from the crook of his arm, both himself and the weapon hidden from the sheriff by the darkness. "Where you goin' so late? Thought everybody was asleep but me."

Corwin handed him the match. "Just ridin' down to see McCullough. Got important business with him, an' reckoned it shouldn't wait 'til mornin'."

The sentry rolled a cigarette and lit it with the borrowed match in such a way that the sheriff's face was well lighted for the moment, but he did not look up. "That's good," he said. "Reckon I'll go along with you. No use hangin' 'round up here, an' I'm shore sleepy. Wait till I get my cayuse," and he disappeared, soon returning in the saddle. His quiet friend in the brush settled back to resume the watch and to speculate on how long it would take his companion to return.

McCullough, half undressed, balanced himself as he heard approaching voices, growled profanely and put the freed leg in the trousers. He was ready for company when one of the night shift stuck his head in at the door.

"Sheriff Corwin wants to see you," said the puncher. "His business is so delicate it might die before mornin'."

"All right," grumbled the trail-boss. "If you get out of his way mebby he can come in."

Corwin stood in the vacated door, smiling, but too wise to offer his hand to the blunt, grim host. "Got good news," he said, "for you, me, an' th' T & C."

"Ya-as?" drawled McCullough, peering out beneath his bushy, gray eyebrows. "Pecos Kane shoot hisself?"

"We got th' fellers that robbed th' bank an' shot Ridley," said the sheriff.

"The hell you say!" exclaimed McCullough. "Come in an' set down. Who are they? How'd you get 'em?"

"That reward stick?" asked Corwin anxiously.

"Tighter'n a tick to a cow!" emphatically replied the trail-boss. "Who are they?"

"I got a piece of paper here," said the sheriff, proving his words. He stepped inside and placed it on the table. "Read it over an' sign it. Then I'll fill in th' blanks with th' names of th' men. If they're guilty, I'm protected; if I've made a mistake, then there's no harm done."

McCullough slowly read it aloud:

" 'Sheriff Corwin was the first man to tell me that———and———robbed the Mesquite bank, and that———killed Tom Ridley. He will produce the prisoners, with the witnesses and other proof in Sandy Bend upon demand. If they are found guilty of the crime named the rewards belong to him.' "

The trail-boss considered it thoughtfully. "It looks fair; but there's one thing I don't like, Sheriff," he said, putting his finger on the objectionable words and looking up. "I don't like 'Sandy Bend.' I'm takin' no chances with them fellers. I'll just scratch that out, an' write in, 'to me.' How 'bout it?"

"They've got to have a fair trial," replied Corwin. "I'm standin' for no lynchin'. I can't do it."

"Yo're shore right they're goin' to have a fair trial!"

retorted the trail-boss. "Twitchell ain't just lookin' for two men—he wants th' ones that robbed th' bank an' killed Ridley. You don't suppose he's payin' five thousan' out of his pocket for somebody that ain't guilty, do you? Why, they're goin' to have such a fair trial that you'll need all th' evidence you can get to convict 'em. Lynch 'em?" He laughed sarcastically. "They won't even be jailed in Sandy Bend, where they shore *would* be lynched. You take 'em to Sandy Bend an' you'll be lynched out of yore reward. You know how it reads."

Corwin scratched his head and a slow grin spread over his face. "Cuss it, I never saw it that way," he admitted. "I guess yo're shoutin' gospel, Mac; but, cuss it, it ain't reg'lar."

"You know me; an' I know you," replied the trail-boss, smiling. "There's lots of little things done that ain't exactly reg'lar; but they're plumb sensible. Suppose I change this here paper like I said, an' sign it. Then you write in th' names an' let me read 'em. Then you let me know what proof you got, an' bring down th' prisoners, an' I'll sign a receipt for 'em."

"Yes!" exclaimed Corwin. "I'll deputize you, an' give 'em into yore custody, with orders to take 'em to Sandy Bend, or any other jail which you think best. That makes it more reg'lar, don't it?" he smiled.

McCullough laughed heartily and slapped his thigh. "That's shore more reg'lar. I'm beginnin' to learn why they elected you sheriff. All right, then; I'm signin' my name." He took pen and ink from the shelf, made the change in the paper, sprawled his heavy-handed signature across the bottom and handed the pen to Corwin. "Now, damn it: Who are they?"

The sheriff carefully filled in the three blanks, McCullough peering over his shoulder and noticing that the form had been made out by another hand.

"There," said Corwin. "I'm spendin' that five thousand right now."

" 'Bill Long'—'Red Thompson'—'Bill Long' again," growled the trail-boss. "Never heard of 'em. Live around here?"

Corwin shook his head. "No."

"All right," grunted McCullough. "Now, then; what proof you got? You'll never spend a cent of it if you ain't got 'em cold."

Corwin sat on the edge of the table, handed a cigar to his host and lit his own. "I got a man who was in th' north stable, behind Kane's, when th' shot that killed Ridley was fired from th' other stable. He was feedin' his hoss an' looked out through a crack, seein' Long sneak out of th' other buildin', Sharp's in hand, an' rustle for cover around to th' gamblin'-hall. Another man was standin' in th' kitchen, gazin' out of th' winder, an' saw Long turn th' corner of th' north stable an' dash for th' hotel buildin'. He says he laughed because Long's slight limp made him sort of bob sideways. An' we know why Long done it, but we're holdin' that back. That's for th' killin'.

"Now for th' robbery: I got th' man that saw Long an' Thompson sneak out of th' front door of th' dinin'-room hall into that roarin' sand storm between eleven an' twelve o'clock on th' night of th' robbery. He says he remembers it plain because he was plumb surprised to see sane men do a fool thing like that. He didn't say nothin' to 'em because if they wanted to commit suicide it was their own business. Besides, they was strangers to him. After a while he went up to bed, but couldn't sleep because of th' storm makin' such a racket. Kane's upstairs rocked a little that night. I know, because I was up there, tryin' to sleep."

"Go on," said the trail-boss, eagerly and impatiently, his squinting eyes not leaving the sheriff's face.

"Well, quite some time later he heard th' door next to his'n open cautious, but a draft caught it an' slammed it shut. Then Bill Long's voice said, angry an' sharp: 'What th' hell you doin', Red? Tellin' creation about it?' In th' mornin', th' cook, who gets up ahead of everybody else, of course, was goin' along th' hall toward th' stairs an' he kicks somethin' close to Long's door. It rustles an' he gropes for it, curious-like, an' took it downstairs with him for a look at it, where it wasn't so dark. It was a strip of paper that th' bank puts around packages of bills, an' there was some figgers on it. He chucks it in a corner, where it fell down behind some stuff that had been there a long time, an' don't think no more about it till he hears about th' bank bein' robbed. Then he fishes it out an' brings it to me. I knowed what it was, first glance."

"Any more?" urged McCullough. "It's *good*; but, you got any more?"

"I shore have. What you think I'm sheriff for? I got two of th' bills, an' their numbers tally with th' bank's numbers of th' missin' money. You can compare 'em with yore own list later. I sent a deputy to their rooms as soon as I had 'em in jail, an' he found th' bills sewed up in their saddle pads. Reckon they was keepin' one apiece in case they needed money quick. An' when th' sand was swept off th' step in front of that hall door, a gold piece was picked up out of it."

"When were you told about all this by these fellers?" demanded the trail-boss.

"As soon as th' robbery was known, an' as soon as th' shootin' of Ridley was known!"

"When did you arrest them?"

"Last night; an' it was shore one big job. They can fight like a passel of cougars. Don't take no chances with 'em, Mac."

"Why did you wait till last night?" demanded McCullough. "Wasn't you scared they'd get away?"

"No. I had 'em trailed every place they went. They wasn't either of 'em out of our sight for a minute; an' when they slept there was men watchin' th' stairs an' their winders. You see, Kane lost a lot of money in that robbery, bein' a director; an' I was hopin' they'd try to sneak off to where they cached it an' give us a chance to locate it. They was too wise. I got more witnesses, too; but they're Greasers, an' I ain't puttin' no stock in 'em. A Greaser'd lie his own mother into her grave for ten dollars; anyhow, most juries down here think so, so it's all th' same."

"Yes; lyin' for pay is shore a Greaser trick," said McCullough, nodding. "Well, I reckon it's only a case of waitin' for th' reward, Sheriff. Tell you what I wish you'd do: Gimme everythin' they own when you send 'em down to me, or when I come up for 'em, whichever suits you best. Everythin' has got to be collected now before it gets lost, an' it's got to be ready for court in case it's needed."

"All right; I'll get back what I can use, after th' trial," replied Corwin. "I'll throw their saddles on their cayuses, an' let 'em ride 'em down. How soon do you want 'em? Right away?"

"First thing in th' mornin'!" snapped McCullough. "Th' sooner th' better. I'll send up some of th' boys to give you a hand with 'em, or I'll take 'em off yore hands entirely at th' jail. Which suits you?"

"Send up a couple of yore men, if you want to. It'll look better in town if I deliver 'em to you here. Why, you ain't smoked yore cigar!"

McCullough looked at him and then at his own hand, staring at the crushed mass of tobacco in it. "Shucks!" he grunted, apologetically, and forthwith lied a little himself. "Funny how a man forgets when he's excited. I bet that cigar thought it was in a vise—my hand's tired from squeezin'."

"Sorry I ain't got another, Mac," said Corwin, grinning, as he paused in the door. "I'll be lookin' for yore boys early. *Adios.*"

"*Adios,*" replied McCullough from the door, listening to the dying hoofbeats going rapidly toward town. Then he shut the door, hurled the remains of the cigar on the floor and stepped on them. "He's got 'em, huh? An' strangers, too! He's got 'em too damned pat for me. It takes a good man to plaster a lie on me an' make it stick—an' he ain't no good, at all. He was sweatin' before he got through!" Again the trousers came off, all the way this time, and the lamp was turned down. As he settled into his bunk he growled again. "Well, I'll have a look at 'em, anyhow, an' send 'em down for Twitchell to look at," and in another moment he was asleep.

CHAPTER XII

Friends on the Outside

WHILE EVENTS were working out smoothly for the arrest of the two men in Kane's gambling-hall, four friends were passing a quiet evening in Quayle's barroom, but the quiet was not to endure.

With lagging interest in the game Idaho picked up his cards, riffled them and listened. "Reckon that's singin'," he said in response to the noise floating down from the gambling-hall. "Sounds more like a bunch of cows bawlin' for their calves. Kane's comin' to life later'n usual. Wonder if Thorpe's joinin' in?" he asked, and burst out laughing. "Next to our hard-workin' sheriff there ain't nobody in town that I'd rather see eat dirt than him. Wish I could 'a' seen him a-climbin' that wall!"

"Annybody that works for Kane eats dirt," commented Quayle. "They has to. He'll learn how to eat it, too, th' blackguard."

"There goes *somethin'*," said Ed Doane as the distant roaring ceased abruptly. "Reckon Thorpe's makin' another try at th' wall." He laughed softly. "They're startin' a fandango, by th' sound of it."

" 'Tis nothin' to th' noise av a good Irish reel," deprecated the proprietor.

"I'm claimin' low this hand," grunted Idaho. "Look out for yore jack."

Johnny smiled, played and soon a new deal was begun.

"Th' dance is over, too," said Doane, mopping off the bar for the third time in ten minutes. "Musta been a short one."

"Some of them *hombres* will dance shorter than that, an' harder," grunted Idaho, "th' next time they pay *us* a visit. They didn't get many head th' last time, an' I'm sayin' they'll get none at all th' next time. Where they take 'em to is more'n we can guess: th' tracks just die. Not bein' able to track 'em, we're aimin' to stop it at th' beginnin'. You fellers wait, an' you'll see."

Quayle grunted expressively. "I been waitin' too long now. Wonder why nobody ever set fire to Kane's. 'Twould be a fine sight."

"You'll mebby see that, too, one of these nights," growled the puncher.

"Then pick out wan when th' wind is blowin' *up* th' street," chuckled Quayle. "This buildin' is so dry it itches to burn. I'm surprised it ain't happened long ago, with that Mick in th' kitchen raisin' th' divvil with th' stove. If I didn't have a place av me own I'd be tempted to do it meself."

The bartender laughed shortly. "If McCullough happens to think of it I reckon it'll be done." He shook out the bar cloth and bunched it again. "Funny he ain't cut loose yet. That ain't like him, at all."

"Waitin' for th' rewards to start workin', I reckon," said Johnny.

Idaho scraped up the cards, shaped them into a sheer-sided deck and pushed it aside. "I'm tired of this game; it's too even. Reckon I'll go up an' take a look at Kane's." He arose and sauntered out, paused, and looked up the street. "Cussed if they ain't havin' a perade," he called. "This ain't th' Fourth of July, is it? I'm goin' up an' sidle around for a closer look. Be back soon."

Johnny was vaguely perturbed. The sudden cessation of the song bothered him, and the uproar which instantly followed it only served to increase his uneasiness. Ordinarily he would not have been affected, but the day's events might have led to almost anything. Had a shot been fired he swiftly would have investigated, but the lack of all shooting quieted his unfounded suspicions. Idaho's remark about the parade renewed them and after a short, silent argument with himself he arose, went to the door and looked up the street, seeing the faint, yellow patch on the sand where Kane's lamps shone through the open door and struggled against the surrounding darkness, and hearing the faint rumble of voices above which rang out frequent laughter. He grimly told himself that there would be no laughter in Kane's if his two friends had come to any harm, and there would have been plenty of shooting.

"Annythin' to see?" asked Quayle, poking his head out of the door.

"No," answered Johnny, turning to reenter the building. "Just feelin' their oats, I reckon."

" 'Tis feelin' their *ropes* they should be doin'," replied Quayle, stepping back to let his guest pass through. "An' 'twould be fine humor to swing 'em from their own. Hist!" he warned, listening to the immoderate laughter which came rapidly nearer. "Here's Idaho; he'll know it all."

Idaho popped in and in joyous abandon threw his sombrero against the ceiling. "Funniest thing you ever heard!" he panted. "Corwin's arrested that Bill Long an' Red Thompson. Took a full dozen to do it, an' half of 'em are cripples now. Th' pe-rade I saw was Corwin an' a bunch escortin' 'em over to th' jail. Ain't we got a rip-snortin' fool for a sheriff?" His levity died swiftly, to give way to slowly rising anger. "With this country fair crowded with crooks he can't find nobody to throw in jail except two friendless strangers! Damn his hide, I got a notion to pry 'em out and turn 'em loose before mornin', just to make things right, an' take some of th' swellin' out of his flat head. It's a cussed shame."

The low-pulled brim of Johnny's sombrero hid the glint in his eyes and the narrowed lids. He relaxed and sat carelessly on the edge of the table, one leg swinging easily to and fro as conjecture after conjecture rioted through his mind.

"They musta stepped on Kane's toes," said Ed, vigorously wiping off the backbar.

Idaho scooped up his hat and flung it on the table at Johnny's side. "You'd never guess it, Ed. Even th' rest of th' gang was laughin' about it, all but th' cripples. I been waitin' for them rewards to start workin', but I never reckoned they'd work out like this. Long an' Thompson are holdin' th' sack. They're scapegoats for th' whole cussed gang. Corwin took 'em in for robbin' th' bank, an' gettin' Ridley!"

Ed Doane dropped the bar cloth and stared at the speaker and a red tide crept slowly up his throat and spread across his face. Johnny slid from the table and disappeared in the direction of his room. He came down again with the two extra Colts in his hands, slipped through the kitchen and ran toward the jail. Quayle's mouth slowly closed and then let out an explosive curse. The bartender brought his fist down on the bar with a smash.

"Scapegoats? Yo're right! It's a cold deck—an' you bet Kane never would 'a' dealt from it if he wasn't dead shore he could make th' play stick. Every man in th' pack will swear accordin' to orders, an' who can swear th' other way? It'll be a strange jury, down in Sandy Bend, every man jack of it a friend of Ridley an' th' T & C. Well, I'm a peaceable man, but this is too much. I never saw them fellers before in my life; but on th' day when Corwin starts south with 'em I'll be peaceable no longer—an' I've got friends! There's no tellin' who'll be next if he makes this stick. Who's with me?"

"*I* am," said Quayle; "an' *I* got friends."

"Me, too," cried Idaho. "There's a dozen hickory knots out on th' ranch that hate Corwin near as much as I do.

They'll be with us, mebby even Lukins, hisself. Hey! Where'd Nelson go?" he excitedly demanded. "Mebby he's out playin' a lone hand!" and he darted for the kitchen.

Johnny, hidden in the darkness not far from the jail, was waiting. The escort, judging from the talk and the glowing ends of cigarettes, was bunched near the front of the building, little dreaming how close they stood to a man who held four Colts and was fighting down a rage which urged their use. At last, thoroughly master of itself, Johnny's mind turned to craftiness rather than to blind action and formulated a sketchy plan. But while the plan was being carried through he would not allow his two old friends to be entirely helpless. Slipping off his boots he crept up behind the jail and with his kerchief lowered the two extra guns through the window, softly calling attention to them, which redoubled the prisoners' efforts to untie each other. Satisfied now that they were in no immediate danger he slipped back to his boots, put them on and waited to see what would happen, and to listen further.

"There ain't no use watchin' th' jail," said a voice, louder than the rest. "They're tied up proper, an' nobody ever got out of it before."

"Just th' same, you an' Harry will watch it," said Corwin. "Winder an' door. I ain't takin' no chances with this pair."

A thickening on the dark ground moved forward slowly and a low voice called Johnny's name. He replied cautiously and soon Idaho crawled to his side, whispering questions.

"Go back where there ain't no chance of anybody hearin' us, or stumblin' over us," said Johnny. "When that gang leaves there won't be so much noise, an' then they may hear us."

At last reaching an old wagon they stood up and leaned against it, and Johnny unburdened his heart to a man he knew he could trust.

"Idaho," he said, quietly, "them fellers are th' best friends I ever had. They cussed near raised me, an' they risked their lives more'n once to save mine. 'Most every-thin' I know I got from them, an' they ain't goin' to stay in that mud hut till mornin', not if I die for it. They come down here to help me, an' I'm goin' to get 'em out. Did you ever hear of th' old Bar-20, over in th' Pecos Valley?"

"I shore did," answered Idaho. "Why?"

"I was near raised on it. Bill Long is Hopalong Cassidy, an' Red Thompson is Red Connors, th' whitest men that ever set a saddle. Rob a bank, an' shoot a man from *be-hind*! Did Bill Long act like a man that had to shoot in th' back when he made Thorpe climb his own wall, with his own crowd lookin' on? Most of their lives has been spent fightin' Kane's kind; an' no breed of pups can hold 'em while I'm drawin' my breath. It's only how to do it th' best way that's botherin' me. I've slipped 'em a pair of guns, so I got a little time to think. Why, cuss it: Hoppy knows th' skunk that got Ridley! An' before we're through we'll know who robbed th' bank, an' hand 'em over to Mac. That's what's keepin' th' three of us here!"

"Bless my gran'mother's old gray cat!" breathed Idaho. "No wonder they pulled th' string! I'm sayin' Kane's got hard ridin' ahead. Say, can I tell th' boys at th' ranch?"

"Tell 'em nothin' that you wouldn't know except for me tellin' you," replied Johnny. "I know they're good boys; but they might let it slip. Me an' Hoppy an' Red are aimin' for them rewards—an' we're goin' to get 'em both."

"It's a plumb lovely night," muttered Idaho. "Nicest night I think I ever saw. I don't want no rewards, but I just got to get my itchin' paws into what's goin' on around this town. An' it's a lovely town. Nicest town I think I ever was in. That 'dobe shack ain't what it once was. I know, because, not bein' friendly with th' sheriff, an' not bein' able to look all directions at once, I figgered I might be in it, myself, some day. So I've looked it over good, inside an' out. Th' walls are crumbly, an' th' bars in th' window are old. There's a waggin tongue in Pete Jarvis' freight waggin that's near twelve foot long, an' a-plenty thick. Ash, I think it is; that or oak. Either's good enough. If it was shoved between th' bars an' then pushed sideways that jail wouldn't be a jail no more. If Pete ain't taken th' waggin to bed with him, bein' so proud of it, we can crack that little hazelnut. I'm goin' back an' see how many are still hangin' around."

"I'm goin' back to th' hotel, so I'll be seen there," said Johnny.

"I'll do th' same, later," replied his friend as they separated.

Quayle was getting rid of some of his accumulated anger, which reflection had caused to soar up near the danger point. "Tom Ridley wasn't killed by no strangers!" he growled, banging the table with his fist. "I can name th' man that done it by callin' th' roll av Kane's litter; an' I'll be namin' th' bank robbers in th' same breath." He looked around as Johnny entered the room. "An' what did ye find, lad?"

"Idaho was right. They've got 'em in th' jail."

"An' if I was as young a man as you," said the proprietor, "they wouldn't kape 'em there. As ut is I'm timpted to go up an' bust in th' dommed door, before th' sheriff comes back from his ride. Tom Ridley's murderer? Bah!"

"Back from his ride?" questioned Johnny, quickly and eagerly.

"Shure. He just wint down th' trail. Tellin' Mac, I don't doubt that he's got th' men Twitchell wants. I was lookin' around when he wint past. This is th' time, lad. I'll help ye by settin' fire to Red Frank's corral if th' jail's watched. It'll take their attention. Or I'll lug me rifle up an' cover ye while ye work." He arose and went into the office for the weapon, Johnny following him. "There she is—full to th' ind. An' I know her purty ways."

"Tim," said Johnny's low voice over his shoulder. "Yo're white, clean through. I don't need yore help, anyhow, not right now. An' because you are white I'm goin' to tell you somethin' that'll please you, an' give me one more good friend in this rotten town. Bill Long an' Red Thompson are friends of mine. They did not rob th' bank, nor shoot Ridley; but Bill knows who *did* shoot Ridley. He saw him climbin' out of Kane's south stable while th' smoke was still comin' from th' gun that shot yore friend. I can put my hand on th' coyote in five minutes. Th' three of us are stayin' here to get that man, th' man who robbed th' bank, an' Pecos Kane. I'm tellin' you this because I may need a good friend in Mesquite before we're through."

Quayle had wheeled and gripped his shoulder with convulsive force. "Ah!" he breathed. "Come on, lad; point him out! Point him out for Tim Quayle, like th' good lad ye are!"

"Do you want him so bad that yo're willin' to let th' real killer get away?" asked Johnny. "You only have to wait an' we'll get both."

"What d'ye mean?"

"You don't believe he shot Ridley without bein' told to do it, do you?"

"Kane told him; I know it as plain as I know my name."

"Knowin' ain't provin' it, an' provin' it is what we got to do."

" 'Tis th' curse av th' Irish, jumpin' first an' thinkin' after," growled Quayle. "Go wan!"

"Yo're friends with McCullough," said Johnny. "Mac knows a little; an' I'm near certain he's heard of Hopalong Cassidy an' Red Connors, of th' Bar-20. Don't forget th' names: Hopalong Cassidy an' Red Connors, of th' old Bar-20 in th' Pecos Valley. Buck Peters was foreman. I want you to go down an' pay him a friendly visit, and tell him this," and Quayle listened intently to the message.

"Bye," chuckled the proprietor, "ye leave Mac to me. We been friends for years, an' Tom Ridley was th' friend of us both. But, lad, ye may die; an' Bill Long may die— life is uncertain anywhere, an' more so in Mesquite, these days. If yer a friend av Tim Quayle, slip me th' name av th' man that murdered Ridley. I promise ye to kape han's off—an' I want no reward. But it fair sickens me to think his name may be lost. Tom was like a brother."

"If you knew th' man you couldn't hold back," replied Johnny. "Here: I'll tell Idaho, an' Ed Doane. If Bill an' I go under they'll give you his description. I don't know his name."

"Th' offer is a good wan; but Tim Quayle never broke his word to anny man—an' there's nothin' on earth or in hiven I want so much as to know who murdered Tom Ridley. I pass ye my word with th' sign av th' cross, on th' witness of th' Holy Virgin, an' on th' mem'ry av Tom Ridley— I'll stay me hand accordin' to me promise."

Johnny looked deeply into the faded blue eyes through the tears which filmed them. He gripped the proprietor's hand and leaned closer. "A Greaser with a pock-marked face, an' a crescent-shaped scar over his right eye. He is about my height an' drags one foot slightly when he walks."

"Aye, from th' ball an' chain!" muttered Quayle. "I know th' scut! Thank ye, lad: I can sleep better nights. An' I can wait as no Irishman ever waited before. Annythin' Tim Quayle has is yourn; yourn an' yore friends. I'll see Mac tomorrow. Good night." He cuddled the rifle and went toward the stairs, but as he put his foot on the first step he stopped, turned, and went to a chair in a corner. "I'm forgettin'," he said, simply. "Ye may need me," and he leaned back against the wall, closing his eyes, an expression of peace on his wrinkled face.

CHAPTER XIII

Out and Away

IDAHO SLIPPED out of the darkness of the kitchen and appeared in the door. "All right, Nelson," he called. "There's two on guard an' th' rest have left. They ain't takin' their job any too serious, neither. Just one apiece," he chuckled.

Johnny looked at the proprietor. "Got any rope, Tim?" he asked.

"Plenty," answered Quayle, arising hastily and leading the way toward the kitchen. Supplying their need he stood in the door and peered into the darkness after them. "Good luck, byes," he muttered.

Pete Jarvis was proud of his new sixteen-foot freighter and he must have turned in his sleep when two figures, masked to the eyes by handkerchiefs, stole into his yard and went off with the heavy wagon tongue. They carried it up to the old wagon near the jail, where they put it down, removed their boots, and went on without it, reaching the rear wall of the jail without incident, where they crouched, one at each corner, and smiled at the conversation going on.

"I'm hopin' for a look at yore faces," said Red's voice,

"to see what they looked like before I get through with 'em, if I ever get my chance. Come in, an' be sociable."

"Yo're doin' a lot of talkin' *now*, you red-headed coyote," came the jeering reply. "But how are you goin' to talk to th' judge?"

"Bring some clean straw in th' mornin'," said Bill Long, "or we'll bust yore necks. Manure's all right for Greasers, an' you, but we're white men. Hear me chirp, you mangy pups?"

"It's good enough for you!" snapped a guard. "I was goin' to get you some, but now you can rot, for all I care!"

Johnny backed under the window, raised up and pressed his face against the rusty bars. "It's th' Kid," he whispered. "Are you untied yet?"

The soft answer pleased him and he went back to his corner of the wall, where he grudged every passing minute. He had decided to wait no longer, but to risk the noise of a shot if the unsuspecting guards could get a gun out quickly enough, and he was about to tell Idaho of the change in plans when the words of a guard checked him.

"Guess I'll walk around again," said one of them, arising slowly. "Gettin' cramped, an' sleepy, settin' here."

"You spit in that window again an' I'll bust yore neck!" said Red's angry voice, whereupon Johnny found a new pleasure in doing his duty.

"You ain't bustin' nobody, or nothin'," jeered the guard, " 'less it's th' rope yo're goin' to drop on." He yawned and stretched and sauntered along the side of the building, turned the corner and then raised his hands with a jerk as a Colt pushed into his stomach and a hard voice whispered terse instructions, which he instantly obeyed. "You fellers ain't so bad, at that," he said, with only a slight change in his voice; "but yo're shore playin' in hard luck."

"Keep yore sympathy to yoreself!" angrily retorted Bill Long.

Idaho, having unbuckled the gun-belt and laid it gently on the ground, swiftly pulled the victim's arms down behind his back and tied the crossed wrists. Johnny now got busy with ropes for his feet, and a gag, and they soon laid him close to the base of the wall, and crept toward the front of the building, one to each wall. Johnny tensed himself as Idaho sauntered around the other corner.

"Makin' up with 'em?" asked the guard, ironically. "You don't want to let 'em throw a scare into you. They'll never harm nobody no more." He lazily arose to stretch his legs on a turn around the building. "You listen to what *I'm* goin' to tell 'em," he said. Then he squawked and went down with Johnny on his back, Idaho's dive coming a second later. A blow on his head caused him to lose any impertinent interest which he might have had in subsequent events and soon he, too, lay along the base of the rear wall, bound, gagged, and helpless.

"I near could feel th' jar of that in here," said Red's cheerful voice. "I'm hopin' it was th' coyote that spit through th' window. What's next?" he asked, on his feet and pulling at bars. He received no answer and commented upon that fact frankly and profusely.

"Shut yore face," growled Bill, working at his side. "He's hatchin' somethin' under his hat."

"Somethin' hatchin' all over me," grunted Red, stirring restlessly. "I'm a heap surprised this old mud hut ain't walkin' off some'ers."

Bill squirmed. "You ain't got no call to put on no airs," he retorted. "Mine's been hatched a long time. I wouldn't let a dog lay on straw as rotten as that stuff. Oh!" he gloated. "Somebody's shore goin' to pay for this little party!"

"Wish th' sheriff would open that outside door about now," chuckled Red, balancing his six-chambered gift. "I'd make him pop-eyed."

Hurrying feet, booted now, came rapidly nearer and soon the square-cornered end of a seasoned wagon tongue scraped on the adobe window ledge. Bill Long grabbed it and drew it between two of the bars.

"Go toward th' south," he said. "That's th' boy! Listen to 'em scrape!" he exulted. "Go ahead—she's startin'. I can feel th' 'dobe crackin' between th' bars. Come back

an' take th' next—you'll have a little better swing because it's further from th' edge of th' window. Go ahead!
It's bendin' an' pullin' out at both ends. Go on! Whoop!
There goes th' 'dobe. Come back to th' middle an' use
that pry as a batterin'-ram on this bar. Steady; we'll do th'
guidin'. All ready? Then let her *go*! Fine! Try again. That's
th' stuff—she's gone! Take th' next. Ready? Let her *go*!
There goes more 'dobe, on *this* side. Once more: Ready?
Let her *go*! Good enough: Here we come."

"Wait," said Johnny. "We'll pass one of these fellers in
to you. If we leave 'em both together they'll mebby roll
together an' untie each other."

"Like we did," chuckled Red.

"Give us th' first one you got," said Bill. "He's th' one
that spit through th' window. I want him to lay on this
straw, too. He's tied, an' can't scratch."

The guard was raised to the window, pushed and
pulled through it and carelessly dumped on Red's bed,
after which it did not take long for the two prisoners to
gain their freedom.

"Good Kid!" said Bill, gripping his friend's hand. "An'
you, too, whoever you are!"

"Don't mention no names," whispered Idaho. "We
couldn't find no ear plugs," he chuckled, shaking hands
with Red. "I'm too well known in this town. What'll we
do with this coyote? Let him lay here?"

"No," answered Johnny. "He might roll over to Red
Frank's an' get help. Picket him to a bush or cactus.
Here, gimme a hand with him. I reckon he's come to, by
th' way he's bracin' hisself. Little faster—time's flyin'. All
right, put him down." Johnny busied himself with the
last piece of rope and stood up. "Come on—Kane's stables, next."

As they crossed the street above the gambling-house,
where in reality it was a trail, Bill Long took a hand in the
evening's plans.

"Red," he said, "you go an' get our cayuses. Bring 'em
right here, where we are now, an' wait for us. Idaho, you
an' Johnny come with me an' stand under th' window of
my room to take th' things I let down, an' free th' rope

from 'em. I'm cussed shore we ain't goin' to leave all of our traps behind, not unless they been stole."

"I like yore cussed nerve!" chuckled Idaho. "Don't blame you, though. I'm ready."

"His nerve's just plain gall!" snapped Red, turning to Hopalong. "Think yo're sendin' me off to get a couple of cayuses, while yo're runnin' that risk in there? Get th' cayuses yoreself; *I'll* get th' fixin's!"

"Don't waste time like this!" growled Johnny. "Do as yo're told, you red-headed wart! Corwin will shore go to th' jail before he turns in. Come on, Hoppy."

"That name sounds good again," chuckled Hopalong, giving Red a shove toward the stables. "Get them cayuses, Carrot-Top!"

Red obeyed, but took it out in talking to himself as he went along, and as he entered the north stable he stepped on something large and soft, which instantly went into action. Red dropped to his knees and clinched, getting both wrists in his hands. Being in a hurry, and afraid of any outcry, he could not indulge in niceties, so he brought one knee up and planted it forcefully in his enemy's stomach, threw his weight on it and jumped up and down. Sliding his hands down the wrists, one at a time, he found the knife and took it from the relaxing fingers. Then he felt for the victim's jaw with one hand and hit it with the other. Arising, he hummed a tune and soon led out the two horses.

"Don't like to leave th' others for them fellers to use," he growled, and forthwith decided not to leave them. He drove them out of both stables, mounted his own, led Hopalong's, and slowly herded the other dozen ahead of him over the soft sand and away. When he finally reached the agreed-upon meeting place he reflected with pleasure that anyone wishing to use those horses for the purpose of pursuit, or any other purpose, would first have to find, and then catch them. They were going strong when he had last heard them.

Idaho had stopped under the window pointed out to him, and his two companions, leaving their boots in his tender care, were swallowed up in the darkness. They opened the squeaking front door, cautiously climbed the squeaking stairs and fairly oozed over the floor of the upper hall, which wanted to squeak, and did so a very little. Hopalong slowly opened the door of his room, thankful that he had oiled its one musical hinge, and felt cautiously over the bed. It was empty, and his sigh of relief was audible. And he was further relieved when his groping hand found his possessions where he had left them. He was stooping to loosen the coil of rope at the pommel of his saddle when he heard a sleepy, inquiring voice and a soft thud, and anxiously slipped to the door.

"Kid!" he whispered. "*Kid!*"

"Shut yore fool face," replied the object of his solicitude, striking a match for one quick glance around. The room was strange to him, since he never had been in it before, and he had to get his bearings. The inert man on the bed did not get a second glance, for the sound and weight of the blow had reassured Johnny. There were two saddles, two rifles, two of everything, which was distressing under the circumstances.

Hopalong had just lowered his own saddle to the waiting Idaho when the catlike Johnny entered the room with a saddle and a rifle. He placed them on the bed, where they would make no noise, and departed, catlike. Soon returning he placed another saddle and rifle on the bed and departed once more.

Hopalong, having sent down both of Johnny's first offerings, felt over the bed for the rest of Red's belongings, if there were any more, and became profanely indignant as his hand caressed another rifle and then bumped against another saddle.

"What'n hell is he doin'?" he demanded. "My God! There's more'n a *dozen* rooms on this floor, an' men in all of 'em! Hey, Kid!" he whispered as breathing sounded suddenly close to him.

"What?" asked Johnny, holding two slicker rolls, a sombrero, a pair of boots, and a suit of clothes. Two belts with their six-guns were slung around his neck, but the darkness mercifully hid the sight from his friend.

"Damn it! We ain't *movin'* this hotel," said Hopalong

with biting sarcasm. "It don't *belong* to us, you know. An' what was that whack I heard when you first went in?"

"Somebody jumped Red's bed, an' wanted to know some fool thing, or somethin', an' I had to quiet him. An' what'n blazes are *you* kickin' about? I've moved *twice* as much as you have, more'n twice as *far*. Grab holt of some of this stuff an' send it down to Idaho. He'll think you've went to sleep."

"You locoed tumble-bug!" said Hopalong. "Aimin' to send down th' bed, with th' feller in it, too?"

A door creaked suddenly and they froze.

"Quit yore damned noise an' go to sleep!" growled a sleepy, truculent voice, and the door creaked shut again.

After a short wait in silence Hopalong put out an inquiring hand. "Come on," he whispered. "What you got there?"

Johnny told him, and Hopalong dropped the articles out of the window, all but the hat, boots, and clothes. "Don't you know Red's wearin' his clothes, boots an' hat, you chump?" he said, gratis. "Leave them things here an' foller me," and he started for the head of the stairs.

They were halfway down when they heard a horse galloping toward the hotel. It was coming from the direction of the jail and they nudged each other.

Sheriff Corwin, feeling like he was master of all he surveyed, had ridden to the jail before going to report to Kane for the purpose of cautioning the guards not to relax their vigil. Not being able to see them in the darkness meant nothing to him, for they should have challenged him, and had not. He swept up to the door, angrily calling them by name and, receiving no reply, dismounted in hot haste, shook the door and then went hurriedly around the building to feel of the bars. One sweep of his hand was enough and as he wheeled he tripped over the wagon tongue and fell sprawling, his gun flying out of his hand. Groping around he found it, jammed it back into the holster, darted back to his horse and dashed off at top speed for Kane's to spread the alarm and collect a posse.

There never had been any need for caution in opening the hotel door and his present frame of mind would not have heeded it if there had been. Flinging it back he dashed through and opened his mouth to emit a bellow calculated almost to raise the dead. The intended shout turned to a choking gasp as two lean, strong hands gripped his throat, and then his mental sky was filled with lightning as a gun-butt fell on his head. His limp body was carried out and dropped at the feet of the cheerful Idaho, who helped tear up portions of the sheriff's clothing for his friends to use on the officer's hands, feet, and mouth.

"Every time I hit a head I shore gloat," growled Johnny, his thoughts flashing back to his first night in town.

"Couldn't you send *him* down, *too*?" Idaho asked of Hopalong. "An' how many saddles do you an' Red use generally?"

"He wasn't up there," answered Hopalong. "We run into him as we was comin' out."

Johnny's match flashed up and out in one swift movement. "Corwin!" he exulted. "An' I'm glad it was *me* that hit him!"

Idaho rolled over on the ground and made strange noises. Sitting up he gasped: "Didn't I *say* it was a lovely night? Holy mavericks!"

"You fellers aim to claim squatter sovereignty?" whispered Red from the darkness. "If I'd 'a' knowed it I'd 'a' tied up somethin' I left layin' loose."

"We got to get a rustle on," said Hopalong. "Some cusses come to right quick. That gent in Red's bed is due to ask a lot of questions at th' top of his voice. Come on—grab this stuff, *pronto*!"

"I left another in th' stable that's goin' to do some yellin' purty soon," said Red. "Reckon he's a Greaser."

They picked up the things and went off to find the horses and as they dropped the equipment Red felt for his saddle. "Hey! Where's *mine*?" he demanded.

"Here, at my feet," said Johnny.

Red passed his hand over it and swore heartily. "This ain't it, you blunderin' jackass! Why didn't you get *mine*?" he growled.

"Feel of this one," grunted Johnny, kicking the other saddle.

Red did so. "That's it. Who's th' other belong to?"

"*I* don't know," answered Johnny, growing peeved. "Yo're cussed particular, you are! Here's two rifles, two six-guns, an' two belts. Take 'em with you an' pick out yore own when it gets light. *I* don't want 'em."

Red finished cinching up and slipped a hand over the rifles. He dropped one of them into its scabbard. "Got mine. Chuck th' other away."

"Take it along an' chuck it in th' crick," said Idaho. "Now you fellers listen: If you ride up th' middle of Big Crick till you come to that rocky ground west of our place you can leave th' water there, an' yore trail will be lost. It runs southwest an' northeast for miles, an' is plenty wide an' wild. If you need anythin' ride in to our place any night after dark. I'll post th' boys."

"We ain't got a bit of grub," growled Red. "Well, it ain't th' first time," he added, cheerfully.

"We're not goin' up Big Crick," said Hopalong, decisively. "We're ridin' like we wanted to get plumb out of this country, which is just what Bill Long an' Red Thompson would do. When fur enough away we're circlin' back east of town, on th' edge of th' desert, where nobody will hardly think we'd go. They'll suspect that hard ground over yore way before they will th' desert. Where'll we meet you, Kid, if there's anythin' to be told; an' when?"

Johnny considered and appealed to Idaho, whose knowledge of the country qualified him to speak. In a few moments the place had been chosen and well described, and the two horsemen pulled their mounts around and faced northward.

"Get a-goin'," growled Johnny. "Anybody'd reckon you thought a night was a week long."

"Don't like to leave you two boys alone in this town,

after tonight's plays," said Hopalong, uneasily. "Nobody is dumb enough to figger that we didn't have outside help. Keep yore eyes open!"

"Pull out!" snapped Johnny. "It'll be light in two hours more!"

"So-long, you piruts," softly called Idaho. "Yessir," he muttered, joyously; "it's been one plumb lovely night!"

Not long after the noise of galloping had died in the north a Mexican staggered from the stable, groping in the darkness as he made his erratic way toward the front of the gambling-hall, his dazed wits returning slowly. Leaning against the wall of the building for a short rest, he went on again, both hands gripping his jaw. Too dazed to be aware of the disappearance of the horses and attentive only to his own woes, he blundered against the bound and gagged sheriff, went down, crawled a few yards and then, arising again to his feet, groped around the corner of the building and sat down against it to collect his bewildering thoughts.

Upstairs in the room Red had used, the restless figure on the bed moved more and more, finally sitting up, moaning softly. Then, stiffening as memory brought something back to him, he groped about for matches, blundering against the walls and the scanty furniture, and called forth profane language from the room adjoining, whose occupant, again disturbed, arose and yanked open his door.

"What you think yo're doin', raisin' all this racket?" he demanded.

"Somebody near busted my head," moaned the other. "I been robbed!" he shouted as the lack of impedimenta at last sank into his mind.

"Say!" exclaimed his visitor, remembering an earlier nocturnal disturbance. "Wait here till I get some matches!"

He returned with a lighted lamp, instead, which revealed the truth, and its bearer swiftly led the way into the second room down the hall. A pair of boots which should not have been there and the absence of the equipment which should have been there confirmed their fears. The man with the lamp held it out of the window and swore under his breath as a bound figure below him gurgled and writhed.

"Looks like Corwin!" he muttered, and hastened down to make sure, taking no time to dress. The swearing Mexican received no attention until the sheriff staggered back with the investigator, and then the vague tale was listened to.

A bellowing voice awakened the sleepers in the big building and an impromptu conference of irate men, mostly undressed, was held in the hall. Sandy Woods returned from the stables, reporting them bare of horses; the investigator from the jail came back with the angry guards, one of whom was too shaky to walk with directness. Others came from a visit to Red Frank's corral, leading half a dozen borrowed horses, and, a hasty, cold breakfast eaten, the posse, led by a sick, vindictive sheriff, pounded northward along a plain trail.

Those who were not able to go along stood and peered through the paling darkness and two deputies left to take up positions in the front and rear of Quayle's hotel where they could see without being seen, while a third man crept into the stable to look for a Tincup horse. Had he been content with looking he would have been more fortunate, but thinking that the master would have no further use for the animal, he decided to take it for himself, trusting that possession would give him a better claim when the new ownership was finally decided by Kane. Reassured by the earliness of the hour and by the presence of the hidden deputy, he went ahead with his plans.

Pepper's flattened ears meant nothing to the exultant thief, for it had been his experience that all horses flattened their ears whenever he approached them, especially if they had reason to know him; so, with a wary eye on the trim, black hoofs, he slipped along the stable wall to gain her head. He had just untied the rope and started back with the end of it in his hand when there was a sudden, sidewise, curving swerve of the silky black body, a grunt of surprise and pain from the thief, pinned against the wall by the impact, and then, curving back again and wheeling almost as though on a pivot, Pepper's teeth crunched flesh and bone and the sickened thief, by a miracle escaping the outflung front hoofs, staggered outside the stable and fell as the whizzing hind feet took the half-open door from its flimsy hinges. Rolling around the corner, the thief crawled under a wagon and sank down unconscious, his crushed shoulder staining darkly through his torn shirt.

The watching deputy arose to go to his friend's assistance, but looked up and stopped as a growled question came from Ed Doane's window.

"Jim's hurt," he explained to the face behind the rifle. "Went in to see if his cayuse had wandered in there, an' th' black near killed him. Gimme a hand with him, will you?"

Quayle had nearly fallen off the chair he had spent the night on when the crash and the scream of the enraged horse awakened him. He ran to the kitchen door, rifle in hand, and looked out, hearing the deputy's words.

"I'll give ye a hand," he said, "but more cheerful if it's to dig a grave. *Mother av God!*" he breathed as he reached the wagon. "I'm thinkin' it's a priest ye want, an' there's none within twinty miles." He looked around at the forming crowd. "Get a plank," he ordered, "an' get Doc Sharpe."

Ed Doane, followed by Johnny and Idaho, ran from the kitchen and joined the group. One glance and Johnny went into the stable, calling as he entered. Patting the quivering nozzle of the black he looked at the rope and came out again.

"That man-killer has got to be shot," said the deputy to Ed Doane.

"I'll kill th' man that tries it," came a quiet reply, and the deputy wheeled to look into a pair of frosty blue eyes. "Th' knot I tie in halter ropes don't come loose, for Pepper will untie any common knot an' go off huntin' for me. It was untied. If you want to back up a hoss thief, an' mebby prove yore part in it, say that again."

"Yo're plumb mistaken, Nelson," said the deputy. "Jim was huntin' his own cayuse, which Long an' Thompson stampeded out of th' stable last night. He was goin' over th' town first before he went out to look for it on th' plain."

"That's *good*!" sneered Johnny. "Long an' Thompson are in jail. I'm standin' to what th' knot showed. Do you still reckon Pepper's got to be shot?"

"They broke out an' got away," retorted the deputy, "an' they shore as hell had outside help." He looked knowingly into Johnny's eyes. "Nobody that belongs to this town would 'a' done it."

"That's a lie," said Quayle, his rifle swinging up carelessly. "I belong to this town, an' I'd 'a' done it, mesilf, if I'd thought av it. Seein' that I didn't, I'm cussed glad that somewan had better wits than me own."

"I was aimin' to do it," said Idaho, smiling. "I was goin' out to get th' boys, an' bust th' jail tonight. I was holdin' back a little, though, because I was scared th' boys might get a little rough an' lynch a few deputies. They're on set triggers these days."

The cook started to roll up his sleeves. "I'll lick th' daylight out av anny man that goes to harm that horse, or me name's not Murphy," he declared, spitting. "I feed her near every mornin', an' she's gintle as a baby lamb. But she's got a keen nose for blackguards!"

Dr. Sharpe arrived, gave his orders and followed the bearers of the improvised stretcher toward his house. As the crowd started to break up Johnny looked coldly at the deputy. "You heard me," he said. "Pass th' word along. An' if she don't kill th' next one, *I* will!"

North of town the posse reached Big Creek and exulted as it saw the plain prints going on from the further bank. Corwin, sitting his saddle with a false ease, stifled a moan at every rise and fall, his head seeming about to split under the pulsing hammer blows. When he caught sight of the trail leading from the creek he nodded dully and spoke to his nearest companion.

"Leavin' th' country by th' straightest way," he growled. "It'll mebby be a long chase, damn 'em!"

"They ain't got much of a start," came the hopeful reply. "We ought to catch sight of 'em from th' top of th' divide beyond Sand Creek. It's fair level plain for miles north of that. Their cayuses ain't no better than ourn, an' *some* of ourn will run theirs off their feet."

Sand Creek came into sight before noon and when it was reached there were no tracks on the farther side. The posse was prepared for this and split without hesitation, Corwin leading half of it west along the bank and the other half going east. Five minutes later an exclamation caused the sheriff to pull up and look where one of his men was pointing. A rifle barrel projected a scant two inches from the water and the man who rode over to it laughed as he leaned down from the saddle.

"It lit on a ridge of gravel an' didn't slide down quite fur enough," he called. "An' it shore is busted proper."

"Bring it here," ordered Corwin. He took it, examined it and handed it to the next man, whose head ached as much as his own and who would not have been along except that his wish for revenge over-rode his good sense.

"That yourn?" asked the sheriff.

The owner of the broken weapon growled. "They've plumb ruined it. It's one more score they'll pay. Come on!" and he whirled westward. Corwin drew his Colt and fired into the air three times at counted intervals, and galloped after his companions when faint, answering shots sounded from the east.

"They're makin' for that rocky stretch," he muttered; "an' if they get there in time they're purty safe."

Not long after he had rejoined his friends the second part of the posse whirled along the bank, following the trail of the first, eager to overtake it and learn what had been discovered.

Well to the east Hopalong and Red rode at the best pace possible in the water of the creek, now and then turning in the saddle to look searchingly behind them. Following the great bend of the stream they went more and more to the south and when the shadows were long they rode around a ridge and drew rein. Red dismounted and climbed it, peering over its rocky backbone for minutes. Returning to his companion he grinned cheerfully.

"No coyotes in sight," he said. "Some went west, I reckon, an' found that busted rifle where we planted it. No coyotes, at all; but there's a black bear down in that little strip of timber."

"I can eat near all of it, myself," chuckled Hopalong. "Let's camp where we drop it. A dry wood fire won't show up strong till dark. Come on!"

CHAPTER XIV

The Staked Plain

PECOS KANE sat behind his old desk in the inner room and listened to the reports of the night's activities, his anger steadily mounting until ghostly flames seemed to be licking their thin tongues back in his eyes. The jail guards had come and departed, speaking simply and truthfully, suggesting various reasons to excuse the laxity of their watch. The Mexican told with painful effort about the loss of the horses, growing steadily more incoherent from the condition of his jaw and from his own rising rage. Men came, and went out again on various duties, one of them closely interrogating the owner of the freight wagon, whose anger had died swiftly by the recovery of the great tongue, which was none the worse for its usage except for certain indentations of no moment. A friend of Quayle and hostile to Kane and for what Kane stood for, the wagon owner allowed his replies to be short, and yet express a proper indignation, which did not exist, about the whole affair. When again alone in the sanctity of his home he allowed himself the luxury of low-voiced laughter and determined to put his crowbar where any needy individual of the future could readily find it.

Bill Trask, because of his short-gun expertness temporarily relieved of guarding the partition door, led three companions toward Quayle's hotel, his face and the faces of the others tense and determined. Two went around to the stable, via Red Frank's and the rear street and one of them stopped near it while the other slipped along the kitchen wall and crouched at the edge of the kitchen door. The third man went silently into the hotel office as Trask sauntered carelessly into the barroom and nodded at its inmates.

"Them fellers shore raised hell," he announced to Ed Doane as he motioned for a drink.

"They did," replied Doane, spinning a glass after the sliding bottle, after which he flung the coin into the old cigar box and assiduously polished the bar, wondering why Trask patronized him instead of Kane's.

"They shore had nerve," persisted the newcomer, looking at Johnny.

"They shore did," acquiesced the man at the table, who then returned to his idle occupation of trying to decipher the pattern of the faded-out wall paper. Wall paper was a rarity in the town and deserved some attention.

"Them guards was plumb careless," said Kane's hired man. Not knowing to whom he was speaking there was no reply, and he tried again, addressing the bartender.

"They was careless," replied Doane, without interest.

Johnny was alert now, the persistent remarks awakening suspicion in his mind, and a slight sound from the wall at his back caused him to push his chair from the table and assume a more relaxed posture. His glance at the lower and nearer corner of the window let him memorize its exact position and he waited, expectant, for whatever might happen. The surprise and capture of his two friends had worked, but that had been the first time; there would be no second, he told himself, especially as far as he was concerned.

"Is th' boss in?" asked the visitor.

"Th' boss ain't in," answered Ed Doane as Johnny glanced at the front door, the front window and the door of the office, which the bartender noticed. "Too dusty," said Doane, going around the bar to the front wall and closing the window.

"When will he be in?"

"Dunno," grunted the bartender, once more in his accustomed place.

"I got to see him."

"I handle things when he ain't here," said Doane. "See me," he suggested, looking through the door leading to the office, where he fancied he had heard a creak.

"Got to see him, an' *pronto*," replied the visitor. "He made some remarks this mornin' about gettin' them fellers out. We know it was done by somebody on th' outside, an' we got a purty good idea of who it was since Quayle shot off his mouth. He's been gettin' too swelled up lately. If he don't come in purty quick I'm aimin' to dig him out, myself."

Johnny was waiting for him to utter the cue word and knew that there would be a slight change in facial expression, enunciation, or body posture just before it came. He was not swallowing the suggestions that it was Quayle who was wanted.

"You shore picked out a real job to handle all alone," said Doane, not letting his attention wander from the hotel office. "Any dog can dig out a badger, but that's only th' beginnin'," he said pleasantly, his hand on the gun which always lay under the bar. He expected a retort to his insult, and when none came it put a keener edge to his growing suspicions.

"I'm diggin' him out, just th' same," said Trask. "There's law in this town, an' everybody's on one side or th' other. Bein' a deputy it's my job to see about them that's on th' other side. Gettin' arrested men out of jail is serious an' I got to ask questions about it. Of course, Quayle don't allus say what he means—we none of us do. We all like to have our jokes; but I got to do my duty, even if it's only askin' questions. Is he out, or layin' low?"

"He's out," grunted Doane, "but he'll be back any minute, I reckon."

"All right; I'll wait," said Trask, carelessly, but he tensed himself. "How's business?" and at the words he flashed into action.

A chair crashed and a figure leaped back from it, two guns belching at its hips. The face and hand which popped up into the rear window disappeared again as the smoking Colt swung past the opening and across Johnny's body to send its second through the office doorway, and curses answered both shots. Trask, bent over, held his right arm with his left hand, his gun against the wall near the front door. The first shot of Johnny's righthand Colt had torn it from Trask's hand as it left the holster and the second had rendered the arm useless for the moment. A shot from the corner of the stable sang through the window and barely missed its mark as Johnny leaned forward, but his instant reply ended all danger from that point.

"Trask," he said, "I'm leavin' town. I ain't got a chance among buildin's again' pot-shooters. I'm leavin'—but th' Lord help Kane an' his gang when I come back. You can tell him I'm comin' a-shootin'. An' you can tell him this: I'm goin' to get him, Pecos Kane, if I has to pull him out of his hell-hole like I pulled Thorpe. Go ahead of me to th' stable—I'll blow you apart if any pot-shooter tries at me. G'wan!"

Trask obeyed, the gun against his spine too cloquent a persuader to be ignored. He knew that there were no pot-shooters yet, and he was glad of it, for if there had been one, and his captor was killed, the relaxation of the tense thumb holding back the hammer of a gun whose trigger was tied back would fire the weapon. The man who held it would fire one shot after his own death, however instantaneous it might be.

Passing through the kitchen Johnny picked up his saddle and ordered his captive to carry the rifle and slicker roll. They disappeared into the stable and when they came out again Johnny ordered Trask into the saddle, mounted behind him and rode for the arroyo which lay not far from the hotel. At last away from the buildings he made Trask dismount, climbed over the cantle and settled himself in the vacated saddle.

"I'm goin' down to offer myself to McCullough," he said. "You can tell Kane that, too. They'll need men down there, an' I'll be th' maddest man they got. An' th' next time me an' you have any gun talk, I'm shootin' to kill. *Adios!*"

He left the cursing deputy and went straight for the trail, where the rising wind played with the dust, and along it until stopped by a voice in a barranca.

"I'm puttin' 'em up," he called. "My name's Nelson an' I'm mad clean through. Get a rustle on; I want to see Mac."

"Go ahead, Bar-20," drawled the voice. "I wasn't dead shore. There's a good friend of yourn down there."

"Quayle?" asked Johnny.

"There's another: Waffles, of th' O-Bar-O," came the reply, and a verse of a nearly forgotten song arose on the breeze.

I've swurn th' Colorado where she runs down clost to hell,
  I've braced th' faro layouts in Cheyenne;
I've fought for muddy water with a howlin' bunch of Sioux,
  An' swallered hot tamales, an' cayenne.

"There's more, but I've done forgot most of it," apologized the singer.

Johnny laughed with delight. "Why, that's Lefty Allen's old song. Here's th' second verse:"

I've rid a pitchin' broncho till th' sky was underneath,
  I've tackled every desert in th' land;
I've sampled Four-X whisky till I couldn't hardly see,
  An' dallied with th' quicksands of th' Grande.

"That's shore O-Bar-O. Lefty made it up hisself, an' that boy could sing it. It all comes back to me now—he called it 'Th' Insult.' Why—here, *you!*" he chuckled. "I said I was mad an' in a hurry. I ain't mad no more, but I *am* in a hurry. See you tonight, mebby. So-long."

Riding on again he soon reached the Question-Mark bunkhouse and dismounted as a puncher turned the corner of the house. They grinned at each other, these good, old-time friends.

"You son-of-a-gun!" chuckled Johnny, holding out his hand.

"You son-of-a-gun!" echoed Waffles, gripping it, and so they stood, silent, exchanging grins. It had been a long time since they last had seen each other.

McCullough loomed up in the doorway and grinned at them both.

"Hear yo're married," said Waffles.

"Shore!" bragged Johnny.

"It ain't spoiled you, *yet*. How's Hoppy an' Red?"

"Fine, now they're out of jail."

Waffles threw his head back and laughed heartily. "I near laughed till I busted when Quayle told us who they was. Hoppy an' Red in *jail*! It was *funny*!"

"Hello, Nelson," said McCullough. "What are you doin' down here?"

"Had to leave town; too many corners, an' too much cover. I'm lookin' for a job, if it don't cut me out of th' rewards."

"She's yourn."

"Wait a minute," said Johnny. "I can't take it. I got to be free to do what I want; but I'll hang out here for awhile."

"You've got th' job instanter," said the appreciative trail-boss smiling broadly. "It's steady work of bossin' yoreself. I've heard of yore work, up Gunsight way. Feed yet? Then come on."

"Shore will. Where's Quayle?"

"Rode back, roundabout; him not courtin' bein' seen; but I reckon everybody in town knows he's been here. He swears by you."

Despite Idaho's boasts to the contrary his ranch again had nocturnal visitors, and there was no lead-flying welcome accorded them. Having spied out the distribution of Lukins' riders the visitors chose a locality free from guards and with the coming of night drifted a sizable herd of Diamond L cattle across an outlying section of the range and with practiced art and uncanny instinct drove the compacted herd onto and over the rocky plateau, where the chief of the raiders obtained a speed with the cattle which always bordered upon a panicky flight, but never quite reached it. All that night they rumbled over the rocky stretch and as dawn brightened the eastern sky the running herd passed down a gentle slope, picked up the waiting caviya and not long thereafter moved over the hard bottom of a steep-walled ravine which could have been called a canyon without unduly stretching the meaning of the word.

The chief of the raiding party cared nothing for the fatness of the animals, or other conditions which might operate against the possibilities of a lucrative sale. There later would be time for improving their condition, plenty of time in a valley rich with grass. All he cared for now was to put miles speedily behind him, and this he was accomplishing like the master cattleman he was. After a mid-day breathing space they went on again, alternately walking and running, and well into the second night, stopping at a water-hole known only to a few men other than these. Some miles north of this water-hole was another, and very much smaller, one, being only a few feet across, and there also was a difference between the waters of the two. The larger was of a nature to be expected in such a locality, but much better than most such holes, for the water was only slightly alkaline and the cattle drank it eagerly. The other was sweet and pure and cold, but rather than to cover the distance to it and back again, it was ignored by all but one man, for the other stayed with the herd. There was grass around both; not enough to feed a herd thoroughly, but enough to keep it busy hunting over the scanty growth. With more than characteristic thought these holes had been named in a manner to couple and yet to keep them separate, and to Kane's drive crew they were known as "Sweet" and "Bitter."

Again on the trail before the sun had risen above the horizon, the herd was sent forth on another day's hard drive, which carried it, with the constantly growing tail herd of stragglers, far into the following night, despite all dumb remonstrances. No mercy was shown to it, but only a canny urging, and if no mercy was shown the cattle none was accepted by the drivers, who rode and worked, swore and panted on wiry ponies which, despite frequent changing, began to show the marks of their efforts under the pitiless sun and through the yielding sands. Both cattle and horses had about reached their limits when the late afternoon of the next day brought them to a rocky ledge sticking up out of the desert's floor, which now was hard and stony; and upon turning the south end of the ridge an emerald valley suddenly lay before their eyes, from whence the scent of water had put a new spirit into cattle and horses for the last few miles; and now it nearly caused a fatal stampede at the entrance to the narrow ledge which slanted down the steep, rock walls.

To a stranger such a sight would have awakened amazed incredulity, and strong suspicion that his sanity had been undermined by the heat-cursed, horror-laden desert miles; or he might have sneered wisely at so palpable a mirage, scorned to be tricked by it in any attempt to prove it otherwise and staggered on with contemptuous curses. But Miguel and the men he so autocratically bossed knew it to be no vision, no trick of air or mind, and sighed with relief when it finally lay before them. While they all knew it was there and had visited it before, none of them, except Miguel, had ever learned the way, try as they might, for until the high ledge of rock, hidden on the west by a great, upslanting billow of sand, came into sight there were no landmarks to show them the way. Each new journey across the simmering, shimmering plateau found fears in every heart but the guide's that he would lose his way. That their fears may be justified and to show them blameless in everything but their lack of confidence in him, it may be well to have a better understanding of this desert and what it meant; and to show why men should hold as preposterous any claim that a cattle herd could safely cross it. Some went even further and said no man, mounted or not, could make that journey, and confessed to themselves a superstitious fear and horror for it and everything pertaining to it.

Before the deep ruts had been cut in the old Santa Fe Trail in that year of excessive rains; before the first wheel had rolled over the prairie soil to prove that wagons could safely make the long and tiresome trip; before even the first pack trains of heavily laden mules plodded to or from the Missouri frontier, and even before the pelt-loaded mules of the great fur companies crossed Kansas soil to the trading posts of the East, Mexican hunters rode from the valley of Taos and Santa Fe to procure their winter meat from the vast brown herds of buffalo migrating over their curious, crescent-shaped course to and from the regions of the Arkansas, Canadian, and Cimarron. They dried the strips of succulent meat in the sun or over fires, the fuel for the latter having been supplied by the buffalo themselves on previous migrations; they stripped the hides from the prostrate bodies and cured them, and trafficked with the bands of Indians which followed the herds as persistently as did the great, gray wolves. Of these *ciboleros*, swarthy-skinned hunters of Mexico, some more hardy and courageous than their fellows, or by avarice turned trader, ventured farther afield and were not balked by the high, beetling cliffs which bordered a great, forbidding plateau lying along and below the capricious Cimarron, in places a river of hide-and-seek in the sands, wet one day and dry the next.

From the mesa-like northern edge, along the warning arroyos of the Cimarron, where erosion, Nature's patient sculptor, carved miracles of artistry in the towering clays, shales, and sandstones, to the great sand hills billowing along its far-flung other edges, this barren waste of dreary sand and grisly alkali was a vast, simmering playground for dancing heat waves and fantastic mirage, and its treacherous pools of nauseous, alkaline waters shrunk daily from their encrusted edges and gleamed malignantly under a glowering, molten sun. Arroyos, level plain, shifting sand, and imponderable dust, with a scrawny, scanty, hopeless vegetation which the whimsical winds buried and then dug up again, this high desert plateau lay like a thing of death, cursing and accursed. It sloped imperceptibly southward, its dusty soil gradually breaking into billowy ridges constantly more marked and with deeper troughs, by insensible gradations becoming low sand hills, ever growing more separate and higher until at last they were beaten down and strewn broadcast by more persistent winds, and limited by the firmer soils which were blessed with more frequent rains to coax forth a thin cover of protecting, anchoring vegetation. To the west they intruded nearly to the Rio Pecos, a stream which in almost any other part of the country would have been regarded as insignificant, but here was given greatness because its liquid treasure was beyond price and because it was permanent, though timid.

Of the first of the Mexicans to push out over this great desolation perhaps none returned, except by happy chance, to tell of its tortures and of the few serviceable water holes leagues apart, the permanency of which none could foretell. But return some eventually did, and perhaps deprecated the miseries suffered, in view of the saving in miles; but their experience had been such as to impel them to drive a line of stakes along the happily chosen course to mark in this manner the way from each more trustworthy water hole to the next, be they reservoirs or furtive streams which bubbled up and crept along to die not far from their hopeful springs, sucked up by palpitant air and swallowed by greedy sands, their burial places marked by a shroud of encrusted salts. In the winter and spring an occasional rain filled hollows, ofttimes coming as a cloudburst and making a brave showing as it tumultuously deepened some arroyo and roared valiantly down it toward swift effacement. The trail was staked, if not by the swarthy traders, then by their red-skinned brothers, and from this line of stakes the tableland derived its name, and became known to men as the Lano Estacada, or Staked Plain.

Of this accursed desert no one man had full knowledge, nor thirsted for it if it were to be had only through his own efforts. There were great stretches unknown to any man, and there were other regions known to men who had not brought their knowledge out again; and what knowledge there was of its south-central portions was not to be found in men with white skins, but in certain marauding redmen fitted by survival to cope with problems such as it presented, and to live despite them. One other class knew something of its mysteries, for among the Mexicans there were some who had learned by bitter pilgrimages, but mostly from the mouths of men long dead who had passed the knowledge down successive generations, each increment a little larger when it left than when it came, who had a more comprehensive, embracing knowledge of the baking tableland; and these few, because what they knew could best be used in furtive, secretive pursuits bearing a swift penalty for those caught in them, hugged that knowledge closely and kept it to themselves. A man who has that which another badly needs can drive shrewd bargains. And of the few Mexicans who were enriched by the possession of this knowledge, those who knew most about it had mixed blood flowing through their veins, for the vast grisly plateau had been a short cut and place of refuge for marauding bands of Apaches, Utes, and Comanches while civilization crawled wonderingly in swaddling clothes.

Of the knowing few Pecos Kane owned two, owned them body and soul, and to make his title firmer than even proof of murder could assure, he threw golden sops to the wise ones' avarice and allowed them seats in the sun and privileges denied to their fellows. One of them, by name Miguel, a small part Spaniard and the rest Mescalero Apache, was a privileged man, for he knew not only the main trails across the plain but certain devious ways twisting in from the edges, one of which wandered for accursed miles, first across rock, then over sand and again over rock and unexpectedly turned a high, sharp ridge to look upon his Valle de Sorprendido, deep and green, whose crystal spring wandered musically along its gravelly bed from the graying western end of the canyon-like ravine to sink silently into the thirsty sands to the east and be seen no more. Manuel, also, knew this way.

Surprise Valley was no terminal, but a place for tongue-lolling, wild-eyed cattle to pause and rest, drink and eat before the fearful journey called anew. No need for corral, fence, or herders here to keep them from straying, but an urgent need for pressing riders to throw the herd back on the trail again, to start the dumbly protesting animals on the thirty-six-hour drive to the next unfailing water, against the instinct which bade them stay. A valley of delight it was, a jewel, verdant and peaceful, forced by man to serve a vicious purpose; but as if in punishment for its perversion the glistening sand hills crept slowly nearer, each receding tide of their slow advance encroaching more and more each year until now the valley had shrunk by half and a stealthy grayness crept insidiously into its velvety freshness like the mark of sin across a harlot's cheek.

Near the fenced-in spring was an adobe building, deserted except when a drive crew sought its shelter, and it served principally as a storehouse should a place of refuge suddenly be needed. It lay not far from the sloping banks of detritus which now ran halfway up the sheer, smooth stone walls enclosing the valley. Across from it on the southern side of the depressed pasture a broad trail slanted up the rock cliffs to the desert above. The cabin, the trail, and the valley itself long ago would have been obliterated by sand but for the miles of rocks, large and small, which lay around it like a great, flat collar. Should some terrific sand storm sweep over it with a momentum great enough to bridge the rocky floor the valley would cease to be; and smaller storms raging far out on the encircling desert carried their sands farther and farther across the stubborn rock, until now its outer edge was closer by miles. Already each rushing wind retained sand enough to drop it into the valley and powder everything.

The pock-marked guide, disdaining the precarious labors of getting the herd down the ledge with no fatalities among the maddened beasts, lolled in his saddle on the brink of the precipice and watched the struggle on the plain behind him, where hard-riding, loudly yelling herders were dashing across the front of the weaving, shifting, stubborn mass of tortured animals, letting them through the frantic restraining barrier in small groups, which constantly grew larger. Here and there a more determined animal slipped through and galloped to the descending ledge, head down and tail up. The cracking of revolvers fired across the noses of the front rank grew steadily and Miguel deemed it safer to leave the brim of the cliff. It was possible that the maddened herd might break through the desperate riders and plunge to its destruction. Had the trail been a few hours longer nothing could have held them.

"Give a hand here!" shouted the trail-boss as the guide rode complacently out of danger. "Ride in there an' help split 'em!"

"I weel be needed w'en we leeve again," replied Miguel. "To run a reesk eet ees foolish. I tol' you to stop 'em a mile away an' spleet 'em there. Eet ees no beesness of Miguel's, theese. You deed not wan' to tak' the time? Then tak' w'at you call the consequence."

Eventually the last of the herd which mercifully was composed of stragglers whose lack of strength made them more tractable, were successfully led to the ledge and stumbled down it to join their brothers standing or lying in the little brook as if to appease their thirst by absorption before drinking deeply. The frantic, angry bawling of an hour ago was heard no more, for now a contented lowing sounded along the stream, where the quiet animals often waited half an hour before attempting to drink. They stood thus for hours, reluctant to leave even to graze and after leaving, left the grass and returned time after time to drink. There were a few half-blinded animals among the weaklings, but water, grass, and rest would restore their sight. Here they would stay until fit for the second and lesser ordeal, and the others in turn.

The weary riders, turning their mounts loose to join the rest of the horse herd, piled their saddles against the wall of the hut and waited for the cook to call them to fill their tin plates and cups. One of them, more energetic and perhaps hungrier than the rest, unpacked the load of firewood from a spiritless horse and carried it to the hut.

The perspiring Thorpe looked his thanks and went on with his labors and in due time a well-fed, lazy group sprawled near the hut, swapping tales or smoking in satisfied silence. At the other side of the building Miguel sat with those of his own kind, boasting of his desert achievements and in reply to a sneering remark from the other group he showed his teeth in a mocking smile, raised his eyebrows until the crescent scar reached his sombrero and shrugged his shoulders.

"Eet ees not good to say sooch theengs to Miguel," he complacently observed. "Eef he should get ver' angree an' leeve een the night eet would be ver' onluckie for Greengos. *Quien sabe?*"

"He got you there, Jud," growled a low voice. "He shore hurts me worse'n a blister, but I'm totin' my grudge silent."

"Huh," muttered another thoughtfully. "A man can travel fast without no cattle to set th' pace. He shore can 'leeve' an' be damned for all *I* care. An' I'm sayin' that if he does there'll be a damned dead Greaser in Mesquite right soon after I get back. Th' place for him to 'leeve' us is at Three Ponds—for then we shore would be in one bad fix."

"I ain't shore I'd try to get away," said Sandy Woods slowly. "There's good grass an' water here, no herdin', no strayin', nobody to bother a feller. A man can live a long time on one steer out here, jerkin' th' meat. Th' herd would grow, an' when it came time to turn 'em into money he'd only have to drive plumb west. It wouldn't be like tryin' to find a little place like this. Just aim at th' sunset an' keep goin'."

"How long would this valley feed a herd like th' one here now?" ironically demanded the trail-boss. "You can tell th' difference in th' grass plain at th' end of a week. Yo're full of loco weed."

"Eef you say sooch things to me I may leeve in the night," chuckled the other. "Wish they'd stampeded an' knocked him over th' eege! One of these days some of us may be quittin' Kane, an' then there'll be one struttin' half-breed less in Mesquite. Tell you one thing: I won't make this drive many more times before I know th' way as well as he does; an' from here on we could stake it out."

Soft, derisive laughter replied to him and the trail-boss thoughtfully repacked his pipe. "It ain't in you," he said. "You got to be born with it."

"You holdin' that a white man ain't got as much brains as a mongrel with nobody knows how many different kinds of blood in him?" indignantly demanded Sandy.

"He's got generations behind him, like a setter or a pointer, an' it ain't a question of brains. It's instinct, an' th' lower down yore stock runs th' better it'll be. There ain't no human brains can equal an animal's in things like that. I doubt if you could leave here an' get off this desert, plumb west or not. You got a big target, for it's all around you behind th' horizon; but I don't think you'd live till you hit it at th' right place. Don't forget that th' horizon moves with you. If there wasn't no tracks showin' you th' way you'd die out on this fryin' pan."

"An' th' wind'll wipe them out before mornin'," said one of the others.

The doubter laughed outright. "Wait till we come back. I'll give you a chance to back up yore convictions. Don't forget that I ain't sayin' that I'd try it afoot. I'd ride an' give th' horse its head. There ain't nothin' to be gained arguin' about it now. An' I'm free to admit that I'm cussed glad to be settin' here lookin' out instead of out there some'ers tryin' to get here to look in. Gimme a match, Jud."

The trail-boss snorted. "Now yo're takin' *my* end," he asserted. "If you ride a cayuse an' give it its head it ain't a white man's brains that yo're dependin' on. That ain't yore argument, a-tall. I'll bet you, cayuse or no cayuse, you can't leave Three Ponds an' make it. A cayuse has to drink once in a while or he'll drop under you an' you'll lose yore instinct-compass."

"I'll take that when we start back," retorted Sandy, "if you'll give me a fair number of canteens. I'm figgerin' on outfittin' right."

"Take all you want at Cimarron corrals," rejoined the trail-boss. "After we leave there I'm bettin' nobody will part with any of theirs." He looked keenly at the boaster and took no further part in the conversation, his mind busy with a new problem; the grudge he already had.

CHAPTER XV

Discoveries

HOPALONG AND Red liked their camp and were pleased that they could stay in it another day and night. They jerked the bear meat in the sun and smoke and took a much-needed bath in the creek, where the gentle application of sand freed them from the unwelcome guests which the jail had given them. Clothing washed and inspected quickly dried in the sun and wind. Neither of them had anything on but a sombrero and the effect was somewhat startling. Red picked up his saddle pad to fling it over a rock for a sun bath and was about to let go of it when he looked closer.

"Hey, did you rip open this pad?" he asked, eying his friend speculatively.

Hopalong added his armful of fuel to the pile near the fire and eyed his friend. "For a growed man you shore do ask some childish questions," he retorted. "Of course I did. I allus rip open saddle pads. All my life I been rippin' open every saddle pad I saw. Many a time I got mad when I found a folded blanket instead of a pad. I've got up nights an' gone wanderin' around looking for pads to rip open. You look like you had sense, but looks shore is deceivin'. Why'n blazes would I rip open yore saddle pad? I reckon it's plumb wore out an' just nat'rally come apart. You've had it since Adam made th' sun stand still."

"You musta listened to some sky pilot with yore feet!" retorted Red. "Adam didn't make th' sun stand still. That was Moses, so they'd have longer light for to hunt for him in. An' you needn't get steamed up, neither. Somebody ripped this pad, with a knife, too. Seein' that it was in th' same camp all night with you, I nat'rally asked. I'm shore *I* didn't do it. Then *who* did?" He swaggered off to get his friend's pad and picked it up. "Of course you wouldn't rip yore own. That—" he held it closer to his eyes and stared at it. "Cussed if you *didn't*, though! It's ripped just like mine. I reckon you'll be startin' on th' saddles, next!"

Hopalong's amusement at the ripping of his companion's pad faded out as he grabbed his own and looked at it. "Well, I'm cussed!" he muttered. "It shore was ripped, all right. It never come apart by itself. *Both* of 'em, huh?" He pondered as he turned the pad over and over.

"They didn't play no favorites, anyhow," growled Red. "Wonder what they thought they'd find? Jewels?"

Hopalong pushed back his hat and gently scratched a scalp somewhat tender from the sand treatment. "Things like that don't just happen," he said, reflectively. "There's allus a reason for things." He grew thoughtful again and studied the pad. "Mebby they wasn't lookin' for anythin'," he muttered, suspiciously.

Red snorted. "Just doin' it for practice, mebby?" he asked, sarcastically. "Not havin' nothin' else *to* do, somebody went up to our rooms an' amused themselves by rippin' open our pads. You got a head like a calf, only it's a hull lot smaller."

"We was accused of robbin' th' bank, Reddie," said Hopalong in patient explanation. "They knowed we didn't do it—so they musta wanted us to be blamed for it. Th' best proof they could have, not seein' us do it, was to plant somethin' to be found on us. This is past yore A B C eddication, but I'll try to hammer it into you. If it makes you dizzy, hold up yore hand. What does a bank have that everybody wants? Money! Why do people rob banks? To get money, you sage-hen! What would bank robbers have after they robbed a bank? Money, you lo-coed cow! Now, Reddie, there's *two* kinds of money. One is hard, an' th' other is soft like yore head. Th' soft has pretty pictures on it an' smells powerful. It also has numbers. Th' numbers are different, Reddie, on each bill. Some banks keep a list of th' numbers of the biggest bills. Reckon I better wait an' let you rest up."

"Too bad they got us out of jail—*both* of us," said Red. "I should 'a' stayed behind. It wouldn't 'a' been half as bad as hangin' 'round with you."

"Now," continued his companion, looking into the pad, "if some of them numbered bills was found on us they'd have us, wouldn't they? We wasn't supposed to have no friends. An' where would a couple of robbers be likely to carry dangerous money? On their hats? No, Reddie; *not* on their hats. In their pockets, where they might get dragged out at th' wrong time? Mebby; but not hardly. Saddle pads, says th' little boy in th' rear of the room. Right you are, sonny. Saddle pads, Reddie, is a real good place. While you go all over it again so you can get th' drift of it I'll put on some clothes. I'm near baked."

"It started some time ago," said Red innocently.

"What did?"

"Th' bakin'. You didn't get that hat on quick enough," his friend jeered. "I've heard of people eatin' cooked calves' brains, but they'd get little nourishment an' only a moldy flavor out of yourn. An' you'd shore look better with *all* yore clothes on. I can see th' places where you've stopped washin' yore hands, feet, an' neck all these years."

Hopalong mumbled something and slid into his under-wear. "Gee!" he exulted. "These clean clothes shore do feel good!"

"*You'd* nat'rally notice it a whole lot more than I would," said Red, following suit. As his head came into sight again he let his eyes wander along the eastern and southeastern horizon. "You know, them bluffs off yonder remind me a hull lot of parts of th' Staked Plain," he observed. "We hadn't ought to be very far away from it, down here."

"They're its edge," grunted Hopalong, rearranging the strips of meat over the fire. Both became silent, going back in their memories to the events of years before, when the Staked Plain had been very real and threatening to them.

At daylight the following morning they arose and not much later were riding slowly southward and as near the creek as the nature of its banks would allow. When the noon sun blazed down on them they found the creek dwindling rapidly and, glancing ahead down the sandy valley they could make out the dark, moist place where the last of it disappeared in the sands. They watered their horses, drank their fill and went on again toward the place where they were to meet Johnny, riding on a curving course which led them closer and closer to the forbidding hills. In mid-afternoon they came to a salt pond and instead of arguing about the matter with their thirsty mounts, let them go up to it and smell it. The animals turned away and went on again without protest. A little later Red squinted eastward and nodded in answer to his own unspoken question.

"Shore it is," he muttered.

Hopalong followed his gaze and grunted. "Shore." He regarded the distant bulk thoughtfully. "Strikes me no sane cow ever would go out there, unless it was drove. It's our business to look into everythin'. Comin'?"

"I shore am. Nobody can buffalo me an' chuck me into jail without a comeback. I'm lookin' for things to fatten it."

"It can't get too fat for me," replied his friend. "Helpin' th' Kid get his money back was enough to set me after some of that reward money; but when I sized up Kane an' his gang it promised to be a pleasure; now, after that jailin', it's a yelpin' joy. If there's no other way I'm aimin' to ride into Mesquite an' smoke up with both guns."

As they neared the carcass Red glanced at his cheerful friend. "Head's swelled up like a keg," he said. "Struck by a rattler."

"Reckon so; but cows dead from snakebite ain't common."

They pulled up and looked at it at close range.

"Shot," grunted Hopalong.

"Then somebody was out here with it," said Red swinging down. "He was tender-hearted, *he* was. Gimme a hand. We'll turn it over an' look at th' brand."

Hopalong complied, and then they looked at each other and back to the carcass, where a large piece of hide had been neatly trimmed around and skinned off.

"Didn't dare let it wander, an' they plugged it after it got struck," said Red.

"Careful, they was," commented his companion. "They was too careful. If they'd let it wander it wouldn't 'a' told nothin', 'specially if it wandered toward home. But shootin' it, an' then doin' *this*—I reckon our come-back is takin' on weight."

"It shore is," emphatically said Red. "Cuss this hard ground! It don't tell nothin'. They went north or south—an' not long ago, neither. Which way are you ridin'?"

Hopalong considered. "If they went either way they'd be seen. I got a feelin' they went right across. Greasers an' Injuns know that desert, an' there's both kinds workin' for Kane. It allus has been a shore-thing way for 'em. Remember what Idaho said?"

"It can't be done," said Red.

"Slippery Trendly an' Deacon Rankin did it."

"But they only crossed one corner," argued Red.

"McLeod's Texans did it!"

"They didn't cross much more'n a corner," retorted Red. "An' look what it *did* to 'em!"

"It's a straight drive for them valleys along th' Cimarron," mused Hopalong. "Nobody to see 'em come or go, good grass to fatten 'em up after they got there, an' plenty of time for blottin' th' brands. I'll bet Kane's got men that knows how to get 'em over. There's water holes if you only know where to look, an' how to head for 'em; an' some of these half-breeds down here know all of that. If they went north or south on a course far enough east to keep many folks from seein' 'em they'd find it near as dry. Well, we better go down an' meet th'

Kid before we do anythin' else. We got our bearin's an' can find th' way back again. What you say?"

Red mounted and led the way. "If I'm goin' to ride around out here I'm goin' to have plenty of water, an' that means canteens. I'm near chokin' for a drink; an' this cayuse is gettin' mean. Come on."

"We might pick up some tracks if we hunt right now," said Hopalong. "If we wait longer this wind'll blot 'em out. I ain't thirsty," he lied. "You go down an' meet th' Kid an' I'll look around east of here. We can't gamble with this: if I find tracks they'll save us a lot of ridin' an' guessin'. Go ahead."

"If you stay I stay," growled Red.

"Listen, you chump," retorted Hopalong. "It's only a few hours more if I stay out here than if I go with you. Get canteens an' supplies. Th' Kid can bring us more tomorrow. I'm backin' my guess: get a-goin'."

Red saw the wisdom of the suggestion and wheeled, riding at good speed to the southwest while his friend went eastward, his eyes searching the desert plain. It was night when Red returned, picking his way with a plainsman's instinct to the carcass of the cow, and he softly replied to a low call which came from behind a billow of sand.

Hopalong arose. "You made good time," he said.

"Reckon so," replied Red, riding toward him. "I only got two canteens an' not much grub. Th' Kid'll be ready for us tomorrow. What about yore cayuse?"

"Don't worry," chuckled Hopalong. "It's th' cayuses that's been botherin' me most. They're all right now. I found a little hole with cold, sweet water, an' there's grass around it for th' cayuses. There ain't much, but enough for these two goats. Th' water hole ain't more'n three feet across an' a foot deep, but it fills up good an' has wet quite a spot around it. An' Red, I found somethin' else!"

"Good; what is it?"

"There's clay around it an' a thin layer of sand over th' clay," replied Hopalong. "I found th' prints of a cayuse an' a man, an' they was fresh—not more'n twenty-four hours old if I'm any judge. I cast around on widenin' circles, but couldn't pick up th' trail any distance from th' hole. Th' wind that's been blowin' all day wiped 'em out; but it didn't wipe out much at th' edge of th' water. I could even make it out where he knelt to drink. There you are: a dead cow, with th' brand skinned off; tracks of a man an' a cayuse at that water hole; no herd tracks, no other cayuse tracks—just them two, an' our suspicions. What you think?"

Red chuckled. "I think we're gettin' somewhere, cussed slow an' I don't know where; but I'm playin' up that skinned cow. If it was all skinned I'd say a hide hunter might 'a' done it, an' that he made th' tracks you saw; but it wasn't. You should 'a' looked better near th' carcass instead of huntin' up th' water hole. You might 'a' seen th' tracks of a herd, or what th' wind left of 'em, 'though I reckon they drove that cow off quite a ways before they dropped it."

"Did you cross any herd tracks after you left me?" asked Hopalong.

"No; why?"

"An' we didn't cross any before you left," said Hopalong. "If there's been any to see runnin' east an' west we'd 'a' found 'em. That was all hard ground; an' there was th' wind. There wasn't none to find."

"Huh!" snorted Red, and after a moment's thought he looked up. "Mebby that feller found th' cow all swelled up with snakebite, away off from water as he thought, an' just put an end to its misery?"

"Then why did he cut out th' brand?" snapped Hopalong.

"What are you askin' *me* for?" demanded Red, truculently. "How'd *I* know? You shore can ask some damn fool questions!"

"Yo're half-baked," growled his companion. "I will be, too, before I get any answer to what I'm askin' myself. I'm aimin' to squat behind a rise north of that water hole an' wait for my answer if it takes a month. I can get a good view from up there."

Red, whose hatred for deserts was whole-hearted,

looked through the darkness in disgust at his friend.
"You've picked out a fine job for us!" he retorted. "If
yo're right an' they did drive a herd across to th' other
side it'll shore be a wait. Be more'n a week, an' mebby
two."

"They've got to drive hard between waters," replied
Hopalong. "They'll waste no time; an' they won't waste
time comin' back again, when they won't have th' cows
to hold 'em down. There's one thing shore: They won't
be back tomorrow or th' next day, an' we both can ride
down an' see th' Kid, an' mebby McCullough. It's too
good a lead to throw away. But before we meet Johnny
we're goin' to have a better look around, 'specially south
an' east."

"All right," agreed Red. "How'd you come to find th'
hole?"

"Rode up on a ridge an' saw somethin' green, an'
knowin' it wasn't you I went for it," answered his friend.
"If it had been made for us it couldn't be better. With
water, an' grass enough for night grazin', an' a good ridge
to look from, it's a fine place for us. We'll take turns at it,
for it won't feed two cayuses steady. Th' off man can
ride west to grass, mebby back to our camp, an' by
takin' shifts at it we can mebby save most of th' grass at
th' hole."

"An' mebby get spotted while we're ridin' back an'
forth?"

"Th' ridge will take care of that, an' I reckon when it
peters out there'll be others to hide us. I'm dead set on
this: I'm so set that I'll stick it out all alone rather than
pass it by. I tell you I got a *feelin'*."

"I ain't quittin'," growled Red; "I ain't got sense
enough to quit. Desert or *no* desert I'm aimin' to do my
little gilt-edged damndest; but I'm admittin' I'll be plumb
happy when it's my time off. We'll get supplies an' more
canteens from th' Kid tomorrow, an' be fixed so we can
foller any other lead that sticks up its head. I shore can
stand more than ridin' over a desert if it'll give us anythin' on them fellers."

"Here we are," grunted his companion, swinging from

the saddle. "Finest, coldest water you ever drunk. I'm puttin' double hobbles on my cayuse tonight, just to make shore."

"Me, too," said Red, dismounting.

In the morning they rode up for a look along the ledge, found that it would answer their requirements and then went southeast, curving farther into the desert, and it was not long before Red's roving glance caught something which aroused his interest and he silently rode off to investigate, his companion going slowly ahead. When he returned it was by another way and he rode with his eager eyes searching the desert beneath and ahead of him. Reaching his friend, who had stopped and also was scanning the desert floor with great intentness, he nodded in quiet satisfaction.

"Think you see 'em, too?" he smilingly inquired. "They're so faint they can't hardly be seen, not till you look ahead, an' then it's only th' difference between this strip of sand that we're on an' th' rest of th' desert. It's a cattle trail, Hoppy; I just found another water hole, a big one. Th' bank was crowded with hoof marks, cattle an' cayuses. Looks like they come from th' west, bearin' a little north. Th' only reason we didn't see 'em when we rode down was because they was on hard ground. That shore explains th' dead cow."

"An' in a few hours more," said his companion, "this powdery dust will blot 'em out. If they was clearer I'd risk follerin' them, even if we only had a canteen apiece. We can ride as far between waters as they can drive a herd, an' a whole lot farther. It's only fearin' that th' trail will disappear that holds me back."

"We don't have to risk it yet," said Red, grimly. "We've found out where they cut in an' how they start across; an' all we got to do is to lay low up there an' wait for 'em to come back, or start another herd across, to learn who they are."

"If we wait for their next drive we can foller 'em on a fresh, plain trail, an' be a lot better prepared," supplemented Hopalong. "I reckon we're shore goin' to fatten our comeback!"

"It's pickin' up fast," gloated his friend. "All we got to do is watch that big water hole an' we got 'em. There ain't so many water holes out on this skillet that they can drive any way they like. We'll camp at th' little one, of course, but we can lay closer to th' big one nights."

"An' from th' ridge up yonder th' man on day watch can see for miles."

"Yes; an' fry, an' broil, an' sizzle, an' melt!" muttered Red. "Damn 'em!"

Hopalong had wheeled and was leading the way into the southwest as straight as he could go for the meeting with Johnny, and Red pushed up past him and bore a little more to the west. They had seen all they needed to see for the day, and they had made up their minds.

At last after a long, hot ride they reached the bluffs marking the side of the plateau and soon were winding down a steep-walled arroyo which led to the plain below, and the country began to change with such insensible gradations that they hardly noticed it. Sage and greasewood became more plentiful and after an hour had passed an occasional low bush was to be seen and the ground sloped more and more in front of them. A low fringe of greenery lay along the distant bottom, where Sand Creek or some other hidden stream came close to the top of the soil, later to issue forth and become the stream into which the Question-Mark's creek later emptied. They crossed this and breasted an opposing slope, followed around the base of a low ridge of hills and at last stopped under a clump of live-oak and cottonwoods in the extreme east end of the Question-Mark valley.

While the two friends were riding toward the little clump of trees west of the Question-Mark ranch visitors rode slowly up to the door of the ranchhouse and one of them dismounted. The shield he wore on his open vest shone in the sun with nickel brightness, but his face was anything but bright. The job which had been cut out for him was not to his liking and had destroyed his peace of mind, and the peace of mind of the two deputies, who needed no reflection upon their subordinate positions to keep them in the sheriff's rear. What little assurance they might have started with received a jolt soon after they had left town, when a gruff and unmistakably unfriendly voice had asked, with inconsiderate harshness and profanity, their intended destination and their business. At last allowed to pass on after quite some humiliation from the hidden sentries, they now were entering upon the dangerous part of their mission.

Corwin stepped up to the door and knocked, a formality which he never dispensed with on the Question-Mark. Other visitors usually walked right in and found a chair or sat on the table, but it never should be said to Corwin's discredit that an officer of the law was rude and ignorant in such a well-known and long-established form of etiquette. So Sheriff Corwin knocked.

"Come in!" impatiently bawled a loud and rude voice.

The sheriff obeyed and looked around the door casing. "Ah, hello, Mac," he said in cheery greeting.

"Mac *who*?" roared the man at the table.

"McCullough," said the man at the door, correcting himself. "How are you?"

"Yo're one full-blooded damn fool of a sheriff," sneered the trail-boss. "Where's them two prisoners I been waitin' for?"

"They got away. Somebody helped 'em bust th' jail. I sent word back to you by yore own men."

"Shore, I got it; I know that. That's no excuse a-tall!" retorted the trail-boss. "I went an' sent word down to Twitchell on th' jump that his fool way worked an' that I was goin' to send him th' men he wanted. Then you let 'em bust out of jail! Fine sort of a fool you made of me! Where's yore reward now, that you was spendin' so fast? An' what'll Twitchell say, an' *do*? He wants th' bank robbers, not excuses; an' more'n all he wanted th' man that shot Ridley. It ain't only a question of pertectin' th' men workin' for him, but it's personal, too. Ridley was an old friend of his'n—an' he'll raise hell till he gets th' man that killed him. What about it? What have you done since they got away?"

"We trailed 'em, but they lost us," growled Corwin. "Reckon they got up on that hard ground an' then lit out, jumpin' th' country as fast as they could. Kane had it on 'em, cold an' proper—but I had my doubts, somehow. I ain't quittin'; I'm watchin' an' layin' back, an' I'm figgerin' on deliverin' th' man that got Ridley."

"You mean Long an' Thompson are innocent?" demanded McCullough with a throaty growl. "Yo're sayin' it yoreself! What was you tryin' to run on me, then?"

"They musta robbed th' bank," replied the sheriff; "but I got my own ideas about who killed yore friend. This is between us. I'm waitin' till I get th' proof; an' after I get it, an' th' man, I'll mebby have to leave th' country between sunset an' dawn. I ain't no dog, an' I'm gettin' riled."

"Then it was Kane who cold-decked them two fellers?" demanded McCullough.

"I ain't sayin' a word, now," replied the sheriff. "Not yet, I ain't, but I'm aimin' to get th' killer. Where's that Nelson?"

"What you want with him?" asked the trail-boss. "Reckon he done it?"

"No; he didn't," answered Corwin. "He only helped them fellers out of jail, an' I'm goin' to take him in."

"What?" shouted McCullough, and then burst out laughing. "I'm repeatin' what I said about you bein' full-blooded! Say, if you can turn that trick I won't raise a hand—not till he's in jail; an' then I'll get him out cussed quick. He's workin' for me, an' he didn't do no crime, gettin' a couple of innocent men out of that mud hut; an', besides, I don't know that he did get 'em out. Go after him, Corwin; go right out after him." He glanced out of the window again and chuckled. "I see you brought some of yore official fam'bly along. Shucks! That ain't no way to do, three agin' one. An' I heard you was a bad hombre with a short gun!"

"It ain't no question of how bad I am!" retorted the sheriff. "We want him alive."

"Oh, I see; aim to scare him, bein' three to one. All right; go ahead—but there ain't goin' to be no pot-shootin'. Tell yore fam'bly that. I mean it, an' I cut in sudden th' minute any of it starts."

"There won't be no pot-shootin'," growled the sheriff, and to make sure that there wouldn't be any he stepped out and gave explicit instructions to his companions before going toward the smaller corral. When part way there he heard whistling, wheeled in his tracks and went back to the bunkhouse, hugging the wall as he slipped along it, his gun raised and ready for action.

Johnny turned the corner, caught sight of the two deputies, who held his suspicious attention, and had gone too far to leap back when he saw Corwin flattened against the wall and the sheriff's gun covering him. Presumably safe on a friendly ranch, he had given no thought to any imminent danger, and now he stood and stared at the unexpected menace, the whistling almost dying on his pursed lips.

"Nelson!" snapped the sheriff, "yo're under arrest for helpin' in that jail delivery. I'll shoot at th' first hostile move! Put up yore hands an' turn 'round!"

Johnny glanced from him to the deputies and thought swiftly. Three to one, and he was covered. He leaned against the wall and laughed until he was limp. When he regained control of himself he blinked at the sheriff and drew a long breath, which nearly caused Corwin to pull the trigger; but the sheriff found it to be a false alarm.

"What th' devil makes you think *I* was mixed up in that?" he asked, laughing again. He drew another long breath with unexpected suddenness, and again the nervous sheriff and the two deputies nearly pulled trigger; and again it was a false alarm.

"I've done my thinkin'!" snapped Corwin. "Watch him, boys!" he said out of the corner of his mouth. "An' if you wasn't mixed up in it you won't come to no harm."

"No; not in a decent town," rejoined Johnny, leaning against the wall again, where Corwin's body somewhat sheltered him from the deputies. The sheriff tensed again at the movement. "But Mesquite's plumb full of liars," drawled Johnny, "trained by Kane. How do I know I'll get a square deal?"

"You'll get it! Put 'em up!" snapped Corwin, raising his

gun to give the command emphasis, and it now pointed at the other's head.

"Long an' Thompson—" began Johnny, and like a flash he twisted sidewise and jerked his head out of the line of fire, the bullet passing his ear and the powder scorching his hair. As he twisted he slipped in close, his left hand flashing to Corwin's gun-wrist and the right, across his body, tore the weapon from its owner's hand. The movement had been done so quickly that the sheriff did not realize what had occurred until he found himself disarmed and pressing against his own weapon, which was jammed into his groin. Johnny's left-hand gun had leaped into the surprised deputies' sight at the sheriff's hip and they lost no time in letting their own guns drop to the ground in instant answer to the snapped command. Corwin's momentary surprise died out nearly as quickly as it was born and, scorning the menace of the muzzle of his own gun, he grabbed Johnny. As he shifted his foot Johnny's leg slipped behind it and a sudden heave turned the sheriff over it, almost end over end, and he struck the ground with a resounding thump. Johnny sprang back, one gun on the sheriff, the other on the deputies.

"Get off them cayuses," he ordered and the two men slowly complied. "Go over near th' corral, an' stay there." In a moment he gave all his attention to the slowly arising officer.

"All this was unnecessary," he said. "You put us all in danger of bein' killed. Don't you *never* again try to take me in till you *know* why yo're doin' it! My head might 'a' been blowed off, an' all for nothin'! You don't know who busted that jail, judgin' by yore fool actions, an' you cussed well know it. You got plenty of gall, comin' down here an' throwin' a gun on me, for that! I'm sayin', frank, that whoever done that trick did th' right thing; but that ain't sayin' that *I* did it. Hope I didn't hurt you, Corwin; but I had to act sudden when you grabbed me."

"Don't you do no worryin' on my account!" snapped the sheriff.

"I ain't blamin' you for doin' your duty, if you was doin'

it honest," said Johnny; "but you ain't got no business jumpin' before yo're shore. I ain't holdin' th' sack for nobody, Corwin; Kane or nobody else. Now then: you can tell what proof you got that it was me that busted th' jail."

Corwin was watching the smiling face and the accusing eyes and he saw no enmity in either. "Then who did?" he demanded.

Johnny shrugged his shoulders. "*Quien sabe?*" he asked. "There's a lot of people down here that would have more reason to do a thing like that, even for strangers, than *I* would. You ain't loved very much, from what I've heard. I don't want any more enemies than I got; but I'm tellin' you, flat, that I ain't goin' back with you; an' neither would you, if you was in my place, in a strange town. Here," he said, letting the hammer down and tossing the gun at the sheriff's feet, "take your gun. I'm glad you ain't hurt; an' I'm cussed glad *I* ain't. But somebody's shore goin' to be th' next time you pull a gun on me on a guess. You want to be *dead shore*, Corwin. We've had enough of this. Did you get any trace of them two?"

The sheriff watched his opponent's gun go back into its holster and slowly picked up his own. "No; I ain't," he admitted, and considered a moment as he sheathed the weapon with great care. "I *ain't* got nothin' flat agin' you," he said; "but I still think you had a hand in it. That's a good trick you worked, Nelson; I'm rememberin' it. All right; th' next time I come for you I'll *have* it cold; an' I'm shore expectin' to come for you, an' Idaho, too."

"That's fair enough," replied Johnny, smiling; "but I don't see why you want to drag Idaho in it for. He didn't have no more to do with it than *I* did."

"I'm believin' that, too," retorted the sheriff; "since you put it just that way. I haven't heard you say that you *didn't* do it. Before I go I want to ask you a question: Where was you th' night th' Diamond L lost them cows?"

"Right here with Mac an' th' boys."

"He was," said McCullough. "Yo're ridin' wide of th' trail, Corwin."

"Mebby," grunted the sheriff. "There's two trails. I mebby am plumb off of *one* of 'em, as long as you know he was down here that night; but I'm ridin' right down th' middle of th' other. When did you meet Long an' Thompson first?" he asked, wheeling suddenly and facing Johnny.

"Thinkin' what you do about me," replied Johnny, "I'd be a fool to tell you anythin', no matter what. So, as long as yo're ridin' down th' middle you'll have to read th' signs yoreself. Some of 'em must be plumb faint, th' way yo're guessin', an' castin' 'round. Get any news about them rustlers?"

"What's th' use of makin' trouble for yoreself by bein' stubborn?" asked McCullough. He looked at Corwin. "Sheriff, I know for shore that he never knowed any Bill Long or Red Thompson until after he come to Mesquite. What news did you get about th' rustlers?"

"Huh!" muttered Corwin, searching the face of the trail-boss, whose reputation for veracity was unquestioned. "I ain't got any news about 'em. Once they got on th' hard stretch they could go for miles an' not leave no trail. I'm figgerin' on spendin' quite some time north of where Lukins' boys quit an' turned back. There's three cows missin' that are marked so different from any I've ever seen that I'll know 'em in a herd of ten thousan' head; an' when they're cut out for me to look at there's some marks on horns an' hoofs that'll prove whose cows they are. I'm takin' a couple of his boys with me when I go, to make shore. Of course, I don't know that we'll ever see 'em, at all. Well," he said, turning toward his horse, "reckon I'll be goin'." He waved to the deputies, who approached, picked up their guns under Johnny's alert and suspicious scrutiny, and mounted. "As for you, Nelson, *next* time I'll be dead shore; an' I'll mebby shoot first, on a gamble, an' talk afterward. So-long."

Watching the three arms of the law ride away and out of sight, Johnny swung around and faced the grinning trail-boss. "You told th' truth, Mac; but I wonder if Corwin heard it like I did?"

McCullough shrugged his shoulders. "Who cares? I'm thankin' you for an interestin' lesson in how to beat th' drop; but I reckon I'm gettin' too old to be quick enough to use it. I reckon Waffles has been tellin' th' truth about yore Bar-20 outfit. Where you goin' now?"

"Off to see a couple of better men from that same outfit," grinned Johnny.

He went on with his preparations and soon rode Pepper toward a gap in the southern chain of hills, leading a loaded pack horse behind him. Emerging on the other side of the pass he followed the chain westward and in due time rounded the last hill and headed for the little clump of trees where he saw his two friends waiting. They waved to him and he replied, chuckling with pleasure.

Red looked critically at the pack animal. "Huh! From th' looks of that cayuse I reckon he figgers we're goin' to be gone some months, like a prospector holin' up for th' winter."

"He never underplays a hand," grunted Hopalong, a warm light coming into his eyes. "Desert or no desert, it's shore good to be with him again. He never should 'a' left Montanny."

Johnny soon joined them, dismounted, picketed the pack horse, pushed back his sombrero and rolled a cigarette, grinning cheerfully. "If you want any more canteens you can have th' pair on my cayuse," he said. "Find anythin'?"

They told him and he nodded in quiet satisfaction. "You shore ain't been asleep," he chuckled. "You've just about found out somethin' that's been puzzlin' a lot of folks down here for some years. I wonder how close they ever come to them water holes when they was scoutin' around? But mebby they never scouted over that way much—everybody was bankin' on 'em stayin' on th' hard stretch over Lukins' way, instead of crossin' it so close to town. You'd never have thought of lookin' for 'em over east if you hadn't remembered Slippery Trendly, now would you?"

"We wasn't lookin' for nothin' nor nobody except you,"

admitted Hopalong. "But when Red saw a dead cow as far out on th' desert as *it* was, we just had to take a look at it. An' when we saw it had been shot we couldn't do nothin' else but look for th' brand. That bein' cut out made us plumb suspicious. One thing just nat'rally led to th' next, as th' mule said when its tail was pulled."

"What you bet that missin' brand wasn't a Diamond L?" Johnny asked.

"Ain't that th' ranch Idaho works for?" queried Red.

Johnny nodded. "They raided Lukins th' night of th' day you an' Hoppy left town. That outfit put in two days ridin' along th' hard ground, half of 'em up an' half of 'em down. They lost over a hundred head."

His friends exchanged looks, each trying to visualize the all but obliterated trail, and both nodded.

"Mebby it *was* a Diamond L," said Hopalong, and he explained their plans to some length.

"That's goin' to win if you can stick it out," said Johnny. "McCullough's steamin' a little, but he's still carryin' out Twitchell's wishes; an' I been arguin' with him, too, to give you fellers a chance. Hey!" he exclaimed, grinning. "I allus knowed I'd get a bad name for hangin' out with you two coyotes; an' I done got it. I'm suspected strong of bein' a criminal, like you fellers, an' I'll mebby be an outlaw, too. Sheriff Corwin just said so, an' he ought to know if anybody does. He arrested me for helpin' to get you fellers out of jail, but he didn't say how he aimed to keep me in it, busted like it is."

"How'd you get away?" asked Red. "Wouldn't you go with him?"

"Mebby he didn't have th' rest of th' dozen," suggested Hopalong.

"Oh, he wasn't real shore about it really bein' me he wanted, so he turned me loose," replied Johnny. "Anyhow, I couldn't 'a' gone with him: I had to get this stuff out to you fellers. An' besides, I knowed if I got in that 'dobe hut you wouldn't have th' nerve to bust me out again."

"I'm honin' to bust Corwin's 'dobe head," growled Red.

"There's four canteens an' plenty of grub, with Mac's

compliments," said Johnny, waving at the pack horse. "When am I to meet you again?"

Hopalong considered a moment. "There's too much ridin', comin' down here unless we has to," he said. "Tell you what: We'll find a hill, or a ridge up on th' plateau where a fire can be lit that won't show to no-body north of them hills you just come around. Take that white patch up yonder: we can see it plain for miles. You ride up to it every day about two hours after sun-up; an' every night just after dark. If you see smoke puffs in day-light, or a winkin' fire at night, ride toward that split bluff behind us. We'll meet you there. If you get news for us, do th' same thing on th' other slope, so it can't be seen from across this valley. As long as it can be seen on a line with th' split bluff we won't miss it."

Johnny scratched his head. "Strings of six puffs or six winks means trouble: come a-latherin'," he suggested. "Strings of three means news, an' take yore time. Better have a signal for grub an' supplies: it'll mebby save ridin'. Say groups of two an' five, alternate?"

Hopalong nodded and repeated the signals to make certain that he had them right. "Two an' five, alternate, for supplies; strings of six, come a-runnin'; strings of three, news, an' take our time. Couple of hours after sun-up an' just after dark. All right, Kid."

"Mac's got an old spyglass. Want it, if I can get it?" asked Johnny.

"Shore!" grunted Red.

"Bring it next time you come," said Hopalong.

"All right. Where you goin' now?"

"Up on Sand Creek, where we're camped," answered Red. "We got a couple of days before we move out on th' fryin' pan, an' we're aimin' to make th' most of it."

"Wait till I get th' glass, an' I'll go along," suggested Johnny, eagerly.

"Get a rustle on—an' take this pack animal back with you," smiled Hopalong as Johnny started without it. "We'll empty out th' canteens, an' we can tote th' sup-plies without it."

CHAPTER XVI

A Vigil Rewarded

THE DAYS passed quietly for the two watchers after Johnny had gone back to the Question-Mark, the hours dragging in monotonous succession. In the Sand Creek camp time passed pleasantly enough, but out on the great, up-slanting billow of sand north of Sweet Spring, devoid of shelter from the blazing sun and from the reflected glare of the gray-white desert around it, was another matter. Prone on his stomach lay Hopalong on the northward slope, his face barely level with the crest of the ridge. Down in the hollow behind him was his horse, picketed and hobbled as well, and at his side on his blanket to keep the cutting sand and clogging dust from barrels and actions lay his rifle and his six-guns, so hot that their metal parts could not be touched without a grimace of discomfort coming to his face. The telescope at intervals swung around the shimmering horizon, magnifying the dancing heat waves until the distortion of their wavering, streaming currents at times rendered the view chaotic and baffling. Strange sights were to be seen in the air and knowing what they were he watched them as his only source of amusement. A tree-bordered lake appeared, its waters sparkling, arose into the air, became vague and slowly dissolved from view, calling from him caustic comment. Inverted mountains reached down from the heavens, standing on snow-covered tops, writhed more and more from their outer edges and melted down from the up-flung bases, slowly fading from view. They were followed by a silvery, winding river, certain features which caused him to think that he recognized it and while he studied it a herd of cattle upside down, and greatly magnified, pushed through into sight as the river scene faded away. Another hour passed and then a steep-walled, green valley inverted itself before his gaze. He could make out a hut and a few trees and then as mounted men began to ride up its slanting bluff trail his attention became riveted on it and he reached for the hot telescope. One look through the instrument made him grunt with disgust, for the figures danced and shrunk and expanded, weaved and became like shadows, through which he looked as though through a rare, discolored vapor. He was mildly excited and tried in vain to search his visual image of the sight for the faces of the men; but it was in vain, and he opened his eyes as the image faded and then closed them again to better search the memory picture. This, too, availed him nothing and he realized that he had not really seen the faces. He was perplexed and vexed, for there was something familiar about some of those riders. About to move for a look around through the telescope, he yielded to a humorous warning and lay quiet for awhile. Was it possible that the mirage had been double-acting, and had revealed each to the other?

"Mebby they won't put as much stock in theirs as I did in mine," he said, and slowly picked up the telescope for a final look all around the horizon before Red should relieve him. East, south, west he looked and saw nothing. Swinging it toward the Sand Creek camp he grunted in satisfaction as a figure very much like Red wavered and danced as it emerged over a ridge of sand. Farther north he swung it and slowly swept the northern horizon. Swearing suddenly he stopped its slow progress and brought it back searchingly over ground it had just covered. Rigid he held it and looked with unbelieving eyes.

"Mirage?" he growled, questioningly. "It's too solid for that—I'm goin' up to see."

Getting his horse he gingerly slipped the hot rifle into its scabbard, hastily dropped the six-guns into their holsters and, mounting, rode to meet his nearing friend.

"Cooked?" queried Red, grinning. "You shore didn't lose no time gettin' started after you saw me! Ain't it hell out here?"

"Hell is right," answered Hopalong, handing over the telescope. "But we got cayuses, full canteens, an' know where we are. Swing that blisterin' tube over yonder," he said, pointing, "an' tell me what you see?"

Red obeyed and the moving glass suddenly stopped and swung back a little. After long scrutiny he raised his head and gazed steadily over the rigid tube as though along a rifle barrel. "I see him, now, without it," he said. "A-foot, he is, staggerin' every-which way. Comin'?"

His companion replied by pushing into the lead and setting a stiff pace through the soft sand and alkali dust. As they drew near they both shivered at the sight which steadily was being better revealed.

The figure of a man, and scarcely more than a figure, stumbled crazily across the sand, hatless, his bare feet covered with dust which had become pasty with the blood exuding through the deepening clefts in the skin and flesh. Progress on such feet would have made him mad from pain if he had not already become so from other causes. His trousers were ripped and frayed to the swollen, dust-plastered knees, the crimson fissures running up and down his swollen legs. Shirt he had none, save the strip which hung stiff and crimson from his belt. His upper body was a thing of horror, swollen, matted with crusts of dried blood, from beneath which more oozed out to in turn coagulate. His burning eyes peered through slits in the puffed face and his tongue, blackened and purplish, stuck out of his mouth.

"God!" muttered Red, glancing awesomely at the tense face of his companion.

"He's gone," said Hopalong, softly. "Nothing can save him. It would be a mercy—" but he checked the words, searching Red's acquiescent eyes.

"Can't do it," said Red. "Can you?"

Hopalong drew in a deep breath and shook his head. "We got to try th' other first," he said. "It's wrong—but there's nothin' else. We ain't doctors, an' there may be a fightin' chance. Hobble th' cayuses. We'll both tackle him—one alone might have to be too rough, for he'll mebby fight."

"He's down," said Red as he swung from his saddle. "Lookin' right at us, too, an' don't see us."

The figure groveled in the sand, digging with blundering fingers worn to the bone by previous digging, and choked sounds came from the swollen throat. Red talked to himself as he hobbled his horse and pushed down the picket pin.

"Lost his cayuse, somehow, or went crazy an' chased it away. Used up his last water an' then threw away everythin' he had. Tore off his shirt because th' neckband got too tight an' th' cloth stuck to th' blood clots an' pulled at 'em. I've seen others, but they warn't none of 'em as bad as him," growled Red more to himself than to his companion.

Hopalong pushed home his own picket pin and stood up. "Comin'?" he asked, starting slowly for the groveling, digging thing on the sand.

They stepped up to him and lifted the unfortunate from the ground. Dazed and without understanding, the pitiful object of their assistance suddenly snarled and reached its bleeding fingers for Red's throat, and for the next few minutes two rational, strong men had as hard a fight on their hands as they ever had experienced; and when it was over and the enraged unfortunate became docile from exhaustion they were covered with blood. Letting a few drops of water trickle down the side of the protruding tongue, which they forced to one side when the drops were stopped by it, they worked over the dying man as long as they dared in the sun and then, carrying him to Hopalong's horse they put him across the saddle, lashing him securely, and covered him with a doubled blankct to cheat the leering sun.

"Go ahead to th' water hole," said Hopalong, straightening up from tying the last knot. "I'll take him to camp an' do what I can. There won't be no trouble handlin' him, tied like he is. Got to try to save him—'though I hope somebody puts a bullet through my head if I ever get like him."

"Bein' crazy, he mebby ain't feelin' it as much as he might," replied Red. "Seems to me he's the one they called Sandy Woods; but he's so plumb changed I ain't shore."

Hopalong thought of the last mirage he had seen, was about to speak of it, but abruptly changed his mind. He conveyed his warning in another way. "Keep a-lookin' sharp, Red," he said. "Th' poor devil shore was one of them rustlers; an' they mebby ain't far behind him. It's gettin' nearer an' nearer th' time they ought to come back. I'll stay with him in camp an' let th' Kid's signal go, if he makes one. This feller ain't got long to live, I'm figgerin'."

"It's a wonder he lived this long," said Red, riding off to take up the vigil.

Hopalong swung his belts and guns over the pommel of the saddle to lighten him, drank sparingly from a canteen and started on foot for the camp, leading his dispirited horse. After a walk through the hot, yielding sand which became a punishment during the last mile he sighed with relief as he stopped the horse on the bank of Sand Creek and tenderly placed its burden on the ground in the shade of a tree. More water, in judicious quantities, and at increasingly frequent intervals brought no apparent relief to the sufferer, and in mid-afternoon Sandy Woods lost all need of earthly care. Kane's thieving trail-boss had won his bet.

Hopalong looked down at the body freed of its suffering and slowly shook his head. "Th' other way would 'a' been th' best," he said. "*I* knowed it; *Red* knowed it— yet, both plumb shore, an' *knowin'* it was better, we just couldn't do it. A man's trainin' is a funny thing."

He looked around the little depression and walked

toward a patch of sand lying near a mass of stones which had rolled down the slope; and before the evening shadows had reached across the little creek, a heaped-up pile of rocks marked the place of rest of one more weary traveler. At the head, lying on the ground, was a cross made of stones. Why he had placed it there Hopalong could hardly have told, but something within him had stirred through the sleep of busy and heedless years, and he had unthinkingly obeyed it.

He looked up at the sun and found it was time to go on watch again. He had been given no opportunity to sleep, but did not complain, carelessly accepting it as one of the breaks in the game. When he reached his friend, ready to go on duty again, Red looked up at him and scrutinized his face.

"Lots of sleep you musta got," said Red. "How's our patient?"

"Gettin' all th' sleep there is," came the reply. "We was right—both ways."

"Spread yore blanket here," said Red. "I'm stickin' to th' job till you have a snooze. Anyhow, somethin' tells me that two won't be more'n we need out here at night, from now on."

"It's my trick," replied Hopalong, decisively. "Spread yore own blanket."

"Him turnin' up like he did was an accident," retorted Red, "an' accidents are shared between us both. Anyhow, I ain't sleepy—an' th' next few hours are pleasant. Get some sleep, you chump!"

"Well, as long as we're both handy, it don't make much difference," replied Hopalong, spreading the blanket. "We can spell each other any time we need to. Hope th' Kid ain't tryin' to signal nothin'."

"We got more to signal than he has," growled Red. "Shut up, now; an' go to sleep," and his companion, blessed by one of the prized acquirements of the plainsman, promptly obeyed; but it seemed to him that he scarcely had dozed off when he felt his friend's thrusting hand, and he opened his eyes in the darkness, staring up at the blazing stars, in surprise.

"Yes?" whispered Hopalong, without moving or making any other sound, again true to his training.

His companion's whisper, a whisper by force of habit rather than for any good reason, reached him: "Turn over, an' look over th' ridge."

Hopalong obeyed, threw off the blanket which Red had spread over him when the chill of the desert night descended, and became all eyes as he saw the faint glow of a distant fire, which rapidly grew and became brighter. "It's them, down at th' other water hole," he said, arising and feeling to see if his Colts had slid out of their holsters while he slept. "I'm goin' down for a better look," and he glanced at the northern sky just above the horizon, memorized a group of stars and disappeared noiselessly into the night.

Nearing the larger water hole he went more slowly and finished by wriggling up to the crest of a sand billow, his head behind a lone sage bush, and his eyelids closed to a thin crack, lest the light of the fire should reflect from his eyes and reveal him to some keen, roving glance.

The greasewood fire blazed under a pair of skillets, while a coffeepot imitated the Tower of Pisa on the glowing coals at one edge. Around it, reclining on the powdery clay, or squatting in the more characteristic attitude of men of the saddle, were a half-dozen of Kane's pets, Miguel and his cronies well to one side. The hidden watcher knew them all by sight and saw several men who had helped the sheriff trick him and Red. In the darkness behind the group he heard their horses moving about as they grazed.

"Do you reckon he made it, Miguel?" asked the trail-boss, apropos of the conversation around the fire.

Miguel turned his face to the light, the scar over his eye glistening against the duller skin around it. "I say no," he drawled. "He change hees horrse at the corrals, no? The-e horrse he took was born at the-e Cimarron corral an' foaled eet's firrst colt there. I would not lak' sooch a horrse eef I did not know my way. But, *quien sabe?*"

The trail-boss looked at him searchingly, wondering how much the half-breed knew about Sandy's reasons for making the change. Kane would not allow fighting in the ranks, and grudges live long in some men. Besides, to lose the bet was to lose his share of the drive profits to a man he secretly hated, and this did not suit the trail-boss.

Miguel smiled grimly into the cold, searching eyes and shrugged his shoulders, his soft laugh turning the cold stare into something warmer. "Eef he deed, then eet ees ver' good," he said; "eef he deed not, then eet hees own fault. But he should not change hees horrse."

"We'll know tomorrow night, anyhow," said a voice well back from the fire. "Get a rustle on you, Thorpe," it growled. "You move around like an old woman."

"Ain't no walls to climb," said another, laughing.

The red-faced cook did not raise his head or retort, but in his memory another name was deeply carved, to replace the one he was certain would be erased when they reached Mesquite. Sandy Woods' dislike for the horse given to him at the corrals had been overcome by the smooth words of the unforgiving cook, who also had a score to pay.

"When do we rustle next?" asked a squatting figure. "We been layin' low too long, an' my pile has done faded; I wasn't lucky, like you, Trask, an' the sheriff," he said, looking at the trail-boss. "Next time a bank is busted *I* aim to be in on it. You fellers can't hog *all* th' good things."

"Don't do no good to talk about it," snapped the trail-boss. "Kane names them he wants. Trask an' me was robbed of half of our share—I ain't forgettin' it, neither. An' as for th' next raid, that's settled. As long as all of us are in it, you might as well know. We're cleanin' up on McCullough's west range, an' there won't be much of a wait." Neither the speaker, his companions, nor the man behind the sage brush knew that Kane already had changed his mind, and because of Lukins' activity had decided to raid McCullough's east range.

"*How* soon?" demanded the questioner.

"Some night this week, I reckon," came the answer. "If we get a good bunch we'll sit back an' take things easy for awhile. Too many drives may cut a trail that'll show, an' we can't risk *that*."

"Too bad we have to drive west an' north before we hit for the plain," said Jud Hill. "Takes two days more, that way."

The trail-boss smiled. "I know a way that would suit you, Jud," he said. "So does Miguel—but we've been savin' it till th' old route gets too risky. It joins th' regular trail right here. Well, at last th' cook has really cooked— pass it this way, Thorpe. I'm eatin' fast an' I'm turnin' in faster. Th' more we beat th' sun gettin' away from here, th' less it'll beat on us. We're leavin' an hour ahead of it."

Not waiting until the camp should become silent, when any noise he might make would be more likely to be heard, Hopalong crept away while the rustlers ate and returned to his friend, who waited under a certain group of stars.

Red cocked his head at the soft sound, his Colt swinging to cover it, when he heard his name called in his friend's voice, and he replied.

Hopalong sat down on the blanket and related what he had seen and heard without comment from his listener until the end of the narrative.

"Huh!" said Red. "You learned a-plenty. An' I'm glad they reached that water hole after dark, an' are goin' to go on again before it gets light. They missed our tracks. I call that luck," he said in great satisfaction. "We wasn't doin' much guessin'. That's shore their drive trail, an' th' best thing about it is that it's th' bottom of th' Y. They've got two ways of leavin' th' ranges without showin' tracks, but they both come together down yonder. I reckon mebby we'll have a piece to speak when they come this way again. Goin' to tell McCullough what's bein' hatched?"

"We ought to," answered his companion, slowly. "We'll tell th' Kid an' leave it to him. They must be purty shore of themselves to rustle Question-Mark cattle at *this* time. If th' Kid tells Mac, an' they try it, Mesquite shore is goin' to be a busy little town. I think I know his breed."

"They ain't takin' much of a chance, at that, if they try it," said Red. "They don't know that we know anythin' about it an' that McCullough will know it, if th' Kid tells him. Mebby they figger that by springin' it right now when th' feelin' is so strong agin' 'em, that it would make folks think they didn't do it, because they oughten't to—oh, pshaw! *You* know what I'm gettin' at!"

"Shore," grunted Hopalong. He was silent a moment and then stirred. "We ain't got no reason to stay out here for a day or two. Let's pull out an' go down where we can signal th' Kid after sun-up. We'll ride well to th' east past their camp. What wind is stirrin' is comin' from th' other way, an' there's no use makin' any fresh tracks in front of 'em."

An hour or so after daylight a small fire sent a column of smoke straight up, the explanation of its smoking qualities suggested by the canteen lying near it. Hopalong and Red slid a blanket over the fire and drew it suddenly aside, performing this operation three times in succession before letting the column mount unmolested for brief intervals. In the west, above and behind a bare spot on a ridge of hills an answering column climbed upward, and then a series of triple puffs took its place. Scattering the fire over the ground the two friends absent-mindedly kicked sand over the embers, and suddenly grinned at each other at the foolishness of their precautions.

When they reached the little grove they found Johnny waiting for them, his horse well loaded with more provisions. As they transferred the supplies to their own mounts they told him what had occurred and he decided that McCullough should be informed of the forthcoming raid, whether or not it would in any way jeopardize the winning of the rewards.

"It's a toss-up whether Mac will wait for them to run it off," he said, "when I tell him. He's gettin' more riled every minute, but he seemed to calm down a little after Corwin visited him. Somethin' sort of pulls him back when he gets to climbin' onto his hind legs, an' he ends up by leanin' agin' th' wall an' swearin'. I'm not tellin' him nothin' about anythin' but th' raid. You aimin' to go back to that water hole?"

Hopalong shook his head. "No, sir," he answered. "There ain't no reason to till th' raid happens. We're campin' on Sand Creek till you signal that it's been run off. Time enough then for us to watch on that cussed griddle."

"Have special signal for that?" suggested Red. "Say two, two an' three, repeated. Mebby won't have time to hear what th' news is. When you get our answer don't bother ridin' down here to tell us anythin'—we'll be makin' tracks *pronto*."

Johnny nodded. "Two, two an' three is OK. I'll be ridin' back to tell Mac there's goin' to be a party on his west range some night soon. I'm bettin' it'll be a bloody party, too. Say," he exclaimed, pulling up, "Lukins an' Idaho was down last night. They're mad as hell, an' they're throwin' a cordon of riders plumb across th' hard stretch every night. Lukins an' Mac are joinin' forces, an' from now on th' two ranches are workin' together as one. With us scoutin' around east of town somethin' shore ought to drop." He pressed Pepper's sleek sides and started back to the sheltering hills.

"Somethin's *goin'* to drop," growled Red, the memory of the jailing burning strongly within him. "Don't forget, Kid—two, two an' three."

Johnny turned in his saddle, waved a hand and kept on going. Rounding the westernmost hill he rode steadily until opposite the white patch of sand on the northern slope and then, dismounting, collected firewood, and built it up on the dead ashes of his signal fire, ready for the match. Going on again he rode steadily until he reached the place in the arroyo which lay directly behind the ranchhouse.

McCullough returned from a ride over the range to find his cheerful friend smoking some of his tobacco.

"Want a job, Nelson?" asked the trail-boss, swinging

from the saddle with an easy agility belying his age and weight.

Johnny smiled at him. "Anythin' that don't take me away from th' ranch too far or too long. Call it."

"One of th' boys, ridin' south of th' hills on a fool's errand, this mornin', thought he saw smoke signals back of White Face," said McCullough. "He says he reckons he's loco. I ain't goin' that far. Think you could find out anythin' about 'em?"

Johnny considered, and chuckled. "Huh!" he snorted. "He's plumb late. *I* saw them before he did, an' know all about 'em. You stuck a couple of jabs into me about bein' lazy, an' likin' to set around all day doin' nothin'. Any chump can wear out cayuses ridin' around discoverin' things, but th' wise man is th' feller that can set around all day, lazy an' no-account, an' figger things out. I don't have to go prowlin' around to find out things. I just set in th' shade of th' house, roll cigarettes an' hold powwows with my medicine bag. You'd be surprised if you knowed what I got in that bag, an' what I can get *out* of it. You shore would."

McCullough looked at him with an expression which tried to express so many uncomplimentary things at once that the composite was almost neutral; at least, it was somewhat blank.

"Ye-ah?" he drawled, his inflection in no way suggesting anything to Johnny's credit.

"Ye-ah," repeated the medicine man somewhat belligerently.

"Oh," said the trail-boss, eyeing his victim speculatively. "You know all about 'em, huh?"

"Everythin'," placidly replied Johnny, rolling another cigarette.

"I wish to heaven you'd quit smokin' them cussed things around here," said McCullough plaintively. "Yo're growed up now, purty near; an' you *ain't* no Greaser. I'll buy you a pipe if you'll promise to smoke it."

"Pipes, judgin' from yourn," sweetly replied Johnny, calmly lighting the cigarette, "are dangerous, unless a man hangs around th' house *all* th' time. When I used to go off scoutin', I allus wished th' other fellers smoked pipes, corncob pipes, like Mister McCullough carries around. Why, cuss it, I could smell 'em out, *up*-wind, if they did. It would 'a' saved me a lot of crawlin' an' worryin'. I knowed you was comin' back ten minutes before I saw you. Now, you can't blame a skunk—he was born that way, an' he's got good reasons for keepin' on th' way he was born. But a human, goin' out of his way, to smell like *some* I knows of," he broke off, shrugging his shoulders expressively.

McCullough slowly produced the corncob, blew through the stem with unnecessary violence, gravely filled and lit it, his eyes twinkling. "Takes a *man*, I reckon, to enjoy its aromer," he observed. "Goin' back to yore medicine bag, let's see what you can get out of it," he challenged.

Johnny drew out his buckskin tobacco pouch, placed it on the floor, covered it with his sombrero and chanted softly, his eyes fixed on the hat. "I smell a trail-boss an' his pipe. They went to th' bend of th' crick, an' they says to Pete Holbrook, who rides that section, that he ought to ride on th' other side of th' crick after dark." He was repeating information which he had chanced to overhear near the small corral the night before, when he had passed unobserved in the darkness.

McCullough favored the hat with a glance of surprise and Johnny with a keen, prolonged stare.

"Pete, he said that wouldn't do no good unless he went far enough north to leave his section unprotected. He borrowed a chew of tobacco before th' man an' th' pipe went away an' let th' air get pure again." The medicine man knew Pete's thrifty nature by experience.

"Yo're shore a good guesser," grunted McCullough. "What about them smoke signals, that you know all about?"

Johnny readjusted the hat a hairsbreadth, passed his hands over it and closed his eyes. "I see smoke signals," he chanted. "There's palefaces in 'em, ridin' cautious at night over a hard plain. They're driftin' cows into a herd. Th' herd is growin' fast, an' it drifts toward th' hard ground. Now it's goin' faster. Th' brands are Diamond L. I see more smoke signals an' more ridin' in th' dark. Another herd, bigger this time, is runnin' hard over that same plain. Th' brands are SV, vented; an' plain Question-Mark. It seems near—within a week—an' it's on yore west range." He opened his eyes, kicked the hat across the room and pocketed the tobacco pouch.

"Mac," he said, gravely. "That's a shore-enough prophecy. Leavin' out all jokin', it's true. Hoppy an' Red told me, a little while ago, that they overheard some of Kane's gang talkin'. They're goin' to raid you like I said. Th' smoke signals was me answerin' theirs. They say Sandy Woods is dead. They ought to know because they buried him. They know three of th' men that robbed th' bank an' they've knowed ever since Ridley was shot, who killed him. They've seen Kane's drive trail crew an' they know a whole lot that I ain't goin' to tell you now; mebby I'll not tell you till we get th' rewards; but if it'll make you feel any better, I'm sayin' that we're goin' to get them rewards right soon. When Kane raids you he springs th' trap that'll clear a lot of vermin off this range."

"How much of all that do you mean?" demanded the trail-boss, his odorous pipe out and reeking more than ever. He was looking into his companion's eyes with a searching, appraising directness which many men would have found uncomfortable.

"All of it," complacently answered the medicine man, rolling a new cigarette. "There's only one thing I'm doubtful about, 'though it was what Hoppy overheard, so I gave it to you that way. They said yore west range. If Kane learns how th' Diamond L riders are spread out, an' I'm bettin' he knew it near as soon as Lukins did, he'll be a fool to drive that way. If it was me, I'd split my outfit an' put half of 'em on th' east end! But I'm a gambler."

McCullough considered the matter. "They'll leave a plain trail if they raid th' east section," he muttered; "an' th' desert'll hold 'em to a narrow strip north *or* south. There's water up th' north way, but there's people scattered all around, an' they're nat'rally near th' water.

South, there's less water, an' more people th' further they go. They might tackle th' desert, but Lukins an' me figger they go west from th' hard ground. I ain't agin' gamblin', but I don't gamble with anythin' *I* don't own. If yore friends heard them coyotes say 'west,' I'm playin' my cards accordin' to their case-rack. I may call it wrong, I may get a split, or I may win—but I'm backin' th' case-keepers, 'specially when they're keepin' th' rack for *me*. West it is—an' west is where hell will pop when they pay their visit. An' lemme tell you this, Nelson: Win, lose or split on th' raid, if it comes off within a week, I'll be dead shore who's behind it, an' there's a cyclone due in Mesquite right soon after. Twitchell had his chance. His game's no good—I'm playin' th' cards I've drawn in my own way when they show their hand in this raid. I'm bein' cold-decked by Corwin—but I'll warm it a-plenty. You hang around an' see th' fireworks!"

Johnny stretched, relaxed, and grinned. "I'm aimin' to touch some off, myself," he replied, "an' I reckon Hoppy an' Red will send up a couple of rockets on their own account. Rockets?" He grinned. "No; not rockets—there's allus burned sticks comin' down from rockets. Besides, they're too smooth an' easy. Reckon they'll touch off some pinwheels. Whizzin', tail-chasin' pinwheels; or mebby jumping-jacks. Most likely they'll be jumping-jacks, th' way some folks'll be steppin' lively to get out of th' way. Don't you bank on this bein' *yore* celebration—you'll only own th' lot an' make th' noise. Th' grand display, th' glorious finish is Bar-20. Just plain, old-fashioned Bar-20. Gee, Mac, it makes me a kid again!"

"It's got an easy job, then!" snorted the trail-boss.

CHAPTER XVII

A Well-Planned Raid

ON NIGHT shift again Pete Holbrook reached the end of his beat, waited until his fellow-watcher on the east bulked suddenly out of the darkness, exchanged a few words with him and turned back under the star-filled sky, his horse having no difficulty in avoiding obstructions, but picking its way with ease around scattered thickets, grass-tufted hummocks, and across shallow ravines and hollows. Objects close at hand were discernible to eyes accustomed to the darkness and Pete's range of vision attained the enviable limits enjoyed by those who live out-of-doors and look over long distances. An occasional patch of sand moved slowly into his circumscribed horizon as he rode on; vague, squatting bulks gradually revealed their vegetative nature and an occasional more regular bulk told him where a cow was lying. These latter more often were catalogued by his ears before his eyes defined them and from the contentment in the sounds he nodded in satisfaction. Soon he felt the gentle rise which swept up to the breeze-caressed ridge which projected northward and forced the little creek to follow it for nearly a mile before the rocky obstruction could be passed.

There had been a time when the ridge had forced the creek again as far out of its course, but on quiet nights a fanciful listener could hear the petulant grumblings of the stream and its constant boast. Placid and slow above the ridge, the waters narrowed and deepened when they reached the insolent bulk as if concentrating for the never-ending assault. They had cut through softer resistance along the edges and now gnawed noisily at the stone itself. Narrower grew the stream and deeper, the pools clear and with clean rock bottoms and sides where the hurrying water, now free from the last vestige of color imposed by the banks further up, became crystal in the light of day. Hurrying from pool to pool, singing around boulders it ran faster and faster as if eager for the final attempt against its bulky enemy, and hissed and growled as it sped along the abrupt rock face. Loath to leave the fight, it followed tenaciously along the other side of the ridge and at last gave up the struggle to turn sharply south again and flow placidly down the valley on a continuation of the line it had followed above.

This forced detour made the U-Bend, so called by Question-Mark riders, and the sloping ground of the ridge was as much a favorite with the cattle as were its bordering pools with the men. Here could be felt every vagrant breeze, and while the grass was scantier than that found on the more level pastures round about, and cropped closer, the cattle turned toward it when darkness came. It was the best bed-ground on the ranch.

The grunting, cud-chewing, or blowing blots grew more numerous as Holbrook went on and when he had reached the crest of the ridge his horse began to pick its way more and more to avoid them, the rider chanting a mournful lay and then followed it with a song which, had it been rightfully expurged, would have had little left to sing about. Like another serenade it had been composed in a barroom, but the barroom atmosphere was strongly in evidence. It suddenly ceased.

Holbrook stopped the song and his horse at the same

instant and his roving glances roved no more, but settled into a fixed stare which drew upon itself his earnest concentration, as if the darkness could better be pierced by an act of will.

"Did I, or didn't I?" he growled, and looked around to see if his eyes would show him other lights. Deciding that they were normal he focussed them again in the direction of the sight which had stopped the song. "Bronch, I shore saw it," he muttered. "It was plain as it was short." He glanced down at the horse, saw its ears thrust rigidly forward and nodded his head emphatically. "An' so did you, or I'm a liar!"

He was no liar, for a second flash appeared, and it acted on him like a spur. The horse obeyed the sudden order and leaped forward, careening on its erratic course as it avoided swiftly appearing obstacles.

"Seems to me like it was further west th' last time," muttered Holbrook. "What th' devil it is, I don't know; but I'm goin' to show th' fambly curiosity. Can't be Kane's coyotes—folks don't usually show lights when they're stealin' cows. An' it's on Charley's section, but we'll have a look anyhow. Cuss th' wind."

The light proved to be of will-o'-the-wisp nature, but he pursued doggedly and after a time he heard sounds which suggested that he was not alone on the range. He drew his six-gun in case his welcome should take that course and swung a little to the left to investigate the sounds.

"Must be Charley," he soliloquized, but raised the Colt to a better position. One would have thought Charley to be no friend of his. The Colt went up a little higher, the horse stopped suddenly and its rider gave the night's hailing signal, so well imitated that it might easily have fooled the little animal to whom Nature had given it. It came back like a double echo and soon Charley bulked out of the dark.

"You follerin' that, too?" he asked, entirely reassured now that his eyes were all right, for he had had the same doubts as his friend.

"Yes; what you reckon it is?"

"Dunno," growled Charley. "Thought mebby it was some fool puncher lightin' a cigarette. It wasn't very bright, an' it didn't last long."

"Reckon you called it," replied Holbrook. "Well, th' only animal that lights them is humans; an' no human workin' for this ranch is lightin' cigarettes at night, *these* nights. Bein' a strange human where strange humans shouldn't ought to be, I'm plumb curious. All of which means I'm goin' to have a closer look."

"I'm with you," said Charley. "We better stick together or we'll mebby get to shootin' each other; an' I'm frank in sayin' I'm shootin' quick tonight, an' by ear. There ain't no honest human ridin' around out here, day *or* night, that don't belong here; an' them that does belong ain't over there, lightin' cigarettes nor nothin' else. That lightnin' bug don't belong, but he may *stay* here. Look! There she is again—*this* side of where I saw it last!"

"Same place," contradicted Holbrook, pushing on.

"Same place yore hat!"

"Bet you five it is."

"Yo're on; make it ten?"

"It is. Shut yore face an' keep goin'. Somethin's happenin' over there."

Minute after minute passed and then they swore in the same breath.

"It's south!" exulted Charley. "You lose."

"He crossed in front of us, cuss him," said Holbrook. As he spoke an answering light flashed where the first ones had been seen and Holbrook grunted with satisfaction. "*You* lose; there's two of 'em. We was bettin' on th' other."

"They're signalin', an' there's mebby more'n two. What's th' difference? Come on, Pete! We'll bust up this little party before it starts. But what are they lightin' lights for if they're rustlin'? An' if they ain't rustlin' what'n blazes *are* they doin'?"

"Head over a little," said his companion, forcing his horse against his friend's. "We'll ride between th' flashes first, an' if there's a herd bein' collected we'll mebby hit it. Don't ask no questions; just shoot an' jump yore cayuse sideways."

South of them another puncher was riding at reckless speed along the chord of a great arc and although his section lay beyond Holbrook's, he was now even with them. When they changed their course they drew closer to him and some minutes later, stopping for a moment's silence so they could listen for sounds of the enemy, they heard his faint, far-off signal and answered it. He announced his arrival with a curse and a question and the answer did not answer much. They went on together, eager and alert.

"Heard you drummin' down th' ridge—you know that rocky ground rolls 'em out," the newcomer explained. "Knowed somethin' was wrong th' way you was poundin', an' follered on a gamble till I saw th' lights. Reckon Walt ain't far behind me. I'm tellin' you so you'll signal before you shoot. He's loose out here somewhere."

When the light came again it was much farther west and the answering flash was north. The three pulled up and looked at each other.

"There ain't no cayuse livin' can cover ground like that second feller," growled Holbrook. "He was plumb south only a few minutes ago, an' *now* will you look where he is!"

"Mebby they're ghostes, Bob," suggested Charley, who harbored a tingling belief in things supernatural.

" 'Ghostes'!" chuckled Holbrook. "Ghosts, you means! Th' same as 'posts'! Th' 'es' is silent, like in 'cows.' I never believed in 'em; but I shore don't claim to know it all. There's plenty of things *I* don't understand—an' this is shore one of 'em. My hair's gettin' stiff!"

"Yo're a couple of old wimmin!" snorted Bob. "There's only one kind of a ghost that'll slow me up—that's th' kind that packs hardware. Seein' as they ain't supposed to tote guns, I'm goin' for that coyote west of here. He don't swap ends so fast. Mebby I can turn him into a *real* ghost. Look out where you shoot. So-long!"

"We'll assay his jumpin' friend," called Charley.

Again the flashes showed, one to the south, the other

to the north, and while the punchers marveled, the third appeared in the southwest.

"One apiece!" shouted Holbrook. "I'll take th' last. Go to em!" and drumming hoofbeats rolled into silence in three directions.

Soon spitting flashes in the north were answered in kind, the reports announcing six-guns in action; in the west a thinner tongue of flame and a different kind of report was answered by rapid bursts of fire and the jarring crashes of a Colt. Far to the south three stabbing flashes went upward, Walt's signal that he was coming. From beyond the U-Bend, far to the east, the triple signal came twice, flat and low. Beyond them a yellow glow sprang from the black void and marked the ranchhouse, where six sleeping men piled from their bunks and, finishing their dressing as they ran, chased the cursing trail-boss to the saddled, waiting horses, their tingling blood in an instant sweeping the cobwebs of sleep from their conjecturing brains. There was a creaking of leather, a soft, musical jingling of metal and a sudden thunderous rolling of hoofbeats as seven bunched horses leaped at breakneck speed into the darkness, the tight-lipped riders eager, grim, and tense.

Through a bushy arroyo leading to Mesquite three Mexicans rode as rapidly as they dared, laughing and carrying on a jerky, exultant conversation. A mile behind them came a fourth, his horse running like a frightened jack rabbit as it avoided the obstructions which seemed to leap at them. A bandage around the rider's head perhaps accounted for his sullenness. The four were racing to get to Red Frank's, and safety. Out on the plain the fifth, and as Fate willed it, the only one of the group openly allied to Kane, lay under his dead horse, his career of thieving and murder at an end. Close to him was a dead Question-Mark horse, and the wounded rider, wounded again by his sudden pitch from the saddle as the horse dropped under him, lay huddled on the ground. Slowly recovering his senses he stirred, groped and sat up, his strained, good arm throbbing as he shakily drew his Colt, reloaded it and fired into the air twice, and then twice more. A burst of firing answered him and he smiled grimly and settled back as the low rumbling grew rapidly louder. It threatened to pass by him, but his single shot caused a quick turn and soon his friends drew up and stopped.

"Who is it?" demanded McCullough, dismounting at his side.

"Holbrook," came the answer, shaky and faint. "They got me twice, an' my cayuse, too. Reckon I busted my leg when he went down—I shore sailed a-plenty afore I lit."

"You got one!" called an exultant voice. A match flared and in a moment the cheerful discoverer called again. "Sanchez, that Greaser monte dealer of Kane's. Plumb through th' mouth an' neck, Pete! I call that *shootin'*, with th' dark an' all—" his voice trailed off in profane envy of the accomplishment.

But Pete, hardy soul that he was, had fainted, a fractured leg, the impact from his flying fall and three bullet holes excuse enough for any man.

The flaring of the match brought a distant report and a bullet whined above the discoverer's head. Someone hurriedly fired into the air and a little later the group heard hoofbeats, which stopped abruptly when still some distance away. A signal reassured the cautious rider and soon Walt joined the group, Bob and Charley coming up later. Two of the men started back to the ranchhouse with Holbrook, the rest of the group riding off to search the plain for the two riders who had not put in an appearance, and to see what devilment they might discover. Both of the missing men were found on the remote part of the western range, one plodding stolidly toward the ranchhouse, his saddle and equipment on his shoulders; the other lay pinned under his dead horse, not much the worse, as it luckily happened, for his experience.

While the outfit concentrated on the western part of the ranch, events of another concentration were working smoothly and swiftly east of the ranchhouse, where mounted men, now free from interference, thanks to their Mexican friends, rode unerringly in the darkness, and drifted cattle into a herd with a certainty and dispatch born of long experience. Steadily the restless nucleus grew in size and numbers, the few riders who held it together chanting in low tones to keep the nervous cattle within bounds. The efficiency of these night raiders merited praise, nefarious as their occupation was, and the director of the harmonious efforts showed an uncanny understanding of the cattle, the men, and the whole affair which belongs to genius. Not a step was taken in uncertainty, not an effort wasted. Speed was obtained which in less experienced hands would have resulted in panic and a stampede. Steadily the circle of riders grew shorter and shorter; steadily, surprisingly, the shadowy herd grew, and as it grew, became more and more compact. Farther down the creek a second and smaller herd was built up at the same time and with nearly the same smoothness, and waited for the larger aggregate to drift down upon it and swallow it up. The augmented trail herd kept going faster and faster, the guarding and directing riders in their allotted places and, crossing the creek, it swung northeast at a steadily increasing pace. The cattle had fed heavily and drunk their fill and to this could be ascribed the evenness of their tempers. Almost without realizing it they passed from the Question-Mark range and streamed across the guarding hills, flowing rapidly along the northern side. Gradually their speed was increased and they accepted it obediently, and with a docility which in itself was a compliment to the brains of the trail-boss. Compacted within the close cordon of the alert riders it maintained a speed on the very edge of panic, but went no further. Shortly before dawn two hard-riding rustlers pounded up from the rear, reported all clear, and fell back again, to renew their watch far back on the trail. For three hours the herd had crossed hard ground and as it passed over a high, dividing ridge and down the eastern slope the trail-boss sighed with relief, for now dawn held no terrors for him. He had passed the eastern horizon of any keen-eyed watchers of the pillaged range. On went cattle and riders, and the paling dawn saw them following the hard bottom of a valley which led to others ahead, and kept them from dangerous sky lines. When the last hard-floored valley lay behind and sloping hollows of sand lay ahead, the trail-boss dropped back, uncorked his canteen of black coffee tempered with brandy, and drank long and deep. It was interpreted by his men to mean that the danger zone had been left in the rear, and they smilingly followed his example, and then leisurely and more critically looked over the herd to see what they had gained. The entire SV trail herd was there, a large number of Question-Mark cattle and a score or more miscellaneous brands, which Ridley from time to time had purchased at bargain prices from needy owners. The trail-boss grinned broadly and waved his hand. It was a raid which would go down in the annals of rustler history and challenge strongly for first honors. At noon the waiting caviya was picked up, and Miguel and his three friends added four more riders to the ranks. He took his place well ahead of the hurrying cattle, and remained there until the first, and seldom visited, water hole was reached, where a short rest was taken. Then he led the way again, abruptly changing the direction of the herd's course and, following depressions in the desert floor, struck for Bitter Spring, which would be reached in the early morning hours. By now the raid was a successful, accomplished fact, according to all experience, and the matter of speed was now decided purely upon the questions of water and food, which, however, did not let it diminish much.

The trail-boss dropped back to his *segundo* and smiled. "Old Twitchell's got somethin' to put up a holler over *now*."

The other grinned expansively. "He'll mebby ante up another reward—he shore is fond of 'em."

Back on the Question-Mark a sleepy rider jogged along the creek, idly looking here and there. Suddenly he stiffened in the saddle, looked searchingly along the banks of the little stream, glanced over a strangely deserted range and ripped out an oath as he wheeled to race back to the ranchhouse. His vociferous arrival caused a flurry, out of which emerged Johnny Nelson, who ran to the corral, caught and saddled his restive black, and scorning such a thing as a signal fire, especially when he feared that he could not start it within the limits of the time specified, raced across the valley, climbed the hills at a more sedate pace, dropped down the farther slopes like a stone, and raced on again for the little camp on Sand Creek.

CHAPTER XVIII

The Trail-Boss Tries His Way

MCCULLOUGH WATCHED the racing horseman for a moment, a gleam of envious appreciation in his eyes at the beautiful action of the black horse, nodded in understanding of the rider's journey and wheeled abruptly to give terse orders.

Charley swung into the saddle and started in a cloud of dust for the Diamond L, to carry important news to Lukins and his outfit; two men sullenly received their orders to stay behind for the protection of the ranch and the care of Pete Holbrook, their feelings in no way relieved by the remark of the trail-boss, prophesying that Kane and his gang would be too busy in town to disturb the serenity of the Question-Mark. The rest of the outfit, procuring certain necessaries for the visit to Kane's headquarters, climbed into their saddles and followed their grim and taciturn leader over the shortest way to town.

Far back on the west end of the northern chain of hills a Mexican collapsed his telescope, hazarded a long-range shot at the hard-riding Charley and, mounting in haste, sped to carry disturbing news to his employer.

The courier looked around as the singing lead raised a puff of dust in front of him, snarled in the direction from whence he thought it had come and, having no time for personal grievances, leaned forward and quirted the horse to greater speed. Whirring across the Diamond L range Charley caused another Mexican, watching from a ridge overlooking the ranch buildings, to run to the waiting horse and mount it, after which he delayed his departure until he saw the Diamond L outfit string out into a race for town, whereupon he set a pace which promised to hold him his generous lead.

In Mesquite a Mexican quirted a lathered horse for a final burst of speed up the quiet street, flung himself through Kane's front door, shouted a warning as he scrambled to his feet and dashed through the partition door to make his report direct to his boss. As he bolted out of sight behind the partition, other men popped from the building like weasel-pursued rabbits from a warren and scurried over the town to spread the alarm to those who were most vitally concerned by it. Two streams forthwith flowed over their trails, the first and larger heading for Kane's; the other, composed entirely of Mexicans, flowed toward Red Frank's, which had been allotted the role of outlying redoubt, to help keep harmless the broken ground between it and Kane's front wall, and was now being put in shape to withstand a siege.

Around Kane's was the noisy activity of a beehive. Hurrying men pulled thick planks from the piles under the floor and hauled them, on the jump, to windows and doors, feeding them into eager hands inside the building. Numbers of empty sacks grew amazingly bulky from the efforts of sand shovelers and were carried, shoulder high, in an unending line into the building. Great shutters were unfastened and swung away from the outer walls, their cobwebbed loopholes soon to play their ordained parts. A feverish squad emptied the stables of horses and food, taking both into the dining-room, and returned, posthaste, to remove doors and certain planks which turned the stables into sieves of small use to an attacking force, even if they were won. That the need for haste was pressing was proved by the sound of a handbell on the roof, where a selected group of riflemen lay behind the double-planked parapet to give warning, and exhibitions of long-range shooting. The shovelers hurled their tools through open windows, the plank carriers shoved the last board into the building and leaped to the shutters, slamming them shut as they hastened along the side of the building, and poured hastily through the front door, which now was protected by a great, outer door of planks, mortised, bolted, and braced in workmanlike manner. From the roof sounded two heavy reports, and grim iron tubes slid into loopholes along the walls. The bartenders carried boxes of ammunition and spare weapons, leaving their offerings below every oblong hole. To threaten Kane was one thing; to carry it to a successful end, another.

Puffs of gray-white smoke broke unexpectedly from points around the building, to thin out as they spread and drifted into oblivion. The cracking of rifles and the echo-awakening, jarring reports of heavy six-guns, were punctuated at intervals by the booming roar of old-time buffalo guns, of caliber prodigious. Punchers, guns in their hands, made the rounds of the town, going from building to building to pick up any of Kane's men who might have loitered, or who planned to hide out and open fire from the rear. Their efforts were not entirely wasted, for although Kane's brood had flocked to its nest, there were certain of the town's inhabitants who were neither flesh nor fish and might become one or the other as expediency urged. These doubtful ones were weeded out, disarmed, and escorted to their horses with stern injunctions as to the speed of their departure and their continued absence. Some of the neutrals, seeing that the mastery of the town at present lay with the ranchmen, trimmed their sails for this wind and numbered themselves with the offense in spirit if not in deeds. Of these human pendulums Quayle had a fair mental list and the owners of certain names were well watched.

The first day passed in perfecting plans, assigning

men to strategic stations, several of these vantage-points remaining tenantless during the daylight hours because of the alertness and straight shooting of the squad on Kane's roof, who speedily made themselves obnoxious to the attackers. The owner of the freight wagon, remembering a smooth-bore iron cannon of more than an inch caliber, a relic of the prairie caravans which had followed the old Santa Fe and other trails a generation past, exulted as he dragged it from its obscurity and spent a busy hour scaling the rust from bore and touchhole. Here was the key to the situation, he boasted, and rammed home a generous charge of rifle powder. To find a suitable missile was another question, but he solved it by falling upon bar-lead with ax and hammer. Wheeled into position, its rusty length protruding beyond the corner of an adobe building, it was sighted by spasmodic glances, an occupation not without danger, for which blame could be given to the argus-eyed riflemen on the roof of the target. Consternation seized the defenders, who had not allowed for artillery, and they awaited its thundering debut with palpitant interest.

The discoverer and groom of the relic was unanimously elected gunner, not a dissenting voice denying his right to the honor, a right which he failed either to mention or press. The powder heaped over the touchhole was jarred off by the impact of a Sharp's bullet and to replace it required a kitchen spoon fastened to a stick, which was an alluring if small target to the anxious aerial riflemen. At last heaped up again, the gunner declined methods in vogue for the firing of such ancient muzzleloaders and used a bundle of kerosene-soaked paper swinging by a wire from the end of the spoon. A few practice swings were held to be fitting preliminaries to an event of such importance, and then the nervous cannoneer, screwing his courage to the sticking-point, swept the blazing mass across the scaly breach and shrunk behind the sheltering corner. He escaped thunderous destruction by an eyelash, for what he afterward found was a third of the doughty weapon whizzed past his corner, taking a large chunk of sun-dried brick with it. From the besiegers arose guffaws; from the defenders, howls of derision; and from the owner of the adobe hut, imprecation and denouncement in fluent Spanish. The wall of his habitation closest to the fieldpiece justified all he said and even all he thought.

"You should ought 'a run it under Kane's before you touched her off," bawled a hilarious voice from cover, "Got another?" he demanded. "Tie it together an' try again."

The cannoneer without a job affected gaiety, drew inspiration from the taunts and hastened home to fashion bombs out of anything he could which would answer his purpose, finally deciding upon a tomato can and baling wire, and soon had a task to occupy the flaming fires of his genius.

Red Frank's, being the weaker of the two defenses and only point-blank range from the old adobe jail whose walls, poor as they were, could be relied upon to stop bullets, formed the favorite point of attack while the offense settled down into better-ordered channels. Idaho and others of his exuberant youth decided that it was their "pudding" and favored it with attentions which were as barren of results as they were full of enthusiasm. Discovering that their bullets passed entirely through the frame second-story and whirred, slobbered, and screamed into the air, they wasted ammunition lavishly, ignorant that for three feet above the second-story floor the walls were reinforced with double planking of hard wood, each layer two inches thick. They might turn the upper two-thirds of walls into a bird cage and do no one any material damage. And so passed the first day, McCullough's efforts unavailing in face of the careless enthusiasm of his men, caused by the novelty of the situation; and not until one man had died and several others received serious wounds did the larking punchers come fully to realize that the game was deadly, and due to become more so.

CHAPTER XIX

A Desert Secret

WHILE MCCULLOUGH argued and swore and waited for sanity to return to his frisking men, three punchers lay on the desert sands north of Sweet Spring, and baked. The telescope occasionally swept the southern horizon and went back between the folds of the blanket, which also hid the guns from the rays of the molten sun. The situation and most of the possible variations had been gone over from every angle and a course of action yet had to be agreed upon. Knowing that a fight in town was imminent, each feared he would miss it and that the reward would be lost to them. From their knowledge of deserts in general they did not wish to assume the labors of driving a herd back across it, even if they were able to capture it; but neither did they wish to let it get entirely away and be lost to McCullough. And so they continued to discuss the problem, jerkily and without enthusiasm, writhing under the sun like frogs on a gridiron. The afternoon dragged into evening and with the coming of twilight came quick relief from the heat, soon to be followed by a cold undreamed of by the inexperienced.

The stars appeared swiftly and blazed with glittering brilliance through the chill air and the three watchers sought their blanket rolls for relief.

Hopalong unrolled from his covering and arose. "Dark enough, now," he said. "I'm goin' down to th' other water hole to wait for 'em. May learn somethin' worth while." He rolled his rifle in the blanket to protect it from sand and stretched gratefully.

"I'm goin' with you," said Johnny, covering his own rifle.

"I reckon I'll have to lay up here an' hold th' sack, like a fool," growled Red, who longed for action, even if it were no more than a tramp through the sand.

"You shore called it, Reddie," chuckled Johnny. "Somebody has got to stay with th' cayuses; an' I don't know anybody as reliable as you. Don't forget, an' build a camp fire while we're gone," and with this parting insult Johnny melted into the darkness after his leader and plodded silently behind him until Hopalong stopped and muttered a command.

"We're not far away now," he said. "Reckon we oughtn't get too close till they come to th' hole an' get settled down. Some of 'em may have to ride far an' wide if th' herd's ornery, an' run onto us. We've got th' trumps, an' they're worth twice as much if they don't know we got 'em. They shoot off their mouths regardless out here."

Johnny grunted his acquiescence and squatted comfortably on his haunches, the tips of the fingers of one hand in the sand. "Never felt more like smokin' than I do now," he chuckled. "Got any chewin'?"

His friend passed over the desired article and Johnny worried off a generous mouthful. "It's got too many stems in it; but bein' th' first chew I've had since I got married I ain't kickin'," he complacently remarked. "Margaret says it sticks to me for hours."

Hopalong grunted. "Gettin' to be real lady-like, ain't you?" he jeered. "Put perfumery on yore shirt bosom?"

"I would if she wanted me to," retorted his companion. "I don't just know what I wouldn't do if *she* wanted me to."

Hopalong snorted. "That so?" he demanded, pugnaciously. "Reckon she might like to know what yo're doin' down here, how much longer you aim to stay, an' if yo're still alive—an' other little foolish things like that. Let me tell you, Kid, you don't know how big a woman fills up yore life till you've lost her."

"I can imagine what it would be without her," said Johnny, slowly and reverently, his heart aching for his friend's loss. "She knows all about it; nearly all, anyhow. I've writ to her every third day, when I could, an' sometimes oftener. She may be worryin', but I'm bettin' every cent I'll ever have that she ain't doin' no cryin'! There ain't many wimmen like her, even in this kind of country."

"Then she's shore got Red an' me figgered for a fine pair of liars," murmured Hopalong; "but just th' same I'm feelin' warmer toward you than I have for a week," he announced. "When did you tell her all about this scrambled mess?"

"When I found that I couldn't tell how much longer I'd have to stay here," confessed Johnny. "I couldn't write letters an' lie good enough to fool her; an' I had to write letters, didn't I?"

"I'll take everythin' back, Kid," said his companion, grinning in the dark.

Johnny grunted and the silence began again, a silence which endured for several hours, such a silence that can exist between two real friends and be full of understanding. It endured between them and was not even broken by the distant, dim flare of a match, nor when low sounds floated up to them and gradually grew into the clicking and rattle of horns against horns, and the low rumble of many hurrying hoofs—hoofs hurrying toward the water which bovine nostrils had long since scented. The rumble grew rapidly as the thirst-tortured herd stampeded for Bitter Spring. A revolver flashed here and there on the edges of the animated avalanche and then a sweet silence came to the desert, soon to be tunefully and pleasantly broken by the soft lowing of cattle leg deep in the saving water.

> *Let th' air blow in up-on m-e-e,*
> *Let me see th' mid-night s-k-y;*
> *Stand back, Sisters, from a-round m-e-e:*
> *God, it i-s s-o-o h-a-r-d to d-i-e.*

wailed a cracked voice, the owner relieving his feelings.

"Thorpe, if you don't wrastle a hot snack damned quick, I'll eat yore ears!"

"Give him anythin' to stop that yowlin'," bellowed another. "Can't he learn nothin' but 'Th' Dyin' Nun'? Thank heaven he never learned no more of it. A sick calf ain't no cheerfuller than him."

"You'll have to eat lively, boys," sang out the trail-boss. "Everythin' is on th' move in an hour. If yo're in such a cussed hurry, Jud, get some wood for him. Take it from that lame pack horse. Reckon we'll have to shoot him if he don't get better in a hurry."

> *Up to my knees in mud I go*
> *An' water to my middle;*
> *Whenever firewood's to be got*
> *I'm Cookie's sec-ond fid-dle,*

chanted Jud, splashing out to where the lame pack horse conducted an experiment in saturation. "Hot, cussed hot," he enlightened the cheerful, but tired group on the bank. "Hot *an'* oozy. Hello, hoss," he greeted, slapping the shrinking shoulder. "You heard what th' boss said about you? Pick up, Ol' Timer; pick up or you'll get shot. What? Don't blame you a bit, not a cussed bit. *I'd* ruther be shot, too, than tote wood over this part of hell. Oh, well; life's plumb funny. You'll fry if you do, an' you'll die if you don't. What's th' difference, anyhow, Ol' Timer?"

"Hey, Jud," called a voice. "Got a new bunkie?"

"I could have worse than a cayuse," replied Jud. "A cussed sight worse."

"There's mocassins, rattlers, copperheads, tarantulas, an' scorpions in that pond!" warned another.

"You done forgot Gila monsters, tigers an'—an'—Injuns," retorted Jud. "Now comes a job. With both arms full of slippin', criss-crossin' firewood, th' rest slidin' from th' pack, I got to hang on to what I got, put th' rest back like it ought to go an' make everythin' tight. Come out here, some damned fool, an' gimme a hand. Better move lively—only got four arms an' six hands. There!" he exploded. "There goes th' shootin'-match off th' hoss. Th' wind'll blow 'em ashore an' we can pick up th' whole caboodle."

"Wind?" jeered the snake-enumerator. "Where's th' wind? Yo're a fool!"

"On th' bank, where yo're settin', you thick-headed ass!" yelled Jud. "You got so cussed much to say, suppose you muddy yore lily-white pants an' do somethin' besides bray!"

"Did you spill any of 'em, Jud?" anxiously asked a voice. "I heard a splash."

Jud's reply was such that the trail-boss snapped a warning which checked some of the conversation, and promised his help. "Wait for me, Jud; I'm comin'," he said.

"Why don't you send that white-washed idol?" asked Jud. "I'll show him who's th' fool; an' what a splash sounds like!"

Hopalong nudged his companion and they crept forward, feeling before them for anything which might make a sound if stepped on. A vibrant *whir* made them spring back and go around the warning snake, and soon they reached the little, sandy ridge which had sheltered Hopalong on his other visit.

"I'm glad you hung on to what you had, Jud," came Thorpe's thankful voice as his match caught the sun-baked wood and sent a tiny flame licking upward among the shavings whittled by his knife. "What you do you allus do right. It's dry as a bone."

"An' so am I," grunted the horse wrangler. "Who's got their canteen?"

"He's askin' for a canteen, with th' whole pond in

front of him!" laughed a squatting rustler. "Here; take mine."

The fire grew quickly and a coffeepot, staunch friend of weary travelers, was placed in the flame, no one caring what it looked like or how hot the handle got. Time passed swiftly in talking of the raid and in consuming the light, hurried meal and soon the wrangler argued to his charges from the bank, and then waded in for his own horse, after which the matter was much simplified. He had them bunched, the next change of horses had been cut out by the men and they were ready to resume the drive when a distant voice hailed them. Soon a lathered horse glistened in the outer circle of light, and the hard-riding courier dashed up to the fire.

"They've hit th' town, boys!" he shouted. "Th' Question-Mark an' th' Diamond L have joined hands agin' us. Their friends in town are backin' 'em. Kane says to drive this herd hell-to-leather to th' valley, leave it there an' burn th' trail back. Where's Hugh Roberts?"

"Here," answered the trail-boss, stepping forward. "Hello, Vic."

"Got strict orders from th' boss," said Vic, leaning over and whispering in the ear of the trail-boss.

Roberts stiffened and swore angrily. "Is *that* all he says for us to do?" he sneered. "I got a notion to tell him to go to hell!"

Eager questions assailed him from the pressing group and he pushed himself free. "He says we are to take Quayle's hotel, their headquarters, from th' rear at dawn of th' day we get back—an' *hold* it! *That's* all!"

An angry chorus greeted the announcement and the shouting courier had a hard time to make himself heard, "That's wins for us!" he yelled. "You get their leaders, you split 'em in two—an' Kane'll turn his boys loose to hit 'em during th' confusion. He's got a wise head, I'm shoutin'. Red Frank's gang smashes from th' west end, an' they'll never know what happened. We'll have 'em split three ways, leaderless, not knowin' what's happened. It'll be a stampede an' a slaughter. Cuss it, *I'll* be with you! That shows what *I* think of it!"

"Throw th' herd back on th' trail," ordered the boss. "We'll drive hard, an' turn th' rest of it over in our minds as we go. So we can have yore valuable assistance yo're goin' with us. Get a fresh cayuse from th' caviya. I say, *yo're goin' with us,* savvy?"

Covered by the noise of the renewed drive Hopalong and Johnny wriggled back until they could with safety arise to their feet, when they hastened back to Red and tersely reported what they had learned. Red's reply was instant.

"One of us has got to learn where that herd is kept; th' others light out for McCullough. Th' herd trailer can go to town when he gets it located. We can't lose them cattle, now."

"Right!" said Hopalong. "I'm puttin' cartridges in my hand. Th' worst guesser goes after th' herd. Odd or even. Red, you first," and he placed his clenched fist in Red's hand.

"Even," said Red, and then he opened the fist, felt of the cylinders and chuckled. There were two.

Hopalong fumbled at his belt and placed his fist in Johnny's hand. "Call it, Kid," he said.

"Even," said Johnny, carelessly. He felt the closed hand slowly open and cast his fingers over its palm, finding two cartridges, and he grunted. "Better take th' extra canteens, Hoppy; an' that spyglass. It'll mebby come in handy. Want Pepper?"

"Just 'cause she's a good cayuse for you don't say that she is for me," chuckled the loser. "She knows you; I'm a stranger," and he led the way to the picketed and hobbled horses. In a few minutes he swung into the saddle, the telescope under his arm, cheerily said his good-byes and melted into the darkness, bound farther into the desert, where or how far he did not know. Passing the southern water hole he drew two cartridges from his belt, placed one in the palm of his right hand and held the other between his fingers. Slowly opening the clenched fist he relaxed the fingers and the second cartridge dropped onto its mate with a little click. There was no need to cough now and hide that slight, metallic noise, so he grinned instead and slowly pushed them back into the vacant loops.

"Fine job, lettin' th' Kid go out on this skillet," he snorted, indignant at the thought. "Me, now—it don't matter a whole lot what happens to me these days; but th' Kid's got a wife, an' a darned fine one, too. Go on, you lazy cow—yore work's just *startin'*."

It was not long before he caught the noise of the hard-driven herd well off to his right and he followed by sound until dawn threatened. Then, slowing his horse, he rode off at an angle and hunted for low places in the desert floor, where he went along a course parallel to that followed by the herd. Persistently keeping from sky lines, although added miles of twisting detours was the price, and keeping so far from his quarry that he barely could pick out the small, dark mass with the aid of the glass, he feared no discovery. So he rode hour after weary hour under the pitiless sun, stopping only once to turn his sombrero into a bucket, from which his horse eagerly drank the contents of one huge canteen, its two gallons of water filling the hat several times.

"Got to go easy with it for awhile, bronch," he told it. "Water can't be so terrible far ahead, judgin' from that herd pushin' boldlike across this strip of hell—but cows can go a long time without it when they has to; an' out here they shore has to. I'm not cheatin' you—there's four for you an' one for me, an' we won't change it."

Mile upon burning mile passed in endless procession as they plodded through hard sand, soft sand, powdery dust, and over stretches of rocky floor blasted smooth and slippery by the cutting sands driven against it by every wind for centuries. An occasional polished boulder loomed up, its coat of "desert-varnish" glistening brown under the pale, molten sun. He knew what the varnish was, how it had been drawn from the rock and the mineral contents left behind on the surface as its moisture evaporated into the air. An occasional "sidewinder," diminutive when compared to the rattlesnakes of other localities, slid curiously across the sand, its beady, glittering eyes cold and vicious as it watched this strange invader of its desert fastness.

Warned at last by the fading light after what had seemed an eternity of glare, he gave the dejected horse another canteen of water and then urged it into a brisker pace, to be within earshot of the fleeing herd when darkness should make safe a nearer approach.

With the coming of twilight came a falling of temperature and when the afterglow bathed the desert with magic light and then faded as swiftly as though a great curtain had been dropped the creeping chill took bold, sudden possession of the desert air to a degree unbelievable. So passed the night, weary hour after cold, weary hour; but the change was priceless to man and beast. The magic metamorphosis emphasized the many-sided nature of the desert, at one time a blazing, glaring thing of sinister aspect and death-dealing heat; at another cold, almost freezing, its considerable altitude being good reason for the night's penetrating chill. The expanse of dim gray carpet, broken by occasional dark blots where the scrawny, scattered vegetation arose from the sands, stretched away into the veiling dark, allowing keen eyes to distinguish objects at surprising distances. Overhead blazed the brilliant stars, blazed as only stars in desert heavens can, seeming magnified and brought nearer by the dry, clear air. His eyes at last free from the blinding glare of quivering air and glittering crystals of salts in the sand; his dry, parched, burning skin free from the baking heat, which sucked moisture from the pores before perspiration could form on the surface; he sucked in great gulps of the vitalizing, cold air and found the night so refreshing, so restful as to almost compensate for the loss of sleep.

The increased pace of his mount at last brought reward, for there now came from ahead and from the right the low, confused noise of hurrying cattle, as continuous, unobtrusive, and restful as the soft roar of a distant surf. So passed the dark hours, and then a warning, silver glow on the eastern horizon caused him to pull up and find a sandy depression, there to wait until the proper distance was put behind it by the thirsty herd, still reeling off the miles as though it were immune to fatigue. The silver band widened swiftly, changed to warmer tints, became suffused with crimson and cast long, thin, vague, warning shadows from sage bush and greasewood—and then a molten, quivering orb pushed up over the prostrate horizon and bathed the shrinking sands with its light.

The cold, heavy-lidded rider glowered at it and removed the blanket which had been wrapped around him, rolling it tightly with stiff fingers and fumblingly made it secure in the straps behind the cantle of his saddle.

"There it is again, bronch," he growled. "We'll soon wonder if th' cold was all a dream."

He stood up in the stirrups and peered cautiously over the bank of the depression, making out the herd with unaided eyes.

"They can't go on another day," he muttered. "This ain't just dry trail—it's a chunk out of hell. They can't stand much more of it without goin' blind, an' that's th' beginnin' of th' end on a place like this. I'm bettin' they get to water by noon—an' then *we* got to wait till th' coast is clear." He shook the canteen he had allotted himself and growled again. "About a quart, an' I could drink a gallon! All right, bronch; get a-goin'," and on they plodded, keeping to the hollows and again avoiding all elevations, to face the torments of another murderous day. Again the accursed hours dragged, again the horse had a canteen of water, a sop which hardly dulled the edge of its raging thirst. Earth, air, and sky quivered, writhed and danced under the jelly-like sun and the few, soft night noises of the desert were heard no more. The leveled telescope kept the herd in sight as mile followed mile across the scorched and scorching sand.

The sun had passed the meridian only half an hour when the sweeping spyglass revealed no herd, but only a distant ridge of rock, like a tiny island on a stilled sea.

"It shore is time," muttered the rider, dismounting. "Seein' as how we're nearly there, I reckon you can have th' last canteen. You shore deserve it, you game old plodder. An' I'm shore glad them rustlin' snakes have their orders to get back *pronto*; but it would just be our luck if that bull-headed trail-boss held a powwow in that valley of theirs. His name's Roberts, bronch; Hugh Roberts, it is. We'll remember his name an' face if he makes us stay out here till night. You an' me have got to get to that water before another sunrise if all th' thieves in th' country are campin' on it—we *got* to, that's all."

An hour passed and then the busy telescope showed a diminutive something moving out past the far end of the distant ridge. Despite the dancing of the heat-distorted image on the object-glass the grim watcher knew it for what it was. Another and another followed it and soon the moving spots strung out against the horizon like a crawling line of grotesque, fantastic insects, silhouetted against the sky.

"There they go back to Mesquite to capture Quayle's hotel an' win th' fight," sneered Hopalong. "I could tell 'em somethin' that would send them th' other way—but we'll let 'em ride with Fate; an' get to that water as quick as yore weary legs can take us. Th' herd is there, bronch; all alone, waitin' for us. It's our herd now, if we want it, which we don't. Huh! Mebby they left a guard! All right, then; he's got a big job on his hands. Come on; get a-goin'!"

Swinging more and more to the south he soon forsook the windings of the hollows and struck boldly for the eastern end of the valley, and when he reached it he hobbled and picketed the horse, frantic with the heavy scent of water in its crimson, flaring nostrils, and went ahead on foot, the hot Sharp's in his hands full cocked and poised for instant action. Crawling to the edge of the valley he inched forward on his stomach and peered over the rim. An exclamation of surprise and incredulity died in his throat as the valley lay under his eyes, for it was the valley he had seen in the mirage only a few days before.

The stolen herd filled the small creek, standing like statues, soaking in the life-giving fluid and nosing it gently. One or two, moving restlessly, blundered against those nearest them and the watcher knew that they had gone blind. The sharpest scrutiny failed to discover any guard, and he knew that his uncertain count of the kaleidoscopic riders had been correct. Hastening back to the restless horse he soon found that it had in reserve a strength which sent it flashing to the trail's edge and down the dangerous ledge at reckless speed. At last in the creek it, too, stood as though dazed and nosed the water a little before drinking.

Hopalong swung into the stream, removed saddle and bridle and then splashed across to the hut, dumping his load, canteens, and all against the front wall. To make assurance doubly sure he scouted hurriedly down one side of the little valley, crossed the creek and went back along the other wall.

Thorpe's carefully stacked firewood provided fuel for a cunningly built-up fire; one of Thorpe's discarded tomato cans, washed and filled in the spring near the hut's walls sizzled and sputtered in the blazing fire and soon boiled madly. Picking it out of the blaze with the aid of two longer sticks the hungry cook set it to one side, threw in a double handful of Thorpe's coffee, covered it with another washed can and then placed Thorpe's extra frying pan on the coals, filling it with some of Thorpe's bacon. A large can of Thorpe's beans landed close to the fire and rolled a few feet, and the cheerful explorer emerged from the hut with a sack of sour-dough biscuits which the careless Thorpe had forgotten.

"Bless Thorpe," chuckled Hopalong. "I'll never make him climb no more walls. I wouldn't 'a' made him climb that one, mebby, if I'd knowed about this."

Looking around as a matter of caution, his glance embracing the stolid herd and his own horse grazing with the jaded animals left behind by the rustlers, he fell to work turning the bacon and soon feasted until he could eat no more. Rolling a cigarette he inhaled a few puffs and then, picking up telescope and rifle, he grunted his lazy way up the steep trail and mounted the ridge, sweeping the western horizon first with the glass and then completed the circle. Satisfied and drowsy he returned to the valley, spread his folded blanket behind the hut, placed the saddle on one end of it for a pillow and lay down to fall asleep in an instant.

When he awakened he stretched out the kinks and looked around in the dim light. He felt unaccountably cold and he looked at the blanket which he had pulled over him some time during his sleep, wondering why he had felt the need for it during the daylight hours in such a place as this.

"Well, I'll cook me some more bacon before it gets dark, an' then set up with a nice little fire, with a 'dobe wall at my back. It'll be a treat just to set an' smoke an' plan, th' night chill licked by th' fire an' my happy stomach full of bacon, beans, an' biscuits—an' coffee, cans an' cans of coffee."

It suddenly came to him that the light was growing stronger instead of weaker, that it was not the afterglow, and that the chill was dying instead of increasing. Shocked by a sudden suspicion he glanced into the eastern sky and stared stupidly, surprised that he had not noticed it before.

"I was so dumb with sleep that I didn't savvy east from west," he muttered. "It's daylight, 'stead of evenin'—I've slept all afternoon an' night! Well, I don't see how that changes th' eatin' part, anyhow. No wonder I pulled th' blanket over me, an' no wonder I was stiff."

With the coming of the sun a disagreeable journey loomed nearer and nearer but, as he told the horse when cinching the saddle on its back, the return trip would not be one of uncertainty; nor would they be held down to such a slow pace by any clumsy herd. A further thought hastened his movements: there was a big fight going on in Mesquite, and his two friends were in it without him. Looking around he saw that he had cleaned up and effaced all signs of his visit and, filling the canteens and fastening them into place, he mounted and rode up the steep slope, turned his back to the threatening sun and loped westward along a plain and straight trail, a grim smile on his face.

CHAPTER XX

The Redoubt Falls

AFTER HOPALONG had ridden off on his desert trailing, Johnny and Red rode to the Question-Mark, reaching it a little after daylight and were promptly challenged when near the smaller corral. The sharp voice changed to a friendly tone when the sentry had a better look at the pair.

"Thought you'd be up with th' circus," said the Question-Mark puncher.

"On our way now," replied Johnny. "Come down here to learn what was happenin'. Meet Red Connors, an old friend of Waffles."

"Howdy," grunted the puncher, looking at Red with a keener interest. "You fellers are lucky—*we* got to stay here an' miss it all. Walt come down last night an' said Kane's goin' to be a hard nut to crack. He's fixed up like a fort."

"Reckon we'll take a look at it," said Johnny, wheeling.

"Hey! If you want to find Mac, he's hangin' out at Quayle's."

Johnny waved his thanks and rode on with his cheerful companion. In due time they heard the distant firing and not much later rode up to Quayle's back door and went in. McCullough was raging at the effectiveness of the sharpshooters on Kane's roof who had succeeded in keeping the fight at long range and who dominated certain strategic positions which the trail-boss earnestly desired to make use of; all of which made him irritable and unusually gruff.

"Where *you* been?" he demanded as Johnny entered.

"Locatin' a missin' herd of yore cattle," retorted Johnny, nettled by the tone. "They're waitin' for you when you get time to go after 'em. Now we'll locate them sharpshooters. Anythin' else you can't do, let us know. Come on, Red," and he went out again, his grinning friend at his heels. At the door Red checked him.

"Looks like a long-range job, Kid. My gun's all right for closer work, but I ought to have a Sharp's for this game."

Johnny wheeled and went back. "Gimme a Sharp's," he demanded.

"Take Wilson's—they got him yesterday," growled the trail-boss, pointing.

Johnny took the gun and the cartridge belt hanging on it, joined Red and led the way to a place he had in mind. Reaching the selected spot, an adobe hut on the remote outskirts of the sprawled town, he stopped. "This is good enough for me," he grunted, "except th' range is too cussed long. Well, we'll try it from here, anyhow."

"I'm goin' to th' next shack," replied Red, moving on. "We'll use our old follow-shootin'—an' make 'em sick. Ready? I'm goin' to cross th' open." At his friend's affirmative grunt Red leaned over and dashed for the other adobe. A bullet whined in front of him, barely heard above the roar of Johnny's rifle. He settled down, adjusted the sights and proceeded to prove title to his widely known reputation on other ranges of being the best rifle-shot of many square miles. "Make a hit, Kid?" he called. "It's mebby further than you figger."

"It is," answered Johnny. "Like old times, huh? Lord help 'em when you get started! Are you all set? I'm ready to draw 'em."

"Wind gentle, from th' east," mumbled Red. "Dirty

gun—got to shoot higher. All right," he called, nestling the heavy stock.

Johnny pushed his rifle around the corner of the building, aimed quickly and fired. A hatted head arose above Kane's roof and a puff of smoke spurted into the air above it as Red's Sharp's roared. The hat flew backward and the head ducked down again, its owner surprised by the luck of the shot.

Johnny laughed outright. "For a trial shot I'm admittin' that was a whizzer. I ain't no slouch with a Sharp's—but how th' devil you can make one behave like *you* do is a puzzle to me."

"I'm still starin'," said a humorous, envious voice behind them and they looked around to see Waffles hugging the end of the building. "If I can get over on Red's right I'll help make targets for him."

"Walk right over to that other shack," called Johnny. "Yo're safe as if you was home in yore bunk. Cover him, Red."

Waffles' mind flashed back into the past and what it presented to him greatly reassured him, but to walk was tempting Providence; he ran across the open and again Red's rifle roared.

"Got him!" yelled Johnny, staring at the body lying over the distant parapet. It was swiftly pulled back out of sight. The rest of Johnny's words were profanely eulogistic.

"Shut yore face," growled Red. "It was plumb luck."

"*Shore* it was," laughed his friend in joyous irony; "but yo're allus makin' 'em. That's what counts."

Waffles, having gained the shelter he coveted, looked around. "Heads was plentiful up there yesterday. There was allus one or two bobbin' up. I'm bettin' they'll be scarcer today."

"They'll be scarcer tomorrow, when we are behind them other shacks," replied Red. "They're easy three hundred paces nearer, an' that's a lot sometimes."

"An' twice as much to them," rejoined Johnny. "Th' nearer you get th' more you make it even terms. You stay where you are—me an' Waffles'll go out there tonight."

When the afternoon dragged to an end Red had another sharpshooter to his credit, and the dominating group on the roof were much less dominant. They cursed the long-range genius who shot hats off of heads, clipped ears, and had killed two men. The shooting, with a rest and plenty of time to aim, would have been creditable enough; but to hit a bobbing head meant quick handling. They were properly indignant, for it was a toss-up with Death to show enough of their heads to sight a slanting rifle. One of their number, whose mangled ear was bound up with a generous amount of bandage, savagely hammered the chisel with which he was cutting a loophole through four inches of seasoned wood, vowing vengeance on the man who had ruined his looks.

The light failing for close shooting, the three friends left their positions and went to the hotel for a late supper, Red receiving envious, grinning looks as he entered the dining-room. Idaho promptly forsook his bosom friends and went over to finish his meal at the table of the newcomers.

"We got Red Frank's place plumb full of holes—you can see daylight through th' second floor," he announced; "but it don't seem to do no good. If I could get close enough to use a bomb I got, we might clean 'em up."

"Crawl up in th' dark," suggested Waffles.

"Can't; they spread flour all around th' place, an' th' minute a man crosses it he shows up plain. Two of us found out *all* about *that*!"

"Go through or over th' buildin's this side of th' place," said Johnny, visualizing the street. "They lead up close to Red Frank's."

Idaho stared, and slapped his thigh in enthusiastic endorsement. "I reckon you called it!" he gloated. "Wait till I tell th' boys," and he hastened back to his friends. Judging from the sudden noise coming from the table, his friends were of the same opinion and, bolting the rest of the meal, they hastened away to forthwith try the plan.

McCullough entered the dining-room and strode straight to Johnny. "Did I hear you say you know where my cattle are?" he asked, sitting down.

Johnny nodded, chewed hurriedly and replied. "I didn't finish it. *I* don't know where they are, but Hopalong is trailin' 'em, an' *he*'ll know when he comes back. Pay us them rewards now, instead of later, an' I'll do some high an' mighty guessin' about yore head—an' bet you th' rewards that I guess right."

The trail-boss laughed. "You've shore got plenty of nerve," he retorted. "When this fight is over there won't be no rewards paid. We got th' whole gang in them two buildin's, an' we got 'em good. You've had yore trouble for nothin', Nelson."

"How 'bout th' gang that are with th' herd?" asked Johnny, a note of anger edging his words.

McCullough shrugged his shoulders. "I ain't worryin' about them—they'll never come back to Mesquite."

"That so?" queried Johnny, sarcastically. "I ought to keep my mouth shut, th' way yo're talkin', but I hate to see good men killed. I'll bet you they'll come back just at dawn, some time in th' next five days. An' I'll bet you they'll sneak up on this hotel an' raise th' devil, while Kane starts a bunch from his place and Red Frank's, to help 'em. Th' minute they start shootin' in here their friends'll sortie out an' carry th' fight to you. Want to bet on it?"

McCullough regarded the speaker through narrowed lids. "How do you figger that?" he demanded suspiciously. "You gettin' that out of your medicine bag, too?" and then he eagerly drank in every word of the explanation. After a moment's thought he looked around the room and then back to the smiling Johnny. "Much obliged, Nelson. I'm beginnin' to see that I owe you fellers somethin', after all. If them fellers we want were loose an' you got 'em, then of course th' reward would stand; but you can't win it very well when we've got 'em corraled. Who-all is in that bunch with th' herd?"

Johnny smiled but shook his head.

"Didn't you say you knowed who killed Ridley?" persisted the trail-boss.

"I know him, an' how he did it. Hopalong saw him while his gun was smokin', but didn't know what he had shot at till later."

"Why didn't you tell me, an' earn that reward right away?"

"That's only half of th' rewards," replied Johnny. "There's money up for th' fellers that robbed th' bank. If we got Ridley's murderer th' others might 'a' smelled out what we was after. You see, I was robbed of more than eleven hundred dollars th' first night I was in town. Th' money belonged to th' ranch. Th' only chance I had of gettin' it back was to make th' rewards big enough to stand three splits that would be large enough to cover it. An' I'm still goin' to do that, Mac. Pay it now an' we'll stick with you till you get th' men an' yore herd. Of course, yo're going to get th' herd, anyhow, as far as we are concerned. I ain't holdin' that over yore head; I'm only tryin' to show you why I can't be open an' free with you."

"I couldn't pay th' rewards now even if I wanted to," said the trail-boss.

"I know that, an' I didn't think you would. I was only showin' you how things are with us."

McCullough nodded, placed a hand on the speaker's shoulder and arose, turning to Red. "Connors," he said, "yo're a howlin' wonder with a Sharp's. Much obliged for holdin' down that roof. If you can clean 'em up there this fight'll go on a cussed sight faster. Th' cover on th' north side of Kane's is so poor that we can't do much out there, but we can do a little better when them sharpshooters are driven down. From what I know of you two, yore friend Cassidy is shore able to trail that herd. I've quit worryin' about everythin' but th' fight here in town. An' lemme make a long speech a little longer: if you fellers can earn them rewards I won't waste no time in payin' up; but there ain't a chance for you. We got 'em under our guns."

"Who was right about where that raid on you was

goin' to take place?" asked Johnny. "You was purty shore about that, too, wasn't you?"

The trail-boss smiled and shook his head. "Yo're a good guesser," he admitted, and went out to consult with Lukins.

The next day found the line a little tighter around the stronghold, thanks to Red's shooting, which increased in accuracy after he had decided to use closer cover and cut three hundred paces out of the range. Better positions had been gained by the attackers during the night, some of the more daring men now being not far from pointblank range, which enabled them to make the use of Kane's loopholes hazardous. To the north another rifleman lay in a hollow of the sandy plain, but too far away to do much damage. The north parapet of the building was hidden from Red by the one on the south and the aerial marksmen made free use of it.

Red Frank's place was in jeopardy, for Idaho and his enthusiastic companions were in the building next on the south, separated from the Mexican's house by less than twenty feet. There was an open window facing the gambling-house and Idaho, chancing quick glances through it, noticed that one of the heavy, board shutters of a window of the upper floor sagged out a little from the top. Signaling the men behind the jail to increase their fire, he coiled his rope and cast it through the window. It struck the upper edge of the shutter, dropped behind it and grew swiftly taut. Two of his companions added their strength to his, while the other two covered them by pouring a heavy revolver fire at the two threatening loopholes. The shutter creaked, twisted, and then slowly gave way, finally breaking the lower hinge and sailing over against the other house to a cheer from the jail. Heavy firing came through the uncovered window, the bullets passing through the opposing wall and driving the Diamond L men to other shelter. Here they waited until it died down and then, picking up the bomb made by the owner of the new freight wagon, Idaho lit the jumpy, uncertain fuse, waited as long as he dared and hurled it across the intervening space and through the shutterless window as the opening was being boarded up. There was a roar, jets of smoke spurt from windows and holes and the wild cursing of injured men rang out loudly. A tongue of flame leaped through a trapdoor on the roof and grew rapidly brighter. At intervals the smoke pouring up became suddenly heavy and thick, but cleared quickly between the onslaughts of the water buckets. Fire now crept through the side of the frame structure and mounted rapidly, and such a hail of lead poured through the smoke-spurting, upper loopholes that it became impossible for the buckets to be properly used. It was only a matter of time before the blazing roof and floor would fall on the defenders in the adobe-walled structure below, and through a loophole Red Frank suddenly shoved out a soiled towel fastened on the end of a rifle barrel.

"Come ahead, with yore hands up!" shouted a stentorian voice from the jail. "Quit firin', boys; they're surrenderin'." Almost on the tail of his words a hurrying line of choking Mexicans, bearing their wounded, streamed from the front door. They were promptly and proudly escorted by the hilarious attackers to safe quarters on the southern outskirts of the town.

CHAPTER XXI

All Wrapped Up

MCCULLOUGH AND Lukins drew men from the cordon around the gambling-hall until the line was thinned and stretched as much as prudence allowed, covering only the more strategic positions, while the men taken from it were placed in an ambuscade at the rear of Quayle's hotel. Both leaders would have preferred to have placed their reception committee nearer the outskirts of the rambling town but, not knowing from which direction the attack would come and not being able to spare men enough for outposts around the town, they were forced to concentrate at the object of the attack. When night fell and darkness hid the movement they set the trap, gave strict orders for no one to approach the rear of the hotel during the dark hours, and waited expectantly.

The first night passed in quiet and the following day found the cordon reenforced until it contained its original numbers. By nightfall of the second day Red, Johnny, and Waffles had cleared the parapet and made it useless during daylight, and as the moon increased in size and brightness the parapet steadily became a more perilous position at night for the defenders. All three marks-

men, now ensconced within three hundred yards of the
gambling-house and out of the line of sight of every
lower loophole, had the range worked out to a foot. Red
and Waffles had discarded their borrowed Sharp's and
were now using their own familiar Winchesters, and it
was certain death to any man who tried to shoot from
Kane's roof on any side but the north one.

Evening came and with it came a hair-brained attempt by Idaho and his irrepressibles to capture and use
the stables. Despite McCullough's orders to the contrary
the group of youngsters, elated by their success against
Red Frank's, made the attempt as soon as darkness fell;
and learned with cost that the stables were stacked
decks. One man was killed and all the others wounded,
most of them so badly as to remove them from the role
of combatants; but one dogged, persistent, and vindictive unit of the foolish attack managed to set fire to the
sun-dried structures before crawling away.

The baked wood burned like tinder and became a
mass of flames almost in an instant, and for a few minutes it looked as though they would take the gambling-
hall with them. It was a narrow squeak and missed only
because of a slight shift of the wind. The scattered line
of punchers to the north of the building, not expecting
the sudden conflagration, had crawled nearer to the
gambling-hall in the encroaching darkness, only to find
themselves suddenly revealed to their enemies by the
towering sheets of flame. They got off with minor in-
juries only because the north side of the building was
not well manned and because the stables were holding
the attention of most of the besieged. When the flames
died down almost as swiftly as they had grown, the
smouldering ashes gave a longer and less obstructed
view to the guards of Kane's east wall and rendered useless certain positions cherished by McCullough.

The trail-boss, seething with anger, stamped up to
Lukins and roared his demands, with the result that
Idaho and the less injured of his companions were sent
to take the places of cooler heads in the ambush party

and were ordered to stay in Quayle's stable until after the expected attack.

In Quayle's kitchen four men waited through the dragging hours, breaking the silence by occasional whispers as they watched the faintly lighted open spaces and the walls of certain buildings newly powdered with flour so as to serve as backgrounds and to silhouette any man passing in front of them. Only the north walls had been dusted and there was nothing to reveal their freshly acquired whiteness to unsuspecting strangers coming up from the south. In the stable Idaho and his restless friends grumbled in low tones and cursed their inactivity. Three men at the darkened office windows, and two more on the floor above watched silently. Outside an occasional shot called forth distant comment, and laughter arose here and there along the alert line.

On the east end of the line a Diamond L puncher, stretched out on his stomach in a little depression he had scooped in the sand during the darker hours of the second night, stuck the end of his little finger in a bullet hole in his canteen and rimmed the hole abstractedly, the water soaking his clothes and making him squirm.

"Cuss his hide," he growled. "Now I got to stay thirsty." He slid a hand down his body and lifted the clinging clothing from the small of his back. "If it was only as cold as that when I *drink* it, I wouldn't grumble. An' I wasn't thirsty till he spilled it," he added in petulant afterthought.

To his right two friends crouched behind the aged ruins of an adobe house, paired off because one of them shot left-handed, which fitted each to his own corner. "Got any chewin'?" asked Righthand. "Chuck it over. Seems to me that they—" he set his teeth into the tobacco, tore off a generous quantity and tossed the plug back to its owner—"ain't answerin' as strong as they was this afternoon."

"No?" grunted Lefthand, brushing sand from the plug. He shoved it back into a pocket and reflected a moment. "It was good shootin' while th' stable burned." Another pause, and then: "Did you hear Billy yell when them fools started th' fire?"

Righthand laughed, stiffened, fired, and pumped the lever of the gun. "I'm gettin' so I can put every one through that loophole. Hear him squawk?" He dropped to his knees to rest his back, and chuckled. "Shore did. Billy, he was boastin' how near he could crawl to them stables. I reckon he done crawled *too* close. Lukins ought to send them kids home."

In a sloping, shallow arroyo to their right Walt and Bob of the Question-Mark lay side by side. Behind them two shots roared in quick succession. Walt lazily turned his head from the direction of the sounds and peeped over the edge of the bank.

"I reckon some coyote took a look over th' edge of th' roof," he remarked.

"Uh-huh," replied Bob without interest and without relaxing his vigil.

"I don't lay out here one little minute after Connors leaves that 'dobe," said Walt. He spat noisily and turned the cud. "I'm sayin' shootin' like his is a gift. I'm some shot, myself, but hell—"

"You'd shore 'a' thought so," replied Bob, grinning as he reviewed something, "if you'd seen that sharpshooter flop over th' edge of th' roof th' other day. I'd guess it was close to fifteen hundred." He changed his position, grunted in complacent satisfaction and continued. "Some folks can't *see* a man's forehead at that distance, let alone *hit* it. Of course, th' sky was behind it."

"Which made it plainer, but harder to figger right," observed Walt. "Waffles says Connors can drive a dime into a plank with th' first, an' push it through with th' second, as far away as he can see th' dime. When it's too far away to be seen, he puts it in th' middle of a black circle, an' aims for th' middle of th' circle. But I put plenty of salt on th' tails of *his* stories."

"Which holds 'em down," grunted Bob. "Who's that over there, movin' around that shack?"

Walt looked and cogitated. "Charley was there when I came out," he answered. "Cussed fool—showin' hisself like that." He swore at a thin pencil of flame which stabbed out from a loophole, and fired. "Told you so!" he growled. "Charley is down!"

Both fired at the loophole and hazarded a quick look at the foolish unfortunate, who had dragged himself behind a hummock of sand. Rapid firing broke out behind them and, sensing what it meant, they joined in. A crouched figure darted from a building, sprinted to the hummock, swung the wounded man on its back, and staggered and zigzagged to cover.

"That was Waffles," said Walt, reloading the magazine of his rifle. "It's a cussed shame to make a man take chances like that by bein' a fool."

Behind the building Waffles lowered his burden to the ground, ripped off the wet shirt and became busy. He fastened the end of the bandage and stood up. "Fools *are* lucky sometimes," he growled; "an' I says you are lucky to only have a smashed collar bone. You try a fool trick like that again an' I'll bust yore head. Ain't you got no sense?"

"Don't *you* go to put on no airs, Waffles," said Red Connors. "I can tell a few things on *you*. I *know* you."

Johnny chuckled. "Tread easy," he warned. "We *both* know you."

"Go to hell!" grunted the ex-foreman of the O-Bar-O, grinning. "Fine pair of sage-hens *you* are to tell tales on me! I got you throwed and hog-tied before you even start." He wheeled at a noise behind him, and glared at the wounded man. "Where'n hell are *you* goin'?" he demanded, truculently.

"Without admittin' yore right to ask fool questions," groaned Charley, still moving, "I'll say I'm goin' to join th' ambush party at Quayle's, an' relieve somebody else." He gritted his teeth and stood erect. "I can use a Colt, can't I?" he demanded.

"Yo're so shaky you can't hit a house," retorted Waffles.

"Which I ain't aimin' to do," rejoined the white-faced man. "You'll show more sense if you'll tie my left arm like it ought to be, instead of standin' with yore mouth open. You'll shore catch a cold if you don't shut it purty soon."

"You stubborn fool!" growled Waffles, but he fixed the arm to its owner's satisfaction.

"If he gets smart, Charley," suggested Johnny, "pull his nose. He allus *was* an old woman, anyhow."

With the coming of midnight the cordon became doubled in numbers as growling men rubbed the sleep from their eyes and took up positions for the meeting of Kane's sortie in case the hotel was attacked by his expected drive outfit.

The hours dragged on, the silence of the night infrequently broken by bits of querulous cursing by some wounded puncher, an occasional taunt from besieger or besieged and sporadic bursts of firing which served more for notifications of defiance and watchfulness than for any grimmer purpose. Patches of clouds now and then drifted before the moon and sailed slowly on. Nature's denizens of the dark were in active swing and filled the night with their soft orchestration. The besiegers, paired for night work, which let one man doze while his companion watched, hummed, grumbled, or snored; in the gambling-hall fortress weary men slept beside the loopholes, the disheartened for a few hours relieved of their fears or carrying them across the borderland of sleep to make their slumbers restless and broken, while scowling, disheartened sentries kept a keener watch, alert for the rush hourly expected.

South of town a group of horsemen pulled up, dismounted, tied their mounts to convenient brush and slipped like shadows toward the nearest house, approaching it round-about and with animal wariness. From house to house, corral to corral, cover to cover they crept, spread out in a fan-shaped line, silent, grim, vindictive and desperate. Not a shadow passed unsearched and unused, not a boulder or thicket was above suspicion nor below being utilized. Nearer and nearer they worked their way, eyes straining, ears, tuned for every sound, high-strung with nerves quivering, keyed to swift reflex and instant decision. The scattered, infrequent firing grew steadily nearer, every flat report was searched for secret meanings and the sharp squeak of a gyrating bat overhead sent every man flat to the earth. The last in the group became cannily slower as opportunity offered and soon managed to be so far behind that his quick, furtive desertion was unnoticed in the tenseness of conjecture as to what lay immediately ahead.

Kane's trail-boss slanted his watch under the moon's rays and gave a low, natural signal, whereupon to right and left a man detached himself and left the waiting group. Minutes passed, their passing marked on nervous foreheads by the thin trickle of cold sweat. Any instant might a challenge, a shot, a volley ring out on any side; hostile eyes might be watching every movement, hostile guns waiting for the right moment, like ravenous hounds in leash. The scouts returned as silently as they had departed and breathed their reassuring words in Roberts' ear. The town lay unsuspecting, every waking eye bent on the bulking gambling-hall. Not a hidden outpost, not a pacing sentry to watch the harmless rear. To the right showed the roof of a two-story building, bulking above the low, thick roofs of scattered, helter-skelter adobes, in any one of which Death might be poised.

Again the slow advance, and breathed maledictions on the head of any unfortunate who trod carelessly or let his swinging six-gun click against buckle or button. Roberts, peering around the end of an adobe wall, held his elbows from his sides, and progress ceased while a softly whistling figure strode across the street and became lost to sight. This was the jumping-off place, the edge of a black precipice of fate, unknown as to depth or what lay below. The savage, thankful elation which had possessed every man at his success in making this border line of life and death faded swiftly as his mind projected itself into the unknown on the other side of the house. Roberts knew what might follow if hesitation were allowed here, and that the conjecturing minds might have scant time to waver he nerved himself and snapped his fingers, leaping around the corner for

Quayle's kitchen door, his men piling after him, still silent and much more tense, yet tortured to shout and to shoot. Ten steps more and the goal would have been reached, but even as the leaping group exulted there came a shredded sheet of flame and the deafening crash of spurting six-guns worked at top speed at point-blank range. The charging line crumpled in mid-stride, plunged headlong to the silvered sands and rolled or flopped or lay instantly still. At the head of his men the rustler trail-boss offered a target beyond the waiting punchers' fondest hopes, yet he bounded on unscathed, flashed around the hotel corner, turned again, doubling back behind the smoke-filled stable and scurried like a panic-stricken rabbit for the brush-filled arroyo, while hot and savage hunters searched the street for him until a hail of lead from Kane's drove them to any shelter which might serve.

When the sheltering arroyo led him from his chosen course Roberts forsook it and ran with undiminished speed toward where the horses waited. At last he reached them and as he stretched out his arm his last measure of energy left him and he plunged forward, rolling across the sand. But a will like his was not to be baffled and in a few moments he stirred, crawled forward, clawed himself into a saddle, jerked loose the restraining rope and rode for safety, hunched over and but half conscious. Gradually his pounding heart caught up with the demand, his burning lungs and spasmodic breathing became more normal, his head steadied and became a little clearer and he looked around to find out just where he was. When sure of his location he turned the horse's head toward Bitter Spring, and beyond it, to follow the tracks he knew were still there to the only safe place left for him in all the country.

He seemed to have been riding for days when he caught sight of something moving over a ridge far ahead of him and he closed his eyes in hope that the momentary rest would clear his vision. After awhile he saw it push up over another low ridge and he knew it to be a horseman riding in the same direction as himself. Again he closed his eyes and unmercifully quirted the tired and unwilling horse into a pace it could not hold for long. Another look ahead showed him that the horseman was a Mexican, which meant that he was hardly a foe even if not a friend. And he sneered as he thought how little it mattered whether the Mexican was an enemy or not, for one enemy ahead and a Greaser at that was greatly to be preferred to those who might be following him. Soon he frowned in slowly dawning recognition. It was Miguel and he had obtained quite a start. Conjecturing about how he had managed to be so far in the lead stirred up again the vague suspicions which had been intruding themselves upon him while he had been unable to think clearly; but he was thinking clearly now, he told himself, and his eyes glinted the sudden anger.

He thought he now knew why the town had been entered so easily, why they had been allowed to penetrate unopposed to its center. It was plain enough why they had been permitted to get within a few feet of Quayle's back door, and then be stopped with a volley at a murderously short range. As he reviewed it he almost was stunned by the thought of his own escape and he tried to puzzle it out. It might be that every waiting puncher thought that others were covering him—and in this he was right. The compact group behind him had drawn every eye. It had been one of those freakish tricks of fate which might not occur again in a hundred fights; and it turned cold, practical Hugh Roberts into a slave of superstition.

On the way to town he had sneered when Miguel had pointed out a chaparral cock which raced with them for several miles and claimed that it was an omen of good luck; but from this time on no "roadrunner" ever would hear the angry whine of his bullets. Thinking of Miguel brought him back to his suspicions and he looked at the distant rider with an expression on his face which would have caused chills to race up and down the Mexican's back, could he have seen them. Miguel, unhurt, riding leisurely back to the herd, with a head-start great enough to be in itself incriminating. And then the Mexican turned in his saddle and looked back, and Roberts let his horse fall into a saner pace.

The effect upon Miguel was galvanic. He reined in, flung himself off on the far side of his horse and cautiously slid the rifle from its scabbard while he pretended to be tightening the cinch. His swarthy face became a pasty yellow and then resumed its natural color, a little darker, perhaps, by the sudden inrush of blood. After what he had done in town Hugh Roberts would be on his trail for only one thing. Miguel's racing imagination and his sudden feeling of guilt for his deliberate, planned desertion found a sufficient reason for the pursuing horseman. Sliding the rifle under his arm he waited until the man came nearer, where a hit would be less of a gamble. The Mexican knew what had happened, for he had delayed until he heard that crashing volley, and knew it to be a volley. Knowing this he knew what it meant and had fled for Surprise Valley and the big herd waiting there. That Roberts should have escaped was a puzzle and he wrestled with it while the range was steadily shortened, and the more he wrestled the more undecided he became. Finally he slipped the gun back, mounted, and waited for the other to come up. He had a plausible answer for every question.

Roberts slowed to a walk and searched the Mexican's eyes as he pulled up at his side. "How'd you get out here so far ahead of *me*?" he demanded, his eyes cold and threatening.

Miguel shrugged his shoulders, but did not take his hand from his belt. "Ah, eet ees a miracle," he breathed. "The good Virgin, she watch over Miguel. An' *paisano*, the roadrunner—deed I not tell you eet was good luck? An' you, too, was saved! How deed eet happen, that you are save?"

"They none of them looked at me, I reckon," replied Roberts. "They got everybody but me—an' *you*. How is it that yo're out here, so far ahead of me?"

"Jus' before the firs' shootin'—the what you call volley—I stoomble as I try not to step on Thorpe. I go down—the volley, eet come—I roll away—they do not see me—an' here I am, like you, save."

"Is that so?" snapped Roberts.

"Eet ees jus' so, so much as eet ees that somewan tell we are comin' to Quayle's," answered Miguel. "For why they do not see us, in the town, when we come in? For why that volley, lak one shot? Sometheeng there ees that Miguel he don' understan'. An' theese, please: Why ees there no sortie wen we come in? We was on the ver' minute—eet ees so?"

"Right on th' dot!" snarled Roberts, his thoughts racing along other trails. "Huh!" he growled. "Our shares of th' herd money comes to quite a sizable pile—mebby that's it. Take th' shares of *all* of us, an' it's more'n half. Well, I don't know, an' I ain't carin' a whole lot now. Think we can swing that herd, Miguel, an' split *all* th' money, even shares?"

The Mexican showed his teeth in a sudden, expansive smile. "For why not? Theese hor-rses are ver' tired; but the others—they are res' now. We can wait at Bitter Spring tonight, an' go on tomorrow. There ees no hurry now."

"We don't hang out at Bitter Spring all night," contradicted Roberts flatly. "We'll water 'em an' breath 'em a spell, an' push right on. Th' further I get away from Mesquite th' better I'm goin' to like it. Come on, let's get goin'."

"There ees no hurry from Bitter Spring," murmured the Mexican. "They ees only one who know beyond; an' Manuel, he ees weeth Kane."

"I don't care a damn!" growled his companion, stubbornly. "I'm not layin' around Bitter Spring any longer than I has to."

Neither believed the other's story, but neither cared, only each determined to be alert when the drive across the desert was completed. Before that there was hardly need to let their mutual suspicions have full play. Each was necessary to the success of the drive—but after? That would be another matter. Fate was again kind to them both, for as they hurried east Hopalong Cassidy hastened west along his favorite trail, the rolling sand between hiding them from him.

Back in the town the elated ambushers buried the bodies, marveled at the escape of Roberts and drifted away to take places on the firing line, which soon showed increased activity. Here and there a more daring puncher took chances, some regretting it and others gaining better positions. Red, Johnny, and Waffles attended strictly to the roof, which now had been abandoned on all sides but the north, where lack of cover prohibited McCullough's men from getting close enough to do any considerable damage. The few punchers lying far off on the north were there principally to stop a sortie or an attempt at escape. As the day passed the defenders' fire grew a little less and the Question-Mark foreman was content to wait it out rather than risk unnecessary casualties in pushing the fighting any more briskly.

Evening came, and with it came Hopalong, tired, hungry, thirsty, and hot, which did not add sweetness to his disposition. Eager to get the men he wanted and to return for the herd, he listened impatiently to his friends' account of the fight, his mind busy on his own account. When the tale had been told and McCullough's changing attitude touched upon he shoved his hat back on his head, spread his feet and ripped out an oath.

"Bastard!" he growled. "All these men, all this time, to clean up a shack like that?"

"Mac's playin' safe—it's only a matter of time, now," apologized Waffles, glaring at his two companions, who already had worn his nerves ragged by the same kind of remarks.

"Hell!" snorted Hopalong impatiently. "We'll all grow whiskers at this rate, before it's over!" He turned to Johnny and regarded him speculatively. "Kid, let Red an' Waffles handle that roof an' come along with me. I'm goin' to start things movin'."

"You'll find Mac plumb set on goin' easy," warned Waffles.

"Th' hell with Mac, an' Lukins, an' you, an' everybody

else," retorted Hopalong. "We're not workin' for nobody but ourselves. All I got to do is keep my mouth shut an' Mac loses a plumb fine herd. Let me hear him talk to me! Come on, Kid."

Johnny deserted his companions as though they were lepers and showed his delight in every swaggering movement. A whining bullet over his head sent his fingers to his nose in contemptuous reply, but nevertheless he went on more carefully thereafter. As they reached the rear of a deserted adobe Hopalong pulled him to a stop.

"I'm tired of this blasted country, an' you ought to be, for you've got a wife that's havin' dull days an' sleepless nights. I'm goin' to touch somethin' off that'll put an end to this fool quiltin' party, an' let us get our money an' go home. By that I'm meanin' th' SV, for it's goin' to be home for me. Besides, it's our best chance of gettin' them rewards. So he's aimin' on cuttin' us out of 'em, huh? All right; I'm goin' to Quayle's, an' while I'm holdin' their interest you fill a canteen with kerosene an' smuggle it into th' stable."

"What you goin' to do?" demanded his companion with poorly repressed eagerness.

"I'm goin' to set fire to that gamblin'-joint an' drive 'em out, that's what!"

"Th' moon won't let you," objected Johnny, but as he looked up at the drifting clouds he hesitated and qualified his remark. "You'll have times when it won't be so light, but it'll be too light for that."

"When I start for th' hotel gamblin'-joint I go agin' th' northeast corner, where there ain't but one loophole that covers that angle. I got it figgered out. When I start, you an' Red won't be loafin' back there where I found you, target-practicin' at th' roof."

Reaching the hotel they found a self-satisfied group complacently discussing the fight. Quayle looked up at their entry, sprang to his feet and heartily shook hands with both.

"Welcome to Mesquite, Cassidy," he beamed. " 'Tis

different now than whin ye left, an' it won't be long before honest men have their say-so in this town."

"Couple of weeks, I reckon, th' way things are driftin'," replied Hopalong, smiling as Johnny left the office to invade the kitchen, where Murphy gave a grinning welcome and looked curiously at the huge canteen held out to him.

"Couple of days," corrected Quayle.

McCullough arose and shook hands with the newcomer. "Hear you been trailin' my herd," he said. "Locate 'em?"

"They're hobbled, an' waitin' for yore boys to drive 'em home. Wish you'd tell yore outfit an' th' others not to shoot at th' feller that heads for Kane's northeast corner tonight, but to cut loose at th' loopholes instead. I'm honin' to get back home, an' so I'm aimin' to bust up this little party tonight. To do that I got to get close."

"That's plumb reckless," replied the trail-boss. "We got this all wrapped up now, an' it'll tie its own knots in a day or two. What's th' use of takin' a chance like that?"

"To show that bunch just who they throwed in jail! Somebody else might feel like tryin' it some day, an' I'm aimin' to make that 'some day' a long way off."

"Can't say I'm blamin' you for that. Whereabouts did you leave th' herd?"

"Where nobody but me an' my friends, on this side of th' fence, knows about," answered Hopalong. "I'll tell you when I see you again—ain't got time now." He nodded to the others, went out the way he had come in and walked off with Johnny, who carried the innocent canteen instead of putting it into the stable.

As they started for the place where Hopalong had left his horse, not daring to ride it into town, they chose a short-cut and after a few minutes' brisk walking Hopalong pointed to a bunch of horses tied to some bushes.

"Th' fellers that owned them played safer than I did," he said, "leavin' 'em out here. I reckon they're all Question-Mark."

Johnny put a hand on his friend's arm and stopped him. "I got a better guess," he said. "I know where all their cayuses are. Hoppy, that rustlin' drive crew musta come in this way. What you bet?"

"I ain't bettin'," grunted his companion, starting toward the little herd, "I'm lookin'. I don't hanker to lose that cayuse of mine, an' they'll mebby get th' hoss I ride after I start for their buildin' tonight. He's so mean I sort of cotton to him. An' he's got some thoroughbred blood in his carcass, judgin' from what Arch said. In a case like this it's only fair to use theirs. Besides, they're fresh; mine ain't."

Johnny pushed ahead, stopped at the tethered group and laughed. "Good thing you didn't bet," he called over his shoulder.

Hopalong untied a wicked-looking animal. "He looks like he'd burn th' ground over a short distance, an' that's what I'm interested in. I'm goin' down an' turn mine loose. If things break like I figger they will there's no tellin' when I'll see him again, an' I don't want him to starve tied up to a tree. He's so thirsty about now that he'll head for McCullough's crick on a bee line."

Johnny nodded, considered a moment and went toward the tie ropes. "Shore, an' not stray far from that grass, neither." He released the horses except the one he mounted and then rode up so close to his friend that their knees rubbed. "No tellin' when anybody will be comin' this way or when they'll get a drink. You look like you been hit by an idea. That's so rare, suppose you uncork it?"

"It's one I've been turnin' over," replied his friend, "an' it looks th' same on both sides, too."

"Turn it over for me an' lemme look."

"Kid, I'm lookin' for somethin' to happen that shore will bother Mr. McCullough a whole lot if he happens to think of it. When that buildin' starts burnin' it's shore goin' to burn fast. They can't fight th' fire like they should with them punchers pourin' lead into them lighted loopholes. Once it starts nothin' can stop it; an' I'm tellin' you it's shore goin' to start right. Th' south side is goin' first. They know there's only a few men watchin' th' north side, an' them few are layin' too far back. It won't take a man like Kane very long to learn that he's got to jump, an' jump quick; an' when he does he'll jump right. Right for him an' right for us. He can't do nothin' else. You said they got their cayuses in there with 'em?"

Johnny nodded. "So I was told. I'm seein' yore drift, Hoppy; an' when Kane an' his friends jump me an' Red shore will have jammed guns an' not be able to shoot at 'em."

"Marriage ain't spoiled yore head," chuckled his companion. "Kane havin' us jailed that way riled me; an' McCullough tryin' to slip out of payin' them rewards has riled me some more. I'm washin' one hand with th' other. Do you think you an' Red could get yore cayuses an' an extra one for me, in case they get this one, around west somewhere back of where yo're goin'?"

"How'll this one do for you?" asked Johnny slapping the horse he was on.

"Plenty good enough."

"Then he'll be there, ready to foller th' jumpers," laughed Johnny.

"Good for you, Kid. You shore have got th' drift. Now, seein' that I may get into trouble an' be too late to go after 'em when they jump, you listen close while I tell you where to ride, an' all about it," and the description of the desert trail and the valley was as meaty as it was terse. He told his friend where to take the horses and where to look for him before the night's work began, and then went back to Kane and his men. "They're bound to head for that valley. There ain't no place else for 'em to go. I'll bet they've had that figgered for a refuge ever since they learned about it."

Johnny laughed contentedly. "An' Mac tellin' me that he's got 'em all tied up an' ain't aimin' to pay no rewards! But," he said, becoming instantly grave, "there's one thin' I don't like. I'm admittin' it's yore scheme, but we ought to draw lots to see who's goin' to use that kerosene. After all, yo're down here to help me out of a hole. Dig up some more cartridges, you maverick!"

"Don't you reckon I got brains enough to run it off?" demanded his friend.

"An' some to spare," replied Johnny; "but I ain't no idjut, myself. Here; call yore choice," and he reached for his belt.

"Yo're slow, Kid," chuckled Hopalong, holding out his hand. "Call it yourself."

Johnny hesitated, pushed back the cartridges and placed his hand on those of his friend. "You went at that like you was pullin' a gun: an' I can't say nothin' that means anythin' faster. Why th' hurry?"

"Habit, I reckon," gravely replied his friend. "Savin' time, mebby; *I* dunno why, you chump!"

"It's a good habit; an' I'm shore you saved considerable time, which same I'm aimin' to waste," replied Johnny. He thought swiftly. Last time he had called "even," and lost. He was certain that Hopalong wanted the task. How would his friend figure? The natural impulse of a slow-witted man would be to change the number. Hopalong was not slow-witted; on the contrary so far from slow-witted that he very likely would be suspicious of the next step in reasoning and go a step further, which would take him back to the act of the slow-witted, for he knew that the cogitating man in front of him was no simpleton. Odd or even: a simple choice; but in this instance it was a battle of keen wits. Johnny raised his own hand and looked down at his friend's, the upper one clasping and covering the lower; and then into the night-hidden eyes, which were squinting between narrowed lids to make their reading hopeless. Being something of a gambler Johnny had the gambler's way of figuring, and this endorsed the other line of reasoning: he believed the chances were not in favor of a repetition.

"Cuss yore grinnin' face," he growled. "I said 'even' last time, an' was wrong. Now I'm sayin' 'odd.' Open up!"

Hopalong opened the closed hands and his squinting eyes at the same instant and laughed heartily. "Kid, I cussed near raised you, an' I know yore ways. Mebby it ain't fair, but you was tryin' hard to outguess me. There they are—pair of aces. Count 'em, sonny; count 'em."

"Count 'em yourself," growled Johnny; "if you can

count that far!" He peered into the laughing eyes and thrust out his jaw. "You know my ways, do you? Well, when we get back to th' SV, me an' you are goin' in to Dave's, get a big stack of two-bit pieces an' go at it. I'll cussed soon show you how much you know my ways! G'wan! Get out of here before I get rough!"

"He's too old to spank," mused Hopalong, kneeing the horse, "an' too young to fight with—reckon I'll have to pull my stakes an' move along." Chuckling, he looked around. "Ain't forgot nothin' about tonight, have you, child?"

"No!" thundered Johnny. "But for two-bits I *would*!" Hopalong's laugh came back to him and sent a smile over his face. "There ain't many like you, you old son-of-a-gun!" he muttered, and wheeled to return to the town and to Red.

His departing friend grinned at the horse. "Bronch," he said, confidently, "he shore had me again. I'm gettin' so cheatin's second nature; an' worse'n that, I'm cheatin' my best friends, an' likin' it. Yessir, *likin*' it! Ain't you ashamed of me? You nod that ugly head of yourn again an' I'll knock it off you! G'wan: This ain't no funeral *yet*!"

CHAPTER XXII

The Bonfire

JOHNNY RODE up to the hotel, got a Winchester and ammunition for it from the stack of guns in the kitchen and then went to the stable for Red's horse and Pepper. As he led them out he stopped to answer a pertinent question from the upper window of the hotel and rode off again, leading the extra mounts.

Ed Doane lowered the rifle and scratched his head. "Goin' for a moonlight ride," he repeated in disgust as he drew back from the window. "Cussed if punchers ain't gettin' more locoed every day. Moonlight ride! Shore—go out an' look at th' scenery. Looks different in th' moonlight—bah! To me a pancake looks like a pancake by kerosene, daylight, wood fire or—or moonlight. I suppose th' moonlight'll get into 'em an' they'll be singin' love-songs an' harmonizin'; but thank th' Lord I don't have to go along!" He glanced around at a sudden *thap!* grinned in the darkness at the double planking on that side wall and sat down again. "Shoot!" he growled. "Shoot twice! Shoot an' be damned! Waste 'em! Reckon th' moonlight's got into you, you cow-stealin', murderin' pup." Filling his pipe he packed and lit it, blew several clouds through nose and mouth and scratched his head again. "Goin' for a moonlight ride, huh? Well, mebby you are, Johnny, my lad; but Ed Doane's bettin' there's more'n a ride in it. You didn't go for no moonlight rides before that missin' friend of yourn turned up; an' then, right away, you ride up on one hoss, collect two more an' go gallivantin' off under th' moon. I'm guessin' close. Eddie Doane, I'll bet you a tenspot them three grizzlies are out for to put their ropes on them rewards. An' I hope they collect, cussed if I don't. That Scotch trail-boss is puttin' on too many airs for me—an' he's rilin' Nelson slow but shore. Go get it, Bar-20: I'm bettin' on you."

There came steps to his door. "Ar-re ye there, Ed?" called a voice.

"Shore; come in, Murphy."

The door opened and closed as the cook entered. "Have ye a pipeful? Mine's all gone."

"Help yourself," answered Doane, tossing the sack. "There it is, by yore County Cork feet."

"I have ut," grunted Murphy. "An' who was th' lad ye was talkin' to from th' windy just now?"

"Nelson. He's goin' ridin' in th' moonlight. Must aim to go far, for he's got three horses."

"Has he, now?" Murphy puffed in quiet satisfaction for a moment. "He's a good la-ad, Ed. Goin' ridin', is he? Well, ridin' is fine for them as likes it. But I'm wonderin' what he's doin' with th' kerosene I gave him?"

"Kerosene? When?"

"Whin he come in with his friend Cassidy—an' a fine bye *that* man is, too. Shure: a hull canteen av it. Two gallons. He says for me to kape it quiet: as if I'd be tellin'! Quayle would have me scalp if he knowed it—givin' away his ile like that. Now where ye goin' so fast?"

"For a walk, under th' moonlight!" answered Doane. "Yo're goin' too—an' we're goin' with our mouths shut. Not a word about th' horses or th' kerosene. You remember what Cassidy said about goin' agin' Kane's northeast corner? Come on—an' see th' bonfire!"

"Shure, an' who's fool enough to have anny bonfires now?"

"Murphy, I said *with our mouths shut.* Come on, up near th' jail!"

The cook scratched his head and favored his companion with a sidewise glance, which revealed nothing because of the darkness of the room. "Th' jail?" he muttered. "He's crazy, he is. Th' jail won't make no bonfire. It's mud. But as long as he has th' 'baccy, I'll go wid him. *Whist!*" he exclaimed as another *thap!* sounded on the wall. "An' what's that?"

"This room's haunted," explained Ed.

"Lead th' way, thin; or let me," said Murphy in great haste. "I'll watch yore mud bonfire."

After leaving the hotel Johnny kept it between himself and Kane's building, rose to the arroyo which Roberts had found so useful and followed it until out of sight of anyone in town. When he left it he turned east, crossed the main trail and dismounted east of the place where he and Red had kept watch on the gambling-house roof. Working his way on foot to his sharpshooting friends he lay down at Red's side and commented casually on several subjects, finally nudging the Bar-20 rifleman.

"I'm growin' tired of this spot an' this game," he grumbled. "They know where we are now, an' that roof's plumb tame."

Red stirred restlessly. "You musta read my mind," he observed. "You've had a spell off—stay here while I take a rest."

"Stay nothin'!" retorted Johnny. "This ain't our fight, anyhow."

"Somebody's got to stay," objected Red.

"Let Waffles, then," rejoined Johnny. "You don't care if we look around?"

"I'd just as soon stay here as go any place else," said the ex-foreman of the O-Bar-O. "Where you fellers aimin' to go?"

"Over west to cover Hoppy," answered Johnny, remembering that this much was generally known. "He aims to make a dash for th' hotel, an' he's so stubborn nobody can stop him. He says th' fight's been goin' on too long; an' you know how he can use six-guns. To use 'em right he'll have to get plumb close."

"Cussed fool!" snorted Red, arising to his knees. "How can he end it by makin' a dash, an' usin' his short guns? Mebby he's aimin' to put his rope on it an' pull it over, shootin' as they pop out from under!" he sarcastically suggested.

"Mebby; better ask him," replied Johnny. "*I* did. Mebby you can get it out of him. When he wants to keep his mouth shut, he shore can keep it shut tight. There's no use wastin' our breath on it. He's got some fool scheme in his head an' he's set solid. All we can do is to try to save his fool skin. Waffles can hold down this place till we come back. Come on, Red."

Red grumbled and stretched. "All right. See you later mebby, Waffles."

Johnny turned. "Don't forget an' shoot at th' feller runnin' for th' east end of th' buildin'," he warned.

"Mac sent th' word along a couple of hours ago," replied Waffles, settling down in the place vacated by Red to resume the watch on the hotel roof, which was fairly well revealed at times by the moon. He seemed to be turning something over in his mind, but finally shrugged his shoulders and gave his attention to the roof. "They've got somethin' better'n six-guns at close range," he muttered. "Well, a man owes his friends somethin', so I'm holdin' my tongue."

Reaching the horses Johnny and his companion mounted and rode northward, leading the spare mount.

"What's he up to?" demanded Red.

"Goin' to set fire to th' shack," answered Johnny, and he forthwith explained the whole affair.

"Huh!" grunted Red. "There ain't no doubt in my mind that it'll work if he can get there an' get th' fire started." He was silent for a moment and then pulled his hat more firmly down on his head. "If he don't get there, I'll give it a whirl. Anyhow, I'd have to leave cover to get to him if he went down—so it ain't much worse goin' th' rest of th' way. An' I'm tellin' you this: That lone loophole is shore goin' to be bad medicine for anybody tryin' to use it after he starts. I'll put 'em through it so fast they'll be crowdin' each other."

"An' while yo're reloadin' I'll keep 'em goin'," said Johnny, patting his borrowed Winchester. "They'll shore think somebody's squirtin' 'em out of a hose."

Some time later he stopped his horse and peered around in the faint light.

Red stopped, also. "This th' place?"

"Looks like it—we ought to get some sign of Hoppy purty soon. Anyhow, we'll wait awhile. Glad that moon ain't very bright."

"An' cussed glad for th' clouds," added Red. "Clouds like them ain't th' rule in this part of the country." He leaned over and looked down at the sand. "Tracks, Kid," he said. "Follow 'em?"

"No," answered his companion slowly. "I'm bettin' they're Hoppy's. Stay with th' cayuses—I'm goin' to look around," and as he dismounted they heard a hail. Red swung to the ground as their friend appeared.

"You made good time," said Hopalong, advancing. "I been off lookin' things over. We can leave th' cayuses in a little hollow about long rifle-shot from th' buildin'. From there you two can get real close by travelin' on yore bellies from bush to bush. Th' cover's no good in daylight, but on a night like this, by waitin' for th' clouds, it'll be plenty good enough."

"How close did you get?" asked Johnny.

"Close enough to send every shot through that loop-hole, if I wanted to."

"Did they see you? Did you draw a shot?"

"No. They ain't watchin' that loophole very close. Ain't had no reason to since th' stables burned. There ain't nobody been layin' off in this direction. Th' cover wasn't good enough to risk it, with only a blank wall to watch, an' with them fellers on th' roof to shoot down. Red couldn't cover th' north part of it from where he was. I been wonderin' if I ought to use a cayuse at all."

"There's argument agin' usin' one," mused Johnny.

"Th' noise, an' a bigger object to catch attention," remarked Red. "If you walked th' cayuse to soften its steps, it still looms up purty big; an' if you cut loose an' dash in, th' noise shore will bring a shot. Me an' th' Kid would have to start shootin' early an' keep it up a long while—an' we're near certain to leave gaps in th' string."

"What moonlight there is shines on this end of th' buildin'," observed Johnny. "That loophole show up plain?" he asked.

"You can't see nothin' else," chuckled Hopalong. "It's so black it fair hollers."

Red drew the Winchester from its sheath and turned the front sight on its pivot, which then showed a thin white line. He never had regretted having it made, for since it had been put on he had not suffered the annoyance of losing sight of it against a dark target in poor light. "Bein' bull-headed," he remarked, "you chumps has to guess; but little Reddie ain't doin' none of it. I told you long ago to have one put on."

"Shut up!" growled Johnny, turning his own Winchester over in his hands.

"I reckon I'm travelin' flat on my stomach," said Hopalong, slinging the big canteen over his head. "I'll go with you till we has to stop, let you get set an' then make a run for it. Seein' that th' Kid has got a repeater, too, you'll be able to keep lead flyin' most of th' time I'm in th' open if you don't pull too fast; an' when you run out of cartridges I'll start with my Colts. I'll be close enough, then, to use 'em right. When you see that I'm under th' buildin' go back quite a ways so th' fire won't show you up too plain, an' *watch th' roof*. I'll start a fire under that loophole before I leave, an' that'll spoil their view through it; an' I ain't leavin' before I've fixed things so them fellers will have so much to do they won't have much time for sharpshootin'. That buildin' will burn like a pine knot."

"Then yo're comin' back th' way you go in?" asked Red.

"Shore," answered Hopalong. "Everythin' plain?"

"Watch me," ordered Red, his hand rising and falling. "If we space our shots like this we ought to be able to reload while th' other is emptyin' his gun. Is it too slow?"

"No," said Johnny, considering.

"No," said the man with the canteen, watching closely. "It'll take that long to throw a gun into th' loophole an' line it up, in this light."

"Not bein' used to a repeater like Red is," suggested Johnny, "I'd better shoot th' second string—that'll give us three of 'em before it's my time to reload. Red can slide 'em in as fast as I can shoot 'em out, timin' 'em like that."

"You can put 'em through that hole as good as I can," said Red. "It's near point-blank shootin'. You do th' shootin' an' I'll take care of loadin' both guns. We can't make no blunders, with Hoppy out there runnin' for his life."

"That's why I ought to do th' runnin'," growled Johnny. "I can make three feet to his two."

"It's all settled," said Hopalong, decisively. "I got th' kerosene, an' I'm keepin' it. Come on. No more talkin'."

They followed him over the course he had picked out and with a caution which steadily increased as they advanced until at length they went ahead only when the crescent moon was obscured by drifting clouds. Ahead loomed the two-story gambling-hall, its windowless rear wall of bleached lumber leaden in the faint light. An occasional finger of fire stabbed from its south wall to be answered by fainter stabs from the open, the reports flat and echoless. A distant voice sang a fragment of song and a softened laugh replied to a ribald jest. A horse neighed and out of the north came quaveringly the faint howl of a moon-worshiping coyote.

The three friends, face down on the sand, now each behind a squat bush, wriggled forward silently but swiftly, and gained new and nearer cover. Again a cloud passed before the moon and again they wriggled forward, their eyes fixed on the top of the roof ahead, two of them heading for the same bush and the other for a shallow gully. The pair met and settled themselves to their satisfaction, heads close together as they consulted about the proper setting of the rear sights. One of them knelt, the rifle at his shoulder reaching out over the top of the bush, his companion sitting cross-legged at his side, a pile of dull brass cartridges in the sombrero on the ground between his knees to keep the grease on the bullets free from sand.

The kneeling man bent his head and let his cheek press against the stock of the heavy weapon, whispered a single word and waited. Twice there came the squeak of a frightened rat from his companion and instantly from the right came an answering squeak as the figure of a man leaped up from the gully and sprinted for the lead-colored wall, the heavy, jarring crash of a Winchester roaring from the bush, to be repeated at close intervals which were as regular as the swing of a pendulum. A round, dark object popped up over the flat roof line and the cross-legged man on the ground threw a gun to his shoulder and fired, almost in one motion. The head dropped from sight as the marksman slid another cartridge into the magazine and waited, ready to shoot again or to exchange weapons with his kneeling friend.

The runner leaped on at top speed, but he automatically counted the reports behind him and a smile flashed over his face when the count told him that the second rifle was being used. He would have known it in no other way, for the spacing of the shots had not varied. Again the count told of the second change and a moment later another extra report confirmed his belief that the roof was being closely watched by his friends. A muffled shout came from the building and a spurt of fire flashed from the loophole, but toward the sky and he fancied he heard the sound of a falling body. Far to his left jets of flame winked along a straggling line, the reports at times bunched until they sounded like a short tattoo, while behind him the regular crashing of an unceasing Winchester grew steadily more distant and flatter.

His breath was coming in gulps now for he had set himself a pace out of keeping with the habits of years and the treacherous sand made running a punishment. During the last hundred feet it was indeed well for him that Johnny shot fast and true, that the five-hundred grain bullets which now sang over his aching head were going straight to the mark. He suddenly, vaguely realized that he heard wrangling voices and then he threw himself down onto the sand and rolled and clawed under the building, safe for the time.

Gradually the jumble of footsteps over his head impressed themselves upon him and he mechanically drew a Colt as he raised his head from the earth. Suddenly the roaring steps all went one way, which instantly aroused his suspicions, and he crawled hurriedly to the black darkness of a pile of sand near the bottom of the south wall, which he reached as the steps ceased. No longer silhouetted against the faint light of the open ground around the building, a light which was bright by contrast with the darkness under the floor, he placed the canteen on the ground and felt for chips and odds and ends of wood with one hand while the other held a ready gun.

There came the sharp, plaintive squeaking of seldom-used hinges, which continued for nearly a minute and then a few unclassified noises. They were followed by the head of a brave man, plainly silhouetted against the open sand. It turned slowly this way and that and then became still.

"See anythin'?" came a hoarse whisper through the open trap.

There was no reply from the hanging head, but if thoughts could have killed, the curious whisperer would have astonished St. Peter by his jack-in-the-box appearance before the Gates.

"If he did, we'd know by now, you fool," whispered another, who instantly would have furnished St. Peter with another shock.

"He'd more likely feel somethin', rather than see it," snickered a third, who thereupon had a thrashing coming his way, but did not know it as yet.

The head popped back into the darkness above it, the trapdoor fell with a bang, and sudden stamping was followed by the fall of a heavy body. Furious, high-pitched

cursing roared in the room above until lost in a bedlam
of stamping feet and shouting voices.

"He ought to kill them three fools," growled Hopalong,
indignant for the moment; and then he shook with silent
laughter. Wiping his eyes, he fell to gathering more
wood for his fire, careless as to noise in view of the free-
for-all going on over his head. Removing the plug from
the canteen he poured part of the oil over the piled-up
wood, on posts, along beams and then, saturating his
neckerchief, he rubbed it over the floor boards. Wriggling around the pile of sand he wet the outer wall as far
up as his arm would reach, soaked two more posts and
another pile of shavings and chips and then, corking the
nearly empty vessel, he felt for a match with his left
hand, which was comparatively free from the kerosene,
struck it on his heel and touched it here and there, and a
rattling volley from the besiegers answered the flaming
signal. Backing under the floor he touched the other pile
and wriggled to the wall directly under the loophole.
Again and again the canteen soaked the kerchief and
the kerchief spread the oil, again a pile of shavings
leaned against a wetted post, and another match leaped
from a mere spot of fire into a climbing sheet of flame,
which swept up over the loophole and made it useless. As he turned to watch the now well-lighted trapdoor, there came from the east, barely audible above
the sudden roaring of the flame, the reports of the rifles
of his two friends, the irregular timing of the shots leading him to think that they were shooting at animated
targets, perhaps on the roof.

The trapdoor went up swiftly and he fired at the head
of a man who looked through it. The toppling body was
grabbed and pulled back and the door fell with a slam
which shook the building. Hopalong's position was now
too hot for comfort and getting more dangerous every
second and with a final glance at the closed trapdoor he
scrambled from under the building, slapped sparks from
his neck and shoulders and sprinted toward his waiting,
anxious friends, where a rifle automatically began the
timed firing again, although there now was no need for

it. Slowing as he left the building farther and farther behind he soon dropped into a walk and the rifle grew silent.

"Here we are," called Johnny's cheery voice. "I'm admittin' you did a good job!"

"An' *I*'m sayin' you did a good one," replied Hopalong. "Them shots came as reg'lar as th' tickin' of a clock."

"Quite some slower," said Red. "That gang can't stay in there much longer. Notice how Mac's firin' has died down?"

"They're waitin' for 'em to come out an' surrender," chuckled Hopalong. "Keep a sharp watch an you'll see 'em come out an' make a run for it."

"Better get back to th' cayuses, an' be ready to foller," suggested Red.

"No," said Johnny. "Let 'em get a good start. If we stop 'em here Mac may get a chance to cut in."

"An' we'll mebby have to kill some of th' men we want alive," said Hopalong. "Let 'em get to that valley an' think they're safe. We can catch 'em asleep th' first night."

The gambling-hall was a towering mass of flames on the south and east walls and they were eating rapidly along the other two sides. Suddenly a hurrying line of men emerged from the north door of the doomed structure, carrying wounded companions to places of safety from the flames. Dumping these unfortunates on the ground, the line charged back into the building again and soon appeared leading blind-folded horses, which bit and kicked and struggled, and turned the line into a fighting turmoil. The few shots coming from the front of the building increased suddenly as McCullough led a running group of his men to cover the north wall. A few horses and a man or two dropped under the leaden hail, the accuracy of which suffered severely from the shortness of breath of the marksmen. The group expanded, grew close at one place and with quirts rising and falling, dashed from the building, pressing closely upon the four leaders, and became rapidly smaller before the steadying rifles of its enemies took much heavier toll.

Before it had passed beyond the space lighted by the great fire only four men remained mounted, and these were swiftly swallowed up by the dim light on the outer plain.

McCullough and most of his constantly growing force left cover and charged toward the building to make certain that no more of their enemies escaped, while the rest of his men hurried back to get horses and form a pursuing party.

CHAPTER XXIII

Surprise Valley

HOPALONG TURNED and crawled away from the lurid scene, his friends following him closely. As soon as they dared they arose to their feet and jogged toward where their horses waited, and soon rode slowly northeastward, heading on a roundabout course for Sweet Spring.

"Take it easy," cautioned Hopalong. "We don't want to get ahead of 'em yet. If my eyes are any good th' four that got away are Kane, Corwin, Trask, an' a Greaser. What you say?"

Reaching the arid valley through which Sand Creek would have flowed had it not been swallowed up by the sands, they drew on their knowledge of it and crossed on hard ground, riding at a walk and cutting northeastward so as to be well above the course of the fleeing four, after which they turned to the southeast and approached the spring from the north. Reaching the place of their former vigil they dismounted, picketed the horses in the sandy hollow, and lay down behind the crest of the ridge. Half an hour passed and then Johnny's roving eyes caught sight of a small group of horsemen as it popped up over a rise in the desert floor. A moment later and the group strung out in single file to round a cactus chaparral and revealed four horsemen, riding hard. The fugitives raced up to Bitter Spring, tarried a few moments, and went on again, slowly growing smaller and smaller, and then a great slope of sand hid them from sight.

Hopalong grunted and arose, scanning their back trail. "They've been so long gettin' out here that I'm bettin' they did a good job hidin' their trail. I can see Mac an' his gang ridin' circles an' gettin' madder every minute. Well, we can go on, now. By goin' th' way I went before we won't be seen."

"How long will it take us?" asked Red, brushing sand from his clothes as he stood up.

"Followin' th' pace they're settin' we ought to be there tonight," answered Hopalong. "Give th' cayuses all they can drink. If them fellers hold us off out there we'll have to run big risks gettin' our water from that crick. Well, let's get started."

The hot, monotonous ride over the desert need not be detailed. They simply followed the tracks made by Hopalong on his previous visit and paid scanty attention to the main trail south of them, contenting themselves by keeping to the lowest levels mile after burning mile. It was evening when they stopped where their guide had stopped before and after waiting for nightfall they went on again in the moonlight, circling as Hopalong had circled and when they stopped again it was to dismount where he had dismounted behind a ridge. They picketed and hobbled the weary, thirsty horses and went ahead on foot. Following instructions Red left them and circled to the south to scout around the great ridge of rock before taking up his position at the head of the slanting trail from the valley. His companions kept on and soon crawled to the rim of the valley, removed their sombreros and peered cautiously over the edge. The faint glow of the fire behind the adobe hut in the west end of the sink shone in the shadows of the great rock walls and reflected its light from boulders and brush. Below them cattle and the horses of the caviya grazed over the well-cropped pasture and a strip of silver told where the little creek wandered toward its effacement. Moving back from the rim they went on again, looking over from time to time and eventually reached the point nearly over the fire, where they could hear part of the conversation going on around it, when the voices raised above the ordinary tones.

"You haven't a word to say!" declared Kane, his outstretched hand leveled at Trask, the once-favored deputysheriff. "If it wasn't for your personal spite, and your damned avarice, we wouldn't be in this mess tonight! You had no orders to do that."

Trask's reply was inaudible, but Corwin's voice reached them.

"I told him to let Nelson alone," said the sheriff. "He was dead set to get square for him cuttin' into th' argument with Idaho. But as far as avarice is concerned, you got yore part of th' eleven hundred."

"Might as well, seeing that the hand had been played!" retorted Kane. "What's more, I'm going to keep it. Anybody here think he's big enough to get any part of it?"

"Nobody here wants it," said Roberts. "Th' boys I had with me, an' Miguel, an' myself have reasons to turn this camp fire into a slaughter, but we're sinkin' our grievances because this ain't no time to air 'em. I'm votin' for less squabblin'. We ain't out of this yet, an' we got four hundred head to get across th' desert. Time enough, later, to start fightin'. I'm goin' off to turn in where there ain't so much fool noise. I've near slept on my feet an' in th' saddle. Fight an' be damned!" and he strode from the fire, keen eyes above watching his progress and where it ended.

The hum around the fire suffered no diminution by his departure, but the words were not audible to the listeners above. Soon Corwin angrily arose and left the circle, his blankets under his arm. His course also was marked. Then the two Mexicans went off, and the eager watchers chuckled softly as they saw the precious pair take lariats from the saddles of two picketed horses and slip noiselessly toward the feeding caviya. Roping fresh mounts, and the pick of the lot, they made the ropes fast and went back to the other horses. Soon they returned with their riding equipment and blankets, saddled the fresh mounts and, spreading the blankets a few feet beyond the radius of the picket ropes, they rolled up and soon were asleep.

"Sensitive to danger as hounds," muttered Johnny.

"Cunnin' as coyotes," growled Hopalong, glancing at the clear-cut, rocky rim across the valley, where Red by this time lay ensconced. "I hope he remembers to drop their cayuses first—Miguel's worth more to us alive."

"An' easier to take back," whispered Johnny. "We want 'em *all* alive—an' we'd never get 'em that way if they wasn't so played out. They'll sleep like they are dead—luck is with us."

Down at the dying camp fire Kane, his back to the hut, talked with Trask in tones which seemed more friendly, but the deputy was in no way lulled by the change. He sensed a flaming animosity in the fallen boss, who blamed him for the wreck of his plans and the organization. Muttering a careless good night, Trask picked up his blankets and went off, leaving the bitter man alone with his bitterness.

Tired to the marrow of his bones, so sleepy that to remain awake was a torture, the boss dared not sleep. In the company of five men who were no longer loyal, whose greed exceeded his own, and each of whom nursed a real or fancied grudge against him and who searched into the past, into the days of his contemptuous treatment of them for fuel and yet more fuel to feed the fires of their resentment, he dared not close his eyes. On his person was a modest fortune compacted by the size of the bills and so well distributed that unknowing eyes would not suspect its presence; but these men knew that he would not leave his wealth behind him, to be perhaps salvaged from a hot and warped safe in the smoking ruins of his gambling-house.

He stirred and gazed at the glowing embers and an up-shooting tongue of flame lighted up the small space so vividly that its portent shocked through to his dulled brain and sent him to his feet with the speed and silence of a frightened cat. He was too plain a target and too defenseless in the lighted open, and like a ghost he crept away into the darker shadows under the great stone cliff, to pace to and fro in an agonizing struggle against sleep. Back and forth he strode, his course at times erratic as his enemy gained a momentary victory; but his indomitable will shook him free again and again; and such a will it was that when sleep finally mastered him it did not master his legs, for he kept walking in a circular course like a blind horse at a ginny.

When he had leaped to his feet and left the hut the watchers above kept him in sight and after the first few moments of his pacing they worked back from the valley's rim and slipped eastward.

"Here's th' best place," said Hopalong, turning toward the rim again. They looked over and down a furrow in the rock wall. "We'll need two ropes. It'll take one, nearly, to reach from here to that knob of rock an' go around it. Red's got a new hemp rope—bring that, too. If he squawks about us cuttin' it, I'll buy him a new one. Got to have tie ropes."

Johnny hastened away and when he returned he threw Red's lariat on the ground, and joined the other two. Fastening one end around the knob of rock he dropped the other over the wall and shook it until he could see that it reached the steep pile of detritus. Picking up the hemp rope he was about to drop it, too, when caution told him it would make less noise if carried down. Slinging it over his shoulder he crept to the edge, slid over, grasped the rope and let himself down. Seeing he was down his companion was about to follow when Johnny's whisper checked him.

"Canteens—better fill 'em while it's easy."

Hopalong drew his head back and disappeared and it was not much of a wait before the rope was jerking up the wall and returned with a canteen. To send down more than one at a time would be to risk them banging together. When they all were down Johnny took them and slipped among the boulders, Hopalong watching his progress. For caution's sake the water carrier took two trips from the creek and sent them up again one at a time. Soon his friend slid down, glanced around, took the hemp rope and cut it into suitable lengths, giving half of the pieces to Johnny and then without a word started for the west end of the valley, treading carefully, Johnny at his heels.

Roberts, sleeping the sleep of the exhausted, awoke in a panic, a great weight on his legs, arms, and body, and a pair of sinewy thumbs pressing into his throat. His struggles were as brief as they were violent and when they ceased Hopalong arose from the quiet legs and released the limp arms while his companion released the throat hold and took his knees from the prostrate chest. In a few minutes a quiet figure lay under the side of a rock, its mouth gagged with a soiled neckerchief and the new hemp rope gleaming from ankles, knees, and wrists.

Corwin, his open mouth sonorously announcing the quality of his fatigue, lay peacefully on his back, tightly rolled up in his blankets. Two faint shadows fell across him and then as Johnny landed on his chest and sunk the capable thumbs deep into the bronzed throat on each side of the windpipe, Hopalong dropped onto the blanket-swathed legs and gripped the encumbered arms. This task was easy and in a few minutes the sheriff, wrapped in his own blankets like a mummy, also wore a gag and several pieces of new hemp rope, two strands of which passed around his body to keep the blanket rolled.

The two punchers carried him between two boulders, chuckled as they put him down, and stood up to grin at each other. The blanket-rolled figure amused them and Johnny could not help but wish Idaho was there to enjoy the sight. He moved over against his companion and whispered.

"Shore," answered Hopalong, smiling. "Go ahead. It's only fair. He knocked you on th' head. I'll go up an' spot Kane. Did it strike you that he must have a lot of money on him to be so hell-bent to stay awake? I don't like him pacin' back an' forth like that. It may mean a lot of trouble for us; an' them Greasers are too nervous to suit me. When yo're through with Trask slip off an' watch them Mexicans. Don't pay no attention to me no matter what happens. Stick close to them two. I'll give you a hand with 'em as soon as I can get back. If you have to shoot, don't kill 'em," and the speaker went cautiously toward the hut.

Johnny removed his boots and, carrying them, went toward the place where he had seen the deputy bed down; but when he reached the spot Trask was not there. Thanking his ever-working bump of caution for his silent and slow approach he drew back from the little opening among the rocks and tackled the problem in savage haste. There was no time to be lost, for Hopalong was not aware that any of the gang was roaming around and might not be as cautious as he knew how to be. Why had Trask forsaken his bed-ground, and when? Where had he gone and what was he doing? Cursing under his breath Johnny wriggled toward the creek where he could get a good view of the horses. Besides the two picketed near the sleeping Mexicans none were saddled nor appeared to be doing anything but grazing. Going back again Johnny searched among the boulders in frantic haste and then decided that there was only one thing to do, and that was to head for the hut and get within sight of his friend. Furious because of the time he had lost he started for the new point and finally reached the hut. If Trask was inside he had to know it and he crept along the wall, pausing only to put his ear against it, turned the corner and leaped silently through the door, his arms going out like those of a swimmer. The hut was empty. Relieved for the moment he slipped out again and started to go toward Kane.

"I'll bet a month's pay—" he muttered and then stopped, his mind racing along the trail pointed out by the word. Pay! That was money. Money? As Hopalong had said, Kane must have plenty of it on him—money? Like a flash a possible solution sprang into his mind. Kane's money! Trask was a thief, and what would a thief do if he suspected that the life savings of a man like Kane might easily be stolen? And especially when he had been so angered by the possessor of the wealth?

"I got to move *pronto*!" he growled. "I'm no friend of Kane's but I ain't goin' to have him killed—not by a coyote like Trask, anyhow. We got to have him alive, too. An' Hoppy?" His reflections were such that by the time he came in sight of Kane his feelings were a cross between a mad mountain lion and an active volcano. He stopped again and looked, his mind slowly forsaking rage in favor of suspicion. Kane was walking around in a circle, his eyes closed; his feet were rising and falling mechanically and with an exaggerated motion.

"War dancin'?" thought Johnny. "What would he do that for? He ain't no Injun. I'm sayin' he's loco. Kane loco? Like hell! Fellers like him don't get loco. Makin' medicine? I just said he ain't no Injun. Prancin' around in th' moonlight, liftin' his feet like they had ropes to 'em to jerk 'em. An' with his eyes close shut! I'm gettin' a headache—an' I'm settin' tight till I get th' hang of this walkin' Willy. Mebby he thinks he's workin' a charm; but if he is he ain't goin' to run it on me!"

He pressed closer against the boulder which sheltered him and searched the surroundings again, slowly, painstakingly. Then there came a low rustling sound, as though a body were being dragged across dried grass. It was to his left and not far away. If it is possible to endow one sense with the total strength of all the others, then his ears were so endowed. Whether or not they were strengthened to an unusual degree they nevertheless heard the rubbing of soft leather on the boulder he lay against, and he held his breath as he reversed his grip on the Colt.

"Hoppy, or Trask?" he wondered, glad that his head did not project beyond the rock. A quick glance at the milling Kane showed no change in that person's antics and he felt certain that he had not been detected by the boss. He froze tighter if it is possible to improve on perfection, for his ears caught a renewal of the sounds. Then his eyes detected a slow movement and focussed on a shadowy hand which fairly seemed to ooze out beyond the rock. When he discerned a ring on one of the fingers he knew it was not Hopalong, for his friend wore no ring. That being so, it only could be Trask who was creeping along the other side of the rock. Johnny glanced again at the peripatetic gang leader and back to the creeping hand, and wondered how high in the air its owner would jump if it were suddenly grabbed. Then he mentally cursed himself, for his independent imagination threatened to make him laugh. He could feel the tickle of mirth slyly pervading him and he bit his lip with an earnestness which cut short the mirth. The hand stopped and the heel of it went down tightly against the earth as though bearing a gradual strain. Johnny was reassured again, for Trask never would be stalking Kane if he had the slightest suspicion that enemies, or strangers, were in the valley, and he hazarded another glance at Kane.

The mechanical walker was drawing near the rock again and in a few steps more would turn his back to it and start away. By this time Johnny had solved the riddle, for although such a thing was beyond any experience of his, his wild guess began to be accepted by him: Kane was walking in his sleep. Where was Hopalong? He hoped his friend would not try to capture the boss until he, himself, had taken care of Trask. This must be his first duty, and knowing what Trask would do very shortly he prepared to do it.

He got into position to act, moving only when the slight sound of Kane's footfalls would cover the barely audible noise of his own movements. Kane's rounding course brought him nearer and then several things happened at once. The owner of the hand leaped from behind the rock and as his head popped out into sight a Colt struck it, and then Johnny started for Kane; but as he reached his feet something hurtled out of the shadows to his right and bore the boss to the ground. Then came the sound of another gun-butt meeting another head and the swiftly moving figure seemed to rebound from the boss and sail toward Johnny, who had started to meet it. He swerved suddenly and muttered one word, just as Hopalong swerved from his own course. They both had turned in the same direction and came together with a force which nearly knocked them out. Holding to each other to keep their feet, they recovered their breath and without a word separated at a run, Hopalong going to Kane and Johnny to Trask. Less dazed by the collision than his friend was, Johnny finished his work first and then helped Hopalong carry Kane to the shelter of the rock.

"Good thing you forgot what I said about watchin' them Greasers," grunted Hopalong. "It's them next, if—" his words were cut short by two quick shots, which reverberated throughout the valley, and without another word he followed his running companion, and scorned cover for the first few hundred yards.

When they got close to the trail they saw two bulks on it, which the moonlight showed to be prostrate horses.

"Where are they, Red?" shouted Johnny. "They're th' only ones free!"

"Down near you somewhere," answered the man above, and his words were proved true by a bullet which hummed past Johnny's ear. He dropped to his stomach and began to wriggle toward the flash of the gun, Hopalong already on the way.

Cut off from escape up the trail the two Mexicans tried to work toward the hut, from which they could put up a good fight; but their enemies had guessed their purpose and strove to drive them off at a tangent.

Red, watching from the top of the cliff, noticed that the occasional gun flashes were moving steadily north-westward and believed it safe to leave his position and take an active hand in the events below. After their experience on the up-slanting trail the Mexicans would hardly attempt it again, even though they managed to get back to the foot of it, which seemed very improbable. The thought became action and the trail guard started to wriggle down the declivity, keeping close to the bottom of the wall, where the shadows were darkest. Because of the necessity for not being seen his progress was slow and quite some time elapsed before he reached the bottom and obtained cover among the scattered rocks. The infrequent reports were farther away now, and they seemed to be getting farther eastward. This meant that they were nearer to the hut, and his decision was made in a flash. The hut must not be won by the fugitives, and he arose and ran for it, bent over and risking safety for speed. After what seemed to be a long time he reached the little cleared space among the rocks, bounded across it, and leaped into the black interior of the hut. Wheeling, he leaned against the rear wall to recover his breath, watching the open door, a grim smile on his face. While keeping his weary watch up on the rim he had craved action, and congratulated himself that he now was a great deal nearer to it than he was before.

Meanwhile the two fugitives, not stomaching a real stand against the men whom they had seen exhibit their abilities in Kane's gambling-hall, had managed to work on a circular course until they were northwest of the hut and not far from it. This they were enabled to do because they were not held to a slow and cautious advance by enemies ahead of them, as were the old Bar-20 pair. They were moving toward the hut, not far from the north wall of the valley, when they blundered upon Trask. In a moment he was released and began a frantic search for his gun, which he found among the rocks not far away. Losing no time he hurried off to release the man he would have robbed, glad to have his assistance. Kane went into action like a spring released and began a hot search for his Colt. When he found it, the cylinder was missing and suspicious noises not far away from him forced him to abandon the search and seek better cover, armed only with a deadly and efficient steel club.

Hopalong and Johnny, guided entirely by hearing, followed the infrequent low sounds in front of them, thinking that they were made by the Mexicans, and drew steadily away from the hut. The Mexicans, motionless in their cover, exulted as their scheme worked out and finally went on again with no one to oppose them. Reaching the last of the rocky cover they arose and ran across the open, leaped into the hut and turned, chuckling, to close the door, leaving Trask to his fate.

Warned by instinct they faced about as Red leaped. Miguel dropped under a clubbed gun, but Manuel, writhing sidewise, raised his Colt only to have it wrenched from his hand by his shifty opponent. Clinching, he drew a knife and strove desperately to use it as he wrestled with his sinewy enemy. At last he managed to force the tip of it against Red's side, barely cutting the flesh; and turned Red into a raging fury. With one hand around Manuel's neck and the other gripping the wrist of the knife-hand, Red smashed his head again and again into the Mexican's face, his knee pressing against the knifeman's stomach. Suddenly releasing his neck hold Red twisted, got the knife-arm under his armpit, gripped the elbow with his other hand and exerted his strength in a twisting heave. The Mexican screamed with pain, sobbed as Red's knee smashed into his stomach and dropped senseless, his arm broken and useless. Red dropped with him and hastily bound him as well as possible in the poor light from the partly opened door.

He had just finished the knot in the neckerchief when a soft, swift rustling appraised him of danger and he moved just in time. Miguel's knife passed through his vest and shirt and pinned him to the hard-packed floor. Before either could make another move the door crashed back against the wall and Kane hurtled into the hut, landing feet first on the wriggling Mexican. He put the knife user out of the fight and pitched sprawling. His exclamation of surprise told Red that he was no friend and now, free from the pinning knife, Red pounced on the scrambling boss.

The other struggles of the crowded night paled into insignificance when compared to this one. Red's superior strength and weight was offset by the fatigue of previous efforts, and Kane's catlike speed. They rolled from one wall to another, pounding and strangling Kane as innocent of the ethics of civilized combat as a maddened bobcat, and he began to fight in much the same way, using his finger-nails and teeth as fast as he could find a place for them. Red wanted excitement and was getting it. Torn and bleeding from nails and teeth, his blows lacking power because of the closeness of the target and his own fatigue, Red shed his veneer of civilization and fought like a gorilla. Planting his useful and well-trained knee in the pit of his adversary's stomach, he gripped the lean throat with both hands and hammered Kane's head ceaselessly against the hard earth floor, while his thumbs sank deeply on each side of the gang leader's windpipe. Too enraged to sense the weakening opposition, he choked and hammered until Kane was limp and, writhing from his victim's body, he knelt, grabbed Kane in his brawny arms, staggered to his feet and with one last surge of energy, hurled him across the hut. Kane struck the wall and dropped like a bag of meal, his fighting over for the rest of the night.

Red stumbled over the Mexicans, fell, picked himself up, and reeled outside, fighting for breath, his vision blurred and kaleidoscopic, staring directly at two men among the rocks but seeing nothing. "Come one, come all—damned you!" he gasped.

Trask, thrice wounded, hunted, desperate, fleeing from a man who seemed to be the devil himself with a six-gun, froze instantly as Red appeared. Enraged by this unexpected enemy and sudden opposition where he fondly expected to find none, Trask threw caution to the winds and raised the muzzle of the Colt. As he pulled the trigger a soaring bulk landed on his shoulders, knocking the exploding weapon from his hand and sending him sprawling. Snarling like an animal he twisted around, wriggled from under and grabbed Johnny's other Colt from its holster. Before he could use it Johnny's knee pinned it and the hand holding it to the ground. A clubbed six-gun did the rest and Johnny, calling to Red to watch Trask, hurried away to see if Roberts and Corwin were loose. The latter was helpless in the blanket, but Roberts had freed his feet and was doing well with the knots on his wrists when Johnny's appearance and growled command put an end to his efforts. He put the rope back on the kicking feet and arose as Hopalong limped up.

"Phew!" exclaimed Johnny. "This has been a reg'lar night! Here, you stay with Corwin while I tote this coyote to th' hut." He got Roberts onto his back and staggered away, soon returning for the sheriff.

Dawn found six bound men in varying physical condition sitting with their backs to the hut, their wounds crudely dressed and their bounds readjusted and calculated to stay fixed. Kane was vindictive, his eyes snapping, and he seethed with futile energy, notwithstanding the mauling he had received. His lean face, puffed, discolored, and wolfishly cruel, worked with a steadily mounting rage, which found vent at intervals in scathing vituperative comments about Trask, whom he still blamed for the predicament in which he found himself. Corwin, sullen and fearful, kept silent, his fingers picking nervously at the buckle and strap on the back of his vest. Roberts was angry and defiant and sneered at his erstwhile boss, sending occasional verbal shafts into him in justification of Trask. The two Mexicans had sunk into the black depths of despair and acted as though they were stunned. Trask, a bitter sneer on his face, glared unflinchingly at the storming boss and showed his teeth in grim, ironical smiles.

"Th' crossbreed shows th' cur dog when th' wolf is licked," he sneered in reply to a particularly vicious attack of Kane's. "What you blamin' me for? You took yore share of Nelson's money, an' took it eager. *You* heard me!" he snarled. "I don't care who knows it—I got it, an' you took yore part of it. It was all right *then*, wasn't it? An' you didn't *know* it was his—you let him make a fool of you an' wouldn't listen to me. But as long as you got yourn you didn't care a whole lot *who* lost it. Serves you right."

"Shut up!" muttered Roberts.

"Shut up nothin'," jeered Trask. "Think I'm goin' to swing to save a mad dog like him? Look at him! Look at th' dog breakin' through th' wolf! *Wolf*? Huh! Coyote would be more like it. Don't talk to me!" He looked at the camp fire and at the man busy over it. "I can eat some of that, Nelson," he said.

Johnny nodded and went on with the cooking.

Sounds of horses clattering down the steep trail suddenly were heard and not much later Red rode up on a horse he had captured from the rustlers' caviya and dismounted near the fire. His face was a sight, but the grin which tried to struggle through the bruises was sincere. He dropped two saddles to the ground, the saddles belonging to the Mexicans, which he had stopped to strip from the dead horses on the trail up the wall.

"Our cayuses went loco near th' crick," he said. "I left Hoppy to take off th' saddles an' let 'em soak themselves," referring to the three animals they had left up on the desert the evening before. "I'm all ready to eat, Kid. How's it shapin' up?"

"Grab yore holt," grunted Johnny. He stood up to rest his back. "Mebby it would be more polite to feed our guests first," he grinned.

Red looked at the line-up. "We'll *have* to feed 'em, I reckon. I ain't aimin' to untie no hands. Who's first?"

"Don't play no favorites," answered Johnny. "Go up an' down th' line an' give 'em all a chance." He faced the prisoners. "You fellers like yore coffee smokin'?" Only two men answered, Roberts and Trask, and they did not like it smoking hot. "Let it cool a little, Red; no use scaldin' anybody."

The prisoners had all been fed when Hopalong appeared on another horse from the rustlers' caviya and swung down. "Smells good, Kid! An' looks good," he said. "I got all th' saddles on fresh cayuses, waitin'—all but these here. We'll lead our own cayuses. That Pepper-hoss of yourn acts lonesome. She ain't lookin' at th' grass, at all." He sat down, arose part way and felt in his hip pocket, bringing out the cylinder of a six-gun. Glancing at Kane, to whom it belonged, he tossed it into the brush and resumed his seat.

Johnny's face broke into a smile and he whistled shrilly. Quick hoofbeats replied and Pepper, her neck arched, stepped daintily across the little level patch of ground and nosed her master.

"Ha!" grunted Trask. "That's a *hoss*!" A malignant grin spread over his face and he turned his head to look at Kane. "Kane, how much money, that money you got on you now, would you give to be on that black back, up on th' edge of th' valley? *All* of it, I bet!"

"Shut up!" snapped Roberts, angrily.

"Go to hell," sneered Trask, and he laughed nastily. "You wait till I speak my little piece before you tell me to shut up! No dog is goin' to ride me to a frazzle, blamin' me for this wind-up, without me havin' somethin' to say about it!" He looked at Red. "What was them two shots I heard, up there on top? They was th' first fired last night."

"That was me droppin' th' Greasers' cayuses from under 'em on th' ledge," Red answered. "They was pullin' stakes for th' desert."

"Leavin' us to do th' dancin', huh?" snapped Trask. "All right; I know another little piece to speak. Where you fellers takin' us?"

Red shrugged his shoulders and went off to get horses for the crowd.

A straggling line of mounted men climbed the cliff trail, the horses of the inner six fastened by lariats to each other, and three saddleless animals brought up the rear. They pushed up against the sky line in successive bumps and started westward across the desert.

CHAPTER XXIV

Squared Up All Around

MESQUITE, STILL humming from the tension of the past week felt its excitement grow as Bill Trask, bound securely and guarded by Hopalong, rode down the street and stopped in front of Quayle's, where the noise made by the gathering crowd brought Idaho to the door.

"Hey!" he shouted over his shoulder. "Look at this!" Then he ran out and helped Hopalong with the prisoner.

Quayle, Lukins, Waffles, McCullough, and Ed Doane fell back from the door and let the newcomers enter, Idaho slamming it shut in the face of the crowd. Then Ed Doane had his hands full as the crowd surged into the barroom.

"Upstairs!" said Hopalong, steering the prisoner ahead of him. In a few minutes they all were in Johnny's old room, where Trask, his ropes eased, began a talk which held the interest of his auditors. At its conclusion McCullough nodded and turned to Hopalong.

"All this may be true," he said; "but what does it all amount to without th' fellers he names? If you'd kept out of th' fight an' hadn't set fire to that buildin' we would 'a' got every one of them he names. Gimme Kane an' th' others an' better proof than his story an' you got a claim to that reward that's double sewed."

Hopalong seemed contrite and downcast. He looked around the group and let his eyes return to those of the trail-boss. "I reckon so," he growled. "But have you got th' numbers of th' missin' bills?" he asked, skeptically.

"Yes, I have; an' a lot of good it'll do me, *now!*" snapped McCullough. "We was countin' on them for th' real proof, but that fool play of yourn threw 'em into th' discard! What'n hell made you set that place afire?"

Hopalong shrugged his shoulders. "I dunno," he muttered. "Was you aimin' to find th' missin' bills on them fellers?" he asked. "Would that 'a' satisfied you?"

"Of course!" snorted the trail-boss. "An' with Trask, here, turnin' agin' 'em like he has it would be more than enough. Any fool knows that!"

Hopalong arose. "I'm glad to hear you come right out an' say that for that's what I wanted to know. I've been bothered a heap about what you might ask in th' line of proof. You shore relieve my mind, Mac. If you fellers will straddle leather we'll ride out where Kane an' th' others Trask named are waitin' for visitors. I don't reckon they none of them got away from Johnny an' Red."

"What are you talkin' about?" demanded McCullough, his mouth open from surprise.

"I mean we've got Kane, Roberts, Corwin, Miguel, an' another Greaser all tied up, waitin' to turn 'em over to you an' collect them rewards. As long as we know just what you want, an' can give it to you, I don't see no use of waitin'. I'm invitin' Lukins an' th' rest along to see th' finish. What you goin' to do with Trask?"

McCullough was looking at him through squinting eyes, his face a more ruddy color. Glancing around the group he let his eyes rest on Trask. Shrugging his shoulders he faced Hopalong. "Take him south, I reckon, with th' others. If he talks before a jury like he's talked up here I reckon he won't be sorry for it." He walked to a window and looked down into the street. "Hey!" he called. "Walt, get a couple of th' boys an' come up here right away. We got somebody for you to stay with," and in a few minutes he and the others left Walt and his companions to guard and protect the prisoner.

The sun was at the meridian when Hopalong led his companions into the Sand Creek camp and dismounted in front of Red, who was watching the prisoners.

"Where's th' Kid?" he asked curiously.

"Don't you do no worryin'," answered Red. He lowered his voice and put his mouth close to his friend's ear. "Th' Greaser on th' end is goin' to pieces. Pound him hard an' he'll show his cards."

The information was conveyed to McCullough, who stood looking at the downcast group. He strode over to Miguel, grabbed his shoulders and jerked him to his feet. Running his hands into the Mexican's pockets he brought out a roll of bills. Swiftly running through them he drew out a bill, compared it with a slip which he produced from his own pocket, whirled the bound man around and glared into the frightened eyes.

"Where'd you get this?" he shouted, shaking his captive.

"Kane geeve eet to me—he owe me money," answered the Mexican.

"What for?" demanded McCullough, shaking him again.

"I lend heem eet."

"You loaned *him* money?" roared the trail-boss. "That's likely! Why did he give it to you?"

Miguel shrugged his shoulders and did not answer.

McCullough jerked him half around and pointed to Hopalong. "This man here saw you sneakin' from Kane's south stable with a smokin' Sharp's in yore hand after you shot Ridley. Trask says you did it. Is *this* all Kane gave you for that killin'?"

"I could no help," protested Miguel, squirming in the trail-boss' grip. "W'en Kane he say do theese or that theeng, I mus' do eet. I no want to but I mus'."

McCullough whirled around and faced Corwin. "That story you told me down in th' bunkhouse that night about how Bill Long shot Ridley is near word for word what Bill says about th' Greaser, an' Trask's story backs him up. How did you come to know so much about it? Come on, you coyote; spit it out! Who told you what to say?" Corwin's silence angered him and he showed his teeth. "There's a lynchin' waitin' for you in town, Corwin, if you don't stop it by speakin' up. Who told you that?"

Corwin looked away. "Miguel," he muttered. "I told you I was hopin' to get th' real one."

"He lie! I never say to heem one word!" shouted the Mexican. "He lie! Kane, he was the only one who know like that beside me!"

"Stand up, *Sheriff*!" snapped McCullough. He searched the sullen prisoner and found two rolls of bills. Going quickly over them he removed and grouped certain of them, and then compared them with his list. "There's five here that tally with th' bank's numbers," he said, looking up. "Where'd you get 'em?"

"Won 'em at faro-bank."

"Won five five-hundred-dollar bills at faro, when everybody knows yo're a two-bit gambler?" shouted the trail-boss. "I'm no damned fool! Don't you forget what I said about th' lynchin', Corwin. I'm all that stands between you an' it. Where'd you get 'em? Like Trask said?"

Corwin's hunted look flashed despairingly around the group. "No," he said. "Kane gave 'em to me, to get changed into smaller bills!"

"Reckon Kane musta robbed that bank all by hisself," sneered McCullough. "I never knowed he had diamond drills an' could bust safes. Didn't you go along to protect an' keep an eye on that eastern safe-blower that Kane had come to do th' job? *Pronto*! Didn't you?"

"I had to," growled Corwin, in a voice so low that the answer was lost to all but the man to whom he was talking.

McCullough gave him a contemptuous shove and wheeled to question Roberts. "Get up," he ordered, and searched the rustler trail-boss. "By God!" he exclaimed when he saw the size of the roll. "You coyotes was makin' money fast! There's near three thousand here!

Let's see how they compare with my list." In a few moments he nodded. "How'd you get these five-hundred-dollar bills? Kane give 'em to you, too?"

"No, Kane didn't give 'em to me!" snapped Roberts in angry contempt. "I earned 'em as my share of th' bank robbery, along with Corwin, th' white-livered snake! Kane didn't give 'em to either of us." He glared at the one-time sheriff. "I'm sayin' plain that if I ever get a chance I'm aimin' to shoot this skunk, along with Trask. You hear me?"

"If you ain't got a gun, hunt me up an' I'll lend you one," offered Idaho.

"Shut up!" snapped McCullough, glaring at the puncher. Whirling he pushed Roberts away. "It'll be a long time before you shoot anybody or anythin'. Now, then," he said, stepping up in front of Kane: "Get up!"

Kane arose slowly, his eyes burning with rage. He submitted to the exploring fingers of the trail-boss and maintained a contemptuous silence as his shirt was whipped up out of his trousers and the two money belts removed from around his waist.

McCullough opened the belts and his eyes at the same time. Neatly folded bunches of greenbacks followed each other in swift succession from the pockets of the belts and, scattering as they were tossed into a pile, made quite an imposing sight. Staring eyes regarded them and more than one observer's mouth gaped widely.

"Seven thousand," announced McCullough, reaching for another handful. "I'm sayin' you wasn't leavin' nothin' behind." He looked up again after a moment. "Eighteen thousand five hundred," he growled and picked up another handful. "Holy mavericks!" he breathed as the last bill was counted and placed on the new pile. "Forty-nine thousand eight hundred and seventy! You was takin' chances, totin' all that with this gang of thieves! Fifty thousand dollars, U.S.!"

Handing his written list to Quayle, he selected the five-hundred-dollar bills and called off the numbers laboriously, Quayle as laboriously hunting through the list. It took considerable time before they were checked off and put to one side, and then he looked up.

"There's still a-plenty of them bills missin'," he announced. "Where did *they* get to?"

Hopalong stepped forward and drew a roll from his pocket. "Here's what I found on Sandy Woods when he died in this camp," he said, offering it to the astonished trail-boss.

McCullough took it, opened and counted it, and called the numbers off to the excited holder of the list.

"They're all on th' list—th' Lord be praised!" said Quayle.

"Where'd Sandy Woods come in this?" demanded McCullough, looking around from face to face.

Roberts sneered. "Huh! He was th' man that took th' safe-blower out of th' country. He didn't have no hand in th' bank job. I'm glad th' skunk died, an' I'm glad it was me that planned his finish. He shore musta held up that feller. How much is there, in th' bank's bills?"

"Five thousand," answered the trail-boss.

"He got it all, cuss him!" snorted Roberts.

McCullough looked at Kane. "I never hoped to meet you like this," he said. "I ain't goin' to ask you no questions—you can talk in court, an' explain how you came to have so many of th' registered bills; an' there's other little things you can tell about, if somebody don't tell it all first." He turned to Hopalong. "We'll be takin' these fellers to th' ranch now."

"Better take th' reward money out of that bundle," replied Hopalong, nodding at the money in the hands of the trail-boss. "We've dealt 'em like you asked, an' gave you th' cards you want. Our part is finished."

McCullough looked from him to the prisoners and then at his friends. "How can I hand it to *you*?" he asked. "Where's Nelson? He's settin' in this."

"He'll show up after th' money's paid," said Red innocently as he arose.

McCullough hesitated and looked around again. As he did so Idaho carelessly walked over to Red, smoothing

out a cigarette paper, and took hold of a paper tag hanging out of Red's pocket and pulled it. Carelessly rolling a
cigarette he shoved the tobacco sack back where he
had found it, but he did not leave Red's side. Blowing a
lungful of smoke into the air he smiled at McCullough.

"Shucks, Mac," he said. "You shouldn't ought to have
no trouble findin' them rewards in that unholy wad. An'
mebby you could find Nelson's missin' eleven hundred
on Trask, if you looked real hard. I like a man that goes
through with his play."

"I'm not lookin' for no eleven hundred at all!" snapped
McCullough. "An' I ain't shore that they've earned th' reward, burnin' that buildin' like they did! They let these
fellers get away, first!"

"I just handed you th' money I found on Sandy
Woods," said Hopalong. "That's like givin' it to you to
pay us with. Hell! You act like you hated to make good
Twitchell's bargain. Well, of course, you don't have to
take this bunch, nor th' money, neither; but I'm sayin'
they don't go separate. Suits us, Mac—we'll keep th'
whole show—money an' all, if you say so."

"Fine chance you got!" retorted the trail-boss, bridling.
"They're here—an' I'm takin' 'em, *with* th' money."

"There ain't nobody takin' nothin'," rejoined Hopalong calmly, "until th' bargain's finished. Don't rile
Johnny, off there in th' brush; he's plumb touchy." His
drawling voice changed swiftly. "Come on—a bargain's
a bargain. Five thousand, *now*!"

"Mac!" said Quayle's accusing voice.

The trail-boss looked at the money in his hand and
slowly counted out the reward amount, careful not to in-
clude any of the registered bills. "Here," he said, handing them to Hopalong. "You give us a hand gettin' 'em to
th' ranch?"

"If three of us could catch 'em, an' bring 'em here,"
said Hopalong, coldly, "I reckon you got enough help to
take 'em th' rest of th' way—if you steer clear of town."

"Don't worry, Mac," said Idaho, cheerfully. "*I'll* go
along with you."

The trail-boss growled in his throat and began, with

Lukins, Waffles, and Quayle, to get the prisoners on the horses. This soon was accomplished and he headed them south, Lukins on the other side, Quayle and Waffles and Idaho bringing up the rear.

"Better come to town for a celebration," called the proprietor, disappointment in his voice. "Ye can leave at dawn."

Johnny shook his head. "There's a celebration waitin' at th' ranch," he shouted, and turned to find his two companions mounted and his black horse waiting impatiently for him. Mounting, he wheeled to face northward, but checked the horse and turned to look back in answer to a faint hail from Idaho, and grinned at the insulting gesture of the distant puncher.

He replied in kind, chuckled, and dashed forward to overtake his moving friends.

"Home!" he exulted. "Home—an' *Peggy*!"